THE ULTIMATE SEDUCTION

BY
DANI COLLINS

All rights reserved including the right of reproduction in whole
or in part in any form. This edition is published by arrangement with
Harlequin Books S.A.

This is a work of fiction. Names, characters, places, locations and
incidents are purely fictional and bear no relationship to any real
life individuals, living or dead, or to any actual places, business
establishments, locations, events or incidents. Any resemblance is
entirely coincidental.

This book is sold subject to the condition that it shall not, by way of
trade or otherwise, be lent, resold, hired out or otherwise circulated
without the prior consent of the publisher in any form of binding or
cover other than that in which it is published and without a similar
condition including this condition being imposed on the subsequent
purchaser.

® and TM are trademarks owned and used by the trademark owner
and/or its licensee. Trademarks marked with ® are registered with the
United Kingdom Patent Office and/or the Office for Harmonisation in
the Internal Market and in other countries.

Published in Great Britain 2014
by Mills & Boon, an imprint of Harlequin (UK) Limited,
Eton House, 18-24 Paradise Road, Richmond, Surrey, TW9 1SR

© 2014 Dani Collins

ISBN: 978-0-263-24673-5

Harlequin (UK) Limited's policy is to use papers that are natural,
renewable and recyclable products and made from wood grown in
sustainable forests. The logging and manufacturing processes conform
to the legal environmental regulations of the country of origin.

Printed and bound in Spain
by Blackprint CPI, Barcelona

"Ryzard Vrbancic?" she managed faintly. *Please no.*

His gorgeous mouth twisted with ironic dismay. "As you can see. Who are you?"

Of course she could see. Now that Tiffany's brain was beginning to function it was obvious this was the self-appointed President of Bregnovia. How did a name like Ryzard go from being something vaguely lethal to something noble and dynamic simply by encountering the man in person? How had she not sensed or realised…?

"There's been a mistake. I've made a mistake."

And yet her body responded to being in his presence. Even though she wasn't drunk, and no music seduced her, her feet didn't want to move and her eyes kept being dragged back to his wide chest, where a sprinkle of hair had abraded her palms. His arms flexed as she watched, forcing memories of being caught protectively against him when the fireworks had started, then carried like a wilted Southern Belle when sex had been the only thing on their minds.

Warily she eyed him. "I didn't know who you were last night."

"No?" His brow kicked up, dismissing her claim as a lie.

"No!"

"You sleep with strangers often?"

"Apparently *you* do, so don't judge me."

THE 21st CENTURY GENTLEMAN'S CLUB

Where the rich, powerful and passionate come to play!

For years there have been rumours of a secret society where only the richest, the most powerful and the most decadent can embrace their every desire.

Nothing is forbidden in this private world of pleasure.

And when exclusivity is beyond notoriety only those who are invited to join ever know its name…

Q Virtus

Now the truth behind the rumours is about to be revealed!

Find out in:

THE ULTIMATE PLAYBOY
by Maya Blake
July 2014

THE ULTIMATE SEDUCTION
by Dani Collins
August 2014

THE ULTIMATE REVENGE
by Victoria Parker
September 2014

Dani Collins discovered romance novels in high school and immediately wondered how a person trained and qualified for *that* amazing job. She married her high school sweetheart, which was a start, then spent two decades trying to find her fit in the wide world of romance-writing, always coming back to Mills & Boon® Modern™ Romance.

Two children later, and with the first entering high school, she placed in Harlequin's *Instant Seduction* contest. It was the beginning of a fabulous journey towards finally getting that dream job.

When she's not in her Fortress of Literature, as her family calls her writing office, she works, chauffeurs children to extra-curricular activities, and gardens with more optimism than skill. Dani can be reached through her website at www.danicollins.com

Recent titles by the same author:

A DEBT PAID IN PASSION
MORE THAN A CONVENIENT MARRIAGE
PROOF OF THEIR SIN
NO LONGER FORBIDDEN?

**Did you know these are also available as eBooks?
Visit www.millsandboon.co.uk**

I've been lucky enough to work with a few different editors at Mills & Boon, London. They're all made of awesome, but I must send a huge shout of appreciation to my current editor, Laurie Johnson. Not only has she made my transition into her care utterly painless, but this is our first book completely midwifed from start to finish by her. No spinal block required! Writer and book are happy and doing well. Thanks, Laurie!

CHAPTER ONE

Tiffany Davis pretended she wasn't affected by the hard stare her brother and father gave her when she entered her father's office. It wasn't easy to let people she loved pass judgment on whether she'd used sufficient concealer on her scars. Sometimes she wanted to throw the bottle of liquid beige into the trash and scream, *There. This is what I look like now. Live with it.*

But her brother had saved her life pulling her from the fiery car. He felt guilty enough for putting her in it. He still grieved for her groom, his best friend, and everything else Tiffany had lost. She didn't have to rub salt in his wounds.

Good girl, Tiff. Keep biting back what you really want to say. It's not like that got you into these skin grafts.

She came to a halt and sighed, thinking it was probably time for another visit to the head doctor if she was cooking up that sort of inner dialogue. But her harsh exhale caused both men to tense. Which made her want to rail all the louder.

Being angry all the time was a character shift for her. Even she had trouble dealing with it, so she shouldn't blame them for reacting like this. But it still fed her irritation.

"Yes?" She clicked her teeth into a tight smile, attempting to hold on to her slipping patience.

"You tell us. What's this?" Christian kept his arms folded as he nodded at the large box sitting open on their father's desk. The lid wore an international courier's logo, and the contents appeared to be a taxidermist's attempt to marry a raven to a peacock.

"The feather boa you asked for last Christmas?" Lame joke, sure, but neither man so much as blinked. They only stared at her as if they were prying her open.

"Be serious, Tiff," Christian said. "Why is the mask for you? Did you request to go in my place?"

A claustrophobic band tightened around her insides. A year in a mask had left her vowing to never feel such a thing on her face again. "I don't know what you're talking about."

The frost in her voice made both men's mouths purse. *Why did all of this have to be so hard?* The touchiness between her and her family was palpable every minute of every day. If she was short, they were defensive. If she was the least bit vulnerable, they became so overprotective she couldn't breathe.

They'd nearly lost her. She got that they loved her and were still worried about her. They wouldn't relax until she got back to normal, but she would never be normal again. It made the situation impossible.

"Where is it you think I want to go?" she asked in as steady a tone as she could manage.

"Q Virtus," her father said, as if that one word sufficed as explanation.

She shook her head and shrugged, still lost. Did they realize she was in the middle of an exchange worth five hundred million dollars? She didn't have much, but she did have a job now. Seeing as it involved running a multibillion-dollar company, she tried to do it well.

"Ryzard Vrbancic," Christian provided. "We put in a request to meet him."

Pieces fell together. *Q Virtus* was that men's club Paulie used to talk about. "You want to meet a puppet leader at one of those rave things? Why? The man's a despot."

"Bregnovia is asking for recognition at the UN. They're a democracy now."

She snorted in disbelief. "The whole world is ignoring the fact he stole the last dictator's money and bought himself a presidency? Okay."

"They're recovering from civil war. They need the sort of infrastructure Davis and Holbrook can provide."

"I'm sure they do. Why go the cloak-and-dagger route? Call him up and pitch our services."

"It's not that simple. Our country hasn't recognized his yet so we can't talk to him openly, but we want to be the first number on his list when recognition happens."

She rolled her eyes. Politics were so fun. "So you've set up this clandestine meeting—"

"It's not confirmed. That happens when you get there."

"That would be the broad 'you,' right? Like the universal 'they'?"

Christian's mouth tightened. He lifted out the feathery contents of the box. It was actually quite beautiful. A piece of art. The blend of blue-black and turquoise and gold feathers covered the upper eyes and forehead and—significantly—splayed down the left side in an eerily familiar pattern. Ribbons tailed off each side.

It was like looking in the mirror, seeing that reflection of her scar. A slithery feeling inside her torso made her heart speed up. She shook her head. She wasn't going anywhere, especially in public, with or without a crazy disguise.

"You understand how *Q Virtus* works?" her brother prodded. "This mask is your ticket in."

"Not *mine*."

"Yeah, Tiff, it is." He turned it around so she could see where her name was inscribed on the underside, along with *Isla de Margarita, Venezuela*. "See? Only you can attend."

His terse tone and shooting glance toward their father made it clear they'd spent some time pondering alternate solutions. Both men showed signs of deep frustration, a level of emotion usually reserved for when approval ratings were low. To see them so bent out of shape activated her don't-make-more-waves genes.

Your father is under a lot of pressure, dear. Do as he asks for now.

No, she reminded herself. She was living her life, not waiting for it to make everyone else's list of priorities. Still, she'd been raised to have civilized conversations, not be outright defiant. "I would think that taking off the mask to show your name defeats the purpose."

"There's a chip embedded. They know which mask belongs to which person, and as you can see, they only fit one face."

"They obviously know a lot about *me.* That's creepy. Doesn't it seem weird they would know how to cover my scars?"

"*Q Virtus* has an exceptional history of discretion and security," her father said, defending it with a kind of pompous grumpiness that surprised her. "Whatever they know about us, I'm sure it's kept very well protected."

A remarkably naive comment from a man who'd been in politics and business long enough to mistrust everyone and everything. Heck, he'd dragged her in here because he thought she'd undermined him with his brotherhood of secret handshakes, hadn't he?

"Dad, if you want to become a member—"

"I can't." He smoothed his tie, one of his tells when his ego was dented.

"Too old? Then Christian—?"

"No."

She was quite smart, had always had better marks than her brother, who fudged his way through just about everything, but she was missing something. "Well, Paulie was a member. What does it take?"

"Money. A lot of it. Paul Sr. was a member and once Paulie inherited, he had the means to pay the fee," her father said in a level tone.

Of course. Therein lay her father's envy and reverence. It must have eaten him alive that his best friend and rival for her mother's affections had possessed something he hadn't.

"When you were still in the hospital, I applied on your behalf, hoping to go as your proxy," Christian explained. "I didn't hear back until today." Glancing at their father, he added, "It is kind of creepy they know Tiff has finally recovered and taken over the reins of Davis and Holbrook."

"Everyone's talking about it. It's hardly a secret," her father dismissed with a fresh heaping of disapproval.

Tiffany bit back a sigh. She would not apologize for grappling her way into running the company now that she was well enough. What else would she do moving forward? Trophy wife and having a family was out of the question with this face.

Still, it was so *unladylike* to work, her mother reminded at every opportunity.

"I don't understand why they've accepted her. It's a men's club," her father muttered.

She eyed the mask, recalling the sorts of stories Paulie used to come home with after attending one of these *Q Virtus* things. "It's a booze-fueled sex orgy, isn't it?"

"It's a networking event," her father blustered.

Christian offered one of his offside grins. "It's a chance for the elite to let their hair down," he clarified. "But a lot of deals are closed over martinis and a handshake. It's the country club on a grander scale."

Right. She knew how that worked. Wives and daughters stood around in heels and pearls planning the Fourth of July picnic while husbands and fathers colluded to keep their money amongst themselves. Her engagement to Paulie, Jr. had been negotiated between the seventh and ninth holes of the top green, her wedding staged on the balcony by their mothers, her cake designed by the renowned chef, and all of it exploded into flames against the wrought-iron exit gate.

"This is all very interesting." It wasn't. Not at all. "But I'm in the middle of something. You'll have to sort this out yourselves."

"Tiffany."

Her father's stern tone was the one that made any good daughter spin, take a stance of dutifully planted feet, knees locked, hands knotted at her sides. She caught her tongue firmly between her teeth. "Yes?"

"Our friends in Congress are hoping for good relations with Bregnovia. I need those friends."

Because his hat was in the ring for the next election. Why was that always the only thing that mattered?

"I don't know what you expect me to do. Pitch our services while wearing a showgirl costume? Who would take that seriously? I can't go into a meeting without it, though. No one likes face-to-face interactions with this." She pointed at where her ear had been reconstructed and a cheekbone implant inserted.

Her father flinched and looked away, not denying that she was hard to look at. That hurt more than the months of screaming burn injuries.

"Maybe I could be your date," Christian said. "I don't know if members are allowed to bring an escort, but..."

"Bring my brother to the prom?" That certainly reinforced how far down the eligibility ladder she'd fallen. Her hands stayed curled at her sides, but mentally she cupped them around her tiny, shrunken heart, protecting it. *Love yourself, Tiff. No one else will.*

"Get me into the club and you won't have to leave your room until it's over," Chris said.

Hide the disfigured beast.

She had to close her eyes against her father's intense stare, the one that willed her to comply.

You weren't going to let yourself be a pawn anymore, she reminded herself.

"How long is this thing?" she heard herself ask, because what kind of family would she have, if not this one? Her friends had deserted her, and dating was completely off the table. Her life would be very dark and lonely if she alienated her parents and brother.

"We arrive at sunset on Friday night, and everyone is gone by Sunday evening. I'll make the travel arrangements," Christian said with quick relief.

"I wear this thing *in* and *out*. That's the deal, because I won't do this if I'm going to be stared at." Listen to her, talking so tough. She was actually scared to her toenails. What would people say if they saw her? She couldn't let it happen.

"As far as I know, everyone wears masks the whole time," Chris said, practically dancing, he was so elated.

"I'll be in my office," she muttered. *Searching for my spine.*

Ryzard Vrbancic abided by few rules beyond his own, but he left his newly purchased catamaran as the shadow of its mast stretched across the other boats in the Venezuelan marina. If he didn't climb the stairs before the red sky had inked purple, he would be locked out of the *Q Virtus* Quarterly.

Story of my life, he thought, but hoped that soon he'd be as welcome worldwide as the famous black credit card.

Security was its usual discreet step through a well-camouflaged metal detector that also read the chip in his mask. One of the red-gowned staff lifted her head from her tablet as he arrived and smiled. "We're pleased to see you again, Raptor. May I escort you to your room?"

She was a pretty thing, but the *petite q's* were off-limits, which was a pity. He hadn't had time to find himself a lover for weeks. The last had complained he spent more time working than with her, which was apparent from her spa and shopping bills. They were as high as his sexual frustration.

His situation should improve now, but he'd have to be patient a little longer. Like the music that set a vacation tone, the *petite q's* provided atmosphere. They could stroke an ego, dangle off an arm, flirt and indulge almost any reasonable request, but if they wanted to keep their job, they stayed out of the members' beds. Being smart and career minded along with attractive and engaging, the *petite q's* tended to side with keeping their jobs.

Such a pity.

His current escort set up his thumbprint for the door then stepped inside his suite for his briefing. "You have a meeting request from Steel Butterfly. Shall I confirm?"

"A woman?" he asked.

"I don't have the gender of our clients, sir."

And if she did know, she wouldn't say, either.

"No other requests?" He was hoping for a signal from international bodies that his petition to the UN was receiving a nod.

"Not at this time. Did you have any?"

Damn. He'd come here knowing he had a meeting request, hoping it would be a tip of the hand on his situation. Now he was under lockdown and liable to be taking a sales pitch of some kind.

"Not at present. I'll accept an introduction on that one, nothing longer." He nodded at her tablet.

"The time and location will be transmitted to your smartwatch. Please let us know if I can arrange anything else to ensure your satisfaction while you're with us."

He followed her out, confident that everything he'd preordered was in the suite. Zeus was exceptionally good at what he did. Ryzard had never had an issue of any kind while at *Q Virtus,* which made the exorbitant membership fee and elaborate travel and security arrangements worth the trouble.

Entering the pub-style reception lounge, he saw roughly thirty people, mostly men in tuxedos and masks. They stood with a handful of gorgeous *petite q's* wearing the customary red designer gowns.

He accepted the house drink for this session, rum over ice with a squeeze of lime and a sugared rim, then glanced at his watch. At his four o'clock, a collection of dots informed him the small conclave of men to his right included Steel Butterfly.

He had no idea where Zeus came up with these ridiculous nicknames, but he supposed Raptor was apt for him, coming from the Latin meaning to seize or take by force. The bones of several dinosaurs in that category had been uncovered in his homeland of Bregnovia, too.

Eyeing the group, he wondered which one was his contact. One accepted a drink from a *petit q* and handed her his watch. It didn't matter, he decided. He wasn't interested in beginning a conversation in public that he was scheduled to have in private tomorrow. He waited until he was out of range in the gambling hall to activate his identity on his own watch. This resulted in an immediate invitation to join the blackjack table.

He sat so he could read the screen mounted near the ceiling in the corner. It subtly manifested and dissolved with blurbs on presentations and entertainment to be held over the course of the *Q Virtus* Quarterly. Tastemakers, trendsetters and thought leaders were flown in to provide rich, powerful, political forces such as himself with the absolute cutting-edge information and samples of global economics and technology. Meanwhile, at tables such as this one, he would pick up the other side of the coin: gossip about a royal's addiction, a cover-up of a coup attempt on a head of state, a lie that would be accepted as truth to stem international panic.

He could only imagine what was said about him, but he didn't let himself dwell on what was likely disapproval and distrust. His people were free, his country independent. That was the important thing.

Still, thoughts of what it had cost him crept in, threatening to inject disappointment and guilt into an otherwise pleasant if staid evening. He folded his hand, left the table and lifted a rum off a passing waiter's tray as he moved outside in search of entertainment.

CHAPTER TWO

TIFFANY WAS STUCK and it was a sickeningly familiar situation, the kind she'd sworn she'd never wind up in again.

She'd love to blame Christian. He had urged her to step through the door when he'd been refused entry. *Go in and ask,* he'd hissed, annoyed.

Since her worst nightmare these days was being stared at, she'd forgone arguing on the stoop and stepped through the entranceway. Inside, pixies in designer nightgowns had fawned over the arriving men in masks. She'd looked around for a bell desk, and a stud named Julio had come forward to introduce himself as a *petite q*.

She, a seasoned socialite, had become tongue-tied over the strapping young man in a red footman's uniform. It was more than two years since she'd been widowed on her wedding day. Even without the scars, that would be bad mojo. Men didn't call, didn't ask her out. If she was in a room with a live one, they rarely looked her in the eye, always averting their gaze. She didn't exist for them as a potential mate.

Julio didn't attract her so much as astonish her. He didn't know what lurked beneath the mask and was all solicitous manners as he offered his services. "I see this is your first visit with us," he said after a brief glance at his tablet. "Please allow me to orient you."

She was completely out of practice with his type—the valet who never overstepped his station, but still managed to convey that he appreciated being in the presence of beauty. She'd haltingly fielded his questions about whether her travel had been pleasant as he smoothly escorted her into an elevator.

When he asked if she had any specific needs he could attend to while she was here, she'd come back to reality. "My brother needs a hall pass, or a mask. Whatever. Can you make that happen?"

"I'll send the request to Zeus, but the doors will be closing in a few minutes. Once we're in lockdown, no one comes or goes. Unless it's an emergency, of course." He'd lifted his head from tapping his tablet.

Lockdown? Alarmed, she'd tried to text Christian only to be informed that external service was cut off while inside the club.

"Cell phones and other cameras are discouraged, as is the sending of photos outside the club. Security will locate him and communicate his options," Julio assured her, then explained that if her requested meeting was accepted, the time and location would be sent to her Inspector Gadget watch.

"Where *are* we? A hollowed-out volcano?" she asked as he set up her thumbprint entry to her room.

"No, but we're working on obtaining one," he said, deadpan. "Now, you'll want to wear your watch throughout your stay. It tells a lot more than time. May I show you?"

Hearing that her scheduled meeting with the Bregnovian dictator wasn't a sure thing was a relief. Her father would be furious if she didn't go in Christian's place, but if the request was rejected, she would be off the hook. Still, she hoped her brother would be granted entry and save her worrying about any of it. She pressed Julio out of her suite with instructions to inform her about Christian as soon as possible.

Her suite was enough of an oasis to calm her nerves. Her

privileged upbringing had exposed her to some seriously nice digs, but she had to admit this was above and beyond. No expense had been spared on the gold fixtures, original art or silk bedding. The new clothes in the wardrobe were a pleasant distraction. Christian had said something about samples of prototypes being handed out to members. *If you don't want them, I do.*

She supposed he was referring to the spy watch Julio had shown her, but she was more interested in the designer gowns. Discreet labels informed her they were from the best of the best throughout South America, all in stunning colors and fabrics. Several were off-the-shoulder, figure-enhancing styles that would cover her scars.

Interesting.

Not that she had anywhere to wear them. She didn't intend to leave her room, but she would make the most of the in-suite amenities, she decided. Call it a vacation from her family. She'd work in peace for a few days.

Work, however, was next to impossible without Wi-Fi service to the external world, and besides, a calypso band was calling to her from below her open French doors. She *loved* dancing.

Full darkness had fallen, so she sidled into the shadows behind a potted fern on her balcony and gazed longingly at the party below, feeling rather like Audrey Hepburn in that old black-and-white. It was such a world beyond her. The pool's glow lit up ice sculptures on the buffet tables. Bartenders juggled open bottles, putting on a cocktail show as they poured fast and free while women in red gowns cha-cha'd with men in tuxedos and masks.

This whole mask thing was weird. As they'd flown south in the company jet, Christian had explained it allowed the world's elite rub shoulders in a discreet way. Sometimes it was best for the biggest players to take their meetings in secret, so as not to cause speculative dips in the stock exchange. Certain celebrities stole these few days to relax without interruption by fans. *Q Virtus* catered to whatever the obscenely rich needed.

I need a new face, she thought sourly, but even the cavernous pockets her husband had left her weren't deep enough to buy a miracle.

She looked to where she'd left her mask dangling off a chair back's spire.

Despite her anxiety with the abrupt change of plans when she arrived, she had felt blessedly anonymous behind her mask as she had walked through the lobby and halls to her room. It had been an extraordinary experience to feel normal again. No one had stared. She had looked exactly like everyone else.

Hmm. That meant she didn't have to stay here like Rapunzel, trapped in the tower with the real world three stories below and out of her reach.

With her heart tripping somewhere between excitement and trepidation, she fingered through the gowns hanging in the wardrobe. The silk crepe in Caribbean blue would expose her good right leg, but not so high as to reveal where her grafts had been taken. After months of physiotherapy, she'd moved back into her old workout routine of yoga, weights and treadmill. She possessed all of her mother's vanity along with the genetic jackpot in the figure department. Only family saw her these days, and she hardly dressed to impress, but she was actually very fit.

Alone in the suite, she held the gown up to her body, then, without her mother there to discourage her, dared to try it on.

Whoever this Zeus guy was, he sure knew how to dress a woman. Especially one with defects to hide. The single sleeve went past her wrist in a point that ended in a loop of thread that hooked over her middle finger. The bodice clung to her waist and torso, plumping breasts that remained two of her best original features. She had to give her backside the credit it deserved, too. When she buckled on new shoes that were little more than sky-high heels and a pair of saucy blue-green straps, it was like being hugged by old friends. She almost wept.

Filtering her image through her lashes as she looked in the mirror, she saw her old self. *Hi, Tiff. It's nice to see you again. 'Bout time, too.*

Makeup didn't completely cover her scars, nothing could, but she enjoyed going through her old ritual after using the concealer, taking her time to layer on shadow and liner, girling herself up to the max. By the time she was rolling spirals into her strawberry blond hair, she was so lost in the good ol' days, she caught herself thinking, *I wonder what Paulie will say.*

The curling iron tagged her cheek where she would never feel it, and she nearly broke down. *You're not Cinderella, anymore, remember? You're the ugly stepsister.*

No. Not tonight. Not when she felt confident and beautiful for the first time since her wedding day. Had she been happy then? She couldn't remember.

Don't go there.

Gathering the top half of her hair over her crown, she tied the mask into place, then let her loose curls fall to hide the strap that circled her skull. Oddly, the mask wasn't as traumatic to wear as she'd feared. It didn't suction onto her face and make her feel trapped in a body that writhed in agony. It stood cocked like a fascinator to cover the left side of her face, while the feathers arranged around her eyes gave an impression of overly long lashes that layered backward to cover her forehead and hairline. She had expected it to be heavy, but it was as light as, well, feathers. They tickled the edges of her scars, where her skin was extra sensitive, making her feel feminine and pretty.

Staring at herself in the full-length mirror, she allowed

that she *was* pretty. After painting on a coat of coral lipstick, she did a slow twirl and caught herself grinning. Smiling felt odd, as if she was using muscles that had atrophied.

She lifted the weighty watch on her wrist, the one that identified her as Steel Butterfly. More like a broken one. Her sides didn't even match.

It didn't have to make sense, she assured herself as she tossed her lipstick into her pocketbook then realized she didn't need either room key or credit card. Such freedom! For a few hours, she would be completely without baggage.

Taking nothing but lighthearted steps, she left to join the party.

Ryzard could drink with the best of them. He'd spent the older half of his childhood in Munich, had managed vineyards in France and Italy, and had lived in parts of Russia where not finishing a bottle of vodka was a gross insult to the host. He was restless enough to get legless tonight, but so far he'd consumed only enough to become mellow and hungry. The cashmere breeze and the scents of beach and pineapple and roasting pig aroused his appetite—all his appetites. He'd mentally stripped the nearest *petite q's* and was considering a pass at one of the female members currently being scouted by every other bachelor here—along with some of the married members.

Not Narciso, aka the Warlock of Wall Street, though. He chatted with his friend long enough to see the man wasn't just here with his wife, but besotted by her. Lucky bastard. Ryzard countered his envy by reminding himself that love was a double-edged sword. He wouldn't ruin his friend's happiness by saying so, but he had once looked forward to marital bliss. Luiza had died before they found it, and the anguish was indescribable. No matter how pleased he was for his friend, he would never risk that toll again.

He'd stick to the less permanent associations one found, enjoyed and left at parties such as this one.

Glass panels had been fitted over the lap pool, turning it into a dance floor that glimmered beams of colored light beneath the bouncing feet. People were having a lively time, keeping the band's quick salsa beat rapping. The drummer stared off to the left, however, his grin male and captivated.

Ryzard followed the man's gaze and his entire being crackled to attention.

Well beyond the pool's light, in a corner mostly blocked by a buffet table and ice sculpture, a woman undulated like a cobra, utterly fascinating in her hypnotic movements timed perfectly with the music. Her splayed hands slid down her body with sexy knowledge, her hips popped in time to the beat, and her feet kick-stepped into motion.

She twirled. The motion lifted her brassy curls like a skirt before she planted her feet wide and swayed her weight between them. The flex of her spine gave way to a roll of her hips, and she was back into motion again.

Setting down his drink, Ryzard beelined toward her. He couldn't tell if the woman had a partner, but it didn't matter. He was cutting in.

She was alone, lifting her arms to gather her hair, eyes closed as she felt the music as much as heard it. She arched and stretched—

He caught her around the waist and used the shocked press of her hands at his shoulders to push her into accepting his lead, stepping into her space, then retreating, bringing her with him. As he moved her into a side step, she recovered, matching his move while her gaze pinned to his.

He couldn't tell what color her eyes were. The light was too low, her feathery mask shadowing her gaze into twin glinting lights, but he reacted to the fixation in them. She was deciding whether to accept him.

A rush of excitement for the challenge ran through him.

After a few more quick steps, he swung her into half pivots, catching each of her wrists in turn, one bare, one clad in silk, enjoying the flash of her bare knee through the slit of her skirt.

How had she been overlooked by every man here? She was exquisite.

Lifting her hand over her head, he spun her around then clasped her shoulder blades into his chest. Her buttocks—fine, firm, round globes as if heaven had sent him a valentine—pressed into his lap. Bending her before him, he buried his nose in her hair and inhaled, then followed her push to straighten and matched the sway of her hips with his own.

Tiffany's heart pounded so hard she thought it would escape her chest. One second she'd been slightly drunk, lost in the joy of letting the salsa rhythm control her muscles. Now a stranger was doing it. And doing it well. He pulled her around into a waltz stance that he quickly shifted so they grazed each other's sides, left, right, left.

She kicked each time, surprised how easily the movements came back to her. It had been years, but this man knew what he was doing, sliding her slowly behind his back, then catching her hand on the other side. He pushed her to back up a step, bringing one of her arms behind his head, the other behind her own. A few backward steps and they were connected by only one hand, arms outstretched, then he spun her back into him, catching her into his chest.

He stopped.

The conga beat pulsed through her as he ran his hands down her sides. Her own flew to cover his knuckles, but she didn't stop him. It felt too amazing. His fingertips grazed the sides of her breasts, flexed into the taut muscles of her waist and clasped her hips to push them in a hula circle that he followed with his own, his crotch pressed tight to her buttocks.

Sensual pleasure electrified her. No one touched her anymore. After being a genderless automaton for so long, she was a woman again, alive, capable of captivating and enticing a man. She nudged her hips into his, flashing a glance back at him.

He narrowed his eyes and held her in place for one deliberate thrust before he spun her into the dance, their energetic quick steps becoming an excuse to look at each other as he let her move to the farthest reach of his hand on hers.

She had been a bit of a tease in her day, secure in the knowledge everyone knew she was engaged. She'd been able to flirt without consequence, enjoying male attention without feeling threatened by it. This stranger's undisguised admiration was rain on her desert wasteland of feminine confidence. Climbing her free hand between her breasts to the back of her neck, she thrust out her chest then let the music snake up and down her spine as she flexed her figure for his visual pleasure.

His feral show of teeth encouraged her while his sheer male sexiness called to the woman in her, urging her to keep the notice of such a fine specimen. He might have started out his evening in a tux, but at some point he'd stripped down to the pants and the shirt, which was open at the collar and rolled back to his forearms at the sleeves. The mask he wore was vaguely piratical in its black with gold trim and wings at his temple, but the nose piece bent in a point off the end of his nose, suggesting a bird of prey.

A hunter.

And she was the hunted.

Her heart raced, excited by the prospect of being pursued. She wanted to be wanted.

Splaying her feet, she allowed her knees to loosen. The slit of her skirt parted to reveal her leg, and she made the most of it, watching him as she rolled her hips in a figure eight, showing off her body, enticing him with a come-hither groove.

He planted a foot between hers, surrounding her without touching her, hands raised as if he was absorbing energy from her aura. The sultry tropical air held an undertone of spicy cologne and musky man. Reaching out, she shaped the balls of his hard shoulders with her hands and climbed them to the sides of his damp neck, sidling close so they sidestepped back and forth, swaying together in time to the music, bodies brushing.

His wide hands flattened on her shoulder blades and slid with deliberation to the small of her back then took possession of her hips. As his unabashed gaze held hers, he pulled her in to feel the firm ridge of his erection behind his fly.

A flood of desire, not the trickles of interest she'd felt in the past, but a serious deluge of passion, transformed her limbs into heavy weights and flooded her belly with a pool of sexy heat. She became intensely aware of her erogenous zones. Her breasts ached and her nipples tingled into sharp, stinging points. Between her thighs, her loins pulsed with a swollen, oversensitive need.

As if he knew, he shifted and his hard thigh pressed into her vulnerable flesh. She gasped and her neck weakened as he bent over her. She dropped her head back and he followed, taking her body weight on his thigh. His nose grazed her chin, then her collarbone. His lips hovered between her breasts. Slowly he brought her up again and leaned his mouth close enough to tease her parted lips.

He was a stranger, she reminded herself, but her lips felt swollen and she desperately wanted the pressure of his mouth—

A clap of thunder exploded in the sky.

Jolted, she found herself smothered against his chest, his hard arms tight around her, one hand shielding the back of her head, fingers digging in with tension. Her mask skewed, cutting into her temple. Beneath her cheekbone, his heart slammed with power.

The claps and squeals and whistles continued and his arms relaxed enough she could fix her mask and look up. Fireworks painted the starscape in flowers and streaks of red and blue and green that dissolved into sparkles of silver and palms of gold.

As people moved into their space, he steered her away from the crowd, into a corner around a partition where they were hidden in an alcove. She set her hands on the concrete rampart and leaned back into the living wall he made behind her, eyes dazzled by the bursts of color reflected on the water as the fireworks continued to explode before and above them. The band switched to an orchestrated classic that matched the explosions, filling her with awe and visceral excitement.

Already fixed in the moment, they became one being, she and this stranger, their bodies pressed tight as they watched the pyrotechnics. His hands moved over her, absently at first, shaping her to his front. She responded, encouraging his touch by rubbing her buttocks into the proof that she could still arouse a man. When his hands cupped her breasts, bold and knowledgeable, she linked her own hands behind his neck, arching into his touch, reveling in the pressure of his palms and the thumbing of her nipples.

Dropping her head to the side, she turned her face and lifted her mouth, inviting his kiss with parted lips. He bent without hesitation, nothing tentative in the way he captured her mouth. Thorough and unhurried, he continued to caress her as he took sumptuous possession of her lips.

She ran her fingers into his hair, greeting his tongue with her own, inhibition melted by pure desire. Distantly she was aware this was out of character, but she wasn't Tiffany. Not the Tiffany of today and not the old one, either. Tonight she was the woman she wished she could have been. She was every woman. Pure woman.

Tonight she had no man to think about but this one. She didn't care that she didn't know him. She and Paulie hadn't known each other, either, not really, not the way a husband and wife should. Not in the biblical sense. She hadn't slept with him or any man.

But she wanted to. She had ached for years to experience sexual intimacy.

A strong male hand stroked down her abdomen and skimmed off to the top of her thigh, making her mewl in disappointment. Then he fingered beneath the slit of her skirt and she had to pull away from his kiss to draw in a gasp as he followed bare skin into the sensitive flesh at the top of her leg.

She stilled.

His arm across her torso tensed and the hand on her breast hesitated briefly before he continued caressing her, lightly and persuasively, both hands teasing her with the promise of continued pleasure.

A moan of craving left her and she shuddered in acceptance.

A streak of light shot skyward and his touch moved into her center, exploring satin and lace that were damp with anticipation. She couldn't help covering his hand with her own, pinning his touch where she ached for pressure.

He seemed to know what she needed more than she did. As he fondled her, her eyes drifted closed and her head fell back to rest against his shoulder. She bit her lip, ripples of delight dancing through her. Was she really doing this? Rubbing her behind into his erection, not caring they were in public, that she didn't know him, that this was all about her pleasure?

He started to draw his hand away and she turned her face to the side, a cry of disappointment escaping her, but he was only hooking her panties down her hip and returning to trace and part and seek and find.

She released a moan of pure joy.

He caught her chin in his other hand and tilted her face up for his kiss while his touch on her mound became deliberate and intimate and determined.

She let it happen. She held very still and kissed him back with naked passion, aware of the light breeze caressing where she was exposed to the shadows of the rampart and the velvety night air. She let him stroke her into delirious intensity, her awareness dimmed at the edges so she was focused on the pleasure he was delivering, plucking and teasing and bringing her closer.

Over the water, the biggest rockets exploded like thunder, sending shock waves through her that made her quiver in stunned reaction. The reverberations echoed inside her, sparking where he stroked, sending a wild release upward and out to the ends of her limbs. He pinched her nipple, and like a flashpoint, she was blind to everything but white light and astonishing pleasure. Glorious waves of joy crashed in, submerging her in tumultuous ripples that he seemed to control, pressing one after another through her with the rub of his fingertip.

As the fireworks dimmed to puffs of smoke surrounding a barge in the bay, her climax receded, leaving her a puddle of lassitude in his steely arms.

He adjusted her panties and started to turn her. She obeyed the command in his hands, wanting to kiss him, to thank him—

Without a word, he drew her across the balcony to a set of shallow stairs leading to the beach. She wobbled, partly because her legs were wet noodles, partly because her heels couldn't find solid purchase in the sand. He scooped her up, carrying her along with easy strength into a cabana encircled by heavy curtains.

Inside he set her on her feet and steadied her with one hand while he raked the cloth door closed behind them. Without a word, he scraped the mask off his face and yanked his shirt open, peeling it off his shoulders and throwing it aside.

She couldn't see his face, not really. It was barely a shade above pitch-black in here, but the glow of satin skin increased as he toed off his shoes and opened his fly, stripping without ceremony.

Sweet Lord, what a man. He stepped closer and she couldn't help reaching out to test the flat muscles of his abdomen, learning them by feel more than sight. Hot and damp, he reacted to her touch with a tense of muscles and a muffled curse, making her smile in the dark, pleased she had an effect on him.

Her hand bumped into his. He was applying a condom.

Curious, she lightly explored his latex-covered shape. As she did, the pressure of her mask shifted.

She knocked his touch away before she thought about what she was doing.

Stillness came over him.

She tried to penetrate the dark and read his face—which was what he was likely doing. He probably thought she was having second thoughts.

Hell, no. She might never have another chance to lose her virginity. Not like this, so caught up in desire she was shaking with it.

"Leave it on," she whispered.

His hands lowered to her shoulders, one skimming down the edge of her bodice under her arm. She knew what he was looking for.

"That, too." Catching his hand away from her zipper, she drew him toward the bed.

In the same way he'd taken her over on the dance floor, he took the lead. A tip of his weight, a knee in the bed and she was lifted and placed half under him in one smooth motion. Her startled exhale clouded between them as a hand sought beneath her skirt, catching at her panties then pausing.

She couldn't help chuckling, understanding the implicit question. Lifting her hips, she invited him to strip them off her. They caught on her shoe, and neither of them bothered to finish the job.

He hitched her skirt then tucked her neatly under him, his legs moving with practiced ease to part her knees wide.

More surprised than shocked, she stilled, bracing herself, wanting this, but not as lost in the moment as she'd been. That was okay. She'd had her fun and she wanted to remember everything about this encounter. Cataloguing the flex of his shoulders under the stroke of her hands, the weight of his hips, the roughened texture of his legs on her smooth inner thighs, she waited.

He teased her, rubbing the head of his erection against her and reawakening her senses. As she hummed a response, he kissed her, deeply, dragging her back into the well of desire she thought she'd left outside on the ramparts.

Sliding her knee up to his hip, she hooked her calf over his buttock and quite suddenly, it was happening. His flesh was pressing for entrance, stretching her. Oh, wow. It hurt, but not bad. She'd experienced pain way worse than this, but it was still very intimate. She bit her lip and concentrated on accepting him, breathing through the sting and countering her instinctive tension—

He swore and the hand in her hair tightened enough to pull, even though she suspected it wasn't intentional. His big body shook with tension.

"I'm hurting you," he said in a voice so gruff she couldn't discern what kind of accent he had.

"It's okay. It feels good. I like it." This was so primeval. Drinking in his scent, she licked his neck, wanting this delicious, mysterious man imprinted on her for all time.

Arching, she discovered there was more of him to take. Squeezing her leg to encourage him, she met resistance. Rather than press into her, he kissed her again, using his tongue, and lifted enough to sidle a hand between them, caressing where they joined. In moments he had her twisting in excitement, and a second later, he slid deep into her.

Ah, *this* was what it was all about.

Eyes wide open to the dark cabana, she hugged his rugged body and learned the dip in his spine and the shape of his buttocks. His tense muscles flexed as he retreated from her depths, pulling strings of sensations through her: echoes of sting, loss, but delicious friction, too. He smoothly filled her again, his big body trembling with strain as he controlled his movements. The smart was still there, but the pleasure was incredible.

Purring, she lifted her hips to his, clasping him with her inner muscles, kissing him with extravagant joy, telling him she loved everything he was doing to her.

For a second, he let her feel his full weight, the full power of his muscles as he caged her beneath him and pressed a hard, hungry kiss on her. The fingers tangled in her hair pulled again, and he held himself in stark possession of her. She could swear she felt him pulsing deep inside her.

Then his fingers massaged her scalp in gentle apology and he lifted slightly, withdrew and slowly began to thrust again. The music dimly entered her consciousness from far away as they danced, him leading her through the erotic steps as he lowered her zip and exposed her breast to his hand and mouth.

She sang breathy notes of acute pleasure and sensual agony, wanting this twisting, exciting play to go on for the rest of her life. But everything he did made the sweet pleasure intensify. Their lovemaking grew better and better, driving her up the scale of passion to exquisite heights. When he ran his hand up the bare thigh that bracketed his hip, and branded her buttock with his palm, lifting her into his quickening thrusts, she moaned in approval, needing that faster pace, that wild stimulation.

Climax arrived suddenly and more powerfully than the first. She clawed at him, stunned by the release, fixated by the intense sensation of his fullness inside her while she orgasmed. He cried out raggedly and shuddered over her and within her, pushing to take deep possession of her, holding them both on that place of ecstatic perfection.

Suffused with bliss, she didn't move afterward, just waited for her heart to slow and listened as his breath settled. In the distance, the music continued and voices rose in conversation and laughter.

At the first shift of his body to relax and leave hers, the first easing of his implacable lock of his hips against hers, she dropped her hands and removed her leg from his waist. Her long history with bandage changes gave her the knowledge that quick and ruthless was best, even though it hurt like hell.

He surprised her by merely shifting his weight off her a little before he pressed a kiss to the corner of her mouth then nuzzled his lips down her bare cheek to her ear. "That was incredible. Thank you."

She couldn't help the smile that grew unseen in the dark, or the way she warmed with pride and eye-stinging gratitude. "Thank *you*. I didn't expect anything like this to happen tonight," she confessed, even though she could hear the delight in her voice. He thought she was *incredible*.

"I'm pleased I could make your first time memorable."

Her heart stopped. "You could tell it's my first time?" She felt like the most gauche girl alive.

"I come to all of these. I know the regulars, and I've

never seen you before. I would have remembered," he added with another buss of warm lips against her cheekbone.

Oh, God, *that's* what he meant. She swallowed her relieved laughter, then stiffened as voices approached their cabana.

"We should go somewhere more private." He gently lifted off her, chivalrously flicking her skirt to cover her as he rolled away.

Everything in her protested, but she sat up on the other side of the narrow bed. As she tucked her breast back into her dress and closed the zipper, his hand curled around her upper arm, hot and commanding, drawing her into tipping back against him.

"I'm on the top floor. Are you closer?"

"I can't," she whispered with genuine regret, senses distracted by the musky scent surrounding him and the damp heat of his chest so close to her nose. She tilted her face to find his lips in a soft kiss of reluctant goodbye.

He didn't move his lips against hers except to say, "Why not?"

"It's complicated. I shouldn't have come out at all." Their breaths mingled. "I hope you *will* remember me," she admitted, feeling safe to reveal the bald longing here in the anonymous dark.

"I'll always wonder why, won't I?" he said with edgy dismay.

"And then you'll remember I wanted to keep this unspoiled by real life."

This time when she pressed her mouth to his, he kissed her back. Hard and thorough, so her heart rate picked up and her arms wanted to snake around his neck.

She wasn't about to hang around until the lights came on, though. She didn't want to see his face when he saw hers.

Pulling away, she stood and shook out her skirt, stepped her underwear off her heel and left them on the mat. Quite the cheeky Cinderella move. Her mother would never quit the slut-shaming if she knew.

Tiffany felt no guilt, however, no shame and no embarrassment as she slipped out of the cabana and up the stairs, past the pool and its raging party, toward the elevators and back to her room. Only sensual satisfaction and poignant *what-ifs* followed her steps.

CHAPTER THREE

RYZARD'S WATCH GAVE a muted beep, reminding him he had a meeting in ten minutes.

Annoyed, he rose from the small table where he'd sat for the last thirty minutes eating a meal he would have preferred to have taken in his room. He swept the breakfast room once more for a certain woman in a mask that made him think of a falcon's smoothly feathered head. A woman who was both gloriously uninhibited, yet had been so tight, he had feared as he entered her that she would call a halt.

A light sweat broke over him as he recalled possessing her, never having felt so—

He cut short the thought, stung by a dart of shame that he was on the verge of elevating a meaningless hookup past the only woman he would ever love. There was no comparison. Forget it all.

Good thing he hadn't allowed the *petite q* to send a message on his behalf. He'd been tempted, but the tight security here did him a favor, preventing him from a weak moment. All he'd had was a description of her mask, but when he had inquired to the nearest *petite q,* she had assured him she could deliver an invitation to the mysterious woman to join him at breakfast. She couldn't, however, divulge the member's name or moniker.

He'd declined, not wanting to look desperate. Not wanting to feel so desperate, but after the blood-chilling thought he'd just had, he *didn't* wish to see her again. Their somewhat literal bumping of two strangers in the night was nothing significant. A letting off of steam. If it had seemed particularly intense, that had been leftover adrenaline from the false alarm when the fireworks had exploded. For a second he'd been back in the heat of Bregnovia's civil war, his life in danger along with the woman in his arms.

Shaking off that terrifying second of *not again,* he assured himself this urgency to see her again was merely his libido looking for another easy pounce and feed.

That's why he'd had to force himself to take his time rising and dressing in the cabana last night, despite a nagging desire to hurry. It wasn't that he'd wanted to catch another glimpse, to actually catch *her* and convince her to strip down completely and stay with him all night. No, he was merely still horny.

Wondering why she hadn't stayed was pointless. He'd never know. Everyone at *Q Virtus* had places to go and people they preferred not to be seen with. Did she know who *he* was, he wondered?

She hadn't been wearing a watch that he'd felt. He'd checked his own as she'd left, trying to read her identifier before she had moved out of range, but no luck. Perhaps she'd run off to rejoin her husband or lover.

That thought infuriated him. Waiting to marry Luiza until it was too late was one of his few regrets. When you did make a lifelong commitment, you didn't break it. If she had…

He refused to dwell on any of it. She was a wet dream and he was awake now. Time to move on. He had an introduction to suffer through—would in fact drag his feet getting there so as to use up most of their time.

Then he would put out feelers for the meeting he really wanted. Someone here would know what was being said in the UN about his country's chances for recognition. Whatever he had to do to bestow legitimacy on his people, he would. They were his priority. It was Luiza's dream. He owed it to all of them to stay focused on that.

Not on some easy piece he'd picked up for a few hours of distraction.

Until the accident, Tiffany had always been fashionably—some would say chronically or even rudely—late. Once she began working, she'd discovered how irritating it was to be on the other side of that. Nowadays she strove to be early, and to that end she followed the directions on her watch, only to come up against yet another set of sliding doors. Rolling her eyes, she watched the timepiece count down how long she'd have to wait until they opened.

"Come on, come on," she muttered, wanting this meeting over with.

She'd almost forgotten it completely and wished she had. Unfortunately, her watch had been returned to her with her breakfast. "It was left in the reception lounge last night," Julio had said. "You have a message. That's what the blue light means."

"It was heavy and men kept coming up to me, saying my watch indicated I was open to being approached," she complained.

"Excellent feedback on the weight. A woman's perspective is so valuable for the manufacturers. But please let me show you how to set your Do Not Disturb."

He'd also shown her how to follow the directions to her meeting.

"Can I wear my mask?" she'd asked, peering at him from behind her feathers while trying to keep them out of her orange juice.

"Of course. Members typically wear their masks the entire time they're here."

With her main argument for blowing off the meeting disintegrated, she'd managed only a quiet, "Thanks."

Biting her thumbnail after Julio left, she'd debated whether to risk leaving her room. What if she saw *him?*

Heated tingles awakened, hinting at how exciting it could be to bump into him, but she tamped down on the wild feelings. Her behavior last night had been a crazy combination of being away from the stifling proximity of her family and, well, she had been a little drunk on rum, having almost finished her second drink by the time she'd begun dancing.

With a stranger.

Her lover.

A burble of near-hysterical laughter almost escaped her as she walked, thinking of their incredible encounter. Part of her reaction was delight that she had it in her to be that bold and daring. Before the accident she might have fantasized about something like that, but it would never be something she could imagine actually doing. There was no such thing as impulse in her family. The consequences to Daddy's career always had to be considered.

The rest of her giddiness had a sharply disappointed edge. This was the sort of secret she might share with a close girlfriend, but she didn't have any. Her friends, some closer than others, had all continued on with their lives during her recovery, living the life she was supposed to have. Hers had stalled and taken a sharp left turn. She would never have much in common with them now except the good old days. That topic just invited pitying stares.

Work was what she had now. A career. She had Paulie's corporation and men in her life who loved her as a daughter and a sister. Last night had been exciting and fun, but she couldn't repeat it. What was she going to do? Come to these events every quarter and sleep with a different stranger each time? The alternative, to expose her scars and hope a lover could overlook them, made her shudder in appalled dread.

No, she had to stay serious and focused and do what she'd been sent here to do. Last night was her personal secret, something to keep her glowing on the inside through the cold years to come. Today she represented Davis and Holbrook, one of the largest construction firms in the world, thanks to her marriage merging her father's architecture firm with Davis Engineering. As the one person with claim to both those names, she supposed she could take ten minutes out of her life to hand over the letter of introduction her brother had prepared.

Even if she didn't entirely approve of this man they wanted to court.

At least she could hide behind her mask. Kinky was her new normal, apparently, since she was becoming really fond of it, but it rejuvenated her confidence.

These gopher burrows under the building she was less sure of.

"Am I in an abattoir?" she asked a *petite q* when she found one.

"Absolutely not," the perky young woman replied, obviously not paid to have a sense of humor. "To ensure complete privacy for our guests, the doors only open if the next hallway is empty. Several people are moving around at this time, causing minor delays. Your meeting room is at the end of this hall and will open to your thumbprint."

As she stepped into the empty meeting room, however, she had to admit that this particular man's world was astounding. Given the industrial decor she'd traversed to get here, she had expected more of the same with the conference rooms. Instead she was in an aquarium—a humanarium—in the bottom of the sea. Stingrays flew like sparrows across the blue water over the glass ceiling and a garden of tropical fish bobbled like flower heads in a breeze, poking from the living reef that fringed the glass walls.

Amazed, she set down her black leather folder on a table between two chairs in the center of the room and walked the curved wall, keeping one hand on it to maintain her equilibrium as the distorted image of swaying kelp made her dizzy. She reminded herself to breathe and oriented herself by turning back to the room to take in the pair of chairs on the white area rug. They faced the windows and were separated by the table that held a crystal decanter of ice water and two cut-crystal glasses.

As she leaned her back against the window, the door panel whispered open and *he* stepped in. Her stranger.

Shock ran through her in an electric current that held her fixed, stunned.

Yes, that was the mask from last night, and she recognized his powerful build even though he was dressed differently. His gray shirt was short-sleeved, tailored close to his muscled shoulders and accentuated his firm, tanned biceps. The narrow collar of his shirt was turned down in a sharply contrasting russet, drawing her eye to the base of his throat.

She watched him swallow and lifted her gaze to his green-gold eyes.

How had he found her?

Behind him, the door whispered closed. The noise seemed to prompt him into motion. He took a few laconic steps into the room, hands going into his pockets. He wasn't taken aback by their incredible surroundings. His eyes never left their lock on hers as he paused next to the chairs, lifted a hand and removed his mask. He dropped it into one of the chairs, still staring at her.

Barefaced, he was beautiful. Not pretty, not vulnerable, but undeniably handsome with his narrow, hawkish face and sharply defined cheekbones. His blade of a nose accentuated the long planes of his cheeks to the rugged thrust of his jaw, making his mouth appear sensual by comparison, even though his lips weren't particularly full.

They weren't narrow, either, and neither were his eyes, but the keen way he watched her spoke of focus and intelligence.

Don't think about last night, she ordered herself, fighting the inner trembling of reaction.

"You could have given me your name last night and saved us taking up a room when they're so highly in demand."

Her throat closed as she processed his thick accent first. It was more pronounced when he spoke above a whisper and charged his deep, stern voice with husked layers. Then his words sifted through her mind, allowing her first to absorb that he recognized her, but didn't know her name. How—? The criticism in his tone penetrated, distracting her. She was rather sensitive to being called thoughtless, willing to admit she'd been quite the spoiled brat before she'd learned that even charmed lives could be hexed.

Finally she grasped the whole of what he'd said, and it sounded as if he thought she had known whom she was messing around with last night. Which meant he hadn't come here because he was looking for her, but because…

Oh. My. God.

"Ryzard Vrbancic?" she managed faintly. Please no.

His gorgeous mouth twisted with ironic dismay. "As you can see. Who are you?"

Of course she could see. Now that her brain was beginning to function, it was obvious this was the self-appointed president of Bregnovia. The leader of a resistance movement turned opportunist who had claimed the national treasury—from a fellow criminal, sure, but claimed it for himself all the same—then used it to buy his seat in his newly minted parliament.

How did a name such as Ryzard go from being something vaguely lethal and unsavory to noble and dynamic simply by encountering the man in person? How had she not sensed or realized—

"There's been a mistake. I've made a mistake." Oh, gawd, she could never tell her family. Her *virginity?* Really? To this man?

And yet her body responded to being in his presence. Even though she wasn't drunk and no music seduced her, her feet didn't want to move and her eyes kept being dragged back to his wide chest, where a sprinkle of hair had abraded her palms. His arms flexed as she watched, forcing memories of being caught protectively against him when the fireworks had started then carried like a wilting Southern belle when sex had been the only thing on their minds.

His wide-spaced feet in Italian leather drew her gaze, making her recall the way he'd shed his shoes and the rest of his clothes so deftly last night. His burnished bronze skin had been anything but cold and hard. He'd been taut and alive.

And generous. He'd touched her with incredible facility completely devoted to her pleasure. She tried not to look for his hands, but she was fervently aware of the way he'd tantalized her so intimately toward orgasm. In public.

Mortified heat burned her to the core, especially because she yearned to know it all again. Everything about him called to her, feathering over her nerves like last night's velvety breeze, not just awakening her sensuality, but exciting her senses into full alert. Why? How? The rapid plunge back into sexual arousal was incredibly confusing. Disconcerting. She needed to get out of here.

Pushing off the glass wall, she took two steps and he took one, blocking her.

Her heart plummeted through the floor. This undersea

garden had suddenly become a shark cage, and she was trapped inside it with the shark.

Warily she eyed him. "I didn't know who you were last night."

"No?" His brow kicked up, dismissing her claim as a lie.

"No!"

"You sleep with strangers often?"

"Apparently you do, so don't judge me."

His head went back a fraction, reassessing her. "Who are you?"

She folded her arms, debating. If she left now, without telling him, Christian might salvage something. She, of course, could never show her face in public again, but she didn't intend to. Except—

Her gaze involuntarily went to the black dossier on the table, the one that held their letter of introduction and a background on the company. She jerked her gaze back to his, panicked that he might have followed her look, but trying not to show it.

His vaguely bored gaze traveled to the table and came back to hers. Intrigue lit his irises, turning their green-gold depths to emerald. A cruel smile toyed with his mouth.

"That's not for you," she said firmly. "I have to go." She took one step toward the table and he reached without hurry to pick the dossier up.

"I said—"

He only flashed her a dangerous look that held her off and opened it with an elegant turn of his long finger. *Don't think about those fingers.*

Leave, she told herself, but there was no point. She couldn't outrun this sizzling mortification, no matter where she went. Her stomach turned over as she waited for a sign of his reaction to what he read.

A muted bell pinged. "Your reserved time has reached

its limit," a modulated female voice said through hidden speakers.

Thank God. Tiffany let out her breath.

"Extend it," Ryzard commanded.

"Will another thirty minutes be sufficient?"

"I can't stay," Tiffany insisted.

Grim male focus came up to hold her in place, locking her vocal chords.

"Send a full report to my tablet on Davis and Holbrook, specifically their director, *Mrs.* Paul Davis. Thirty minutes is plenty."

"Very good, sir." The bell pinged again and Tiffany thought, *run.* The threat he emanated seemed very real, even though he didn't move, only stared at her with utter contempt.

Bunching her fists at her sides, she lifted her chin, refusing to be anything less than indignant if he was going to jump to nasty conclusions about her. *He* could be married for all she knew—which was a disgusting thought. Her brain frantically tried to retrieve knowledge one way or another. She was no poli-sci major, but she'd always kept up on headlines, usually knowing way more than she wanted to about world politics because of her father's ambitions. There were gaps because of the accident, of course, months of news she'd missed completely that coincided with the coup in Bregnovia.

She had no memory about his marital status, but something told her he wouldn't be nearly so scornful of her if he had his own spouse in the wings.

Ryzard tossed the folder into the empty chair and hooked his hands in his pockets to keep from strangling the woman who wanted to play him for a fool. Her being married was bad enough. She might shrug off little things like extramarital affairs, but he did not.

The fact she thought she could buy his business was even more aggravating, partly because he was so affected by last night. As much as he wished he wasn't, his body was reacting to her even though she was dressed very conservatively. Her loose, sand-colored pants grazed the floor over heeled sandals he'd glimpsed when she had moved. They were clunky-looking things, but their height elongated her legs into lissome stems he wanted to feel through the thin fabric of her pants. Her yellow top was equally lightweight and cut across her collarbone, hiding skin that had seemed powder white last night.

What he'd seen of it, anyway. He couldn't see much today and found that equally frustrating. He might have detected her nipples poking against the fine silk of her top, but while her flat green jacket nipped in to emphasize her waist, it also shielded her breasts from his view.

Nothing about her appearance hinted at the exciting, sensual woman he'd met last night. Even her wild curls had been scraped back, which might have been an elegant display of her bone structure if he could see her face.

"Take off your mask," he ordered, irritated that his voice wasn't as clear as he'd like.

"No."

The quietly spoken word blasted into his eardrums. It was not something he heard often.

"It's not a request," he stated.

"It's not open for discussion," she responded, body language so hostile he could practically taste her antagonism.

Curious.

No. He wouldn't allow himself to be intrigued by her. Pulling himself together, he did his best to reject and eject her from every aspect of his life in one blow.

Glancing away as if his senses weren't concentrated upon her every breath and pulse, he said dismissively, "Tell your husband you failed. My business can't be bought. He might enjoy your second-rate efforts that offer no real pleasure, but I'm more discerning."

Her sharp inhale, as if she'd been stabbed in the lung, drew his gaze back to her. Her lips were white and trembled just enough to kick him in the conscience.

He forced himself to hold her hurt gaze, surprised how effective his insult had been. Her startling blue eyes deepened to pools of navy that churned with angry hatred. He didn't flinch from it, but instead held her gaze as if he was holding a knife in a wound, ensuring he would fully sever himself from a repeat performance of his weakness.

"How do you propose I tell him?" she asked with a bitterness that bludgeoned him, implacable and final. "Hire a psychic? He's dead." She pivoted to the door.

A blinding flash, like white light, shot through him. Not an external thing, but an inner slice of laser-sharp pain that he felt as an echo of hers. He knew that sort of grief—

Before he realized what he was doing, he'd moved to catch her arm and spin her around to him.

She used her momentum to bring her free hand up, sending it flying toward his face.

He caught her wrist and jerked back his head, his reflexes honed by war and a natural dominance that always kept him on guard. Still, a heavy blanket of regret suffocated him as he held her while she wordlessly struggled. He'd insulted her because he was angry, but he would never wound someone by dangling such a loss over them. An apology was needed, but holding on to her was like trying to wrestle a feral cat into a sack.

"Stop fighting me," he ground out, surprised by her wiry strength and unflagging determination.

"Go to hell!"

He got her wrists in one hand behind her back, her knee scissored between his own tightly enough to prevent it rising into his crotch. Squeezing her enough to threaten her breathing, he loosened off as she quieted.

"Big man, overwhelming a helpless woman," she taunted in a pant.

"You're not that helpless," he noted, admiring her fighting spirit despite his inherent knowledge that he shouldn't like anything about her.

She was widowed. That was tremendously important, even though he refused to examine too closely why he was so relieved. Or why he was now determined to learn more about her. He'd been serious about not being corruptible, no matter how his body longed to be persuaded.

Her shaken breaths caused her breasts to graze his chest, increasing the arousal their struggle had already stimulated. She recognized his hardness and squirmed again, forcing him to pin her even closer to hang on to her.

"Let me go," she said in a furious voice that provoked more than intimidated.

"In a minute." He reached to remove her mask—

She tried to bite him. He narrowly snatched his fingers from the snap of her teeth.

"You little wildcat." He couldn't help but be amused by her streak of ferocity. Her bared teeth were perfect, her pinched nostrils as refined as a spoiled princess's.

"I'm reporting this assault," she told him.

"I have a right to see whose body I was in last night," he told her, unconsciously revealing with the low timbre of his voice how disturbed he was by the memory.

"No, you don't. I'm discerning about who sees any part of me. And maybe I didn't bring my best game last night because I was bored and wanted it over with. Did you think of that?"

"I suppose I deserved that," he murmured, but her insult still landed like a knee in the gut, making his abdominal muscles clench in offense.

Digging his fingers around the knot of her hair, he tugged lightly, deliberately overwhelming her with his strength, exposing her throat and making her aware she was at his mercy. Not because he got off on hurting women. Never. But she needed to understand that even though she was utterly vulnerable to him, he wouldn't harm her.

"Now we've both said something cruel, and neither of us will do it again."

Her outraged "Ha" warmed his lips, making him deeply conscious of the shape of her Kewpie-doll mouth with its peaks in her top lip over a fat strawberry of a bottom one. Her scent, like Saponaria, somewhere between dewy grass and sun-warmed roses, threatened to erase all thought but making love to her again.

"I only said what I did because I thought you were married. And you tricked me. I don't like your trying to take advantage of me. To even the playing field…" He reached for the tailing ribbon that held her mask.

"Noooo." The sharp anguish in her voice startled him. She was genuinely terrified, straining into a twist to escape his loosening of the mask.

He let go of the ribbon and her, horrified that he'd scared her so deeply, but he couldn't help reaching to steady her when she staggered as she tried to catch the falling mask. Her shaking hands fumbled it before her, turning it around and around, trying to right it so she could put it on again. A desperate sob escaped her.

It was too late. He'd seen what she was trying to hide, and the bottom dropped out of his heart. He touched her chin, wanting a better look.

She knocked his hand away and flashed a look of fury at him. With her jaw set in livid mutiny, she stopped trying to replace her mask and stared him down with the kind of aggression that would make him fear for his life if she'd been armed.

"Happy?" she charged.

Not one little bit.

As he took in the mottled shades of pink and red, all he saw was pain. He'd been in battle. He knew what bullets and flames and chemicals could do to the human body. That's why his world had stopped last night when he'd thought a bomb was landing on the ramparts of the club.

But these were healed injuries, as well as they'd ever get anyway. The ragged edge of the facial scar followed a crooked line like a country's border on a map, sharply defining rescued flesh from the unharmed with a raised pink scar. It hedged a patch from over her left eye into the corner of her lid—she might have lost her sight, he acknowledged, cold dread touching his internal organs. Under her eye, it cut diagonally toward her nose before tracing down to the corner of her mouth and under her jawline, and then wound back to her hair.

The side of her neck was only a little discolored, but the way the color fanned at the base of it made him suspect the scarring went down her arm and torso, too, maybe farther.

As he brought his gaze back up to her face, he met eyes so bruised and wounded, he was struck with shame at causing her to reveal herself. He hadn't been trying to humiliate her. This wasn't meant as a punishment.

The hatred in her eyes took it as such anyway, stabbing him with compunction.

"I wouldn't work for you if your country was knocked back into the Stone Age and we were overinventoried in animal fur and flint. I'm leaving. Now."

He didn't try to stop her, sensing he'd misjudged her on a grand scale.

She tied her mask into place without looking at him. When she pressed the button to open the doors, they didn't cooperate, remaining closed while she swore at her watch.

"Tiffany," he cajoled, pulling her name from what he'd read, but not sure what he would say if he could persuade her to stay.

"Die," she ordered flatly.

The doors opened and she walked out.

CHAPTER FOUR

For the first time in months, Tiffany cried. Really cried as she hugged her knees in the shower and released sobs that echoed against the tiles. They racked her so hard she thought she'd throw up. She hated her life, hated herself, hated him.

She'd still been processing his remark about her efforts being second-rate when he'd yanked back her curtain and looked at her as if she was an object of horror. As though he was repulsed.

Sex was not worth this. Men weren't. She was old enough, and educated enough, to know that having a husband and kids were not necessary ingredients to a woman's happiness. Why then was she so gutted every time she was forced to face that no man would ever want her? That a family life would never be hers?

It was self-pitying tripe, and she had to get over it.

Forcing her weak legs to support her, she turned off the shower and leaned against the wall, cold and dripping until she worked up the energy to pull on a robe. As she moved into her room, she felt empty. Not better, not depressed, just numb.

That was okay. She could live with numb.

Perching on the foot of the bed, she stared at her wrinkled fingers and wondered what she should do. Hide in her room until this ridiculous clubhouse opened its doors again? Fake appendicitis for a helicopter ride to the mainland? She felt sick. She was damp and feverish, aching all over, weak and filled with malaise.

A yawn took her by surprise and she thought, *Siesta*. One small thing in her favor. Crawling up to her pillows, she escaped into unconsciousness.

The sun crept around the edge of his balcony, likely to begin blistering his bare toes soon, but Ryzard was ready to stretch away the stiffness in his body anyway. He'd been motionless for over an hour as he read through the report he'd been provided by the *Q Virtus* staff.

Davis and Holbrook was an exceptional organization, very well regarded in the international construction industry. He could definitely do worse as he looked at rebuilding the broken roads and collapsed buildings in his city centers. They had wanted to land on his radar as he moved toward those sorts of goals, and now they were.

The rest of the report, about Mrs. Paul Davis, was even more interesting. She had started out as a wealthy society darling. Her marriage to a family friend had all the markings of a traditional fairy tale, right up to the wedding gown with a train and the multitiered cake.

Except a wedding gift from the bride's brother of a prestigious sports car had been more temptation than the drunken groom could resist. He'd taken it up to ninety between the courtyard and the gates of the golf and country club, detonating it against a low brick wall before the guests had stopped waving.

After a flurry of death and memorial announcements accompanied by touch-and-go mentions of the bride, the reports had dried up. Fast-forward two years and his widow was taking the reins of her dead husband's corporation. Her brother had held her power of attorney during her recovery, but his talents were better suited to hands-on architectural engineering. The plethora of awards he'd earned spoke to that very loudly.

All of this would have been flat information if it didn't reinforce to Ryzard that he'd made a mistake in assuming she'd been trying to influence him with sex. What reason would she have? Her company was flourishing—somewhat surprisingly, given that her credentials amounted to an arts degree and attitude, but her grades were exceptional. She was certainly intelligent.

And he could personally attest that she was a ballbuster, he allowed with irony. He had no doubt she was more than a figurehead. If she had a vision, quite likely one formed in her husband's name, she would achieve it.

Turning from that disturbing thought, he allowed that if Bregnovia had already attained recognition, she might have tried for an advantage while he had a wider playing field to draw from, but it would be a risky move until his government was recognized.

Did their interest in his business mean an acknowledgment for Bregnovia was in the works? Or was their rendezvous exactly what it seemed to be: two healthy people enjoying the pleasures of the mating ritual.

Heat pooled in his lap as he dwelt on the possibility she'd welcomed him because she'd been as caught up as he had in their physical compatibility.

A twinge of conscience followed, but he had long ago rationalized that his heart and his body were separate when it came to sex. He had the same basic needs as any living thing, requiring nutrition, a sheltered environment and a regular release of his seed. If a peculiar mix of chemistry intensified his reaction when that last happened, well, he couldn't be held responsible. It was hormones, not emotion.

It was not infidelity against Luiza.

And Tiffany would have no reason to pursue him for sex

to gain his business. It would only complicate what might otherwise be a wise and lucrative association.

Something he should take under consideration, he supposed, scraping the side of his thumb against the stubble coming in on his jaw. It didn't matter how he cast their tryst. It shouldn't happen again.

Except there was one other fact from this report that kept teasing him.

Mr. Holbrook, Tiffany's father. An architect by education, he'd quickly become a career politician who'd worked his way up the ranks of local councils into a senator's mansion. He was now running for the presidency.

Suppose last night had been pure coincidence. Why then had the Holbrooks requested he meet them here, under the discreet curtain of *Q Virtus?* If they feared making a play for his business would hurt the senator's chances, they wouldn't have met him at all. No, it must mean they knew the United States was leaning toward recognition.

A flush of excitement threatened to overtake him, but Ryzard reminded himself to be patient. Backing from the United States would influence many other countries to vote in his favor, but nothing was confirmed.

Still, one thing was clear: he needed another meeting with Tiffany Davis.

Tiffany woke foggy-headed to a noise in the main room like dishes rattling on a cart. Leaping from the bed, she staggered to the door into the lounge and found Ryzard Vrbancic directing one of the *petite q's* to set a table on the balcony.

"What are you doing?" She turned the lapel of her robe up against her cheek.

"I thought you were showering, but apparently you went back to sleep."

"What?" Tiffany scowled at him. "How do you know

what I've been doing? I thought these rooms were completely secure," she charged the woman in the red gown.

"I used my override to bring in the meal you ordered... didn't you?" The young woman looked suspiciously at Ryzard, but he was quick.

"We did, thank you. I'll manage from here. You can go." To Tiffany, he said, "Don't confuse the staff just because we've had a tiff." A mild snort and, "You're aptly named, aren't you?"

"Get out of here," she cried.

The *petite q,* already hurrying, ran to the door and out.

Goggling at Ryzard, whose mouth twitched, Tiffany said, "Seriously?"

"You're overreacting."

"I want you to leave."

"I'm about to make you an offer you can't refuse. Quit hiding and accept."

She narrowed her eyes on his back as he moved onto the balcony, not interested in anything from him except assurances her family would never find out what had happened between them. Not that she was willing to say so.

It took everything in her to stand tall and say, "What kind of offer?" She was writhing inside at everything that had happened, yet had wound up dreaming about him. It had been erotic until it had turned humiliating.

"I can't hear you," he called from the balcony.

Clenching her teeth, she wavered in the doorway, hanging back while telling herself not to let him get away with this manipulation. At the very least, she ought to cover up. She didn't so much as go for milk in the middle of the night without concealer for fear of frightening the staff at home. The only reason she'd forgone it this morning was because she'd expected to keep her mask on.

Ryzard Vrbancic had seen her, however, and she was

still flopping like a fish out of water, gasping for air, waiting for the boot that would send her careening off the boat.

Everything in her cringed with a need to hide, but maybe seeing her again like this would repel him into moving along.

Yanking tight the tie on her robe, she marched to the open French doors and said, "I'm not interested in any offers from you. Please leave."

"I thought you were dressing," he remarked, squeezing fresh lemon across raw oysters in their half shell. They were arranged on a silver tray of ice. Next to them sat a tapas platter of fritters, flatbread, shredded meat, guacamole, salsa and something that looked like burritos but they were wrapped in a type of leaf.

Her stomach growled. She tried to cover the sound with her hand, but he'd heard.

"You're hungry. Eat," he urged magnanimously. As if he wasn't trespassing in her room.

"I prefer to eat alone." She indicated the door, not subtle at all.

He picked up an oyster and eyed her as he slurped it into his mouth, chewed briefly, then swallowed. Raw oysters were supposed to be an aphrodisiac. She'd always thought they were disgusting, but what he'd just done had been the sexiest thing she'd ever seen. She followed the lick of his tongue across his lips, and a wobbly sensation accosted her insides.

Reacting to him made staring him down even more difficult than it already was, but she held his gaze, inner confidence trembling as she waited for another flinch to overtake him like the one this morning. His expression never wavered, though. He let his gaze slide to her scarred cheek, but then it went south into her cleavage, where the swells of her breasts peeped from between her lapels. His perusal continued over her hips, lingered on the dangling ends of her belt and ended at her shins, one white, one mottled.

Involuntarily, her toes curled as she reacted to his masculine assessment. She couldn't tell if she was passing muster or being found wanting. She told herself it didn't matter, that she didn't want his approval or any man's, but in her heart she yearned for a hint of admiration.

He pulled out a chair. "Sit down."

Swallowing, telling herself to keep a straight head, she deliberately provoked a reaction to her flaws by saying, "I'm not supposed to go in the sun."

He shrugged off the protest. "It will set in twenty minutes."

"Look, I'm running out of ways to tell you to get lost without pulling out the big one. I don't want anything to do with you. I was against giving you that letter in the first place, and I'm sorry I came here at all. We won't work for you."

He finished another oyster, but she had his full attention. She could feel it. When his tongue cleaned his lips, she imagined he was licking her all over.

Ignore it, she chided herself.

"Why?" he asked.

Why what? Her brain had lost the plot, but she quickly picked it up, reminding herself of *his* flaws.

"Because I don't like your methods. You're no better than the criminal you replaced."

"I'm a lot better than the criminal I replaced. Check my human-rights record," he growled while a flush of insult rose to his cheeks.

It was enough antagonism to give her pause and make her reconsider deliberately riling him, but despite how much she hated herself for having sex with him, she was still aware of a pull. She desperately needed to cut him down and out.

"You're living pretty large while your countrymen starve. How many people died so you could eat raw oysters and watch the sun set?"

"You know nothing about what I've lost so my people can eat," he said in a lethal tone.

As he spoke, he turned aside to toss his empty shell on the cart, but she glimpsed such incredible pain she caught her breath against an answering stab of anguish. She quickly muffled it, but something in her wavered. Was she misjudging him?

She shook off the thought, scoffing, "Did I strike a nerve? Do you not like having your repulsive side exposed?"

He shot her a fierce look and she thought, *Shut up, Tiffany.*

"You're acting out of bitterness, and it's not with me. We promised not to be cruel."

That gave her a niggle of guilt, which she didn't like at all. She looked at her perfectly manicured nails.

"You might have promised," she said haughtily. "I didn't."

"You like to deliberately hurt people? You do have an ugly side."

That lifted her gaze, and his expression made her heart tremor where it clogged the base of her throat. He had very patrician features. Very proud and strong. Right now they were filled with contempt.

Shame lunged in her. She might have been spoiled and self-involved, but she never used to be mean. But she was angry. So angry. And there was no one to take it out on. She had to look away from the expression that demanded she apologize.

She wavered, uncertain of her footing, but she had enough unscrambled brain cells to remember he was a dictator, not some do-good pastor.

"What do you expect, a welcome mat?" she hazarded, tucking her fists behind her upper arms, affecting a bravado she didn't feel. "You've invaded my territory—"

"You're not angry I'm here. You're angry you had to face the man you made love to last night. That I saw your secret. You're not repulsive, Tiffany."

"As I said, you're stepping into places you haven't been invited."

"I was invited." He picked up an oyster, and his tongue curled to chase and catch the slippery flesh before he pulled the morsel into his mouth.

Inner muscles that were still vaguely tender from their lovemaking clenched involuntarily, sending a shimmer of pleasure upward to her navel and down the insides of her thighs.

When he took a step toward her, she took a hasty one back, bumping into the rail of the balcony.

He raised his brows as he pulled out her chair another inch, reading way too clearly what kind of nervousness she'd just revealed.

"I want you to leave," she insisted.

"We'll clear the air first."

She almost mumbled an adolescent, *I don't want to clear the air.* Because she didn't. She wanted to hit and bite and push away.

She wanted to be left alone to die of loneliness.

Oh, don't be such a baby, Tiffany.

It was true, though. She was like a wounded animal that snarled at anyone who tried to help it. It was the source of the horrible tension with her family. They didn't know what to do with this new Tiffany who hated her life and everything in it.

She glared at Ryzard, loathing him for being the man to show her how twisted she'd become. He'd caught her in a moment of terrible weakness last night, playing pretend that she was normal. He'd sliced past the emotional scar tissue she'd grown, and he seemed to still be doing it. That made him dangerous.

"The sun is about to set. It won't hurt you to be out here," he said.

She whipped around to see how close it was to the horizon. She hadn't been in the sun for more than a handful of steps between a house and car in two years. As she stepped into its rays, the heat on her face felt good. The fading red ball filled her with rapture as it lowered toward the sea.

Holding her breath, she strained her ears.

The band started below, making her slap a hand on the rail in disappointment. "I wanted to hear it!"

"Hear what?" he asked, standing next to her.

"When the sun touches the water."

He gave her a skeptical look that said, *Aren't you a bit old for that?*

She turned away, hiding that yes, she clung to certain childish fantasies that reminded her of easier, simpler times. Being lighthearted and silly didn't come naturally to her anymore, and she desperately longed to find that part of herself again. Tiny moments of happiness were like bread crumbs, hopefully leading her back to a place of acceptance. Maybe even contentment.

"You're really quite sensitive, aren't you?" he mused.

"No."

"And contrary." He waved at the chair he'd pulled out for her. "I have some questions for you. They're important. Sit."

"I'm not a dog."

"No, you're as aloof and touchy as a wet cat. The purring version is worth all the scratching and hissing, though."

"I don't want to talk about that," she rushed to state, unnerved by the suggestiveness in his remark.

"We won't. Not yet," he agreed, and his touch on her shoulder nudged her to sit.

She did, mainly to avoid the way the light contact of his hand made her stomach dip in excitement, and partly because her mother was lecturing her in her head. The members of their family, in all their greatness, were ambassadors, obligated to set an example of good manners and rising above the unpleasant. Such an annoying legacy.

She was also starving. Taking care of herself had become a habit through her recovery. Good food was one of her few real pleasures these days, and this stuff looked awesome.

He watched her build a flatbread into a soft taco, not being shy with the high-calorie avocado paste, either.

"What?" she asked defensively.

"I'm not used to seeing a woman eat like that."

She bit back a spiteful, *Too busy watching them starve?* She really didn't want to be that person, but she didn't know how else to handle him.

"Why are you here?" she asked instead.

He paused in preparing his own flatbread. "Why are *you* here, Tiffany? Why did your family send you to meet me?"

The weight of his gaze turned her shrug into a shiver. "Apparently I'm the only one who is a member."

His brows went up in surprise.

"I inherited my husband's fortune. My father isn't exactly struggling, but he doesn't qualify."

"I read about your accident. I'm sorry for your loss."

She prickled, waiting to see if he would make more of it, dig deeper, question how a married woman could have been a virgin.

"I'm also a member and was one long before our civil war. The money you accuse me of stealing is Bregnovia's. It's earmarked to fund our recovery."

She eyed him, seeing a contrary mix of Euro-sophistication and obdurate leader. When he caught her looking at him, her heart skipped. She looked away.

"I'll have to request a report on you from the powers that be. Find out how you made your fortune," she said.

"I'll tell you. It's a spigot system I developed for the oil industry, inspired by what I learned working in vineyards after finishing my engineering degree."

Despite her inner warnings to hold him off, she was intrigued. "That seems an odd choice. What was an engineer doing in a winery?"

"Rebelling," he said flatly, not inviting more questions as he reached to the wine bucket and drew out a dripping green bottle. "This is from my country. You'll enjoy it."

Of course she would. Who would dare not?

His arrogance was growing on her if she was finding it more amusing than annoying.

"What do you mean, you were rebelling?"

He drew a subtle breath, as though gathering himself for something difficult. "If you were to order a report on me, you would learn my parents sent me to live in Germany when I was six. For my safety and to give me a better life. Our country has been annexed by one neighbor or another since before the First World War. There were constant outbreaks of independence-seeking followed by terrible repression. My parents couldn't leave, but they smuggled me out to friends. I can't complain. My foster parents were good people. The husband was an automotive engineer who pressed me to follow in his footsteps. As a vocation I didn't mind it, but when I graduated I felt as most young people do. That this was my life and I could do as I liked." He shrugged, mouth twisting in self-deprecation. "I'm not proud of abandoning my potential to pick grapes, but it allowed me to bring a fresh perspective when I went to Russia, planning to make my fortune drilling for oil."

"Where you fashioned this doodad that is so popular it made you into a bazillionaire?"

"Da," he confirmed with a nod.

"Humph." She reached for her wine. "Does the rest of the world know this?"

He lifted a shoulder dismissively. "The press prefers to sensationalize what I did with my money."

"Which was to fund a war."

"I freed my country."

"And now you own it."

"I lead it. What do you think of the wine?"

She was no sommelier and didn't bother with sniffing and swirling, but she thought the light color was appealing and she enjoyed the way the initial tang, almost fruity, eased into something more earthy. Not oaky. Vanilla?

She tried again, wanting to determine what it was. But as much as she loved wine, alcohol had been off-limits as her body had needed every advantage to recover. That made her a lightweight. She had to be careful about losing her head around him.

As the memory of their dirty dancing and everything that followed bathed her in heat, the proximity of a bedroom and sitting here in her robe suddenly seemed incredibly dangerous and intimate.

Ryzard watched a glow of awareness brighten Tiffany's skin, filling her compelling blue eyes even as she looked into the crisp white wine she set aside. Her reaction might be in response to the alcohol, but his male instincts read her differently.

He shifted in his chair, widening his knees to make room for the growing reaction tugging insistently between his legs.

Tricking the waitstaff into granting him entry to her room had been the oldest one in the book, but as he'd suspected, she wouldn't have seen him otherwise and he wanted answers. At this precise second, however, he found himself with only one thing on his mind: her. She was more complex than he'd given her credit for, both when he'd lost himself in the mecca of her flesh and when he'd assumed she was attempting to manipulate him.

She was far more beautiful than he'd taken the time to notice this morning, too. Then his attention had been drawn to the scarring, his focus on the pain it indicated. Now he could see what had existed before discoloration and a raised jagged line had bisected her cheek. Blonde, blue eyed, with skin like a baby and the bone structure of an aristocrat, she was Helen of Troy.

Not that he was prepared to go to war ever again, but he could imagine men who would. Her young husband must have been intimidated, knowing how coveted she was.

"It's rude to stare," she said, growing redder in one cheek.

"I'm not staring. I'm admiring."

Her mouth shrank in rejection, and so did his brain. He forced himself to look away from thick lashes that swept down to hide her eyes. This meeting wasn't about kindling an affair that had barely started, no matter how much the thought appealed.

It appealed far too much. He could barely concentrate as memories of her pushing her ass into his groin as she writhed with pleasure under his slippery touch filled his head. The heady power of fondling her to orgasm had made him drunk and was overshadowed only by how good she had felt squeezing him in her hot, perfect depths.

But his country came first. He couldn't forget that. Couldn't forget anything.

He shook himself out of his fascination and spoke briskly.

"Your father seems exceptionally well connected in Washington. By sending you to speak to me, he is signaling that your country is likely to support my petition for recognition at the UN, is he not? Has he told you this is forthcoming?"

"He's under that impression, but who knows what the attitude will be tomorrow? Welcome to politics. You know how these things work."

He did, and the hardest lesson he had learned after being in a war was when to back off and use diplomacy instead of force to get what he wanted. It was also standard practice to weigh a person's impact on an agenda before developing a relationship.

Maybe he hadn't properly examined how their affair could affect his goal before he made love to her, but Tiffany's knowledge and connections suggested she could have a very positive influence.

A wild rush of excitement flew through him as he found a rationale to continue their affair, but he forced himself to hold on to a cool head and gather information first. "Does your father have any sway over your country's decision makers?"

"He has followers. Believers in his vision. Isn't that how you got elected, by cultivating the same?" The remark was somewhere between haughty and ironic.

"You don't seem to be one of them. His followers, I mean. It's quite obvious you're not one of mine. Yet."

"Ha," she choked, but she lowered her lashes as if to prevent him reading something different in her eyes. "Never yours and while I'll always cheer for Dad, I'm tired of living my life by his career," she said with dour humor and popped a cherry tomato into her mouth, pursing her lips in a pout as she chewed.

"When is the election?" he asked, trying not to watch her plump lips too closely.

"Not for a year, but the campaigning is well under way. He was leaving for Washington as we were coming here."

"We?" he asked sharply, territorial instincts riled.

"My brother and I."

"Ah. That's fine then." He frowned. Whatever relief he felt in knowing there wasn't another man in her life was buried under the discomfort of revealing he saw himself in the role. What was it about her that not only affected him but also lowered his ability to hide how much?

She lifted her brows. "Jealous?" Her smile was taunting, but her voice thinned across the word, suggesting a vulnerability that further undermined his resistance to her.

He shouldn't want her this badly, but he did. Last night had been exceptional, and she was a practical connection to cultivate. Where was the sense in fighting it?

"Possessive," he corrected. "You have a lover, *draga*."

Her shocked expression masked into something complex. Her lips tightened in dismay while her brow flinched in pain. A stark yearning drew her features taut while her swallow indicated a type of fear. Then it all smoothed away, leaving him unsettled, wondering if an affair with her could become more complicated than it needed to be.

"Had," she said in a husky voice. "Past tense."

"I'm not talking about your husband," he growled, stirred to jealousy after all.

The blank look she sent him disappeared in a raspy laugh. "Neither am I."

His sharp brain caught a hidden meaning, but she kept talking, distracting him.

"Last night was a departure from my real life, not something I'll ever do again. Why would you even want to—" Dawning comprehension waxed her features before her face gradually tightened in rejection and something more disturbing. Anguish. "Wow. Nice to know some things haven't changed," she said bitterly.

"What do you mean?" Clammy palms seemed an overreaction to being rejected as a one-nighter. He'd done it himself in the past, but he didn't like it. Not from her.

"I'm still capable of being used," she answered. "You think that if you keep me close, you'll keep my father's cronies closer."

A pinch of compunction gave him pause, but that's not all that was going on here. And now she'd piqued his curiosity.

"Who used you in the past? How?" It was a tender point for him. Only a blind fool would fail to see the advantage to him in associating with her, but there were lines, especially with women. When Luiza was taken, it was to use her as leverage against him. She'd ended her life to prevent it. He never took manipulation of the unwilling lightly.

"Who *hasn't* used me?" she demanded. "I thought if there was one silver lining to this—" she drew a circle around her face "—it was that I was no longer a pawn. Thanks for dinner." She stood up, tossing him a pithy look. "A girl in my position is lucky when a man shows her a bit of attention. You're a helluva guy, Ryzard."

Her contempt burned like acid as it dripped over him. It might not have seared so deeply if he hadn't grasped at the advantages of an affair to justify exactly how badly he wanted to continue theirs.

He didn't want to admit how fierce his hunger for her was, but the hurt beneath her words told him she didn't see any at all. Wounding her, especially when she was so sensitive about her desirability, had a disturbing effect on him. Guilt assailed him and provoked something deeper. A compulsion to draw her close and make up with her.

He didn't want to be so enthralled. It went against everything he'd promised himself and Luiza's memory. Nevertheless, he reacted to the way she rejected him with a pivot of her body. It incited him to strike fast to keep from being shut out. Fear that had nothing to do with the best interests of his country goaded him to act.

"Don't underestimate what's between us, Tiffany." He

inwardly cringed at revealing so much, but he was even more averse to her thinking he was capable of low motives. "The attraction between us is real and very strong."

"Oh, give it up! You don't want me. You—"

"Shall I prove it?" He rose and easily stalked her across the tiny space of the balcony, using her outstretched hand to tug her close and pulling her resistant body into to his own.

"What do you think you're doing?" she demanded, wriggling for freedom then stilling when she felt his arousal. "You—" Confusion stilled her and she searched his expression.

"As I said." He lowered his head, setting a determined kiss over her protesting mouth.

Tiffany continued to press for distance, but he wasn't being mean, just insistent. Still, she was awfully confused. The way he'd given her that moment of hope that she could be attractive to someone before she realized it was all a ruse had been devastating. Now he was coming on strong, making her want to melt into him. Really, seriously, turn to mush in his arms. It was so frightening to be this affected. She did the only thing she could think to do. She tried to bite him.

He jerked his head back. "Are we playing rough, *draga?*" He shot his hand beneath her robe, grasping her breast in a firm hand, dislodging the slippery tie of her robe so it started to fall open.

"Don't!" she cried, hunching and scrambling to keep as much cloth in place as possible. "Please, Ryzard, don't do this. Not out here where anyone could see."

He froze, then slowly withdrew his hand. The tips of his fingers grazed a distended nipple, sending a pulse of pleasure-pain through her. She was too humiliated to respond and too shaken by the fear of exposure to appreciate his obeying her plea.

"Tiffany," he scolded as he held her in loose arms. "I'm not trying to hurt you."

Pushing back until he reluctantly let his hold on her drop away, she ensured she was completely covered, but couldn't lift her head.

"I've seen battle scars, you know." The hand he used to smooth her hair back from her bad cheek was surprisingly compassionate.

Rather than turn into his caress, she averted from it.

"I'm your first lover since the accident? That's why you're so shy?" Ryzard was still trying to catch up to the way her shield of toughness had fallen away so quickly into such tremendous vulnerability. One second she'd been a worthy adversary, the next a broken fawn in need of swift protection.

"Yeah." Her snorted word held a hysterical note. She tried to step over the chair he'd upended, trying to move away from him. Tears sheened her eyes, her emotions so close to the surface he knew she was near a tipping point.

He bent to right the chair, allowing her to move away into privacy because pieces were falling into place in his mind in a way he couldn't quite believe. Her back seemed incredibly narrow and bowed under a weight as she entered the suite. He could hardly countenance what he was thinking, but her gasp of pain last night rang in his ears. He had thought she just wasn't quite ready, but...

Cautiously he followed, one hand going to the door frame to steady himself as he asked, "Tiffany. Am I your *only* lover?"

She didn't turn around, but her shoulders seemed to flinch before she lifted her head to say cockily, "So far, but with my looks and connections, I'm encouraged to believe there's more in my future."

He bit back a curse while his free hand clenched into a

fist at his side. He wanted to shake her out of sheer frustration with her cavalier attitude, but at the same time he had a deep compulsion to cradle her against him. The erotic memory of their coming together grew sweeter even as he struggled with the ramifications of being a woman's first. He'd done it once before. He knew the emotional ties it pulled from both parties.

A splintering sensation accosted him as he once again compared her with Luiza. His first instinct was to walk away. Confusing emotions tumbled through him like a rockslide, tainted with the intense grief he'd managed to avoid as the aftermath of war had consumed him. He once again hated himself as a traitor for having more than a passing interest in Tiffany, but learning he was her first changed things. He wasn't so archaic he thought virginity was a seal of quality, but losing it was an important marker in a woman's life. He couldn't be dismissive of her or what she'd offered him, even if she was trying to be.

"Can you explain to me how this is possible, *Mrs. Davis?*"

Tiffany looked to the ceiling, battling back stupid tears and a deeper sense of vulnerability than she'd ever felt. There had been a time when her confidence, her belief in her own superiority, had been unflagging. In an instant she had become weak and broken and dependent. Finding her way back from that seemed impossible, and she hated that Ryzard saw her at this low point. He was so strong and sure of himself. Where had he been when she'd had all her defenses in place and could have handled his forceful, dynamic personality?

A dozen sarcastic responses to his question came to her tongue, but the nearest she could get to flippant was to say, "I was afraid I'd fall in love with someone else if I didn't save myself for Paulie."

She tightened her belt and turned, surprised to catch him in an unguarded moment.

The faraway look in his eye suggested he had dark thoughts of his own. Seeing he might not be as completely put together as he seemed gave her the courage to continue with more outspokenness than she'd ever allowed herself.

"Our marriage was written in stone. Our fathers were friends, and his mother was my mom's maid of honor. Paulie and my brother, Christian, were inseparable through childhood. The architect and engineer designed the bridge between our families when Paulie and I were still in diapers. By the time I was in high school, no other boy had the guts to ask me out. They knew I was already taken."

"You didn't date? Didn't sleep with him?"

"*Paulie* dated. He sowed enough wild oats for the both of us. He took me to the Friday night dances, and on Monday I would hear what had happened at the parties he went to after he dropped me at home. He came *here* and had affairs."

"And you put up with that?"

She sighed, hugging herself. "I believed him when he told me he was getting it out of his system. He swore that once we were married, he would never stray. I still believe he meant it. He encouraged me to do the same," she offered with a shrug, "but like I say, no one offered and I told myself it would be romantic to wait."

"Did you love him?"

She sighed, chest aching as she admitted what she'd never told anyone. "I adored him like a best friend. That's a good foundation for a marriage, right?" She had needed to believe it, but hearing it now only made her hug herself tighter.

She tried to stem the emotions swelling in her, but the rest of her feelings, the churning doubts and anger and grief, gathered and poured out. "I miss him like crazy. He's the one person who would have been right beside me through all of this, keeping my spirits up, saying all the right things. But I don't know if I'd even be speaking to him because I'm so angry. I hate him for dying, really truly hate hi—"

A sob arrived like a commuter train with a whoosh and a suck of air. She held herself steady as grief rose and peaked. She blinked and trembled until she could assimilate it. After a long minute, she found control again and managed to continue.

"I hate him for getting behind the wheel that night. I hate Christian for giving him the car. I hate myself for thinking one spin up the drive when we were all so drunk would be okay."

Something tickled her jaw, and she realized a tear had bled down her numb cheek to burn her chin. She swiped it away and sniffed back the rest.

Through blurred eyes, she saw Ryzard looked gray, but she was coming back from a dark place. The whole world looked dull and bleak.

"I've never admitted that to anyone," she confessed. "I think it needed to come out. Thank you." She rubbed her arms, becoming aware she was frozen and achy.

Ryzard's long legs and wide chest appeared unexpectedly before her. He drew her into his arms even as she drew a surprised breath. His expression was stark and filled with deep anguish.

"Don't say anything," he said heavily, overcoming her automatic stiffening and pressing her into the solid strength of his body. "Just be quiet a minute."

He smoothed hands along her back to mold her into him, warming her. It wasn't a pass. It was comfort. After a hesitant moment, she let her head settle into the hollow of his shoulder and closed her eyes. He stroked her hair and she let her arms wrap around him, hugging him so the bruise that was her heart still ached, but felt covered and protected by the shield of his solid presence.

"Sometimes anger and hatred are the only things that get you through the injustice," he said so quietly she wasn't sure she really heard him, but the tickle across her hair told her his voice was real. "I envy people of strong faith. They never seem tortured by the why of it."

She swallowed, floored to realize they were sharing a moment, something so deep and personal it didn't need a name of a lost one for her to know he understood her utterly and completely. He suffered as she did.

Her hand moved on his back, soothing the tension in the muscles alongside his spine. She relaxed into him and they held each other for a long minute.

Gradually she realized he was becoming aroused. He wasn't overt about it, but she knew and an answering thread of response began subtly changing her own body. Her internal organs felt quivery and her breasts grew sensitive. Awareness of their stark physical differences expanded in her mind along with how intimately they'd fit themselves together last night.

As heat suffused in her, she tried to pull away and keep her head ducked so he wouldn't see how she was reacting.

He kept her close and tilted her face up. His mouth twitched ruefully, but his eyes remained somber. "You see?" he murmured. A sensation of pressure made her think he might have stroked his thumb over the scar tissue on her cheek. "We're a good fit. You should let me give you the after-party you deserved before your wedding."

"Tempting," she said, backing out of his hold because a resurgence of warmth that had its feet in embarrassed longing tingled through her. "But I'm not a charity case you need to offer a pity lay. Give me your email and I'll let you know if my father learns anything."

"My desire for you has nothing to do with my political

agenda," he dismissed with a heavy dollop of annoyance. "I want you."

She snorted. "Why?"

"Because, Tiffany, if you had any experience with men, you would know that last night was remarkable. There are people who have been together years and not been so attuned to each other." He flinched a little as he said that, but she was too busy reacting to his outrageous claim.

"That's not what you said this morning." She tried to sound unaffected, but she was still feeling unfairly spanked. It reflected in the raspy edge on her tone and filled her with debasement long after the insult had landed. She couldn't even look at him.

"I was under a wrong impression and behaved unpleasantly. I apologize."

She eyed him, skeptical.

"I don't apologize often. I suggest you accept it."

"No doubt," she allowed with a twitch of her lips. His arrogance ought to turn her off, but he seemed to have a right to it. His inner strength was as compelling as his obvious physical virility. When it wasn't turned against her, that combination was lethally attractive.

"Come here," he cajoled in a smoky invitation, even though he stood within touching distance and only had to reach out if he really wanted to.

"Why?" She stayed where she was, but everything in her gravitated to him.

"I want to kiss you. Show you how good we are together."

"Seduce me?"

He offered a masculine smile so tomcattish and predatory, it made her stomach dip in giddy excitement. "I would very much like to make love to you again," he said.

An image of her naked body, the one she avoided in the

mirror every day, flashed in her mind. She drew the lapels of her robe together and shook her head.

"Find someone else. I'm not playing hard to get. I just don't see the point."

Rather than argue, he pursed his mouth in regret. "I've damaged your trust in me."

"There wasn't much to begin with," she assured him with a tight smile.

"And the claws are revealed once again." He seemed more amused than irritated. "You trusted me enough to share your—what does your American singer call it? The wonderland that is your body."

"Yes, well, I was pretending to be someone else," she dismissed with false breeziness, inner foundations unsteady as she recalled how completely she'd deluded herself into believing what she'd done was okay.

"Do it again," he commanded.

"Ha!" She couldn't help it. The man was so lofty and single-minded.

"I'm serious," he insisted. "Put on your mask. We'll go downstairs and find that woman capable of such delightful spontaneity."

"It's—no. I can't."

But she couldn't think why. At least, not fast enough to have an answer ready when he demanded, "Why not?"

"Because..." She searched for a reason.

"We could dance again. We both enjoyed that. Of course, we could do that here." He glanced to where the balcony doors stood open. The music from the band below drifted in with the sea-scented air and the swish of waves on the shore.

The mood and music came across as a lazy, exotic throb.

"No," she said firmly, smart enough to be wary of his power once he got his hands on her. The way he'd felt her up on the dance floor last night had obviously been a spell of some kind.

"Downstairs it is. Shall we say one hour? I can shave and change in fifteen minutes, but you women need twenty just to find a pair of shoes."

"He said," she mocked, "demonstrating his vast experience with the opposite sex."

"I won't apologize. We're adults. We can enjoy each other if we want to." He moved forward to set a brief but profound kiss on her startled mouth. "Sure you don't want to stay in?" he asked in a private tone that made her blood flutter in her arteries.

Oh, she was tempted, but she shook her head. "I'm not sure I even want to see you again."

"Meet me downstairs, Tiffany, or I'll come looking for you. But I don't want to waste time searching. Set your watch."

She shook her head. "I don't like people thinking they can talk to me. I'd rather leave it on Do Not Disturb."

"Set it so *I* can find you." At her blank look, he gave her a head shake of exasperation. "Where is it? I'll show you."

A few minutes later she stood in her empty suite wondering how she'd gone from crying in the shower to having a date, one that made her feel more awake and alive than— this was dangerous—any other time in her life.

Oh, Tiffany, be careful. You could still fall for the wrong man.

No, she wasn't that pathetic and vulnerable, she assured herself. Nor was she strong enough to stay in her room and risk his coming for her. Besides, she had enjoyed feeling normal. There was no crime in that, was there?

She liked even more the idea of making him see her as beautiful. Turning, she went to see what treasures the designers might have left her.

CHAPTER FIVE

RYZARD MOVED THROUGH the three-dimensional images of a *carnivale* parade. He had to be careful. There were real people, *Q Virtus* members and *petite q's,* dressed as colorfully as the fake partiers, but for the most part he walked right through projections of extravagant floats and scantily clad women wearing beaded bikinis and feather headdresses. He stopped for a troupe of men in checkered pants and neon elephant masks when they began a tumbling routine in front of him, nearly convinced they were real.

His watch hummed, indicating Tiffany was close by, but *where?*

His need to see her again, to know she'd come down here for him, was out of proportion to any normal sort of anticipation. He brushed it aside, thinking if he could have her just once more, he'd be able to forget about her. It didn't matter that she'd revealed more about herself than he'd ever heard from all other *Q Virtus* members combined. Like most of the happenings here, their private conversation would stay locked in his own personal vault, not even to be revisited by him.

He especially refused to dwell on their comforting embrace when her mixture of grief and anger and self-blame had struck a chord in him. Even though, for the better part of a minute while he held her, he'd been at peace for the first time in a long time.

He stepped on a man's hands and looked through the feet that would have struck him in the nose if the vision was real. Music blared, voices cheered, and the holographic players were so dense he might as well have been in a crowd on the street.

There. All the hairs stood up on his body as he took her in.

She had her head bent to study her watch and pivoted as though trying to orient herself with a compass. The movement allowed him to take her in from all sides.

She really was strikingly beautiful. Tall and slender, but generously curved in the right places. He swallowed. She wore some kind of jumpsuit that clung from knees to elbows, then flared into ruffles down her forearms and over her shins. It had a subtle sparkle in its midnight blue color and clung to her ass so lovingly, his knees weakened.

He mentally recited the populations of Bregnovia's cities, trying to keep hold of his control as he approached her. Sidling up behind her, almost touching, he inhaled where she'd left the right side of her neck bare, gathering her hair to the left so it covered the scars.

"What the hell are you wearing?"

Her head came up. "You don't like it?" She jiggled the watch in her hand. "This thing was buzzing at me, but I couldn't figure out if you were over there or over there."

"I'm here," he growled, wanting so badly to palm the firm globe near his crotch his hand burned.

"So you are." She turned to study his mask from behind her own. "Hello again, Mystery Man. Buy me a drink? I've had a terrible day with the most arrogant, self-aggrandizing jerk you can imagine."

Few people could get away with insulting him so openly, but he found her brashness refreshing. Maybe even reassuring. She wasn't as vulnerable as she'd seemed in her suite. Good.

Testing the waters, he said, "I'm looking forward to one myself. I was stuck all evening with the most infuriating female, smart as a whip, but *blonde*. No offense." He tugged one of her ringlets.

For a moment her mouth stayed flat and humorless, just long enough for doubt to creep over his conscience. Then her lips twitched and a pretty, feminine chuckle erupted, sounding a shade rusty, as if she hadn't laughed unreservedly in a long time, but it engaged him in a way he hadn't expected. He instantly wanted to hear it again.

"None taken," she assured him breezily, turning to grasp his arm above his elbow, demonstrating how much self-assurance she possessed when she wasn't paralyzed by self-consciousness. "Can you believe this parade? I thought it was real."

Despite wanting to remark on the sudden change in her, he decided to go with it.

"The first time I saw this technology, it was a rain forest. It wasn't as robust as this, but the rain effect was quite something."

"You've been coming to these shindigs for a while?"

"This is my twenty-fifth. I earned a pin." He lifted his lapel to draw her eye to the small gold button.

"Nice. What does it do? Beam you up? Shoot lasers?"

"It tells people I belong."

Ryzard's mouth tightened after he spoke, as if he hadn't meant to reveal that, which piqued her curiosity all the more. "What do you mean?"

He shook his head, trying to dismiss her curiosity. "They have a live performance on the beach tonight. Shall we check it out?"

"Are you sensitive to not belonging because of the UN thing? You must know how slowly the wheels of political progress can turn. If the old boys' network is refusing to pick you for their team, tell them to stuff it."

His mask annoyed her. He was already pretty stoic, and now she had to try reading his emotions from the way the corner of his supersexy mouth flattened with disgust.

"I've learned to do exactly that, Tiffany. And it really doesn't matter to me if I'm rejected or found wanting, but I can't bear for my country to be discriminated against."

Discriminated. There was a big word. As a woman she'd been on the short end of that nastiness even in her own home in favor of her brother, but she couldn't imagine it happening to a man who showed so few weaknesses. He wasn't a typical representative of the people she understood to suffer the worst end of biases.

"When were you picked on? Why?" she asked, allowing him to steer her through the shower of candies that should have landed with a sting or crunched under her platform shoes.

He shrugged as if the details were inconsequential. "Different times. When I was a child and didn't yet speak German. I was late to sprout and quick to fight, angry that I couldn't see my parents. My temper was a problem. Getting a legitimate passport was a nightmare, so I was forever in a country illegally. That's one of the reasons I picked grapes. Things like visas can be overlooked when the fruit is ripe and a transient offers to help. But when I tried to go to America, they wanted nothing to do with me."

"So you went to Russia."

"There are parts as wild as your early frontier. Misfits are the rule."

"Which country's passport do you travel on now?"

"Bregnovian," he asserted, as if that should be obvious.

"But it's not recognized? That still keeps you from entering America?"

"I wouldn't be allowed into Venezuela."

"But you're welcome here." She pointed at the floor of the club.

He nodded once, still seeming bristly.

She considered how that might feel, always being separated and left out. Being who she was had always ensured her entrée into virtually any situation. For all her father's faults and detractors, he was still welcome everywhere. Even with her scars, she wasn't locked out. It was her choice to stay home.

She looked up at Ryzard, wanting to ask how he'd come to finally go home and fund a war, but they had arrived on the beach. Bending, she removed her shoes and allowed him to take them so she could walk barefoot in the cool, powdery sand.

"That's an excellent cover band," she said as they moved toward the music.

"It's the real band," he told her, making her chuckle.

He looked at her and the corners of his mouth curled again, but his mask and the strobing lights made it hard to tell if he was smiling because he was in a good mood, or if he was laughing at her.

"I can't get used to this," she excused. "It's a lot to pay just for an exclusive concert, isn't it? The membership fee, I mean."

"If you hadn't been sulking in your room, you could have attended some of the lectures. There was an excellent one on the situation in Africa. Last quarter, I brokered a free trade agreement that will ease a lot of strain on our wheat and dairy production."

She weighed that, seeing new value in these meetings and wondering if she would come to another. Maybe see him again.

Or see him with someone else.

The chasm that thought opened in her chest was so great,

she quickly distracted herself by declaring with false crossness, "I wasn't sulking."

"You're still pouting," he claimed and took her jaw in a firm hand, nipping her bottom lip with the firm but tender bite of his.

A zing of excitement shot straight down her breastbone into her abdomen, then washed tingles into her limbs. Her hands instinctively lifted to his waist, but she held him off by proclaiming, "I've heard that all my life. I can't help it if my bottom lip is fat."

He drew back enough to sweep a gaze of masculine appraisal across her masked features, then bent to take a slower, more detailed tour of her mouth, allowing them both the luxury of a small feast. Absently she shuffled toward him, knees and thighs shifting so he could fit their frames together. His erection pressed into her stomach and her breasts ached as she flattened them to his chest. The music seeped through her and he began to rock them in a slow dance.

More like making love to her in public again, but who cared? No one even knew who they were. God, he felt good under her roaming hands.

"Come to my room," he intoned against her good ear.

She had her hands fisted in his shirt beneath the jacket of his tuxedo. Everything in her wanted to hang on to him forever. It was such a dangerous precipice to stand on, so threatening of a bad fall. But she couldn't escape how good it felt to feel wanted and beautiful and capable of giving him pleasure.

Without even doing much soul-searching—just like last night—she offered a shaky nod and let him guide her back into the club then into an elevator where they kissed with barely schooled passion. A minute later, he thumbed the sensor that opened his door and pivoted her into the foyer of his suite. It was grander than her own, but he *was* a twenty-five-visit member. Still, she barely saw it. One second later, she was in his arms.

Knocking off his mask, he dipped his head and kissed her again, discipline abandoned as he let her know with the thrust of his tongue exactly what he wanted to do to her. His hands roamed over her restlessly and he finally jerked back to say, "What the hell is this thing? I can't find a zipper."

Which was why she'd chosen it, she recalled dimly. Even the neckline was a difficult entry point. She didn't have the courage to be naked with him, but she wanted to make love to him.

Smiling secretively, she fingered open the buttons of his shirt and gazed appreciatively at the sleek bronze chest plate she revealed. A narrow line of hair delineated the center of his chest and outlined his squared pecs, which were flat, firm statements of strength.

Above his left nipple, a scrolled phrase in blue ink gave her pause. Some of the letters were oddly accented, but she thought she read the word *Bregnovia*. Framing it with the finger and thumb of her splayed hand, she asked, "What does it say?"

Tension stole through him. He seemed to expend a lot of effort drawing in a pained breath. "Luiza, Martyr of Bregnovia."

"Like our Lady Liberty?"

She drew a circle around his nipple and he jerked, making her smile.

"Yes," he rasped. "She's revered—damn. By all."

Other questions crowded into her mind, but she was too distracted by his gorgeous physique. Her hands couldn't resist smoothing over the hot satin of his skin. "You're so perfect, Ryzard. It's intimidating."

"Take off your clothes," he urged, plumping her breasts through her spandex suit.

Cruising her hand from his waist to his belt and lower,

she explored the shape of him. He grunted with pleasure and was so hard against her palm, her internal muscles clenched in anticipation. She swallowed and used her other hand to fumble his pants open.

He tried to remove her mask, but she pulled away and shook her head. "Not yet." She was too intent on being the anonymous Tiffany, the one who followed impulse and seduced a man if she wanted to. Lowering his fly, she managed to expose him, and *oh*. She went to her knees because he made her so deliciously weak.

"Tiffany," he groaned raggedly.

She was barely touching him, too new at this to do more than brush light fingertips over him. His breaths were audible hisses of anticipation, his erection jumping in reaction to her caresses. When she smoothed her lips against silky skin over steel, the weight of his hand came to rest on her head. The other stroked her exposed cheek, fingers trembling.

An experimental lick imprinted her with the taste of him. This was new territory for her, something she'd always been curious about, but it was so much more enthralling than she'd expected. She could sense how much power she had as she learned his shape with her tongue and openmouthed kisses

When she took the tip into her wet mouth, he growled a string of foreign words, guttural and tortured, but sexy and thick with pleasure. If she could have smiled, she would have. Instead, she focused on finding his sensitive points, wanting this to be something he would never forget.

She never would.

Ryzard managed to hitch his pants back into place, but wasn't capable of much else. His head was swimming, his muscles trembling, and he was too wrung out to properly close his fly. He needed the wall to keep himself upright.

Water ran in the powder room, but he was barely aware of anything else. What Tiffany had just done to him had blown his mind. Her inexperience had been obvious in her tentative touch and first nervous licks, but after that she'd been so generous and given over to what she was doing, he'd lost it completely.

The door latch clicked and he turned his head. She walked out of the powder room with her clothes and mask in place, but there was an adorable self-conscious flush on her exposed cheek and an even more exquisite glow of arousal coming off her like an aura. Her nipples were pencil tips beneath her second-skin jumpsuit, and the way she walked held the hip sway of the sexually aroused.

Unbelievably, he twitched back to life below his unbuckled belt. He instantly wanted to strip her and have her under him.

"I'm going to eat you alive," he warned her.

She shook her head. "I have to go."

"The hell you do." He'd tie her up if he had to.

"No, I do," she insisted.

"What happened?" He looked to the powder room, wondering what had changed between seconds ago and now.

"Nothing. I just... This was really nice, but I want to leave it like this. As a nice memory for both of us."

"We can keep the lights off," he blurted in a burst of panic.

"Ryzard, please." There were tears in her eyes. "Just this, okay?"

He swiped his hand down his face, unable to think where he'd gone wrong. *Why the hell was she shutting him out?*

"I won't force you to make love with me. You don't have to go." Hell, the last thing he was capable of right now was *talk,* but it would be better than her leaving.

"I know you wouldn't, but I want to. Thank you again."

She skittered a wide circle around him and slid through the cracked door.

She'd got him off and thanked him twice. *What the hell?*

Tiffany was still trembling when she slid between her sheets, both angry with herself and relieved. Maybe she should have stayed with him. Maybe this was her chance to get over her scars so she could pursue a relationship with another man in the future.

But she didn't want anyone else, and she didn't have the courage to expose herself to Ryzard.

With a moan of despair, she rolled onto her stomach and groaned into a pillow.

A muted bell sounded. She lifted her head and noticed a light flashing on the bedside phone. Picking it up, she said a wary, "Yes?"

"It's me. Where are you?"

His voice sent a race of erotic excitement through her veins and into her loins. "In my room, obviously," she said, unable to control the husky edge on her voice.

"In bed?"

"Sleeping, yes," she lied.

"Liar."

She rolled her eyes. *So* arrogant.

"What are you wearing?" he asked.

"Flannel jammies and a nightcap."

"Well, take them off, *draga*. I'm about to tell you what you missed by running out of here."

"You're going to force me to have phone sex?"

"Hang up any time."

"I might have enough without adding more," she murmured in a considering tone.

"Hmm? Oh. Clever," he said with dry amusement. "I never know what to expect from you, Tiffany. Although

I'm quite sure you're still aroused. Have you been thinking of how you nearly killed me tonight?"

"Did I?" She couldn't help smiling.

"So smug. Yes, you did. I didn't thank you, and I should have. You're a delightful lover."

She curled on her side so the phone was tucked under her ear. "Thank you for saying that."

"Are you naked yet? Because if my hands will not be stroking your gorgeous body, then I will listen as you do it."

"You wish." But she tingled at the thought. He was right about sexual excitement hovering under the surface. Her skin prickled to sharp life, making her feel sensual and deeply aware of all her erogenous zones.

"Satisfy my curiosity," he said in a low voice. "Are your nipples still hard?"

"It's dark, I can't see."

"Feel them."

She closed her eyes, tempted, but, "Ryzard, I meant it when I said we should leave it at tonight."

Silence.

Had he hung up on her?

"Are you still there?" she asked, hearing a forlorn note in her voice.

"At least tell me why you're cutting me off." Underlying the brisk frustration in his tone was an edge of something she'd heard this evening when he'd said, *It shows I belong.* She'd hurt him.

Through an aching throat, she managed to blurt out the worst cliché around. "It's not you, it's me. I'm the biggest head case going."

"You're concerned that I will be repulsed by these scars of yours."

"Yes," she admitted, breathing a little easier at his understanding.

"Why would that bother you if I was?"

"I— What?" Her whole body tensed. *Did* she disgust him?

"Why would you care about my opinion? Who am I to you? Just some stranger you slept with on a wild night, right?"

So many protests choked her, she couldn't speak. He wasn't just anyone, not after some of the conversations they'd had and the physical intimacies they'd shared, but she couldn't admit that to him. He was already way too close to sensing he meant more to her than their brief association should warrant. His opinion mattered a lot.

"You're expecting me to get naked, be as exposed as I possibly could be, and risk being rejected," she said in a strained voice. "Wouldn't that bother you?"

"It bothered the hell out of me when you walked out tonight. I was as naked as a man needs to be the first night." His anger blistered off the receiver, making her squinch her face in a cringe. "You've done it to me twice."

"I'm sorry." The words burned from all the way in the pit of her sick stomach. "I didn't look at it from your perspective. I wasn't rejecting you."

"You need to start looking beyond yourself, Tiffany."

"I just apologized. That doesn't happen often. I suggest you accept it."

He sighed with frustration, then said with austerity, "You have been dealt a cruel blow from life. I won't dismiss that. But it didn't kill you, so start learning to live with it."

Wow. He didn't pull any punches, did he?

"How?" she demanded in a burst of angry despair. "You're not telling me anything I don't know, but how do I just get over it?"

"You want to be with a man, Tiffany. You like it when I touch you. Be with me."

He did make her feel more confident, but it would take

about a hundred of these heart-to-hearts before she'd be able to face being naked in front of him.

"We could meet for breakfast," she offered. The inside of her cheek stung and she realized she was biting it, feeling very insecure at putting herself out even this much.

"Where?" he asked.

"I assume they have a buffet or a restaurant downstairs."

"I meant your place or mine, but I see. Yes, they have a breakfast room. Nine?"

He wasn't making any effort to hide his disappointment, but she only confirmed, "Downstairs at nine. It's a date."

Ending the call, she rolled onto her back and stared at the dark ceiling. What was she doing? There was even less point in seeing him at breakfast on their last morning. They'd never see each other again after that.

Still, just thinking about seeing him made her body feel ripe and wanton. Running her hands over the hard swells of her breasts with their taut tips poking sharply against her rippling fingertips, she tried to erase the sensations nagging at her. The hunger deepened, provoking memories of Ryzard leaning on the wall, disheveled pants barely containing flesh she had memorized with her mouth, his eyes heavy lidded and voracious.

Rolling a frustrated moan into her pillow, she wished she'd said yes to the phone sex.

When she arrived in the dining room, Ryzard was standing in the entrance talking to another woman.

It was a low blow and nearly made her turn in retreat, but he lifted his hawkish mask and held out a hand to her even before he locked his gaze on her.

Stupid watches. Hers was shivering at its nearness to his, just like her to him. As she walked across, she experienced a little thrill at how good he looked in simple black pants and a white shirt open at the throat. His hair, clipped so short you could barely tell it curled, was still damp.

A dip of insecurity accosted her at the same time. The woman gesturing so passionately in front of him wore a light cover-up over a bikini that barely contained her flawless figure. Her mask was equally spare, just a sleek line from temple to temple.

Tiffany felt overdressed in her pants suit and elaborate mask as well as intrusive as she arrived, causing the woman to break midsentence.

Ryzard grasped her hand in a firm, warm grip, drawing her a step closer while continuing to give his attention to the other woman. "Please continue."

"I—" She was obviously disconcerted by Tiffany's arrival. Her body language changed from enticing to standoffish. "I just wonder if the sudden rumors being spread about this weekend, talk of dirty deals and Greek Mafia connections, could be true. Zeus's reputation is important for all of us, and if he's no better than a crook we should talk about it. Figure out what to do."

Tiffany was a little lost, coming in late and distracted by the strength and heat of her *lover*. He smelled freshly showered, and his flimsy white shirt was hardly any barrier, allowing her to nearly taste the texture of his skin.

Still, being excluded niggled at her. She'd been The Family Behind Him too many times for her father, a required face in a photo, but heaven forbid she open her mouth. Being relegated to arm candy here, where she was supposed to be an equal, was the final straw.

"Who *is* Zeus?" Tiffany asked.

"No one knows," the woman said, dismissing her with a patronizing jerk of her shoulder, adding, "Which is part of the problem. He should identify himself so we can decide if we want to continue associating with him."

Tiffany followed the entreating glance the woman sent

to Ryzard. She was obviously trying to pull him over to her side for reasons other than any real concern about the club.

"That seems hypocritical, doesn't it?" Ryzard said calmly. "When we keep our own identities secret?"

"I have to agree. It's quite possible to have a wrong impression about someone until you know them better," Tiffany said with a significant look upward to Ryzard.

"Well, we don't keep any secrets from Zeus, do we?" the woman insisted. She wavered with indecision a moment as her gaze touched on his hand holding Tiffany's so possessively. Then she made a noise of impatience and muttered, "I'm just saying," before she walked away.

Tiffany raised her brows, not that Ryzard could see them and appreciate her pique at coming upon a woman hitting on him so blatantly.

"Good morning," he said before swooping to kiss her.

She stiffened, but he took his time, working swirls of reawakened passion down through her torso and into her belly until she softened into his loose embrace. When he lifted his head, he said, "I'm starving. You?"

Food was the last thing on her mind, but she followed him through the indoor/outdoor dining room to a table near the lagoon-shaped pool. They accepted coffee and placed their orders before she lost her ability to stay silent and asked, "Do you pick up women at all these things?"

Setting down his coffee, he regarded her with a hard look. "Your pretty blue eyes have gone quite emerald, *draga*."

"Who is she?"

"That's a question I can't answer. Members do not out other members. That's why I didn't introduce you."

She narrowed her eyes. "If I had looked at my watch, would I have seen her nickname?"

He shrugged. "Possibly. Mine is turned off except for

you. She only spoke to me because we happened to meet at the door and have spoken before."

"About?" she prompted.

"It's confidential."

"Have you seen her away from these things?"

"Also confidential."

"So you won't tell me anything."

"This is how the club works. That's why it works. But I will tell you that I have never had a sexual relationship with her."

"And she would never admit to one if you had because members don't out other members. I'm just supposed to trust that you're telling me the truth."

"Yes," he said firmly. "I do expect you to trust me."

Her gaze dropped to the button he'd only half pushed through its hole in the middle of his chest.

"If you had let me make love to you last night, you would not be feeling so insecure this morning," he added.

Her heart skipped at that, but she only said, "I'm not insecure. I don't *know* you."

"Exactly."

Oh, he was infuriating. And sexy. Her eyes were eating up the way his shirt was perfectly tailored across the line of his shoulders and hugged the strength in his arms. Her fingers itched to unbutton the whole shirt and expose his very promising chest again.

It's just hormones, she tried to insist to herself, not wanting to succumb to feelings that were a lot more complex than mere lust.

"I'm jealous of her for being pretty," she admitted in an undertone, ashamed that she was this shallow, but, "I used to be and it gave me confidence. Don't deny that being physically attractive is powerful," she warned with a point of her finger. "My mother still turns heads and uses it every day. And she places so much importance on looks."

The weight of that knowledge slumped her into her chair.

"Sometimes I wonder if that's why she chose Dad and not Paul Sr. He wasn't ugly by any stretch, but Dad's got that Mr. President, all-American look. Mom wanted the best-looking kids in the state and she got them. Now, when she looks at me..."

Time to shut up. Her throat was closing and it was impossible to fix.

"Your mother sounds very superficial." His tone of quiet observation told her he'd heard and weighed every word she'd said. Being such a tight focus of his concentration made her feel oddly vulnerable and safe at the same time. It made her think he genuinely cared about what she was revealing.

"She's the wife of a politician. Her world revolves around how things look. You're judged on everything in that position. Looks matter."

"I suppose," he allowed with a negligent tilt of his head. "Did she push your father into politics?"

"No, it was something he wanted, but maybe that's the real reason she married him." Tiffany considered her parents' marriage a moment. "Dad is a good father, a super husband, a really good man, but he aspires to be a Great Man and Mom aspires to be the wife of one. She set me up to..." want? demand? "expect the same thing."

"Was your husband planning to go into politics?"

"If our parents had anything to do with it, yes." She curled her mouth in mild distaste.

"You didn't want him to."

Once again she was able to speak a truth to him that she couldn't say aloud to anyone else.

"I honestly didn't think I had a choice. But I've seen how that life has affected my mother over the years. Every word she says is guarded. Half the time she's Dad's mistress. His work is his wife. Our family day at the fair was always a photo op with Dad glad-handing everyone except us. He couldn't buy me the candy floss I wanted. A taffy apple was a better message." She sighed, still more bewildered than bitter. "My life was staged to look like the life I wanted, but we weren't allowed to actually live it that way."

"Another reason why I will never marry. Too much sacrifice on a family's part."

"'Another' reason? You don't intend to marry? Don't you want children? That's the one thing I looked forward to when I agreed to marry. I wanted to give my kids the childhood I hadn't had."

As the words left her mouth, she realized how leading they sounded. As if this was a conflict they'd have to resolve before proceeding with their relationship. She never talked this openly, except maybe to her therapist, but who else did she talk to these days? She was out of practice with hiding her real thoughts and feelings.

"You can still have a family," he said with a calm blink of his eyes within the holes of his mask. "Why couldn't you?"

Behind her own mask, she burned with self-consciousness, her gaze fixed to his. Her finding that kind of happiness wasn't as easy as he made it sound, and he knew it. With her teeth bared in a nonsmile, she said, "Why don't you want to marry?"

"I'm married to my country," he stated. "As you said, my work is my wife. Everything I do, I do for my people."

She tried to ignore the dull pain that lodged in her chest. That was good, wasn't it? She admired patriotism, and that certainly kept things simple between them. No false expectations.

"How did you become, um, president?" she asked, faltering because it was an impulsive question that sounded a lot more loaded than she'd meant it to.

"I was elected," he said coolly.

She waited while their meals were delivered, then said, "I meant, how did people come to know who you are and want to vote for you? I'm sure it was covered in the news, but as you've said, that's usually slanted, and quite frankly I've had other things on my mind for the last few years. I missed how it all happened. I'm really asking what drew you back to your country and into representing it."

"My mother was killed in a random attack. I went back for the funeral and my father was determined to fight. I couldn't leave him to it. I was angry with myself for not returning sooner, for thinking someone else would sort out the trouble and I could return when there was peace."

"You're either part of the solution, or part of the problem," Tiffany murmured. "I'm sorry about your mom." Was that whom he'd been talking about yesterday, she wondered, when he'd held her in shared grief? "At least your father is safe."

"He died, as well. Fighting."

"Oh. I'm so sorry."

He waved that away with a lift of two fingers. "I believe he wanted it that way. To be with my mother."

"Still…" She swallowed, ready to cry for him because he seemed so withdrawn and contained. Tears would never dare to seep from his bleak eyes. "I'm sure he would be very proud of you for what you've achieved."

"Once you've paid the price of a loved one, you don't stop until the job is done. I managed to bring enough of our various factions together to throw over our corrupt government and campaigned on a promise of peace. There is still a very long road. The biggest challenge is keeping the country from falling back into fighting, but we had some corruption charges work through the courts recently that gave people confidence. Small things like that matter."

She nodded, tipping a little further into the primordial

world of deeper feelings for him. Genuine admiration. Awe. Empathy.

Careful, Tiffany.

"Shall we take the art walk?" he asked when they finished eating.

"I didn't know they had one." She looked around, expecting artists with pads and a jumble of still lifes and caricatures had arrived to line the stones near the pool.

"They set it up inside to avoid sun and humidity damage."

"Really? What are we talking about? Priceless artifacts? Da Vinci?"

"If something like that is on the market, absolutely. Most of it is contemporary, but they're all good investments."

Moments later, they entered a gallery of comic book art competing with old-world landscapes and elegantly carved wooden giraffes. She fell in love with a stained glass umbrella, mostly because it was so ridiculously useless.

"How much is it?" she demanded, searching for a tag.

"The auction is in a few hours."

"We'll come back?"

"If you like."

"I want to use it as a parasol against the sun." It had to weigh fifty pounds. It was the most impractical object ever created and she *had* to own it.

"You have a beautiful laugh," he remarked, tugging her into a space behind a giant sculpture of ladies' shoes. "I'd like to see you smiling under this umbrella of yours, your face painted by the colored glass. I'd like to see you sunbathe naked under it," he added in a deeper tone that seemed to stroke beneath her skin and leave a tingle.

At the same time his words put a pang in her heart. She wished…

He bent to kiss her, pulling her into his aroused body as if they were the only two people in the room. A second later, as his tongue invaded her mouth, she forgot everything except the feel of him, shoulders to thighs, branding her.

"I want you in my bed," he told her huskily, as he found her bare earlobe and drew it between his lips.

Her body felt as if it swelled to fill his arms, breasts aching, all her skin thin and sensitized. Willpower and self-protection fell away as she confided in a whisper, "I want that, too."

He lifted his head. His possessive hands stilled and firmed on her. "Yes?"

Her heart stalled. He wouldn't accept any more waffling. She swallowed, still terrified by the idea of being naked in front of him, but she would hate herself forever if she refused him out of sheer cowardice. With breath held, she gave an abbreviated nod.

His smile should have alarmed her. It bordered on grim, but a light of excitement behind his eyes made her tremble with anticipation. He really did want her.

Blood rushed in her ears so she barely heard him speak to a *petite q* as they made their way back to the main floor.

"Early checkout?" she repeated as he led her through the door the *petite q* released with a thumbprint and security override card.

"Gold membership has its privileges," he said drily. "But they'll only let me leave early. They won't allow us back in."

"Oh, but what about my things—?" She paused on the ramp down to the marina, where several eye-popping luxury yachts bobbed like toys in a bathtub.

"Our luggage would be packed for us regardless. That's the level of service we pay for, Tiffany." He waved and called something in Bregnovian to a young man as they approached a catamaran. It was called the *Luiza* and had an orange sail wrapped around its single mast. The body was such a brilliant white she had to squint.

"We'll remain docked a few hours yet," Ryzard said in

answer to a question from his crewman. "Unless we have to move to let someone out." He nodded at the boat they'd traversed to reach this one. "Tell the captain we're aboard and will order lunch when we're ready, but we don't wish to be disturbed."

Tiffany blushed behind her mask, thinking Ryzard was making it incredibly obvious what they were about to do. He didn't seem concerned, however, as he led her through the interior salon of sleek curved lines, the colors a soothing mix of bone and earth tones. Panoramic windows slanted over the lounge and bar, bringing splashes of turquoise water and cerulean sky into the room. Bypassing a short staircase that led to an elevated pilothouse of some kind, he brought her down a half flight of steps into the master stateroom.

"This is amazing," she couldn't help blurt. No stranger to the finer things in life, she was awestruck by the simple elegance and understated masculinity in the surprisingly spacious room. Drawers and cupboards in blond teak lined the space below the windows that provided a one-eighty view. A door led to an exterior deck on this side and into a well-organized head on the other. One curved radius corner of the room was a scrupulously efficient work space, the other a rounded sofa that looked to a flat-screen television set into the wall offset from the bed.

The bed itself was a king-size statement of power, tall and stalwart, its linens almond colored with a bold chocolate stripe across the foot. She dragged her eyes away from it as she heard a whispery sound and the light changed.

Ryzard moved with deliberation to draw woven shades down into a clip, allowing filtered sunlight to penetrate, but giving them privacy.

Her stomach swooped and she put out her hand, not sure where to find purchase when the floor was dipping at the same time.

"I thought we'd go to a room in the club," she said, linking her hands before her to hide that she was trembling with nerves. And excitement.

He turned from the last window and brushed away his mask, tossing it aside. "As I said, I don't want to be interrupted."

By staff wanting to pack their belongings, she imagined he meant, but couldn't speak because he came close enough to remove her mask.

She stopped him.

"I've seen your face, Tiffany."

"I don't want you to see how scared I am."

He frowned. "Of me?"

"Your reaction."

He shook his head, dismissing her fear as he trailed light fingertips over her clothing, grazing the sides of her breasts and settling warm hands on her waist. "I'm afraid I'll hurt you again. I wish you'd warned me the other night. I wasn't nearly as gentle as I could have been."

"I know pain, Ryzard. That was nothing."

"It was something," he told her, pulling her close enough to brush his mouth against hers, not properly kissing her. Teasing. "I'll never forget it."

An odd expression spasmed across his face before he controlled it, as if he hadn't meant to admit that to her, but she drew in his confession like air, deeply affected, wanting to hold on to this special feeling he provoked in her. Everything in her yearned so badly to please him, and she was so sure she wouldn't.

Get it over with, she told herself. She had to let him see and judge and reject before she climbed too high in optimism and desire. A long fall from excitement to disgust would be more than she could bear. If she did it now, before they'd gone too far, she'd still be able to dress and trudge into the nearest town to phone her brother—the one she kept forgetting about.

For now, she had to gather her courage.

Gently removing Ryzard's hands from her waist, she took a step back. The mask seemed like a tiny bit of necessary protection so she kept it, reaching first for the single button that held her linen jacket closed.

Removing it exposed her arm, marbled in streaks of red and pink, some parts geometric patterns from the grafts, other edges random and white. Not looking at him, she opened her pants and stepped out of them. Her left leg was as bad as her arm, and the top of her good right thigh was peppered with rectangles where they'd taken skin to patch the bad. Her stomach had the same types of scars. She threw off her sleeveless silk top and stood there in her cherry red bra and underpants and gold gladiator sandals.

For the life of her, she couldn't lift her chin. Her eyes were glued to the floor, her mind full of the rugged road map her body had become. No ivory virgin here.

"You do know pain, Tiffany," he said quietly.

That brought her eyes up. He studied her gravely, all the way to her toes, and gradually climbed his gaze back to her face. Stepping closer, he touched her chin to bring her face up and looked into her eyes. His were somber, but glowing with something fierce.

"You humble me. I don't know if I could have fought through such a thing."

She had to bite her lips to keep them from trembling.

Gently he removed her mask and let it fall. She felt incredibly vulnerable, standing before him nearly naked when he was clothed.

"Do not be ashamed of your courage to survive."

She had wanted to be told she was pretty despite her scars, but what he said was better, filling her with an emotion she couldn't describe. Tipping into him, she hugged him tight.

And realized he was aroused. His hand swept her bare back down to where her thong exposed her naked cheek. With a purposeful clench of his fingers into the firm flesh, he tilted her hips into pressing where he grew harder by the second.

"You're turned on," she breathed in wonder.

"I've got you naked next to a bed. How the hell else would I react?"

That made her laugh, then she squealed as he picked her up and lightly tossed her onto the mattress. Coming up on her elbows, she accused, "Caveman."

"Believe it," he confirmed, yanking off his shirt and dropping it away. His pants came off with similar haste. "Off with the rest," he ordered, jerking his chin at her lingerie. "This time we're both naked."

He was, in record time, and pulled off her shoes without ceremony.

"Don't wreck them. I like those," she protested, pausing in finding the clip between her breasts to reach for the strap of her shoe.

"What about these?" he asked, hooking two fingers in her panties at her hip. "Special favorite? Because I'm out of patience." He snapped them.

"Oh!" Why his primitive act turned her on, she couldn't imagine, but the way he loomed over her, practically overwhelming her with his strength, gave her a thrill. Probably because she felt totally safe despite his resolute expression and proprietary touch. He was impatient, but not without discipline. He threw away her bra, but then he simply held her, his weight on one elbow as he studied her breasts.

"Does this hurt?" he asked, tracing where her scar licked like a flame up the side of her breast.

"I can barely feel anything. Just a bit of pressure. Nerve

damage. You know how your face feels after the dentist and the freezing is just starting to come out?"

"Good to know. I'll focus where you can feel it." He cupped her breast and flicked her nipple with his thumb.

The sensation was sharper than she anticipated, and she flinched.

"No?" he prompted.

"I— No, it's good, just really..." She blushed. This was surreal, lying in full light with a gorgeous man naked against her. Twin desires to curl into him and to stop and give herself time to take it in accosted her.

He lowered his head to lick, and her inner muscles clenched like a fist, tearing a sound of reaction out of her.

Almost experimentally, he switched to her other breast, teasing and making her shift restlessly. It felt incredible, but wasn't quite as intense as the other.

He moved to her left one again and another shot of extreme sensation went through her, flooding her loins with a heated rush of pleasure. She didn't know if her nerve endings were compensating for others nearby that had ceased to work, but the way his tongue toyed so delicately made her pinch her thighs together.

"That one is really sensitive," she panted, smoothing her hand over his short, thick hair and clutching at his shoulders, not sure if she wanted him to stop or take her over the edge.

"I can tell," he said with smoldering approval. Opening his mouth on her, he sucked delicately, nearly levitating her off the bed.

"Ryzard," she cried, knee bending and thighs opening as she tried to grasp more of him. With a growl, he slid down and bit softly at her inner thigh. "Do you know how many things I want to do to you?"

Moaning, she threw her arm over her eyes and surrendered. "Do anything. I love everything you do to me."

For a second he did nothing. She wondered if she'd done something wrong and started to drop her arm away. Then she felt his touch delicately parting her. His mouth. Pressing the back of her wrist against her open mouth, she muffled her throaty groan of abject joy. To be wanted like this, so deliciously ravished, brought tears of happiness to the seams of her closed eyes.

And *oh* that was nice. Pleasure coiled and built on itself through her middle, winding her into the sweetest tension. She wanted release and she wanted this to go on and on. Then he slid a testing finger in her, and she knew exactly what she wanted.

And told him.

"I can't wait, either," he said in a raw voice, as if the truth stunned him. In a sliding lunge across her, he nearly yanked the bedside drawer from its table and seconds later smoothed latex down his length.

When he pressed into her, she welcomed him with a gasp, nails tightening into his skin as he possessed her with ruthless care, slow and inexorable. Through her lashes, she watched him watching her and bit her lip, feeling deeply exposed, but moved by the intimacy at the same time.

"I can't believe I'm the only man who knows how amazing you are," he said gutturally, hands holding her head as he rocked side to side, settling deep inside her, sealing their connection.

Her body didn't feel like her own. She trembled in arousal, limbs both weak and strong, clinging to him. Her mouth offered itself, parting and begging for his.

With a tortured growl, Ryzard kissed her, thrusting his tongue into her, wanting more and more of her. All of her. Indelibly.

But that intense, deep possession couldn't be sustained forever. Eventually, he drew back enough for ecstasy to strum through him as her sheath stroked and clenched around him. She smelled incredible, felt even better, tasted like forbidden substances. He became animalistic, purely in his physical state, senses captured and held by this creature who entranced him. Nothing entered his vision except the expression of exquisite torture against the unique pattern on her face.

In a rare moment of unguarded openness, he removed his internal shields so he could fully absorb the pure, sweet light of her. His only thought was to fill her with the same all-encompassing rapture that held him in its grip.

She sobbed his name and he increased his tempo, reacting to her need and compelled to fulfill it. She met him thrust for thrust, their bodies so attuned they scaled the cliff together and soared into the abyss with perfect affinity. Clutching her tight under him, buried deep in her shivering depths, he let out a ragged cry of triumph as he gave in to pulse-pounding release.

CHAPTER SIX

RYZARD ROLLED AWAY, then settled on his back, his body brushing hers, but only incidentally. He wasn't embracing or meaning to touch her that Tiffany could tell.

She turned her head to see his profile was unreadable. Not displeased, but not...

Oh, she didn't know what she was looking for. A spear of inadequacy impaled her. While she had been caught up in their lovemaking, she'd been fine, but now she was back to being scared and self-conscious of her scars. She sat up.

"Don't go anywhere," he said, hand loosely cuffing her wrist.

Ha. Where could she go? They weren't allowed back into the club. *Hello, big brother, can you pick me up at the docks?*

Glancing over her shoulder, she tried to read his mood behind his heavy eyelids, but his spiky lashes made it impossible.

"You seem..." She didn't want to reveal how sensitive she was to disapproval right now. They might have been intimate in other ways before, but this was different. It wasn't just the physicality or revealing of her scars. She'd been incredibly uninhibited, exposing the very heart of herself.

"It's probably best if I go," she managed in a husky voice.

"I don't know what I seem, but I'm only trying to assimilate something that—" He breathed a word in his own language. She suspected it was a curse, but his tone was kind of awed and self-deprecating at the same time.

Facing forward, she closed her lids against a sudden sting, biting back an urge to beg him to continue what he'd almost said. It sounded as if he was as moved by their lovemaking as she was, which was balm to her tattered soul.

He released her wrist to stroke her lower back, making her lift her head from where she'd let it droop to rest on her knees.

"Are you okay?" he asked.

"Just trying not to act like a first-timer."

"This is unique for both of us."

She tried not to drink too deeply of that heady assessment. She was already falling for him in little ways and couldn't afford to become too enamored. This was merely an extension of their one-night stand.

"You keep condoms in the drawer by the bed," she pointed out. "I'm not that unique."

A beat of dark silence, then, "*I* never claimed to be a virgin."

She wanted to glare at him, but couldn't risk him seeing how hard it was for her to acknowledge his experience. Why? What right did she have to possessive feelings? She was lucky to be included in his special club at all.

"And this won't be the only bed I'll ever be in, so—hey!"

He had her on her back and under him before she realized he could move that fast.

"Here's a tip for someone new to this," he growled. "We don't discuss past and future lovers, particularly when we're still making love to each other."

She blinked in shock, heart hammering.

His aggression fell away to a baffled, tender caress that he smoothed along her good cheek. "Don't make me feel guilty for my life before I met you. How could I have known that what I thought was pleasure…" His expression clouded with a look of such angst, it made her heart hurt.

"It's just chemistry," she assured him, teetering inwardly against her own words even as she attempted to comfort him with them. The remark went directly against her girlish desire to hear that she was actually very special to him.

She held her breath, hoping against logic that he'd offer such a pledge.

"Exceptional chemistry," he agreed. His hungry gaze followed his hand as he caressed from her lips to her collarbone, across the damp underside of her breast and down to her hip where his thumb aligned to the crease at the top of her leg. "But you do understand this is simply an affair? It can't lead to anything permanent. I'm not the sort of life partner you're looking for."

His blunt statement fell between them like a metal wall, softened only by the expression of regret on his face.

"Glad you said it first," she said with a poignant smile, hoping it hid the way she tensed internally. She was as wary of certain fantasies as he was, but not nearly as adept at cutting her emotions out of her heart. "I told you what I think of being the woman behind the man. You're merely a guilty indulgence, like cheating on a diet."

His brow winged, indignant but amused. "Let's fatten you up then."

Ryzard gave up trying to work. They'd been sailing three hours already, so he had another word with his captain, then remained at the helm while his instructions were carried out. As the wind whipped his shirt through the open windows of the pilothouse, he once again congratulated himself on having the wisdom to switch from a single-hulled sailboat to the double construction of a cat. The three-sixty views and flexibility with anchorage were worth the ribbing he received from traditionalists.

Hell, if he had allowed his concentration to wander like this on his old schooner, they'd all be dead, but here he could indulge himself with recollecting every delicious minute of his day. He'd devoted several hours to learning each and every one of Tiffany's pleasure triggers, stimulating both of them as he expanded both of their educations in physical delight. Sweetest of all had been her generous straddling of him, broken voice asking for direction as she tugged him along her path to bliss.

They'd been like drunkards at that point, sheened in perspiration. Her eyes had been glassy, her pouted lips reddened by a thousand kisses. Her breasts had swayed with their undulations, her hips an instrument of torture he wielded on himself as he guided her with hands clamped tight in ownership.

He'd been sure he would die, it had been that good.

Rubbing his face, he dragged himself back to reality, yanking open his collar in search of a cool breeze to take his libido down a notch. They were flying over the waves, skipping at a light angle, demanding he pay attention, but all he could think was, how could he be this aroused again? She'd drained him dry. They'd collapsed into unconsciousness, utterly exhausted from making love.

He'd woken soon after, sweaty and thick with recovery, wanting her again.

When he'd shifted, she'd grumbled without opening her eyes, "Don't move. My hip hurts. I need to keep my leg propped."

He didn't doubt it. His joints had protested his rising from the bed, and he'd never crashed and burned in a roadster. He'd substituted a pillow under her thigh and watched her settle back into sleep before taking his insatiable libido for a cold shower in a spare cabin.

Then he'd made a decision he was still second-guessing, but it was done. She was his.

I love everything you do to me. The power of that statement unexpectedly exploded in his mind again, but that first bit, *I love...*

He scratched his chest where a sensation gathered like sweat trickling. The tickle was behind his breastbone, uncomfortable and impossible to erase. *It's just chemistry,* she'd said as he'd been reeling from a depth of pleasure he'd never experienced before.

He'd agreed with her, clinging to that simple explanation, but it was harder to blame chemistry when he'd found himself unable to wake her and send her on her way.

Why not? Why was his response to her, on every level, so much more intense than it had been with the woman he'd loved, the one he'd pledged to marry? He hated himself for it, but he couldn't deny it.

He and Luiza hadn't had the luxury of time and privacy to soak themselves in sexual intimacy, though. Their bond had been forged by shared secrets and ideals. She had loved him when he'd had no one else. Her vision had become his.

She'd died before her dream could become reality, but he was still striving to make it come true. There was no reason to suffer pangs of infidelity just because he wanted to play out an affair with a particular woman for a little longer than a weekend.

He clenched his hands on the wheel, telling himself that the fact Tiffany had been a virgin weighed into his decision to extend their association. No man wanted to be a woman's first and her worst. He owed her more time and consideration than the average jaded socialite.

And she happened to have a sexual appetite to match his own. He kept mistresses when it suited him for that very reason. This was still a temporary arrangement, and Tiffany understood that's all he ever intended to have with any woman. His heart belonged to Luiza. If he couldn't marry her, he wouldn't marry anyone.

Having relegated Tiffany to her rightful place in his mind, he was ready to see her again. He nodded at the first mate, and the young man swung the sail to catch more gust.

Tiffany was falling out of bed.

She woke with a cry and a start, arms splayed to orient herself on the mattress. The room glowed a brassy yellow, the bed was a wreck and her body felt as if she'd been thrown down a flight of stairs. She held very still, trying to come to grips with the odd feeling the boat was not just bobbing in its slip, but moving.

It was. They were at sail!

She'd been on sailboats, but unlike the sharp angle that resulted in stumbling around to grip her way across a deck, this catamaran was only a hair off level, allowing her to rush the window and snap up the blind. Yep. Not another boat in sight. Just a speck of land on the horizon and glittering waves in every other direction.

"What the hell, Ryzard?" she said aloud.

Glancing around for her clothes, she caught sight of herself and cringed. Her hair was naturally straight, and all that sweaty sex had weighed it down into a droopy haystack. The side of her breast felt raw where it had been abraded by stubble and when she turned her nose to her shoulder, she could swear she smelled Ryzard's unique scent on her skin.

An odd, sexy feeling overcame her, making her want to loll in bed and call him to her, but she gave herself a firm shake. Where the hell was he taking her?

A very quick shower later, she dressed in her pants and sleeveless top to go in search of him. She forced herself not to be so cowardly as to wear the mask, but she still peered around corners, avoiding his staff.

She found him lounging in the shade of the aft deck,

taking up all the cushions of the built-in sofa as he read his tablet and sipped a drink made with tomato juice. A stalk of celery rested against its salted rim. He set it down when she appeared.

"I thought a few sharp turns might shake you out of bed," he said.

"Are you familiar with the term *kidnapping?*"

"I have business in Cuba."

"You're taking me to Cuba?" She gave a wild look around. Nope, not one hint of assistance in sight.

"Much as I'd love to anchor somewhere private and shirk my responsibilities, I can't. My weekend was booked for *Q Virtus,* but now we'll have to carve out our time around other commitments."

"Commitments like the one I made to get on a plane with my brother two hours ago? He'll be frantic." Dumbfounded, she braced a hand on her forehead trying to gather her scattered wits enough to formulate a plan.

"My staff spoke to him when they collected your things."

"Your staff collected my things. And brought them here?" She pointed to the deck, so astounded she could barely form words. "After they informed my brother that I was carrying on with you?"

"They're discreet enough to simply say you're my guest. Naturally he needed to be told why you weren't meeting him as arranged. Why are you upset? Relax. I realize you avoid the sun, but you can enjoy the view from the shade. I have a masseuse aboard, if you need."

"Ryzard," she said with a ring of near hysteria in her tone. "You said we'd stay in dock."

"For a few hours. We did. You overslept."

"You should have woken me! Not said things to my brother. He doesn't need to know about this. No one does. It's nobody's business but mine!" She splayed a hand on the place in her chest where he was taking up way more room than he should. Where he was lodged very close to places no one was allowed to go.

"When you called me your dirty little secret, I didn't realize you meant it," he replied stiffly.

Oh, she would *not* feel guilty. Maybe she was overreacting, but he didn't realize what kind of firestorm he would have set off with her family. This was bad.

"You should have asked me," she insisted. "And let *me* talk to my brother. Is there some way I can contact him?" Panic gripped her.

"If your mobile doesn't work, ask the captain for the ship to shore." He still sounded stung, but dealing with Ryzard came second to smoothing things over with Christian. What would he think of her?

She'd left her mobile in her room at the club and found it in her purse in the cabin where her things had been unpacked. Not Ryzard's cabin, she noted, but a separate one—and why did that bother her? She was upset with him, not supposed to be mooning about what it meant if he set her up to sleep apart from him.

Keying her code into her phone, she saw that her brother had left her a dozen messages.

"What the *hell,* Tiff," were his first words when she reached him.

"I know." She closed her eyes. She really should have thought this through before dialing. She was just so frantic to undo what had been done. But how?

"How does something like this even happen?" he demanded.

His askance reaction crystallized the confused self-consciousness inside her, so she felt very fragile and very brittle all of a sudden. Ryzard, despite his assumptions and autocratic ways, was not the villain. The problem with her family knowing about their affair, she realized, was the impossible vision she was supposed to live up to.

"You're the expert on picking up women. You know how it works," she retorted. "He came on to me with a great line. I fell for it."

The door clicked and Ryzard entered in time to hear most of what she said.

She averted her gaze from his darkening expression, prickling as her brother said, "You're too smart for that."

"Am I? Maybe I'm weak and desperate. Maybe I'm grateful for attention from *any* man."

In her periphery, Ryzard's arms folded and he said in an ominous undertone, "Is that true?"

"I knew it. He's taking advantage of you."

She sucked in a jagged breath, more hurt than words could express, but it was the ugly truth they'd all been dancing around since her accident. She wasn't worth a man's attention.

She flashed a look of resentment at Ryzard, angry that he was witnessing her humiliation. At the same time, she wished he didn't look so thunderous. She was desperately in need of backup. Instead, he'd probably leave her on a sandbar somewhere, but that was almost better than sending her back to the bosom of her kin.

"Thanks, Chris," she choked. "Thanks for letting me know there's no way he could possibly be attracted to me. I'm some broken, awful thing that ceased to be valuable when I ceased to be perfect. Shame rains upon us and it's my fault. Has Mom taken to her room?"

A weighted pause. She didn't dare look at Ryzard.

"I didn't say that," Christian said quietly.

"But it's true! Tell me something. How many times have you stolen a weekend with someone? Hundreds," she quickly provided. "How many times have you had to answer for it? *None.* And I never worked up the nerve to even kiss another man because I had a reputation to uphold. Not just mine, but the entire family's. Paulie's even."

He swore. "Okay, I get it. You're entitled to a private life, but this isn't exactly the time, is it?" he seethed. "Or the man."

"You haven't told Mom and Dad, have you?"

"I didn't know what to think, Tiff! This isn't like you."

"When have I ever had a chance to be who I am?" she cried. "I've been Dad's daughter, Paulie's intended. The bride who wore bandages. For God's sake, I'm an adult. A married, *widowed* woman. I shouldn't have to defend myself like I've committed a federal crime."

"No, you're right, I'm sorry. Truly."

"How bad is it?" she asked, hanging her head, weighted by guilt despite all she'd just said. "Do I have to talk to them or better to wait?"

"They don't know what to think, either. But they don't want to see you get hurt in any way, ever again. Is this thing serious with Vrbancic?"

She glanced at Ryzard. He didn't look quite so much as if he wanted to wring her neck, but he had an air of imperative surrounding him. As if he didn't intend to wait much longer for her to give her attention back to him.

"Not, um, really," she murmured.

Christian's sharp sigh grated in her ear.

"Oh, I'm sorry, did I miss where you married everyone you ever slept with?" she railed.

"So it's gone that far."

He didn't have to take a tone like the septic was backed up!

"Goodbye, Chris. Tell Mom and Dad whatever you want." She stabbed the end button and threw her phone onto the bed. Then dropped a pillow on top of it for good measure. And added a punch that left a deep indent.

"I'd like to say I'm above caring what people think of me, but when my family judges me, it hurts." Her baleful gaze met one that didn't so much judge as measure.

"You knew they would disapprove. That's why you were upset."

"Not because it's you. They would have been scandalized no matter who I slept with. Although, I'm sure there's some shock value that they sent me to talk to you and here I am. As God is my witness, I'll never, ever tell my mother I didn't even see your face the first time, let alone know your name." She buried her hot face in her clammy hands, reacting to all that had happened since she'd woken so abruptly. "This isn't the way I usually behave, Ryzard. I can't blame them for being shocked."

"Be careful how much you hate your parents, *draga*. They're the only ones you have."

"You're going to judge me now?" She lifted her face in challenge.

"I'm only offering the benefit of my experience."

"You hated your parents?" She didn't believe it.

"I was angry with them for sending me away. Keeping me away from my home. It felt like a rejection."

He hadn't explained that part before. A pang struck at how lonely and discarded he must have felt.

Beneath the pillow, her phone burbled. Tiffany made a noise and started from the room, then said, "Actually, I want to change. It's too hot for long pants."

Ryzard closed the door, but remained in the room. Apparently he intended to watch. Hell. The man gave her goose bumps without making any effort at all.

Skimming past the one-shoulder and long-sleeved shirts and dresses, she pulled out a skimpy sundress she would have worn only in the privacy of her suite yesterday. It was patterned busily in neon pink and green and yellow, hopefully bright enough to draw attention from her equally busy skin patterns.

The scared mouse in her wanted to hide under layers, but a spunky, more daring part of her wanted to test whether she still held his interest.

Stripping unceremoniously, even dropping her bra, she shrugged her arms under the spaghetti straps and tugged it into place, then picked up the flared skirt in a little curtsy, spinning under the direction of his twirled finger.

"Adorable. Now come here."

"And risk making love on that telephone? Possibly landing on buttons that could have serious consequences? No. You promised me a meal and we skipped lunch."

"Yet I recall being very satisfied with everything I tasted," he mused, one hand on the door latch. The other caressed her bottom as she exited in front of him.

Her blood skipped in her arteries, and she was blushing hard as she led him outside to where a table was set and chilled wine was ready to be uncorked. The sun sat low on the horizon, ducking beneath the shade to strike off the silver and crystal.

Ryzard held a chair in a corner for her and asked for a filtered shade to be drawn.

"I'm sorry I was such a pill," she said contritely. "You took me by surprise with this." She indicated the extravagance of the cat. "I thought we'd part ways this afternoon and maybe I'd see you with someone else at a future *Q Virtus* event. This is better," she allowed, but met his gaze with a level one. "But I do have to work."

"Apology accepted. And I've already instructed my crew to set up a work space in the cabin where your things were unpacked. It should be completed by morning."

"They're going to work while I'm sleeping in there?" she asked, already anticipating his reply.

"You won't be in there, *draga*. And you won't be sleeping."

* * *

Ryzard flipped through his emails on his tablet while he waited for Tiffany to finish her call. They'd had a surprisingly productive morning, despite lazing in bed first thing. An easy, affectionate companionship had fallen between them after her rather explosive reaction to waking at sea yesterday.

He still chafed a little, recalling it, even though he now understood it to be her own baggage with her family that had caused her to push him away like that. His reaction, however, continued to niggle at him no matter how much he wanted to ignore it. Her claim that she was with him out of desperation had slapped him with a surprisingly sharp hand.

She was volatile. A woman as sexually passionate as she was would have strong feelings in every aspect of her life, he supposed. He could only imagine what kind of mama bear she'd be about her children.

Sucking in a breath at having taken such a bizarre turn in his mind, he lifted his head to see her set aside her phone.

"Done. Really sorry," she said.

"Don't apologize. We both have to work. I made you wait this morning."

She gave him a look that said, *Seriously?* and slid her eyes to the crewman setting out their air tanks.

He grinned, amused by her blushing over his referring to the way they'd been driving each other into a frenzy, fresh out of the shower, when he'd had to take a call that couldn't be put off. Afterward, they'd nearly ripped each other apart, and breakfast had been a quietly stunned affair when her bare foot atop his had pleased him well beyond what was reasonable.

They'd parted ways after, each moving to their separate work spaces, but he'd been distracted by her proximity. With most women, that would signal the end for him. Not with Tiffany. His brain couldn't even contemplate an end to this. It had barely started. She was too extraordinary.

Her phone rang and she turned from removing her wrap, clad only in her bikini as she stepped toward the table where she'd left the phone. "I don't have to get that. We'll pretend we're already in the water and— Oh shoot, it's my brother. I should answer. Why are you staring?" She followed his gaze to her torso, then sent an anxious look to the crewman who had lifted her tank, ready to strap it onto her.

"I'm staring because you're hot as hell," Ryzard prevaricated. "Take your call or you'll be wondering what he wanted."

Somewhat flustered, she stabbed the phone, then held the screen before her for the video call. "Hey," she said as she picked up her wrap and shrugged her arm into it.

Ryzard sighed inwardly. He hadn't meant to make her feel sensitive. He'd been looking at her scars, yes, but only thinking that a woman with less zeal for life would have succumbed to such injuries. Tiffany's ferocious spirit was the reason she'd survived, and he was very glad she had.

"You're naked?" Her brother frowned. "It's the middle of the day. I thought it would be safe to call."

"Excuse me, darling," Tiffany said to Ryzard. "My brother has called to ask if the sun is over the yardarm. Could you lift the sheet and see?"

Christian sputtered, Ryzard looked to the sky for patience and his crewman buried a snort of laughter into his shirt collar. Although Ryzard had to admit it was nice to know she gave others a hard time, not just him.

"We're about to go swimming, you idiot," she said to her brother. "See? Bathing suit." She ran her phone down her body as if she was scanning for radioactivity, showing him the strapless band and itsy slash of blue. Then she turned the phone to show him the equipment on the deck. "There are the breathing tanks and scuba flippers. There's the mask that's going to give me an anxiety attack so Ryzard will have to buddy-breathe me to the surface. Is my virtue restored? Want to tell me now why you called?"

"Dad hasn't come across anything useful yet, but said he'd ask around."

"Motivated, is he?" The way Tiffany's blond lashes lifted to send a resolute look toward Ryzard made his blood kick into higher gear. "Tell him I appreciate anything he's able to pass along."

"As do I," Ryzard told her as she hung up. "If you're talking about what I think you are."

"I asked Christian to put a bug in his ear. Dad's not speaking to me directly right now, but I don't know if that's because he's in Washington and doesn't have time for the kind of conversation he thinks we need to have or if he's genuinely angry. I hope you don't mind, but I was worried Dad might—" She shrugged apologetically. "I'm his little princess. I didn't want any grumpiness he felt toward you to come out with anyone in a position to affect your situation. If he knows I have an interest in the outcome, he'll take care to support your petition. Or at least not damage it."

His ears rang with the impact of what she was saying. "He has that kind of influence?" It wasn't like him to underestimate people, but his sexual enthrallment had temporarily shortened his sight of the bigger picture.

"He's very well connected. And I'm being overcautious," she assured him, moving to put a hand on his arm. "Don't worry. He wouldn't do anything rash. Something like throwing support behind a leader who hasn't been recognized… It's too big a gamble going into an election. If anything he'll be even more circumspect, couching his reaction while trying to find out everything he can. He's not going to stir up a lynch mob or anything."

"No shotgun wedding?" he prompted, throat dry. How far would her father go for his daughter's groom?

"Absolutely not," she assured him.

He should be relieved. He couldn't betray Luiza's memory by contemplating marriage to another woman, but in the back of his mind a voice whispered, *If it was for your country...*

He brushed the thought aside, trying to remind himself this was a simple fling. Two people enjoying sexual compatibility and the luxury of Caribbean waters. If he took a moment to reassess Tiffany, not just because she was lissome and golden, not simply because she had a quick, intelligent mind and a clear understanding of politics, but because she could soon be first daughter of the United States of America, that didn't mean he was being disloyal to his one true love. Luiza had had a dream for their country, and he was obligated to consider any avenue to achieve it. That's all he was doing.

He watched her frown at her diving mask, lips white where she pinched them together. She'd told him about her aversion to wearing things tight against her face, but he watched her draw in courage with a deep breath and wrestle the mask onto her face.

"I'm really worried I'll freak out down there," she said in a tone made nasal by the mask covering the upper half of her face. Her eyes behind the glass were anxious.

"You're tough," he told her, pride and regard moving in him. "You'll handle it."

"You don't know that." She set a hand on her bare chest. "My heart's going a mile a minute."

"But you're trying anyway, despite your anxiety. That's why I know you'll be fine," he assured her.

He quickly slipped into his own gear, not wanting to make her wait for the distraction of reef and shipwreck to take her mind off her fears. Holiday fun, he insisted to himself. Nothing so complex as wanting to coax her past bad memories because he felt compelled to share the wonder below the surface with her.

Why it mattered to him that she go with him was a puzzle he didn't study too closely. He could just as easily dive with one of his crew and had in the past, but he was aware of a preference for staying aboard with her over diving without her.

That wasn't like him. He was not a dependent person. Tiffany had been surprised the other day when he'd told her he didn't want a wife or children. He understood the reaction. Everyone in the world wanted a lifetime companion and offspring, but after Luiza, he'd closed himself off to the idea.

He *didn't* want emotional addiction to another being. It made a person vulnerable, and he couldn't afford such weaknesses.

But the thought of marrying Tiffany kept detonating in his mind, trailing thoughts of sleeping with her every night for the rest of his life.

It was because of the advantages she offered him. It would be a practical move, not something he did out of a need to connect himself irrevocably to her. He didn't want or need *family*.

He needed to stabilize his country and make good on his promise of peace.

"You look like a frog," she said as they readied to jump.

"So kiss me, Daddy's Little Princess. See what I turn into."

She did, quick and flirty, then bit her smile onto her mouthpiece and fell back into the water.

He leaped after her.

CHAPTER SEVEN

"That was fantastic!" Tiffany panted, still breathless from their ascent from a shipwreck covered in coral and barnacles, populated with colorful fish darting in and out of fronds. Ryzard had carried a spotlight so the wash of blue-green from the filtered sunlight had disappeared, revealing the true brilliance below.

He handed off his tank to his crewman, then heaved himself to sit on the platform at the stern of the boat, legs dangling beside her. "Up?" He offered a hand.

"Still recovering. Give me a sec," she said breathlessly.

He relayed their gear as they both stripped, lifting her tank off her back, muscles flexing under the glistening latte of his tan. His black bathing suit was ridiculously miniscule, making American men such as her brother seem like absolute prudes with their baggy trunks. She'd heard people refer to those teensy tight suits as banana hammocks and budgie smugglers, but on the right man, they were sexy as hell.

A crooked finger came under her chin, and he lifted her face to look him in the eye. Beneath the water, his foot snaked out to catch her at the waist and guide her into the space between his knees.

"What?" she challenged, hands splaying on the steely muscles of his flexing thighs.

"Are we staying in the water a little longer?" he asked suggestively. "You can't look at me like that and not provoke a response."

She flicked her gaze downward and saw he'd filled out the tight black fabric to near bursting.

"Don't ever let anyone tell you you're not beautiful, *draga*. When you smile, you light up the room, and when you're aroused, I can't take my eyes off you."

The water should have bubbled and fizzed around her, she grew so hot and flushed with joy.

"Will you come to Bregnovia with me?"

Oh. It was an out-of-the-blue question with huge implications, the most important being, *he wanted to keep her with him.*

Surging upward, she straightened her arms and let her chest plaster into his, meeting his hot kiss with open-mouthed, passionate joy.

"Yes," she agreed.

One big hand came up to cradle the back of her head and the other dug into her waist, holding her steady while his calves pinched her thighs, bracing her in the awkward position. Their kiss went on for a long time, sumptuous and thorough.

With a tight sound of frustration, he jerked back. "No condom," he muttered.

"What? There's plenty of room in that suit for one."

"Not much room at all, actually," he growled. "You'll take the lead into the cabin."

Laughing unreservedly, she let him pull her the rest of the way out of the water and onto his lap. "At least we know what you turned into down there."

He raised his brows in query.

She whispered, "Horny toad."

He pinched her bottom as he urged her inside.

* * *

The landscape from the airport was one of a country in recovery. When her brother had said Bregnovia could use their firm's expertise, he hadn't been kidding. They left the partially bombed-out tarmac, wound past a scorched vineyard and turned away from one end of a shattered bridge that spanned a canyon to zigzag into the riverbed, where they four-wheeled over a makeshift crossing before climbing the hairpin curves on the far side to enter a city that looked like a child had kicked over his blocks.

But what a city it had been. Bregnovia's capital, Gizela, was a medieval fairy tale on a river that, until dammed for electricity and irrigation, had been a trading arm in and out of the Black Sea. Low canals still lapped at the stone walls in its village square. Beyond that quaint center, stark communist housing stood next to even more modern shopping malls, but nothing escaped the wounds of recent war. Rubble punctuated in a small landslide off a facade here, crooked fencing kept children out of a teetering building there.

Fascinated by the contrast of beauty and battle, Tiffany barely spoke until they drove through gates that were twelve feet high and thirty-six feet wide. Their ornate wrought-iron grillwork with gold filigree appeared startlingly new and grand.

"This is your home? It looks like Buckingham Palace."

"It is a palace," Ryzard confirmed casually. "Built as the dacha for a Russian prince during tsarist times. The communists spared it—a KGB general appropriated it—but it was the last stand for my predecessor. We're still repairing it from the siege. It's only mine while I'm president, but I'm paying for the refurbishment, as my legacy."

Despite the bullet holes and the pile of broken stones that might have once been a carriage house, the palace made the White House look like a neglected summer cottage, especially with its expansive flower bed that formed a carpet beneath a bronze statue of a woman with an arm across her breast, the other outstretched in supplication—

Tiffany read the nameplate as the limo circled it. Inexplicably, her heart invaded her throat, pulsing there like a hammered thumb. *Luiza.*

Ryzard had said she was his country's martyr, revered like their Lady Liberty, but this statue wasn't staid. It didn't project a state of peace and optimism with a torch to light the way forward. It was anguished and emotional and raised all the hairs on her body. This statue wasn't a symbol or an ideal. She was a real person.

Whose name was tattooed on Ryzard's chest.

Not wanting to believe the suspicion flirting around the periphery of her consciousness, Tiffany left the car and walked inside to confront an oil portrait of the same woman in the spacious drawing room. Here, Luiza's serene smile was as exquisite as Mona Lisa's, only eclipsed by her flawless beauty.

Again it didn't seem like a commemorative pose that a country hung in the National Gallery. There was a wistful quality to the painting. It was the kind of thing someone lovingly commissioned to enshrine a memory.

Luiza's eyes seemed to follow Tiffany as she accepted introductions to Ryzard's staff. Thankfully they quickly left her behind as Ryzard and his porters took her up the stairs and along the colonnaded walk that circled the grand entrance below and brought her to a place he called the Garden Suite.

"It's the only one in the guest wing that's habitable," he said with a minor twist of apology across his lips. "But your work space is here." He left the bedroom and crossed the hall to push through a pair of double doors into a sitting room that had been tricked out with office equipment and a replica desk that Marie Antoinette would have used if she had run a modern international construction firm. "You won't have any problem working outside your country? With the different time zone?"

"We're global and I've been working from the family mansion. The advantage to living like a recluse is that no one will expect me to show up in pers— My umbrella!" The stained glass piece hung at a cocked angle in front of the window, just high enough for her to stand under it. "You said we slept through the auction," she accused.

"I placed a reserve bid before we left."

Moving in a slow twirl, she closed her eyes and imagined she could feel the colors as they caressed her face. "You're spoiling me."

"I want you to be happy. You will be?"

She opened her eyes to the window and the back of Luiza's bronzed head beyond the glass. Her floating spirits fell like a block of lead. She couldn't shake the feeling that Ryzard had a statue of his old girlfriend on the lawn.

"Tiffany?" he queried, voice coming closer.

"Where will you be?" she asked, leaving the window and leading him back across the hall to the bedroom. Here, at least, the windows faced the river.

"Too damned far away," he replied.

"Why? Security? No outsiders in the president's bedroom?" she guessed.

"Certain customs remain quaintly adhered to."

"Mmm." She pushed her mouth to the side, hiding that she was actually quite devastated. "I don't suppose our president could get away with bringing women home, either." The porter had gone so she jerked her chin at the door, saying, "See if that door locks."

"Subtle," he said drily, "but I can't."

"I don't know what you think I'm suggesting," she challenged, tossing her head to cover up that she rather desperately needed to reconnect physically. The emotional hit of what looked quite literally like a monumental devotion to Luiza shook her tenuous confidence. Badly. Now he was rejecting her, inciting a quiet panic. "I only meant that if I'll be sleeping alone, I need to feel safe."

"You won't be alone."

"I can have a guard with me?"

"That would be detrimental to the state of peace I'm trying to maintain," he stated with one of his untamed smiles. "No, I will sleep with you, but right now I have to go outside and salute my flag. It's a custom I observe when I return after being away. People gather to see it. It reassures them of my commitment. Would you do me the favor of putting on something suitable and joining me? They'll be curious."

Here we go again, she thought with an unexpected faceplant into dread.

I bet Luiza would do it, a taunting voice sang in followup.

"Problem?" he asked, obviously reading something of her reluctance.

"Just disappointed we can't test the bed," she prevaricated.

"They stand at the gate, if you're worried they'll see you close up."

"It's fine," she assured him.

It was. When she stood outside thirty minutes later, face shaded by a hat from the surprisingly hot sun, her entire being swelled with admiration as she watched Ryzard in his presidential garb stand tall and make a pledge to his flag. He wasn't a man going through the motions. His motives were pure, his heart one hundred percent dedicated.

With tears brimming her eyes, she watched him step away from the flag with a bow, taking his respectful leave. Then he turned and saluted the statue of Luiza, first pressing the flats of his fingertips to his mouth then offering the kiss to her in an earnest lift of his palm.

Tiffany stood very still, fighting not to gasp at the slice of pain that went through her. It wasn't the gesture that struck her so much as the anguish on Ryzard's face.

Her suspicions were confirmed. He loved Luiza, really loved her as a strong man loves his soul mate. His pain was so tangible, she could taste its metallic flavor on her tongue.

She reached out instinctively, longing to comfort him, but he stiffened under her touch, catching her hand and gently but firmly removing it from his sleeve.

"When I asked about your tattoo, you never said—"

"I know," he cut in, releasing her and taking one step away. "It's difficult to talk about."

"Of course," she managed, curling her fingers into a fist even though the blood was draining from her head, making her feel faint. Would she have come here if she'd known? The starkness of his rejection felt so final she could barely stand it. "I'm so sorry."

She meant she was sorry for overstepping, but he heard it as a lame platitude and dismissed it with an agitated jerk of his shoulder.

"I never want to go through anything like it again. To love like that and lose— Never again," he choked, flashing her a look that was both adamant and apprehensive.

He quickly looked away, but that glimpse of his resolve struck like a blow. She knew what it meant: he would never *allow* himself to love again. It would make him too vulnerable.

Making another quarter turn, he bowed his head toward the gates.

That's when Tiffany noticed the crowd of fifty or sixty people with faces pressed through the uprights of the gate, witnessing his rebuff and her humiliation. They didn't applaud, didn't wave, just stared at them for a few moments before slowly beginning to disperse.

Even they seemed to know she had no place here.

As she followed Ryzard back into the palace, she couldn't tell if Luiza's portrait met her with a smug smile, or a pitying eye. Thankfully, they both had work to catch up on. She needed space, even one situated with a prime view of Luiza's last haircut.

Oh, don't be bitter, Tiffany.

Ha, she laughed at herself. Bitterness had been her stock in trade after the pain of her recovery had receded from blinding to merely unrelenting. She really had believed her life was over, but Ryzard had shown her she could have a measure of happiness.

She considered the boundaries of her happiness later, as she soaked in a tub of bubbles. Ryzard had had to take a call, leaving her to dine alone, and she felt very much as her mother must have for much of her marriage. Not so much slighted as resigned. This was the reality of living with someone in his position. If he had loved her, the sacrifice might be worth it, but he didn't.

His heart belonged to Luiza. Indelibly.

A tiny draft flickered the candles in the corner of the tub and sudden awareness made her glance toward the door, then sit up in a startled rush of water and crackling bubbles.

Ryzard slouched his shoulder against the frame, arms folded, hip cocked. The most decadently wicked glint of admiration gave his shadowed expression a sexy cast.

She'd set a stage for him if he chose to come looking for her. A delicate lily-of-the-valley scent hovered in the humid air and a low-volume saxophone hummed sensuously from the music player. That hadn't prepared her for the impact of his tousled hair, wrinkled collar under a pullover sweater, or the way her heart leaped when he reached to tug his sweater over his head.

"I came to sneak you down to my room, but you've made me an offer I can't refuse. Before I forget, though…" He leaned over her, one broad hand cradling her chin while he crushed her mouth in a hard, thorough kiss that made her murmur in surprised delight.

"You were in danger of forgetting to do that, were you?" she asked breathlessly as he straightened to take off his shirt and kick away his pants.

"An undersecretary from your State Department called. It's not a promise to vote in favor, but it's a promising sign they're leaning that way."

"Oh!" The impulsive clap of her hands sent bubbles exploding like flakes off a snowball. "That's wonderful."

"That's thanks to you." He eased into place behind her, his muscular body buoying hers as he pressed her to relax back into him.

"I didn't do anything."

"I'm sure it was your father's influence at play."

"Mmm." She let her head loll against his shoulder, absently playing with his fingers where he roped his forearm across her collarbone. Her brow pleated. She wanted him to be happy, wanted peace for his country—who wouldn't wish peace for everyone in the world? But a pang sat in her chest. She wished something more personal had brought him to her this evening.

"It's a very big step," he said, drifting his hand down the slippery slope of her breast. "Do you know how many countries hesitate to make a move because they fear instigating something with yours? If America supports us, the other two-thirds of the votes I need would fall into place fairly quickly. I know I said I wouldn't force any dress-up on you, but there may be a few state dinners in our future."

She bit back a huffing laugh. *So* not surprised.

Just say no, Tiffany.

But refusing to play her part meant refusing this relationship. Despite it's misty future, she wasn't ready for it to end.

Especially when Ryzard lightly toyed with her nipple, making her murmur approval and slide against him. Was he manipulating her with her own responses, she wondered distantly? He was hardening against her, so he *did* want her.

Still, she hated herself a little for being so weak and easily managed. If she couldn't have the same effect on him, she at least wanted to break through his control. Rolling over, she grasped him in a firm hold, the way she'd learned he liked, and nipped his bottom lip.

He jerked his head back. The gold flecks in his green eyes glinted like sparks off a sword. "It's like that, is it?" he growled.

She grinned and sent a small tsunami across the ledge as she dragged herself onto her knees and straddled his thighs. As she kissed him with all the passion releasing inside her, she used her whole body to caress him, wiggling her hips to encourage the palms that shaped her backside.

Licking into his mouth, she reached to caress his thick erection again and started to take him into her.

"*Draga,* wait," he rasped against her open mouth. "Protection." He leaned away to reach for his pants.

Inhaling anguish along with a small dose of shame, she wondered what she had been thinking, offering unprotected sex. Was she that desperate for something permanent with him?

"Actually, let's go to the bed," he said, pulling away to leave the tub and let water sluice off him onto the floor. "It'll be more comfortable." He reached to draw her onto her feet, then lifted her out, carrying her wet and dripping into her bedroom, where he followed her onto the bed.

She bit him again as he tried to kiss her.

"What has got into you?" he asked, pulling her scratching nails off him and pinning them above her head in one hand.

"Not you," she taunted, inciting him with the arch of her body into his. "What's taking so long?"

With a bite of the packet and a stroke of a finger and

thumb, he was covered and pushing into her, not rough, but not gentle. Inexorable. She was ready, but not entirely. The friction caused her to draw in a breath of both surprise and anticipation.

"Better?" he asked, holding himself so deep inside her, she released a little sob. He eased back. "Tiffany, what's wrong?"

She shook her head. "Just make love to me."

Ryzard did, because he couldn't be with her like this and not thrust and withdraw and savor and bask. But he held out, making it last a long time for both of them, sensing a wall that needed prolonged lovemaking to erode. He blamed himself for the distance. He was struggling with having her here. It had been an impulse to ask her and he didn't regret it, but he was still having a hard time adjusting.

For the moment, however, he closed his mind to his inner conflicts and opened himself to Tiffany.

She writhed beneath him, so beautiful in her struggle to resist the little death of orgasm, clinging to him as she hung on to their connection. It couldn't last forever, though. Nothing could. His heart stopped. The whole world did. Ecstasy overtook them and nothing existed for him except her.

He stayed in that trance for hours, trying to sate their appetite for each other with repeated joinings. The wall between them receded and he didn't worry about it again until the next morning, when she woke in his bed.

She glanced around with the perplexed befuddlement of the bubbleheaded blonde he sometimes teasingly called her. "Where am I?"

"The Presidential Bedroom," he answered, shrugging into his suit jacket while he enjoyed the show.

The sheet slipped as she sat up. Her blue eyes blinked and she smoothed a hand over her tangled hair. "Why?"

"Your bed was wet," he reasoned, distantly aware that wasn't the whole truth. He had wanted her in here before he'd ever gone looking for her, but he was distracted by the shadow that passed behind her clear-sky irises as she looked around.

"Problem?"

She only lifted the sheet and glanced at her naked body. "Please tell me you put clothes on me when you carried me here."

"You were awfully heavy. I couldn't manage another ounce."

Her baleful gaze held a dire warning that made him grin. He picked up her robe from the chair and tossed it to the foot of the bed in answer.

She stood to pull it on, not returning his smile. The niggling sense of being held off returned full force.

"Are you all right, *draga?*" he asked, moving forward to cup her cheek and force her to look up at him.

She didn't quite meet his eyes, only saying with an ironic twist to her mouth, "Let's just say it's a good thing I had a warm bath to loosen my muscles before we played for gold in that triathlon last night."

"Shall I rub you down?" he offered, stroking a hand down her back in concern. He was ready to insist, wanting the physical connection to her even if it wasn't a sexual one. The way she stayed resistant to his touch bothered him.

"I thought it was verboten for me to be in here? I'll be fine. I'll have a hot shower and do my stretches." She kissed him, but it was a minimal brush of her lips against the corner of his mouth before she disappeared.

He frowned as he crossed to pick up his phone from the nightstand. Absently he straightened the snapshot of him and Luiza on horseback, wondering if he was imagining the wedge between him and Tiffany.

It was probably for the best if there was one, he reasoned. This was an affair. They couldn't afford to develop deeper feelings.

Still, he left his room with a pain cleaved into his chest.

CHAPTER EIGHT

TIFFANY TRIED TO ignore the fact that Ryzard was in love with a dead woman and soak up what he offered her: generous lovemaking and a boost to her confidence.

On his catamaran, she'd quit trying to hide herself from his crew. Three days in Bregnovia and she was even more comfortable in her own skin. He kept threatening to take her along on his public appearances and she always managed to talk him out of it, but part of her longed to go on a date the way they had at *Q Virtus*.

Pressing a strapless dress in sunset colors to her front, she decided to have a pretend date with him tonight. She imagined that like all men he had a thing for short skirts and low necklines. She'd knock his socks off.

An hour later, she'd run the straightening iron over her hair to give it a sheen and applied a final layer of glossy pink to her lips, making them look pouty and ripe. The dress offered her breasts in half cups, hugged her waist and clung so tightly across her hips she could barely walk. The gladiator sandals didn't help, but man did she look hot. The fact her scars were fully revealed by the itty-bitty dress didn't faze her.

She paused to consider that. A light coat of concealer downplayed the mottled scar on her face, but she wasn't about to smear her whole body with the stuff. Ryzard wouldn't notice or care either way. He thought she was gorgeous exactly as she was. It was such a painfully sweet knowledge, she had to stop and cradle it and blink hard or ruin her carefully applied makeup.

Digging her nails into her palms, she focused on the sting to clear her head, aware she was dangerously close to tumbling into love with him. It was because he was her first, she reasoned. He was gorgeous and smart and *so* patient with her moodiness and baggage. He commanded everything around him with calm ease, and that would make anyone feel safe and protected and cherished.

The real tell would be when they separated. She couldn't hide from her parents forever. The one stilted conversation with her mother had centered on exactly how long she intended to be away.

Tiffany hadn't wanted to admit she was afraid to leave. Would Ryzard miss her if she went home for a week? Or would it be the end of their associations?

She shook her head, having learned to be present in a moment, especially if it lacked pain. No one had a crystal ball telling what would come next. For now, she and Ryzard were together and happy.

With a calming breath, she searched him out in his office. He was watching his favorite newscaster and remained behind his desktop screen as she entered, head bent in concentration as he listened, expression grim and contained.

"What's happening in the world to make you look so severe?" she teased as she sidled up to him. "A beautiful woman just walked in. Whatever you're watching, forget it and notice *me*."

His arm came around her waist, grasping her close and tight, but his other hand caught hers before she could press his head down for the kiss she wanted. The look in his eyes was not easily interpreted, and the voice beside her startled her out of trying.

"Should we continue this later?" the newscaster asked.

"No," Ryzard answered.

Tiffany cried out in surprise and jerked against Ryzard's arm, but he held on to her without laughing.

"I thought you were watching a broadcast," she gasped, covering her heart.

The familiar face on the screen gave a tight smile of acknowledgment.

"I didn't realize I was walking into a video call. I apologize. Oh, gosh," she realized with a belated hand going to the bad side of her face. "I can't imagine what you think of me, making an entrance like that."

"I was already aware you two were close," the talking head said. He was a globally known face, one who'd elevated from foreign-correspondence stories to hard-hitting investigative stories and in-depth analyses of world politics.

At the moment she didn't have much choice with regard to how close she was to Ryzard. His arm was like a belt of iron, pinning her to his side, his tension starting to penetrate as she read zero amusement in his expression over her mistake.

"What's wrong?" she asked, instinctively bracing herself.

"We had company after our dive," he replied.

"Paparazzi?" She tried to step back, but he kept a tight grip on her.

"It doesn't matter, Tiffany."

"Of course it matters! Otherwise your friend here wouldn't be calling to warn you. Is it photos or video?"

"Photos." Ryzard fairly spat the word.

"The photographer knew I would never touch something purely to incite sensation," the newscaster said. "So they didn't offer them to me or I would have kept them off the market completely. Instead I heard about it secondhand and I've suggested a countermeasure to draw attention from their release."

"What kind of countermeasure? What are they saying?" She looked between the screen and Ryzard, panic creeping into her bloodstream.

"They don't sell clicks by being kind," Ryzard said brutally. "We'll meet in Rome," he told his friend on the screen. "You're right that a face-to-face broadcast interview will have more impact than something thrown together remotely."

"I'm not going on camera!" Tiffany cried.

"No," Ryzard agreed with the full impact of his dictatorial personality. "But you'll accompany me to the interview—"

She shook her head, growing manic. Part of her wanted to explode in rebellion, the other desperately needed to crawl away and hide.

"I need to go home." Had her father heard yet? She struggled against Ryzard's steely grip, then froze, thinking of her mother's reaction. "My family will be livid. They're already barely speaking to me—"

"Calm down." He thanked his friend and promised to be in touch with his travel arrangements, then turned off the screen. "The sun will still rise tomorrow, Tiffany. No one has died."

"It would be better if I had. That's what they'll be thinking."

"Don't talk like that. Ever." He gripped her arms and gave her a little shake.

She quit struggling, but kept a firm hand of resistance against his chest. "We're not one of these families who has a disgrace every minute, Ryzard. My accident was the worst thing Dad has ever had to field with the press. Given it was more tragedy than scandal, it didn't do him any harm in the polls, but it was still a monumental circus. He won't appreciate this."

The look of wild outrage Ryzard savaged over her made

her shrink in his hold. "Your father enjoyed some kind of political *benefit* from your near death?"

"He didn't mean to! I'm just saying that's how it works. Chris and I know that. We don't go off and sleep with people who are shaking up the maps of an atlas, putting the UN on notice, then get ourselves photographed for the gossip rags so Dad has to make explanations for our behavior. This, what you and I are doing, has to stop. I have to go home." She tried again to push away.

"So you can be shunned and cloistered? No," he gritted through his teeth, holding her in place. "The photographer is the villain here, not you. Not us."

"I'm still about to be vilified, aren't I? And I don't want..." Her voice wavered. Her muscles ached where she still held him off. "Home is my safe place, Ryzard. I'd rather be there when— How bad are they? The photographs, I mean."

"Don't think about them," he commanded. "You'll never see them if I have anything to do with it." His voice sent a wash of ice from her heart to her toes, it was so grim. "But I can't allow you to be away from me when they're released. They'll say I've rejected you, and that's not true. Besides, it doesn't sound as if your family will support you, so no, you stay with me."

She drooped her head. "They would support me," she insisted heavily. "The wagons get circled at times like this. And after it blows over, they would still be there for me. They do love me. It's just complicated."

"I will *ensure* it blows over," he said, forcing her chin up and looking down his nose from an arrogant angle, but his touch on her gentled even if his voice didn't. "You're coming to Rome with me, Tiffany."

She held back from pointing out she was perfectly capable of booking a charter flight and getting herself anywhere she darned well wanted to go. If he was only being authoritarian, she probably would have, but he sounded concerned. He sounded as if her feelings mattered, not just his image. That softened all the spikes of umbrage holding her stiff, making her shudder in surrender.

"Okay," she acquiesced.

"Good girl."

"Don't push it," she warned, but turned her face toward the caress of his fingertips as he smoothed her hair back behind her ear. Her eyes drifted closed.

"I'd like your father's contact number."

"Oh, no, I'll call Dad." She straightened, but found herself still in the prison of his hold.

"No, Tiffany. This is my fault. I should have taken more care to shield you. He's already uncomfortable with our relationship. I should have introduced myself before something like this made our first conversation an unpleasant one."

"I really think—"

"We're not negotiating, *draga*. We'll stand here until you've given me his number, but I'd like to get to Rome sooner than later, so make this easier on both of us."

"You're unbelievable," she choked.

"His people will have questions about the arrangements I've made. Quit being stubborn," he pressed.

Her? Stubborn? Kettle. *Black*.

With a sigh of defeat, because she really didn't want to face down her father *and his people,* she offered up his private mobile number.

How could he kiss something so hideous?

She didn't know why she looked it up. She should have known better, but she'd been compelled to know what they were saying. It was horrid. Beyond cruel.

Ryzard had been furious when he had emerged from

his shower and found her with his tablet in her lap, fingers white, throat dry, eyes unable to meet his.

"Why would you take a dose of poison? It's self-destructive, completely against everything you are," he'd growled, nipping the tablet away from her and tossing it across the room onto the bed.

Somewhere in his words she supposed a compliment lurked, but all she heard was disapproval. It made her cringe all the more.

The flight to Rome was exhausting and silent, his mood foul, but she hadn't wanted to speak, either. She didn't want him to notice her. She seemed like a burden, something he was carrying with him because he had to, not because he wanted her. How could he want anything to do with her when she was bringing shame on him like this?

Like sleeping with snakeskin. She shuddered at the headlines and comments from trolls that would stay in her mind forever. *Her husband was lucky he died and didn't have to stay married to that.*

Ryzard's interview was staged in a hotel room, the pristine white decor too bright for her gritty, bloodshot eyes. Neither of them had slept despite lying next to each other for a few hours. He'd stroked her for a time, but she hadn't been able to respond, too frozen inside. Feeling betrayed. Her parents hadn't called, not even replying to her text that she was available if they wanted to talk. The only friend she had right now was Ryzard, and he was so remote he might as well have stayed in Bregnovia and sent a wax double in his place.

She'd been too afraid to ask what he intended to say and wound up standing at the side of the room, staring dumbly from the shadows into the light as he took his seat. The interview began.

Her father had done a million of these things, so she wasn't surprised to hear them tiptoe through a variety of political tulips on the way to the meat of the interview. Ryzard's devotion to his country was on full display, and she imagined the whole world was reevaluating him as he spoke passionately about Bregnovia's desire for peace and plans for prosperity. She hoped so. He deserved to be taken seriously.

She grew more and more tense as the interview dragged on, however. Didn't they realize the audience was waiting for the mention of her name?

Twenty-five minutes in, the question finally came.

"Photos have circulated showing you with American heiress Tiffany Davis. Is it serious?"

"I take very seriously that your bottom-feeder colleagues are making their fortune on photos that for all we know have been manipulated for a higher profit."

Nice of him to defend her with such an implication, but the photos had not been airbrushed. She genuinely looked that bad.

The interviewer smiled tightly. "I meant is the relationship serious?"

"That's between us. We're private people," Ryzard stated implacably.

Tiffany caught back a harsh laugh. Did he really think he'd get away with as little as that?

"My sources tell me you met at the notoriously secret *Q Virtus*," the newscaster continued.

See? she wanted to cry. The press never rested until they drew as much blood as possible, even when they called themselves a friend.

"That's true," Ryzard allowed.

"*Q Virtus* is a rather exclusive club, isn't it? What can you tell me about it?" the journalist pressed.

"I'm sure contacting them would get you more information than you'd ever get out of me," Ryzard said smoothly.

Oh. Ha. That was smart. She relaxed under a ripple of

humor. The public's insatiable curiosity would now turn to the club. Papers could trot out as many before-and-after photos of Tiffany Davis as they wanted, but viewers and readers would be more interested in learning the names of other people in the secret club. They'd hungrily eat up the scant yet salacious details of what went on there. She and Ryzard would be old news before the credits rolled on this broadcast.

In fact, when she watched later that evening, she noted that while the names rolled, her own image came forward to Ryzard's reaching hand. She shook hands with the newscaster and thanked him, all of them standing in friendly banter. Her good side was angled to the camera. Her hair was done and her makeup was decent. Wearing a simple alabaster suit, she looked…normal. Pretty even.

Ryzard clicked it off as it went to commercial. She collapsed on the foot of the hotel bed, emotionally exhausted. Could it really be over as easily as that?

Ryzard watched Tiffany as he unknotted his tie and released first the cuffs, then the front buttons of his shirt. As tough as she was, he'd seen what a toll this attack had had on her. She'd been shutting him out as a result, and that infuriated him. Her talk of running away where he couldn't reach her had nearly put him out of his mind.

He was still beside himself that this incident had happened at all. His captain had warned him that an unidentified boat kept turning up in their radar, but he'd shrugged it off. None of his mistresses in the past had warranted much attention, but he supposed his own profile was elevated to the international stage these days. Tiffany's family was certainly of a level to feed the appetite of her country's gossip columns.

And she's not just a mistress, is she? The question beat in warning like a jungle drum in his chest, ominous and dark.

His plans for his relationship with Tiffany were changing, but he hadn't wanted to allude to anything more in his interview. The last time his link to a woman had been public and indelible, she'd been used as a pawn in his country's civil war and the outcome was fatal.

Seeing Tiffany beaten and wounded by words shook loose his nightmare of losing Luiza. He'd grasped at anger to counter his resurgence of helplessness, hating that he couldn't stem the damage being done to her, but agony and guilt were constant. He should have protected her better. If he could have stopped Tiffany from searching out what they were saying about her, he would have. Humanity's capacity for ugliness astounded him. His job, the one he'd taken on for his country, for his own sanity, was to push brutality and attacks to the furthest fringes of existence that he could.

And keep himself apart so the pain of life couldn't reach inside him and wring him into anguish.

It wasn't easy when Tiffany sat with her spine slouched and her golden hair trailing loose from its neat bun, seeming incredibly delicate, like a dragonfly that had its wings crushed. When she was like this, she stirred things in him that needed to stay in firmer places. The chin-up, spoiled and cheeky Tiffany he could easily compartmentalize as a friendly partner in a game of sexual sport. Like a tennis opponent who gave him a run for his money, athletic and quick.

The vulnerable Tiffany frightened him. She made him feel so ferociously protective he would do violence if he ever found the photographer who'd reduced her image to a commodity in filthy commerce.

Shaken by the depth of his feelings, he tried to pull them both out of the tailspin with a blunt, "Dinner out or in?"

She sighed and looked up at him. Her heartrending expression was both anguished and amused. His heart began to pound in visceral reaction, and he swayed as though struck with vertigo, not sure why.

"My first thought is, *Duh, Ryzard*. Of course I'd never dine in public, but how could I be such a coward when you've just defended me so fiercely? No one else has. I can't tell you how much that means to me."

A sensation of wind rushing around him lifted all the hairs on his naked chest, as if he was free-falling into space. Her gaze was so defenseless, he couldn't look away. She reached inside him with that look, catching at things he couldn't even acknowledge.

"You already know I would only wish away your scars because I hate that you were hurt at all. But I see them as a badge of your ability to overcome," he heard himself admit. "Your sort of willpower, your deep survival instinct, is rare, Tiffany. You probably don't realize it because it's such an integral part of your nature to fight, but not everyone accepts such a life blow and makes herself live through it."

Luiza hadn't, he acknowledged with a crash of his heart into his toes. Thinking about her when he was with Tiffany, contrasting them, was wrong. Setting aside Luiza in his mind was like ripping an essential part of him away and abandoning it, but he had to do it. They couldn't occupy the same place inside him, and right now Tiffany needed him.

"All my life I heard, 'You're so pretty.' Like that was the most important thing to be. You're the first person to compliment me on having substance. I really thought I'd lost everything by losing my looks."

Where Luiza had built him into the man he was with vision and belief in him, Tiffany slayed him with honesty and vulnerability. His heart felt as though it beat outside his chest. When she rose and came to him, and went on tiptoe to brush soft lips against his jaw, he closed his eyes in paralyzed ecstasy. Deep down, at a base level, it felt wrong to be this gripped by her, but he couldn't help it. In this moment, she was all he knew.

"Thank you for wanting me exactly as I am."

He did. God help him, he wanted her in ways he couldn't even describe.

They shouldn't come together like this, with hearts agape and defenses on the floor, but he couldn't *not* touch her. Pulling her in, he settled his mouth on hers, tender and sweet. The animal in him wanted to ravish, but the man in him needed to cherish.

She drew an emotive breath and kissed him back in a way that flooded him with aching tenderness. The sexual need was there, strong as ever, but it sprang from a deeper place inside him. Hell, he thought. Hell and hell. Lingering feelings of infidelity fell away. This woman was the one he had to be faithful to. *This one.*

The rending sensation inside him hurt so much he had to squeeze her into him to stop what broke open, fearing his lifeblood would leak away if he didn't have her pressed to the wound. Her arms went around his neck, light palms cradling the back of his skull as she fingered through his hair, soothing and treasuring and filling the cavernous spaces in him with something new and golden and as unique as she was.

When they stripped and eased onto the bed and came together, it was with a shaken breath from him and a gasp of awe from her. She gloried in his possession, and he bent his head to her breast in veneration, golden lamplight burning the vision of her into his memory with the eternity of a primordial being caught in amber.

Twin fingers traced on each side of her scar, the sensation dull on one side, sweet on the other. She stretched in supreme pleasure and reached for him without opening her eyes, finding only cool, empty sheets where he was supposed to be.

"I'm already showered and dressed, *draga*," he said on her other side. "You said to let you sleep and I did as long as I could, but we have to leave soon. We have a dinner engagement in Zurich."

"Are you serious?" She rolled onto her back so she could see him where he stood over her, his knife-sharp suit of charcoal over a dove gray shirt set off with a subdued navy tie. He looked way too buttoned-down, hair still damp, chin shiny and probably tasting spicy and lickable. She skimmed the sheet away and invited, "Come back to bed."

"Your parents are expecting us. I already agreed to see them, but if you'd like to send our regrets…"

"They're in Zurich?" She sat up, bringing the sheet to her collarbone as if her father had just walked in the room. "How? Why?"

"I left it to our collective staff to work out the how. I simply extended the invitation when I informed him about the photos. He wanted you to come back to America. I said you were accompanying me to Rome and that I had a commitment in Switzerland, but that we'd be pleased if they could meet us there."

"How delightfully neutral. I guess that explains why they haven't been in touch. They've been traveling." She threw off the sheet and walked naked to find her phone, pleased at the way he pivoted to watch her.

Sending him a saucy smile over her shoulder, she clicked her screen and tapped in her code, reading aloud the message she found. "'Staying with the deHavillands in Berne.' That's the American ambassador. Mom went to school with her. Longtime friends of the family. 'Where will you be staying?'" She looked to him.

"At the hotel where the banquet will be held. My people should have sent the details already. I'll ask them to extend the invitation to include your parents' friends." He reached inside his jacket pocket for his mobile.

Tiffany heard only one word and lowered her phone, barely hanging on to it with limp fingers as she repeated, "Banquet?"

He gave her a long, steady look. "Something I arranged months ago. I've been trying to ease you into the public eye, *draga*. Don't look so shocked. It's not something I can miss since it's a charity I personally fund. We remove land mines and petition to stop their use completely. They're an appalling weapon."

She felt as though she stood on one, but he didn't coddle her over what attending would mean. Given everything that had happened, she supposed it was time to set aside her fear of being in public. As long as she had him by her side, she'd be okay, wouldn't she?

CHAPTER NINE

A FEW HOURS LATER, she wasn't so sure. She'd taken an *in for a penny, in for a pound* approach and forgone the one-shouldered gowns that would have disguised a lot of her scarring, deciding instead to let her freak flag fly. Her halter-style gown set off her breasts and hips beautifully and was the most gorgeous shade of Persian blue that glistened and slithered over her skin as she walked.

...snakeskin...

Stop it. She pretended she was her old self, the somewhat infamous fashionista who had graced more than her share of best-dressed lists. With her trained yoga posture reaching her crown to the ceiling, shoulders pinned back with pride, she entered the lounge and took the druglike hit that was Ryzard in a tuxedo.

"I knew you wouldn't disappoint me," he said. His smile was sexy and smug, but held a warmth of underlying approval.

Winded, she dissembled by checking her pocketbook, trying to grasp hold of herself as she reacted to him and the effect he had on her. Did he know how defenseless she was around him? She suspected he did. He was coming to know her very well, maybe too well. There was an imbalance there because he could see right past her defenses, but he remained unpredictable to her.

As if to prove it, he came forward and threaded a bracelet up her marred arm until it wrapped in delicate scrolls against her biceps. It was a stunning piece of extravagant ivy tendrils fashioned from platinum. Diamonds were inset as random pops of sparkling dew, fixating the eye.

"It's beautiful."

"When people stare, you can say, 'Ryzard gave it to me. He thinks I'm a spoiled brat, but wouldn't change a thing about me.'"

She wanted to grin and be dismissive, but she was too moved. Her voice husked when she admitted, "You do spoil me. I have no idea why."

"You inspire me," he confided, then swooped to set a kiss against the corner of her mouth. "Lipstick, I know," he muttered before she could pull away in protest. "In the future, don't put it on until I've finished kissing you."

"Then we'd never leave the room, would we?"

"And how is this a problem?" He held the door as he spoke, the light in his eye making her laugh, reassuring her the evening would turn out fine.

They stopped by another suite on their way downstairs. He'd arranged it for her parents and the ambassador. Her father greeted her with a long hug before he set her back. Then he looked between her and Ryzard, not seeming to know where to start.

She quickly introduced them and included the ambassador's husband, Dr. deHavilland, using Ryzard's title as the president of Bregnovia, and heard the crack in her voice as she queried, "Mom didn't come?"

"The ladies are fussing down the hall," the doctor said after kissing her cheeks. Taking her chin, he turned her face to eye her scar. "The specialist did wonders, didn't he? It's good to see you out, Tiffany. Ryzard, what's your poison? We're having whiskey sours."

He accepted one and she squeezed his arm. "Do you mind if I…?"

"Of course, go say hello, but we need to be in the ballroom to greet the guests in fifteen minutes."

"Five," she promised with a splayed hand and hurried in search of her mother, nervous of the confrontation, but experiencing the homesick need to reconnect.

Following voices through a bedroom to the open door of a bathroom, she approached and set her hand on the inner door only to hear a makeup compact click over her mother's voice. "Are we supposed to believe he's in love with her? Any fool can see he's using her for our connections."

"Any fool except me?" Tiffany blurted, pushing the door farther in while outrage washed over her. It was followed by a stab of hurt so deep she could barely see.

Nevertheless, her vision filled with the flawless image of her mother turning from the mirror. Shock paled her mother's elegantly powdered cheeks. An automatic defense rose to part her painted lips, but first she had to draw a breath of shock as her gaze traveled her daughter's appearance and measured the amount of exposure. A trembling little head shake told Tiffany what her mother thought of this gown.

"You won't be comfortable in that."

"You mean *you* won't," Tiffany volleyed back and turned to leave. A type of daughterly need for her mother's bosom had driven her in here, and now she wished Barbara Holbrook had stayed home.

"Tiffany Ann." The strident voice didn't need volume to stop Tiffany in her tracks. "He told your father he wanted to marry you. You met him last *week*. What are we supposed to think?"

Tiffany spun back, thrown by the statement. "He did not."

Her mother held her lady-of-the-manor pose, the one that had too much dignity to descend into a did-so, did-not quibbling match. Instead, she gave Tiffany another once-over and asked primly, "How on earth did you come to be his guest? I mean, if he had brought a party aboard, I'd understand you being swept along, but obviously he wants us to believe he has a romantic interest in you. What sort of promises has he made you?"

Tiffany heard the strange lilt in her mother's voice. Concern, but something else. Something shaken and protective...

She felt her eyes go wider and sting with dryness as understanding penetrated. Her mother genuinely believed she was being used—and was too blind to see it.

If her high school diary had been passed around the football locker room, she couldn't have felt more as though her deepest feelings were being abused. If only she could have defended Ryzard. If only she believed he had deeper feelings for her beyond the physical and amusement with her "great personality."

God, maybe he didn't even feel that much for her. Maybe it *was* all about who her father was. Insecurity nearly drove her to her knees, but she made herself stand proud and state what she'd let herself believe.

"He hasn't made any promises. He wants me for my body. It's mutual."

Dumbly she turned and walked out, floored by what her mother had said about Ryzard wanting to marry her. Was it true? Because if it was, her mother was right. It wouldn't be love driving his interest in her. They *had* met only ten days ago.

She tried to swallow away the painful lump of confusion that lodged itself high behind her breastbone.

Ryzard set down his drink as she appeared and held out his crooked arm. "Ready? We'll see you downstairs," he said to the men.

"Tiffany," the ambassador scolded, following her with a

swish of skirts. "You can't speak to your mother like that. She's been telling me how worried she's been for you, not just because you dropped out of sight with a stranger—I apologize if that sounds rude," she added in an aside to Ryzard. "But since—"

"I *know*. The accident. I've been a great burden on them, but can you understand how sick I am of having that define me? I'm better now. It's time for both her and Dad to butt out of my life."

She yearned for everyone to leave her alone so she could lick her wounds in private. It pained her horribly that everyone could see how weakly she'd fallen for this incredibly handsome, indulgent charlatan who had soothed her broken ego and wormed his way toward her heart. All in the name of advancing his own agenda.

"Where is this rebellion coming from?" her father clipped in his sternest tone. "You were never like this before. Your mother and I can't fathom what's got into you. Letting you go to work has obviously put too much stress on you."

"*Letting* me." She jerked up her chastised head, filling with outrage.

Beside her, Ryzard took her good arm in a warm, calming grip. "If you'll pardon an outsider's observation? Every child has to leave the nest at some point, even one who was blown back in and needed you very badly for a time. Your daughter is an adult. She can make her own decisions."

Despite that statement of her independence, she found herself letting him make the decision for both of them to leave. A crazy part of her even rationalized that even if he *was* using her, he was also helping her find the state of autonomy she longed for.

As they waited for the elevator, a jagged sigh escaped her. "I can't do this, Ryzard."

She meant the banquet, the evening, but he misunderstood.

"Don't let this upset you. Listen, I visited Bregnovia after finishing university. I could have stayed. My mother wanted me to, but I chose to drift across Europe like pollen in the wind. I was making a statement. They had forced me to leave as a child, but they couldn't make me stay as an adult."

"And now you hate yourself for not spending time with them. You think I should go back and apologize?" She looked back down the hall, hating the discord with her family even as she dreaded facing them again.

The elevator car arrived and Ryzard guided her into it.

"I don't hate myself as much as I should. Everyone does need to leave the nest at some point, *draga*. But be assured that your parents are operating from a place of love. Your father had some very pointed questions for me. He is the quintessential father who feels a strong need to protect his baby girl."

With bloodless fingers clinging to her pocketbook, she lifted her gaze to meet his. "Did you tell him you want to marry me?" Her voice sounded flayed and dead, even more listless than the tone she had used to discuss her prospective marriage to Paulie.

Surprise flashed across his expression before he shuttered it into a neutral poker face. "He asked me about my intentions when I called. I said they were honorable. What else could I say?"

"You told me this relationship wouldn't lead to anything permanent. When did you decide it could?"

He turned his head away, profile hard with undisguised impatience, then looked back, fairly knocking her over with the impact. "What are you really asking, *draga*?"

The car stopped and she swayed, stomach dipping and clawing for a settled state. "You weren't ever going to marry, but then you realized exactly how useful my father could be. Is that right?"

"Yes." No apology, just hardened, chiseled features that were so remote and handsome she wanted to cry.

"We talked about how much I enjoy being used, Ryzard."

The doors of the elevator opened. His handlers were waiting, one reaching to hold the door for them.

"We need a moment," he clipped.

"No, we don't." Her voice was strangled, but she stepped from the elevator into the bubble that was its own bizarrely familiar shield against reality. Her skin burned under the stares of his people, but she allowed only Ryzard to see how much that tortured her as she turned to glare up at him. "If this is what I'm here for, then let's do it. I'm probably better on stage than you are. Smile. Nothing matters except how this looks."

"Tiffany," he growled.

Arranging the sort of warm, gracious smile her mother had patented, she sidled beyond his reach and asked a handler, "Where would you like me to stand in relation to the president?"

Talk about land mines. Ryzard felt as though he stood in a field of them as he welcomed his guests and waited for the misstep that would cause Tiffany to discharge. She was the epitome of class though, greeting people warmly as he introduced her, maintaining a level of poise that made his heart swell with pride even as his blood ran like acid in his veins.

We talked about how much I enjoy being used.

He struggled to hide how much his conscience twisted under that. Did she think he couldn't see what this evening was costing her? He was so deeply attuned to her that he felt her tension like a high-pitched noise humming inside his consciousness, keeping him on high alert. It was fear, he realized with a *thunk* of dread-filled self-assessment. She would run given an opportunity, and that kept him so fixated on her he could hardly breathe, braced as he was to catch her before her first step.

He ought to let her go if that's what she really wanted, but he couldn't bear it when she hadn't even given him a chance to explain. The way she'd thrown her accusation at him in the elevator had been a shock. He'd answered honestly out of instinct, because any sort of subterfuge between them was abhorrent to him.

But distance was equally repugnant to him, and she was keeping an emotional one that didn't bode well for sifting through things he'd barely made sense of himself.

As for her pithy suggestion that all he cared about was his image, she was dead wrong there. He cared about her. Thinking about how much he cared made him feel as though the elevator's cable had been cut and he was still plummeting into the unknown.

They didn't have a chance to speak freely again until they were dancing after dinner. He kept his gaze off her, dangerously close to becoming aroused from holding her. Every primordial instinct in him wanted to drag her into the nearest alcove and stamp her as his own. The way they moved perfectly together no matter what they did seduced him unfailingly.

"Another one bites the dust," she murmured.

"What does that mean?" he asked with a flash of his glance into furious eyes that scored him with disdain.

"You can't keep your eyes off my mother. I told you she was beautiful."

He realized he'd been staring at the distraction of white hair swept in a graceful frame around aristocratic bone structure. Mrs. Holbrook's blue eyes stood out like glittering sapphires on the sateen of flawless skin as she watched them. Where Tiffany had a seductively full bottom lip, her mother's was narrow and prim, but that hint of severity lent her countenance keen intelligence. She was the height of elegance when she smiled and scrupulously well-mannered. She had thanked him warmly for inviting them even as her gaze consigned him to hell.

"She's not the one giving me a hard-on, *draga*. She's keeping it from becoming obvious. I'm in danger of catching pneumonia from her glare. I take it she doesn't approve of our affair?"

"I thought we were engaged." Limpid eyes, as capable of beaming frost as her mother's, glared up at him.

He involuntarily tightened his hands on her. "Not here, Tiffany. Not now."

She snorted, lashes quivering in a flinch, but it was her only betrayal of how much his deferral stung. He silently cursed, realizing he was forcing the taffy apple upon her.

"We'll talk upstairs as soon as I can get away," he promised.

"Mom and Dad are going back to Berne with the deHavillands first thing in the morning. They want me to come, so it would probably be better if I stayed with them—"

"Like hell," he said through his teeth. She was so stiff in his arms, he thought she'd shatter if he held her too tightly, but the idea she'd leave him made everything in him clench with possessiveness.

She showed him her good cheek, the skin stretched taut across it. Her voice wavered. "You were so appalled at the idea that Dad would use my accident for his own gain, but the minute you saw an advantage to your own precious country, you—"

"Enough," he seared quietly through gritted teeth. "Marriage is not something I take lightly. Even thinking of marrying you is the breaking of a vow I made to myself and a dead woman. You have no idea what it costs me."

With a little gasp, she stopped moving, forcing him to

halt his own feet. He looked down at her, as appalled by what he'd revealed as she seemed to be.

"Luiza," she stated under her breath, lips white.

He flinched. Hearing her say his beloved's name was a shock.

"Da," he agreed, nudging her back into dancing, feeling cold.

The air of thick tension surrounding them threatened to suffocate Tiffany, but she was a trained pony. The dance continued and her company smile stayed in place while all she could think about was the snippets of information he'd revealed about his tattoo, his lady liberty, his marriage to his *country*.

The rest of their waltz passed in a blur of tuxedos and jewel-colored gowns, glittering chandeliers and tinkling laughter. When he returned her to their table, her parents rose with their friends, ready to take their leave.

"Goodbye, Ryz—" she began.

"Don't even think it," he overrode her tightly.

"I have a headache," she lied flatly. "I'd like to leave."

"Then we will," he said with equal shortness. "Let me inform my team while you say good-night to your parents."

Seconds later he cut her from the herd and whisked her up to their suite.

"You're not making friends behaving like this, you know," she whirled to state as he closed the door behind them. "My father won't have your back in any arena if you continue to kidnap his daughter."

"I know your father hates my guts, but you will not let him separate us. If you're angry with me, then you stand here and tell me so," he railed with surprising vehemence, yanking off his tuxedo jacket to throw it aside. "Do not put yourself out of my reach. That is the one thing I will not tolerate."

Deep emotion swirled from his words at hurricane force, buffeting her. She unconsciously braced her footing, absorbing his statement with a wobble of her heart in her chest that left all the hair standing up on her body. It wasn't fear exactly. More of a visceral response to his revelation of intense feeling. Her body was warning her not to take his outburst lightly. He was startlingly raw right now, and anything but taking great care with how she reacted would be stupid and possibly hurtful to both of them.

She could hurt him.

A reflexive shake of her head tried to deny the thought. His face was lined with grief, emotions he felt for someone else, but a glint of something else in the stark, defensive gaze stilled her. A strange calm settled in her mind despite the racking pain of being used still gripping her.

The suspicion he feared being wounded by her was so stunning, she could only stand there hugging herself, not knowing what to say.

She had to say or do something. His hurting destroyed her. It was particularly intolerable because it had its roots in his love for another woman, but as much as she wanted to sublimate that knowledge, a masochistic part of her had to know the details. It was like assessing an injury so she'd know how to treat it.

"Was…" She cleared her throat. "Will you tell me about her?"

He turned away to the wet bar. Glass clinked as he poured a drink, drained it, then refilled his glass and poured one for her. When he brought hers across to her, his face was schooled into something remote while his eyes blazed with suppressed, but explosive emotion.

"Were you married?" she asked in a strained whisper. *Did you love her?* She couldn't bring herself to ask it.

"Engaged. She wanted to focus on winning the war, not planning a wedding. She was a protestor, an idealist, but very passionate and smart. I met her when I came back for my mother's funeral. I was beside myself, ready to seek retribution, but Luiza helped me develop a vision that people would rally behind. She was the velvet glove to my iron fist."

"You said she was your country's icon. That everyone revered her. What happened?"

He brought his glass to his lips, took a generous swallow then hissed, "She was captured and would have been used against me. She took herself out of the equation."

Appalled horror had her sucking in a pained breath, one she held inside her with a slap of her hand across her mouth. *Once you have paid the price of a loved one, you do not stop until the job is done.*

She stared at Ryzard over her hand, brutally aware there were no words to compensate for what he'd just told her. She didn't need the details. The horrifying end was enough. The truly shocking part was that he wasn't twisted into bitterness and revenge by loss.

He was stricken with guilt and anguish, however. It showed in the lines that appeared on his face before he turned away again.

"I'm so sorry," she breathed, reaching toward him.

He shrugged off her touch. "There's nothing that can be done. We both know that death is final. Nothing in the past can be reversed."

"No," she agreed, staring at her mottled arm folded across her good one. "You can only learn to live with the consequences. And preserve their memory," she added, feeling as though her chest was scraped hollow like a jack-o'-lantern. "That's what you want to do, isn't it? Achieve what she sacrificed herself for? That's why you'll do anything to bring peace to Bregnovia. You're doing it for her."

"I'm not the only one who lost people, Tiffany. I want it for all of us."

She swallowed, understanding, empathizing, yet feeling very isolated. Her heart ached for him, but for herself, too, because she instinctively wanted to help him. Maybe he was using her, but as he kept demonstrating, his goal was noble. And she loved him too much to refuse him outright when his need and grief were very real.

She loved him.

Staring at the red flecks in the carpet between their feet, she absorbed the bittersweet ache that pulsed through her arteries and settled in her soul. Part of her stood back and mocked herself for having such strong feelings after a mere week and a half of knowing this man. Surely her mother was right and this was a type of Pygmalion infatuation. God knows it was a sexual one.

But when she compared it with what she'd felt for Paulie—exasperated affection and the security of friendship—she knew this was the deeper, more dangerous shade of love. The mature kind that was as threatening as it was fulfilling because it made her needs less important than his. It gave him the power to cripple her with nothing more than his eternal love for another woman.

"I told myself if I couldn't marry Luiza, I wouldn't marry at all." He drained his drink and set it aside, turning to push his hands in his pockets. "Then I met you."

And realized how useful she could be.

"I understand." She fought to keep her brow from pulling.

"Do you? Because I don't. It wasn't a vow of celibacy. I'm not dead. I gave myself permission to have affairs. That ought to be enough. With every other woman it has been."

A strand of something poignant thrummed near her heart. She tried to quell it for the sake of her sanity, trying not to read anything into what he was saying. In a lot of ways what he'd offered her was more than she'd imagined she'd ever find, so she shouldn't be yearning so badly for more.

"I realize you have to look out for your country's best interest, Ryzard. You've been very kind and supportive of me—"

"Oh, shut *up*, Tiffany. Looking out for my country's best interest is how I've been rationalizing your presence in the presidential bed, but even that doesn't work. Do you think I can use you in good conscience after Luiza *died* as a pawn? *Hell, no.* But allowing you to push her out of my heart would be an even greater betrayal."

She could see the tortured struggle in him. He might never love her, not when to do so would mean accepting the debilitating guilt that accompanied it. Who could accept such a deep schism to their soul?

As she absorbed that reality, her breath burned in her lungs like dry smoke.

"But each time you talk of leaving for America, I start thinking about a length of chain about this long." He showed her a space between his hands of two or three feet. "With a cuff here and here." He pointed from his smartwatch to her wrist.

She couldn't help a small smile.

"For such a sophisticated, educated man, you're incredibly uncivilized. You know that, right?" She rubbed the goose bumps off her arms, trying to hide how primitive she was at her core, responding to his caveman talk like some kind of kinky submissive.

"Your parents have every right to be suspicious of me," he allowed drily. "But it's important to me that you know my intentions toward you are not dishonorable."

That's exactly what she had feared after overhearing her mother. It had gutted her. Meeting his gaze was really hard with that specter still haunting her.

"I don't expect you to love me, Ryzard." The words fractured her soul. "But I have to insist on honesty. If you're really just with me because of my father, please say so and I'll—"

"I can't believe I'm going to say this," he cut in impatiently, "but sometimes I wish to hell you'd had other lovers so you would appreciate what we have. *I* do."

"Oh, well, let me just accommodate that right now."

He grabbed her before she'd taken two steps toward the door.

"Gorilla! Brute! You're hurting me," she accused as she found herself bouncing over his shoulder toward the bedroom.

"Honesty, Tiffany," he reminded in a scolding tone. "You just demanded it, and so do I. Lie to me and so help me, I'll spank you. That is not a bluff." He flopped her onto the bed and retreated to slam the bedroom door.

"You scare me," she cried, sitting up. "Not like scared you'll hurt me," she protested with an outstretched hand, trying to forestall the outrage climbing in his expression. "The way you make me feel. I'm terrified you'll stop wanting me. You saw what I was like before you came along. I don't want to be that person again. I don't know how to handle how important you are to me, or how horrible I'll feel when this ends."

The tense line of his shoulders eased. "I can't imagine that happening."

"But I don't know how honorable *my* intentions are. I told you how I feel about living in the public eye. If it's just an affair…"

She trailed off, distracted as he joined her, his big body crowding and overwhelming, sending her onto her back under him with the force of his personality, barely even touching her. She melted in supplication, slave to his authority and the tenderness in his eyes.

"This is more than an affair," he insisted.

That didn't allay any of her misgivings, but she wasn't sure what she wanted him to say. She rather wished she had more experience with relationships herself, but from everything she'd observed, she doubted anyone was truly confident with whatever sorts of relationships they had. It came down to trust, and as much as she wanted to believe in Ryzard, she didn't have much faith in herself.

She touched the pad of her fingertip to his lips, tracing the masculine shape that so entranced her.

"Where do we go from here?" she asked, meaning emotionally, but he took her literally.

"I have quite a few appearances. I would like you to accompany me. Will you?"

Her heart stalled, but refusing meant bringing The End forward to now, and she could already see it would be horribly painful. She wasn't ready for that, so she said the only thing she could.

"Of course."

CHAPTER TEN

DESPITE TIFFANY'S AGREEMENT, despite the unflagging passion between them, she grew less like the cheeky woman he'd come to know and more like the chilly mother he'd met in Zurich.

Of course he was pressing her inexorably into her mother's role. He couldn't help it. The opportunity was too ripe, the timing at hand, and she was damned good at it. She stepped forward with a gracious remark when needed and backed off the rest of the time. No matter what came up or when, she accepted the pull of his attention with equanimity. If she didn't like it, no one could tell, not even him. When he asked, she assured him everything was "Fine."

A sure sign that it wasn't.

But neither of their schedules had room for the type of downtime that had brought them together in the first place. She'd been up for several hours two nights in a row trying to resolve a problem with her firm. Now he'd dragged her to Budapest for an Eastern European conference. A black-tie reception opened the event, and her best makeup couldn't hide the exhaustion around her eyes.

Still she smiled, always ignoring startled reactions to her scars or simply moving past an awkward moment with a calm "Car crash." Then she would distract with a compliment or question, her warm manner disguising the fact she maintained a discreet bubble of distance.

So why was she currently clasping two hands over a stranger's? Her expression was uncharacteristically revealing, not the cool mask she usually wore at these events. The man was older than Ryzard, somewhere in his fifties, but not someone he recognized. Tiffany was sharing deep eye contact with him, and her profile was somber.

He excused himself and crossed over to them, possessive male hackles rising to attention, especially when they both stiffened at his approach and lowered their gazes.

"Ryzard, this is Stanley Griffin, minister of international trade in Canada and my late husband's cousin. Well, cousin to my mother-in-law, Maude."

Despite the legitimate reason for familiarity, he used the introduction to extricate Stanley's hand from Tiffany's grasp.

They briefly chatted about his country's mission to, "Do what we did with the EU here in Eastern Europe." Ryzard expressed his desire to participate, but first he needed recognition so if that message could be conveyed to Canada's prime minister...?

Stanley left with a promise to do so, but made a point to ask Tiffany, "Please stay in touch." Once again, Tiffany had proved her worth to him politically, but her coziness with the man rankled Ryzard for the rest of the evening.

"You seemed very familiar with that Canadian," he said later when they were undressing in the hotel suite. He was tired of being away and wished they were home.

Home. Did she regard his country the way he did? She wasn't happy here in Hungary, despite her expressed desire to see the country and her interest in this city's history. He couldn't be sure she'd been happy in any of the places they'd been recently.

"He was at my wedding. I didn't remember him, to be honest, but he certainly remembered me. He started to tell me how much he loved it when Paulie had spent summers with their family, when the boys were young, and I thought we were both going to—" She clamped her lips together, then pressed a knuckle to her mouth, turning away.

Stricken by her edging toward breakdown, he moved to grasp her shoulders in bracing hands. "Shh. Don't talk about him."

She reacted with a violent twist away from his grip and glared up at him with eyes full of tears and betrayal. "Oh, that's rich. Why can't I talk about my husband? Luiza is right *there* every time we're naked." She poked two fingers into his chest.

Her hostility took him aback, as did the underlying challenge. He bristled, but managed to keep himself from pointing out her scars were an equally indelible reminder that she had had a life before he entered it.

"I didn't say you couldn't talk about him, but it's obviously upsetting you so you should stop," he managed, barely hanging on to a civil tone.

Her jagged laugh abraded his nerves, plucking his aggression responses to even higher alert. "Yeah, well, if that's the criteria, there's a lot of things I should stop doing."

Don't ask, he told himself, but the elephant in the room had grown large enough to put pressure on both of them. A few weeks ago she hadn't had the courage to go to the grocery store in her hometown. Today she was being shoved into a supporting role on the world stage. If she didn't want to do it, she ought to have said so by now, but apparently that was up to him.

"You're not happy in the spotlight. I understand that." He removed his belt and flung it away, angry with himself for turning a blind eye to what was obviously damaging their relationship, but he couldn't undo who he was any more than he was willing to have Luiza's name erased from his chest.

"Stanley said Paulie's mother was always jealous of my

mom because she looked like she had it all, but at least Maude had privacy. All I could think is, *What am I doing? Why am I here?*" She lifted helpless hands.

"Tiffany, you're good at this," he began.

"I'm good at sex. Should I do that with every man who asks?" she snarled back.

He recoiled, shocked by her vehemence and scored by a remark that made it sound as if she only tolerated sleeping with him. "As I said—" The words ground from between his clenched teeth. "You shouldn't do anything that fails to give you some level of enjoyment."

Her fierce expression flickered toward remorse, before she collapsed in a chair, elbows on her knees, head in hands, shoulders heavy with defeat. "I'm sorry. I know better than to have this fight. It accomplishes nothing because at the end of the day, you still need me beside you."

"I *want* you beside you, Tiffany. I don't need you. If you're feeling used then you know my feelings on that. I'll achieve my two-thirds votes with or without you."

She lifted her head out of her hands to stare at him, face like a mask, half of it tortoiseshell reds, the other side white. Slowly her flat gaze moved to the floor while her hands twisted together. She forced herself to sit upright, but her shoulders remained bowed.

"That certainly tells me where I stand."

The ice maiden was back, causing cold fire to lick behind his heart, leaving streaks of dead, black tissue.

"I'm saying you don't have to participate if you don't want to. We can still be together. It doesn't have to change anything," he said rather desperately, sensing things slipping away without any chance to control it.

"It changes everything, Ryzard! What am I going to do? Sit in your presidential castle waiting for you to come home? *There's* a departure from turning into my mother," she said with a caustic laugh. "What else could I do? Follow you around but never be seen? That would be living as a recluse again. If you—" She bent her head to stare at her pale knuckles, but he saw the pull in her brow of deep struggle. "If we loved each other, it would be different."

He couldn't help his stark inhale of aversion. Marriage he might rationalize. Pulling his heart from the grave where he'd buried it next to Luiza was impossible. There, at least, it was safe from another blow of great loss.

Silence coated the room in a thick fog for a long minute. Tiffany was the first to move, swiping at her cheek before speaking haltingly.

"I thought my life was over, that I'd never be able to have a husband and family. I even reconciled myself to it and figured out how to fill my life with other things. I could live unmarried and childless with you, Ryzard. But you're the one who made me believe I shouldn't sell myself short. If someone could love me, if I have a soul mate out there, I shouldn't settle for anything less than finding him."

He clenched his hands into fists, trying to withstand a pain so great it threatened to rend him apart. She *did* deserve to be loved. He couldn't keep her here to serve his passion while he withheld parts of himself. It would wear on her self-esteem. If he wasn't capable of giving her all of himself, he had to let her go.

But the agony was so great he wanted to scream.

The weariness and misery in her eyes when she lifted them to meet his gaze was more than he could bear though.

"It's time for me to go home," she said gently.

He nodded once, jerkily, incapable of any other response. His throat was blocked by a thick knot of anguish, the rest of him caved in on itself so his skin felt like a thin shell, ready to crack and turn to powder.

"I'll go make the arrangements," her voice thinned over the last word as she stood and rushed from the room.

She didn't return.

When he couldn't stand it any longer, he went looking for her and came up against a locked door. He could hear her sobbing inside the bedroom, but he didn't knock. He silently railed at her for shutting him out, but the truth was, he was close to tears himself. Drowning himself in a bottle of vodka looked like a really good idea.

Taking one to his room, he sat on the bed then left it untouched on the nightstand as he stayed awake through the long, dark night, willing Tiffany to come to him.

CHAPTER ELEVEN

BARBARA HOLBROOK WANTED to know exactly what had happened.

"Mom," Tiffany protested, feeling cornered in her room, jet-lagged and wondering how she still had a doll propped on the pillows of her made bed. It was an antique, granted, but seriously. "I'm about ten years too late for having my heart broken by my first crush. That's all it was."

That's what she kept telling herself anyway. She sure as heck didn't want to deconstruct everything that had happened with Ryzard. It was too painful.

But she missed him. Sleeping alone sucked and stalking him on the web only made her heart ache. Or laugh aloud.

Mrs. Davis and I remain on excellent terms. Print something negative about her at your own peril, she read over breakfast one Saturday morning and got herself goggled at by her entire family for her outburst.

"What," she hedged, amusement fading. "It's funny," she insisted after reading it to them. She wanted to kiss his austere image, feeling as though he was flirting with her from far, far away. He'd been so contained that last night, so willing to let her go without a fight. That had made her feel insignificant, but reading that they remained "on excellent terms" bolstered her.

"You'll be seeing him again, then?" her father asked, sipping his coffee.

"Why? Does sleeping with him help your approval rating?"

"Tiffany," her mother gasped.

Christian sent her a hard look. "Come on, Tiff."

Setting her cup into its saucer like a gavel announcing a judge's decision, Tiffany said, "That was out of line. I apologize. But I'm tired of being a bug under a microscope. It's time I went into the office."

"You've been in there every day since you came home," her mother said with confusion.

"Not my office here, Mom. The real office. In the city."

"What? When?" Chris asked swiftly. "I can't drive you for a week at least. I told you I'm working from here until I get that design done, so I'm not interrupted."

"And I have to be in Washington," her father said with apology.

"I have an appointment in New York at the end of the month, darling," her mother offered. "You can come in for the day with me, but are you sure you're ready?"

She wished she'd had her tablet set to record. Ryzard would shake his head at this display and probably claim this coddling was the reason she was such a spoiled brat. She suspected he'd also remind her how lucky she was to be so loved.

Misty emotion washed over her in a flood of gratitude for the family she had and an ache of longing for the man she didn't.

"You guys are awesome. I love you," she said, meeting each pair of eyes in turn to let her sincerity sink in. She silently thanked Ryzard as she did it, finally able to see herself as a whole, independent adult because he had treated her as one. "But it's time for me to be a grown-up. I'll drive myself to New York and stay in the company flat until I find my own place."

Her mother's gasp and near-Victorian collapse didn't

sway her. On Monday she walked through the glass doors of Davis and Holbrook, palms clammy and half her face hidden behind giant sunglasses. By Thursday the worst of the buzzing and staring was behind her. Friday morning she was interrupted by a delivery of flowers.

"Wow," she couldn't help saying, stunned by the bouquet arranged to look like a culmination of fireworks. Her heart began to gallop in her chest. "Who is that from?"

"I couldn't say, ma'am." The uniformed man tapped the subtle *Q Virtus* crest on his shirt pocket. "I work for their concierge service. All I get is a pickup and delivery address."

"Oh, um, would it be from *Q Virtus* itself, then?" That was disappointing. And made the significance of portraying fireworks a little creepy.

"There's usually a 'compliments of Zeus' card if it is. Without one, I'd guess it's from one of their members, but I really couldn't say. I'm not privy to much that goes on there. *You* could be a member for all I know," he added with a shrug.

"I imagine there are members who don't know they belong," she murmured ironically, thanking him with a generous tip, then burying her face in the perfume of the bouquet. She wanted to gather the fragrant leaves and butter-soft petals into herself, trying to feel closer to Ryzard.

How could he be this sweet, this pleased by her stepping out of her comfort zone and taking control of her life, and not love her a little?

Luiza, she thought with a pang. She could never compete with a woman who had shown such a level of bravery.

Taking a page from Ryzard's book, she had *Q Virtus* arrange a nice lunch when her mother came to visit at the end of the month. Being scrupulously efficient, they located it in a penthouse that fit exactly what Tiffany was looking for as a new home. The decor was a bit too colorless for her taste. It needed a stained glass umbrella to jazz it up, but the floor plan and views were astonishing.

Her mother pronounced it excellent for entertaining, which only made Tiffany think of holding court with Ryzard and miss him all over again.

She sat across from her mother in tall wingbacks at a circle of white marble facing a floor-to-ceiling view of Central Park, sipping from crystal water goblets with brushed gold trim, thinking she'd rather be staring at that heart-wrenching statue if it put her back in his proximity.

"This isn't at all how I imagined things turning out for you," her mother murmured.

She seemed surprised that the words had escaped her and glanced toward the kitchen, where the noise and staff were well contained beyond a small service pantry.

Tiffany set down her glass and linked her fingers together, subtly bracing for reaction as she admitted, "I think it might have come to this eventually. I didn't love Paulie. Not in a way that would have kept us together forever."

"I know," Barbara sighed.

"You did?"

Her mother's perfectly coiffed head tilted in acknowledgement. "Not until you started up with that Bregnovian fellow, but once I saw the lengths you were willing to go for him, I realized you and Paulie never stood a chance. I should have seen it from the outset, but it would have been so convenient, Tiffany."

She sputtered a laugh at that. "Yeah, well, the situation with Ryzard was more convenience on his part. You were right about that much." Deep angst threatened to rise up and squeeze her in its clawed grip.

"Is that true? He seemed so protective of you. Still does."

"I think that's his nature," Tiffany said shakily, finding it really hard to hold on to her control. "He was so supportive, made me feel so good about myself, but when it came down to it he said he didn't need me or my connections. He—" Her voice broke, but she had to say it aloud so she could get over it and move on. "He doesn't love me."

"But you love him."

Through blurred eyes, Tiffany saw her mother's hand cover her own. The gesture was bittersweet and made her think of all the times her mother had held her hand through her recovery. Through her whole life. She was the wrong person to be mad at.

"I shouldn't have pushed you away so much lately," she husked.

"Shush. Your brother did it when he was eleven. I've been lucky enough to keep you close this long. I'm just glad I can be here for you when you need me."

"Are you going to tell me there's plenty more fish in the sea?"

"I'd like to, but there are so few worth reeling in," her mother bemoaned, making Tiffany chortle past her tears. "It's so good to see you smiling again," her mother added with her own misty smile.

She didn't know how often Tiffany cried. How she combed for news and photos of Ryzard, how she quietly kept tally of the countries recognizing him. She was doing exactly that one afternoon before going into a meeting, getting her fix to get her through one more day without him, when she came across a horrifying update.

Coal Mine Explosion in Northern Bregnovia, Dozens Unaccounted For, one hour ago.

Leaping to her feet, she shouted for her assistant.

Even though sabotage was not suspected, it was war conditions all over again. Ryzard could hardly bear it, but quick response on the recovery effort was critical. There was no time to ask the fates why his country should suffer this way. No way to reassure his people that they could live without fear. There were only feet on the ground, hands digging into the rubble, people trying to save people into the night.

Dark was receding, exhaustion setting in and spirits low when a throaty drone began climbing on the air. The latest batch of survivors, many badly burned, had just left on what aircraft he'd been able to muster on short notice. They hadn't had time to drop and be back so soon. That didn't bode well.

Squinting into the silver horizon, he saw what looked like an invasion, and his heart stopped. Then the hospital crosses on the underbellies of three of the helicopters became visible and he relaxed. Someone asked if the Red Cross was finally here. He had no idea. His phone was charging in the one small shack that had a power generator for electricity.

Jerking his chin at someone to greet and direct them, he threw himself back into the work at hand.

Sixteen hours later, he was knee-deep in rubble, numb and almost asleep on his feet, losing the light, when his eye—and half-dead libido—was caught unexpectedly by a pair of skintight jeans tucked into knee-high black boots. A blond ponytail swung against the back of a black leather jacket as the woman nodded at whomever she was speaking to.

He was seeing things. He clambered across to her, swaying on his feet as he pulled her around by a rather despondent grip on her arm, distantly surprised to catch at a solid person and still not believing his eyes, even when he saw the familiar patch of color on the side of her face.

"You're real," he said dumbly.

She smiled tenderly and set a hand against his cheek. Her touch was surprisingly warm, making him aware how cold he was. How utterly empty and frozen he'd been for weeks.

"All I could think was that no country would be equipped for this many burn injuries. We have a triage set up. I hope you don't mind, but I'm sending the victims with their families to whoever can take them."

He couldn't speak, could only string clumsy arms around her and drag her into him. Closing his eyes, he drank in the sweet, familiar scent of her hair.

Tiffany ran soothing hands over him, feeling the chill on his skin beneath his shirt, trying to ease the shudders rippling through his muscles. He was heavy, leaning into her, beyond exhausted.

"Come with me," she urged, dragging him stumbling across the trampled yard to the tent where cots and coffee were on hand for the rescuers.

His arm was deadweight across her shoulders. When he sat, he pulled her into his lap.

"You need to sleep," she insisted as she tried to extricate herself.

He said something in Bregnovian, voice jagged and broken. He snugged her closer, his hold unbreakable.

Not that she really wanted to get away. It felt so good to be near him. He was grimy and sweaty, but he was Ryzard. She blinked damp eyes where he was keeping her face trapped against his chest, surrounded in his personal scent.

"You need to lie down, Ryzard. You're not even speaking English."

He brought her with him so the cot groaned beneath them. When she tried to rise, he threw a pinning leg across her and tangled his fingers in her hair. "Don't leave," he murmured and the lights went out. He became a lead blanket upon her.

Since she was jet-lagged and had been on her feet for hours, she relaxed and dozed until activity around them woke her. Then she managed to climb free of his tentacle-like hold and carry on with the rescue effort. The trapped miners had been reached and the final victims would need transport.

* * *

Ryzard woke thinking he'd dreamed her, but the jacket draped across his chest told him he wasn't crazy. She was here, somewhere.

Coffee in one hand, jacket in his other, he went in search and found her trying to comfort an anxious wife as an injured miner was packaged into a helicopter. The woman clutched a baby and had a redheaded boy by the hand, and Tiffany held a matching toddler on her hip.

"Oh, Ryzard," she said when he draped her jacket over her shoulders, "Please tell her I'm sure her husband will live. The burns are bad, but they didn't find internal injuries. I've lost my translator and she's so upset."

Together they reassured the woman and made arrangements for her to catch up with her husband at the burn unit in Paris.

Calm settled as everyone was accounted for. There was a longer journey ahead to bring the mine back into operation, but the immediate crisis was over. Tiffany stifled a yawn as she thanked people and gave them final directions for breaking down the field hospital they'd erected.

"I can't thank you enough for this," Ryzard said.

"When you're part of a club, you pitch in to help your fellow members when they need it, right?"

She was being her cheeky self, but he wasn't in a frame of mind to take this gesture so lightheartedly.

"I'm being sincere, Tiffany. I hope your motives were not that superficial."

She sobered. "I told you last night that this struck close to home for me. But I don't suppose you remember, being pretty much sleepwalking at the time."

Was it only empathy for fellow burn victims that had brought her here? He flinched, wondering where he got off imagining she could have deeper feelings for him when he'd pushed her from his life the way he had.

"Hey, Tiff," some flyboy called across. "You catching a lift in my bird or...?"

"Oh, um—"

Ryzard cut her off before she could answer. "You'll come to Gizela with me."

"Will I," she said in the tone she used when she thought he was being arrogant, but he only cared that she acquiesced. He did *not* care for the way she hugged the pilot and kissed his cheek, thanking him for his help.

Ryzard lifted his brows in query when she turned from her goodbye.

"He grew up with Paulie and my brother. I've known him forever," she defended. "We needed pilots so I called him."

It was petty and ungrateful to think, we didn't need them *that* badly, but he was still short on sleep and deeply deprived of her. His willingness to share her, especially when he was so uncertain how long he'd have her, was nil.

His own transport arrived. They fell asleep against each other in the back of the 4x4 for the jostling four-hour drive back to Gizela.

The palace looked better than ever, Tiffany noted when she woke in front of it. Its exterior was no longer pockmarked by bullet holes and the broken stones were gone, giving the grounds a sense of openness and welcome. Inside, she went straight up the stairs next to Ryzard, both anxious for a shower. They parted at the top and she went to her room, where, he had assured her, everything she'd left was still there.

She wasn't sure what it meant. A dozen times she'd thought about asking for the items to be shipped, but she'd been afraid that contacting him would be the first step toward falling back down the rabbit hole into his world. Or it would have been final closure, something she hadn't been ready for. Had he felt the same? Because he could have had the things shipped to her at any time.

The not knowing hung like a veil over the situation, making her wonder if she was being silly and desperate when she dressed for his flag salutation, or respectful and supportive. He wouldn't have brought her here if he didn't want her here, she told herself, but she faltered when they met at the top of the stairs.

He wore his white shirt, black suit and presidential sash. His jaw was freshly shaved and sharply defined by tension as he took in her houndstooth skirt and matching wool jacket. "You don't have to," he said for the second time.

She almost took him at his word, almost let herself believe that he only wanted her, didn't need her, but his eyes gave him away. They weren't flat green. They burned gold. As if he was taking in treasure. As if she said she wasn't ready, he would wait until she was.

"I want to," she assured him, wondering if she was being an imaginative fool. Why would she want to do this? Pride of place, she guessed. It made her feel good to be with him no matter what he was doing. She admired him as a man and took great joy in watching him rise to his position.

Outside, it was blustery and tasting of an early-fall storm with spits of rain in the gusting wind. Leaves chased across grass and their clothes rippled as they walked to the pole. The flag snapped its green and blue stripes as he made his pledge and saluted it.

A burst of applause made them both turn to the crowd gathered at the gate. It was a deeper gathering than Tiffany had seen any other time. Hundreds maybe. A fresh rush of pride welled in her.

"Your predecessor wouldn't have cut up his hands freeing trapped miners," she said, picking up his scabbed hand. It was so roughened and abused, she instinctively lifted it to her lips.

The cheering swelled, making her pull back from touching him. "Sorry. That was dumb."

"No, they liked it. They're here for you as much as me. They know what you did for us." He faced the crowd and indicated her with a sweep of his hand and a bow of his head.

His people reacted with incendiary passion, waving flags and holding up children.

"They're thanking you, Tiffany." He lifted her hand to his own lips, and another roar went up.

They stood there a long time, hands linked, waving at the crowd. No one walked away. They waited for her and Ryzard to go in first.

"Are you crying?" he asked as they entered the big drawing room. It was such a stunning room with its gorgeous nineteenth-century furniture and view overlooking the sea, but she still wasn't comfortable in it.

Averting her gaze from Luiza's portrait, she swiped at her cheeks. "That was very moving. I didn't expect it. I had the impression they thought of me as an interloper." Now she couldn't help straying a glance at Luiza, as if the woman might be eavesdropping.

For a long moment he didn't say anything, only looked at the portrait with the same tortured expression she'd seen on him before, when his feelings for Luiza were too close to the surface.

She looked away, respecting his need for time to pull himself together, but taking a hit of despair over it, too.

"It's my fault you felt that way," he said in a low, grave voice. "But please try to understand what she meant to me. Luiza made me see that Bregnovia is my home. That if I fought for it and made it ours, *mine*—" he set his fist over the place where her name was inked forever "—I would always belong here. That was deeply meaningful after so many years of being rootless and displaced."

She nodded, unable to speak because she did understand and felt for him.

"I needed her love after losing my parents. I would have shut down otherwise. Become an instrument of war."

Instead of a leader who had retained his humanity. It was one of the qualities she admired most in him, so she could hardly begrudge the woman who'd kept his heart intact through the horrors of battle and loss.

"When I lost her, I couldn't let myself become embittered and filled with hatred. It would have gone against everything she helped me become, but I couldn't face another loss like it. The vulnerability of loving again, knowing the emotional pain of grief if something were to happen… It terrifies me, Tiffany."

He said it so plainly, never faltering even when he was exposing his deepest fear.

She wanted to look to the ceiling to contain the tears gathering to sting her eyes. It killed her to hear that he couldn't give up his heart, but she couldn't look away from him.

"It's okay. I admire her, too," she managed. Her voice scraped her throat with emotion, but she was being sincere. "I wish I'd met her. She had amazing willpower. I wouldn't have had the guts to do what she did."

"Guts." The harsh sound he made was halfway between a laugh and a choke of deep anguish. "Luiza had ideals. Now she is our martyr and a symbol of our sacrifice and loss. I would do her a disservice to forget or dismiss that, but it doesn't make you an interloper for living where she died, Tiffany. She had a vision. When I look at you, I see reality. Our reality. Scarred by tragedy, but so beautiful. So strong and determined to carry on."

His tender look of regard had its usual effect of striking like an unexpected punch into her solar plexus, making her breath rush out. She had to cover her lips to still them from trembling.

"I don't like comparing you. It's disrespectful to both of you, but you're right. You and Luiza are very different. You wouldn't have killed yourself. Given the same situation, you would fight with everything in you to stay alive until I came for you, no matter what happened. That's who you are. Your courage astounds me."

He ran his hand down his face only to reveal an expression of profound regret.

"When I sent you away, all I could think was that I didn't want to risk the pain of loss again. And did you crawl back in your cave even though I'd hurt you? No. You went on with your life without me, and I was so hurt and so proud at the same time."

She lowered her head, touched beyond measure, and saw a teardrop land on the hardwood. She swiped at her numb cheek, finding it wet. "Thank you for the flowers."

"The flowers were an apology. You made me feel like a coward, refusing to embrace love when it's as precious as life. I wanted to come to you and to hell with your Customs and Immigration, but I had to finish my obligation to Luiza first. I've done that. Official announcements will be made later in the week. I have the votes I need."

"Oh, Ryzard, that's wonderful!" She was elated for him, but still reeling from his mention of embracing love. Did that mean…? She searched his inscrutable expression.

"After the last few days, this country needs good news." He sighed and rocked back on his heels, regarding her. "It also means the worst is over for a time when it comes to state functions. I won't run in the next election. Could you live with two more years of being in the public eye, knowing it would be temporary?"

"What?" Her nails cut into her palms as she tried to stay grounded, not leaping too high on what he was saying. Not reading too deep. Definitely not wanting to hold him back in any way. "Ryzard, you *are* Bregnovia. It's barely on its feet. You can't hand it over to someone else so soon. I couldn't live with myself if all this stability you've fought for crumbled."

"I don't want to wait that long to marry you, *draga*. I ache every night and barely get through my days. I need you."

"You do?" Her voice hitched and stayed awfully small, but the world around her seemed to expand in one pulse beat, stealing the oxygen and filling the air with sparks. "You really want to marry me? *Me?*"

"*You*. Not the daughter of the next American president, not Davis and Holbrook, not the woman who charms heads of state without even trying. You."

"Because you love me?" she hazarded, curling her toes and pulling her elbows in, bracing for the worst.

"Because we love each other."

His tender gaze held hers, gently demanding she give up her heart to him. She did, easily.

"If I hadn't been trained from birth to pretend everything was fine no matter how miserable I was, I couldn't have got through these last weeks. I love you so much, Ryzard, and I hated myself for not letting my love be enough to keep us together."

"I shouldn't have made you feel like it was all up to you," he said, coming across to draw her into him. With his lips pressed to her forehead, he added, "I will never hold back from you again. I thought I was being noble, letting you find the man who would love you like no other could, but that man is me. I love you with every breath in me, Tiffany. A different man loved Luiza. This one is yours."

She relaxed her forehead against his nuzzling lips, touched to her soul. Fulfilled. Hopeful. *Happy*.

He traced a soft kiss along the raised line of her scar,

following it down to the corner of her eye and across her cheek until he was almost at her mouth.

"We should take this upstairs," she said against his lips. "I have a feeling it won't stay PG rated for long."

He quirked a rueful grin and led her upstairs. In his bedroom, he took a moment to lift the snapshot from his bedside table and walk it into his sitting room.

When he returned he found her seated on the bed, hands tucked in her lap.

"We have to talk about one more thing before we go any further," she said.

"What's that?" he queried.

"Children."

"At least two. I want them to have each other if something happens to us," he affirmed.

"I was going to say six, but okay. Coward."

"Ambitious," he remarked in a drawl. "I can keep up if you can." His smile was a slow dawn of masculine heat that twitched with amusement. "I've missed you, Tiffany. You make me laugh."

She threw herself into his arms.

EPILOGUE

THE MILKY WAY stretched from one edge of the horizon to the other, diffusing into more stars against Zanzibar's indigo sky than Tiffany had ever seen in her life. If Ryzard hadn't kept her pressed firmly against his side as he steered them down the jetty toward the island bar, she likely would have stumbled into the lagoon.

"What the hell are you up to?"

"I know, I'm sorry, but I've never seen anything like— wait, what?" She realized Ryzard had been talking to a man in a mask who'd just passed them on the jetty. She glanced back the way they'd come to see the member break off his lip-lock with a *petite q* and hurry her toward the interior of the club.

"Who was that?"

"A friend. One who knows better than to play with Zeus's toys." He dragged his puzzled gaze to her expectant one. With a low sigh, he bent to whisper, "His name is Nic." Straightening, he added, "Don't ask me to say more than that. Even though you're my wife, I still have an obligation to respect other members' privacy."

She grinned, pleased more by her title of "wife" than anything else.

The DJ's electronica pulsed louder as they finished their walk into the open-air bar. *Q Virtus* members and *petite q's* danced and jumped to the beat, making the wooden floor bounce.

Tiffany refused a drink offered by a passing *petite q,* but Ryzard drew her to a side bar. "Iced coconut. Nonalcoholic," he said.

Her condition wasn't official, especially since they'd been married only a day, but they'd stopped using protection weeks ago. She was pretty sure, and they were both so quietly, ferociously happy it was criminal.

The server tilted his array of cones for her to peruse. They were stunning, not merely shaved and frozen coconut with a splash of color, but intricately decorated works of art in more shades, flavors and hues than the stars above them.

Tiffany almost picked the one that looked like a bouquet of sweet peas, but maybe the mandala was prettier. The paisley?

"It just hit me," Ryzard said in a tone of discovery. "It was never about the taffy apple being better optics. You couldn't decide what color candy floss you wanted."

Grinning, she admitted, "You caught me."

"I'm convinced it's the other way around, *draga,*" he retorted.

She laughed in delight, but contradicted, "I distinctly remember a kidnapping on the high seas."

"I remember fireworks," he said with a smoky look from behind his mask. "Choose something or we'll miss these ones."

Face warm with pleasure behind her own mask, she took two cones and gave him one, leaning her weight into him as he hooked his arm across her shoulders and steered her toward the rail overlooking the Indian Ocean.

"I see them every night, you know. Fireworks. 'Cause I'm spoiled."

"You are," he agreed, leaning down to bite at her cone before he offered his. "So am I."

"Mmm. We're in the right place for the privileged, aren't we?" she mused, licking clove-and-orange-flavored coconut from her lips.

He stopped and turned her so they held each other in a way that felt perfect and familiar and right. "As long as I'm with you, I'm exactly where I belong."

* * * * *

*If you enjoyed this book,
look out for the next instalment of*
THE 21ST CENTURY GENTLEMAN'S CLUB:
*THE ULTIMATE REVENGE
by Victoria Parker
Coming next month!*

Sloan surprised her by sliding his hands into her hair and covering her lips with his own.

Ziara's eyes slid shut as an explosion of sensation overwhelmed her and reason and logic disappeared. He could do what he wanted with her.

Just don't stop touching me.

Never one to do things by half measures, Sloan deepened the kiss, igniting a flash of longing through her body. Only after the last of her intelligence had leaked from her brain did he pull back a fraction. His hands remained anchored in her hair, his minty breath fanning across her face.

Forcing her heavy lids upward, she made her eyes meet his. "What was that for?" she asked, embarrassed by the husky whisper of her voice.

His hands tightened against her head for a moment, as if to draw her forward for another kiss, but instead he spoke. "For keeping my secrets."

Dani Wade astonished her local librarians as a teenager when she carried home ten books every week—and actually read them all. Now she writes her own characters, who clamour for attention in the midst of the chaos that is her life. Residing in the southern United States, with a husband, two kids, two dogs and one grumpy cat, she stays busy until she can closet herself away with her characters once more.

*This is Dani's dazzling debut—
we hope you love it as much as we do!*

**Did you know this is also available as an eBook?
Visit www.millsandboon.co.uk**

HIS BY DESIGN

**BY
DANI WADE**

All rights reserved including the right of reproduction in whole
or in part in any form. This edition is published by arrangement with
Harlequin Books S.A.

This is a work of fiction. Names, characters, places, locations and
incidents are purely fictional and bear no relationship to any real
life individuals, living or dead, or to any actual places, business
establishments, locations, events or incidents. Any resemblance is
entirely coincidental.

This book is sold subject to the condition that it shall not, by way of
trade or otherwise, be lent, resold, hired out or otherwise circulated
without the prior consent of the publisher in any form of binding or
cover other than that in which it is published and without a similar
condition including this condition being imposed on the subsequent
purchaser.

® and TM are trademarks owned and used by the trademark owner
and/or its licensee. Trademarks marked with ® are registered with the
United Kingdom Patent Office and/or the Office for Harmonisation in
the Internal Market and in other countries.

Published in Great Britain 2014
by Mills & Boon, an imprint of Harlequin (UK) Limited,
Eton House, 18-24 Paradise Road, Richmond, Surrey, TW9 1SR

© 2013 Katherine Worsham

ISBN: 978-0-263-24673-5

Harlequin (UK) Limited's policy is to use papers that are natural,
renewable and recyclable products and made from wood grown in
sustainable forests. The logging and manufacturing processes conform
to the legal environmental regulations of the country of origin.

Printed and bound in Spain
by Blackprint CPI, Barcelona

HIS BY DESIGN

One

This was not how her morning was supposed to play out.

Ziara Divan rushed down the hallway of Eternity Designs, her brain pounding with the knowledge that she was late. Her cheeks burned as a result of her jog from the parking garage in workday pumps, and her suit skirt rode up the panty hose strangling her legs.

She threw her purse under her desk and grabbed her tablet from the drawer, turning it on as she continued down the hall with more speed than decorum. Rounding the corner into Vivian Creighton's outer office, Ziara ground to a halt. Vivian's assistant's desk was empty.

Breathe, Ziara. Pull yourself together.

She straightened her clothes in an attempt to regain her prized professional facade. But the agitated urgency to move, to get into the office quickly, still pounded in her chest. She wasn't perfect, but she made sure she came pretty dang close as an executive assistant in training, no matter how many minutes she spent stuck on a backed-up Georgia interstate.

As she struggled to regulate her breathing, Ziara heard

voices from beyond the door to the inner sanctum. At first, she couldn't grasp the idea that someone was yelling, because this was Vivian's office. Vivian didn't yell. It went totally against the traditional Southern rules of behavior for all ladies. But Vivian's voice was definitely raised. Ziara inched closer.

The other voice was male, deep. *Oh no.*

"...will not let you ruin my father's company..."

Sloan Creighton. Vivian's stepson. He came into the office rarely, but when he did he brought a tornadic level of energy and caused an unwanted tingle of awareness at the base of Ziara's spine. Though she studiously avoided him on his rare visits, he always seemed to find her. And flirt with her. And just generally turn her sense of professionalism upside down. The best reason to avoid him.

Vivian's own voice was muffled, but parts of Sloan's words came through the solid wood.

"...our biggest buyer rejected all the designs..."

Ziara's heart sank, threatening to drop out of her chest. Her knees went weak enough to force her to grab the frame of the door.

Ziara had suspected that last week's meeting with their largest retail account hadn't gone as planned, but the few who had attended were keeping quiet. Losing that buyer could mean ruin for Eternity Designs, something Ziara didn't want to see happen. She loved her job; this place, these people had also provided the stability and acceptance that had been lacking her entire life.

"...you have no choice..."

And neither did Ziara. She had to go through that door. Vivian had said to be in her office at eight sharp; it was now 8:17 a.m. But the thought of Sloan and the way his cool, effortless good looks and flirty attitude affected her body and her psyche made her want to return to the crowded freeway.

But backing down wasn't an option. With a deep breath to fortify herself, she headed through the doorway.

Sloan stood tall over Vivian, his voice ringing clear in the room. "I *will* have more voice in Eternity Designs, starting now. I'll need the next three months. If my fall line is a hit with our buyers, you will sign over enough of your shares for me to own fifty-five percent...and relinquish complete creative control. To. Me."

Ziara paused just inside the door, her mind absorbing those incredible words, while Sloan and Vivian glared at each other across Vivian's desk. For a moment Ziara's panic overrode everything, even the tempting sight of Sloan's strong shoulders and firm backside.

As the tension crept higher and higher, Ziara finally broke. Into the silence, she said, "Would you like me to come back, Vivian?"

Like pushing Play on a paused DVD, Vivian and Sloan both turned and looked in her direction. She met Vivian's eyes first, checking in with her boss and mentor. The narrowed glare and tight mouth signified a frustration that radiated like a cracked web through Vivian's normal composure. As if she realized how she must look, Vivian straightened, smoothing her elegant close-cropped curls into place. "Good morning, Ziara. Please sit."

"Now, Sloan," she said, turning her attention back to him. "Explain to me why I would ever agree to such ridiculous demands."

Sloan was too happy to comply. "Let me guess, commissions are down, creditors are closing accounts and you don't have a clue how to get yourself out of this situation." He straightened with confidence. "But I do."

"I'm sure I can find someone else to do the same."

"In enough time to make a difference? I don't think so."

She conceded to her stepson's ultimatum by leaning back in her chair, her composure shaken enough that she fiddled with the wedding band still gracing her left hand.

At least she didn't seem to notice—or care—that Ziara was late. Sloan, on the other hand, started cataloging everything about her. His gaze traveled down the length of her body to her toes, then back up with leisurely enjoyment.

Dragging her own composure around her like a cloak that

granted her invisibility, Ziara walked with measured steps across the carpeting to a chair beside Vivian's desk. A glance from under her lashes caught Sloan's interested stare zeroing in on the V of her suit jacket, where the modest edge of a lacy camisole peaked into view. With a great struggle, she forced herself not to adjust, to hold still while his eyes wandered back up to her vulnerable neck. The knowing smirk on his contoured lips sparked arousal beneath her irritation, confusing her further.

Damn man. She could see why Vivian found him so infuriating—professional behavior seemed to be a foreign concept to him. She'd seen the spark of interest before, though never quite this blatantly. Of course, his simple presence had always created an uncomfortable heat in her core that prompted her to keep any previous meetings as short and far apart as possible.

If she'd simply passed him on the street, Ziara would never have suspected him of the professional dedication he was displaying now. His collar-length, sun-streaked hair and the slight crook of his previously broken nose said "surfer boy" more than it did "hard-hitting negotiator." But the perfectly tailored dress shirt and pants, paired with his take-no-prisoners attitude, demonstrated the real man inside. His electric-blue eyes confirmed her suspicions that his core was pure steel.

She was thankful when he turned back to his stepmother. "This is my father's legacy we're talking about, Vivian. I save other people's businesses every day. Resurrecting Eternity Designs is right up my alley," he said.

"Yes," Vivian said, letting the word draw out. "Your...fix-it-up business."

"You could call it that. I call it the very lucrative process of taking failing companies and turning them into profit-making machines. Too bad you didn't get in touch with me sooner, but then you'd have to admit that you screwed up."

The slap of Vivian's hand on her desk made Ziara jump. She watched her with wide eyes, shocked by the venom scarring Vivian's normally genteel facade.

"Your father didn't trust you to take care of his legacy enough to leave it all to you. Why should I?"

Sloan stalked back and rested his hands on the desk, so he could loom over his stepmother. "And whose fault was that? Who slipped poisonous thoughts into his mind from day one, turning him against me so he could be yours and yours alone? Hell, Vivian, if I didn't know better, I'd think you set his whole will up. You're the one who made him insist I go for my MBA instead of continuing to pursue my own plans of fashion design, aren't you?"

"I don't know what you're talking about."

"Of course you do. After all, going from Daddy's assistant to his wife meant you got to control his entire life and not just his business, didn't it?"

Oh. Dear. Ziara's lungs shut down, trapping the air inside. Vivian's early involvement with Eternity Designs had never been explicitly discussed. Ziara had simply assumed she'd started working with the company sometime after she'd married Mr. Creighton.

The knowledge left Ziara reeling. How many times had Vivian admonished her that only tramps got involved with their coworkers? Ever since her childhood, when Ziara had been bullied because of her mother's lack of morals, she'd avoided anything that would suggest she was the same. Vivian's lessons had simply reinforced Ziara's focus on professionalism and the building of a flawless reputation.

Vivian's hand shook as she pointed at her stepson. "Don't talk to me that way, Sloan. It's disrespectful. Your father would never approve of your tone."

Sloan leaned in, hard. "Well, he's not here to reprimand me. If you wanted my respect, you should have tried earning it a long time ago. Now it's too late."

"It's never too late to expect you to be a gentleman. But we just couldn't get those lessons to stick."

Sloan laughed, collapsing into the chair as his body shook with a tainted kind of humor. Ziara felt like she was watching a tennis match. Sloan clearly thought he was the winner.

Vivian conceded with less graciousness than Ziara had ever seen her display, but then again, she'd learned quite a few new things about her mentor in the past ten minutes. Vivian hadn't always been a lady. Disbelief still ricocheted throughout Ziara like the ball inside a pinball machine.

"Fine, Sloan. Do whatever it is you do," Vivian forced out through clenched teeth.

"I'll have that in writing, I think," Sloan said.

"As demanding as you are, I'm amazed anyone will work with you."

"Oh, I'll manage," he said with a cocky quirk of his shapely lips.

"Not alone, you won't. The last thing I need is you wandering around unattended."

"Aw, Vivian. I didn't know you cared. Oh wait, you don't," Sloan said with saccharin sweetness.

"I care about Eternity Designs," she said.

His gaze scanned Vivian's face as if to determine the catch. "Anyone you saddle me with better know what they're doing and how to take orders."

"Oh, I have no doubt she'll work like a charm…and be able to keep you in line."

Ziara's heart picked up speed when Vivian's elegant, bejeweled fingers waved in her direction. *No. No, no, no.* The effort to hide her sudden panic and appear in control might just give her a heart attack.

Vivian's voice trickled through her consciousness, breaking her inward focus. "Your history with assistants is well-known, Sloan. They crawl all over you like bees in honey. That won't be an issue with Ziara. I've trained her well. She knows more about how we conduct business here than anyone except my own assistant. And her behavior is impeccable—unlike yours."

What was she—a slave girl at auction? *Would the buyer prefer pretty and pliable or plain but talented?* Though dependable was exactly the look she was going for, the thought still disconcerted her.

"Well, Vivian, isn't that thoughtful of you?" he said.

Ziara glanced up to find Sloan's gaze directed her way. His earlier anger had turned his bright blue eyes icily sharp, his body rigid, his jaw tight. But now he eased back in a chair, propping his elbows on the arms. His fingers absently stroked the upper ridge of his lip, drawing her attention to the sensuous curve of his mouth. His turbulent look suddenly softened like ice thawing beneath a heat lamp.

Her emotions seesawed as his gaze traveled south, visually caressing the extra length of leg exposed by her hasty drop into her chair. She could almost feel his touch sliding along the edge of her skirt, tickling the sensitive skin on the backs of her legs.

Bit by bit, Ziara used up her willpower forcing herself to sit impassively. The twitch of her thighs urged her to shift her feet, but she resisted. That would tell him just how much he affected her. Tightening her muscles, she tried to crack down on the spreading fire, to no avail. Ignoring physical desire had never been a problem before him.

Her new boss.

Her soothingly subtle gray business suit, so comfortable in the luxurious air-conditioning only moments ago, now felt heavy, itchy. Her nipples peaked against their confinement. She felt that he peered through her professional armor to the woman she kept hidden deep inside.

How could a simple look make her so aware, too aware? As if she lacked something only he could provide.

As casually as possible, she adjusted her position and her skirt, covering her legs down past her knees.

Knowledge leaked into his eyes, as well as smug satisfaction. *He did that on purpose.* Feeling a need to defend herself, she met him with a flick of her lashes. Slowly she lifted her left brow.

He grinned, not at all intimidated by her challenge. "Be in my office and ready to work first thing tomorrow morning."

She could handle his antagonistic, dismissive tone; she welcomed it to counteract her strange reaction to him. Unlike efficient orders and professional expectations, the sensations created with that hot, hard stare set her nerves on edge.

But she could handle it. She'd pulled herself up from a sludge-pile existence and become a woman with goals and dreams and skills. She could control herself for the three months it would take to get Eternity Designs back in the spotlight and earn her stripes as an executive assistant. But how was she going to control him?

Ziara. Her classic beauty and calm demeanor distracted Sloan from Vivian's condescension. Staring his new assistant down made him hotter than he'd been in a long time. Vivian's insistence that Ziara wouldn't follow the path of his previous assistants didn't worry him. As annoying as it had been to replace three employees in less than two years because they insisted they were *in love* with him, he might have to pursue this woman. Her pretend lack of interest challenged him, but turning Ziara's head could provide plenty of ammunition in his war with Vivian.

How ironic that the very thing he'd avoided in his professional life—intimate involvement with an employee—could give him a leg up in this situation. It felt wrong even thinking that way, but winning her loyalty could give him the freedom to do whatever he wanted without Vivian's interference. He needed every advantage to fight against Vivian. His stepmother was totally immune to his charm, which drew cheeky toddlers, blue-haired dames and women of every age in between. If Vivian had been a typical trophy wife, at least Sloan could have fallen back on his practiced grin and genuine appreciation of the female species, but, instead, dear old Dad had the foresight to marry a savvy woman. One steeped in Southern tradition and brimming with a Southern belle's ingenuity to survive. Too bad her temperament had always favored Scarlett's machinations as opposed to Melanie's sweetness.

She viewed his father's memory and Eternity Designs as hers; Sloan was a threat to her reign as queen. His frustration had been building over this situation for years and he let it out for once.

"We need to shake things up," he said. "We can't afford to

lose our biggest account because we're afraid to break out of the mold. Reliance on tradition is getting you nowhere. Eternity Designs needs a modern edge, a new designer, a revamped portfolio. Pronto."

That was exactly what Vivian didn't want to hear. "Your father prided himself on the tradition inherent in this company and its designs," she said, elegantly restrained anger sharpening her tone. "This discussion demonstrates exactly why he chose me to continue the legacy of Eternity Designs."

Not you.

The wedding gown design firm had been in his family for three generations—if his current 40 percent share of it counted for anything. With Vivian, it didn't. But the words of the accountant told him now was the time to insist on the control she'd denied him for so long.

"The whole company will go under if something isn't done immediately."

"Sixty percent ownership doesn't mean you're God," he said, ignoring the burn of betrayal. "It's a good thing dear ol' Dad isn't alive to see how you've run it into the ground." Yep. Payback was a bitch.

A quick glance revealed Ziara stiffening, in surprise or defense he wasn't sure. If she knew what the posture did for her magnificent breasts, she'd hunch in on herself for eternity. He paced back and forth in front of Vivian's desk, arousal and frustration fueling his restlessness. The business expert in him was tired of talking.

The man in him begged for a totally different kind of action.

Watching Ziara's reactions to his and Vivian's little fight fascinated him more than he would have thought. Her exotic, raven-haired beauty brought to mind sensual, spice-scented nights. What would she look like with that thick bun let loose around her shoulders? With that suit jacket loosened up a few buttons? Seducing her out of her loyalty to Vivian was going to be such guilty fun.

He'd avoided getting involved with his employees like a contagious disease, to the point that he hadn't even had an assistant for six months. But his desperation called for outrageous actions—like storming into Vivian's office this morning. Finding out Ziara had given up company loyalty for carnal indulgence would probably mean a quick dismissal, but he couldn't let that stop him. For Ziara this was a job; she'd find another one soon enough.

For Sloan, Eternity Designs was a legacy.

Vivian's haughty belle persona reappeared. "You're awfully sure of yourself, Sloan. Overconfidence leads to nasty downfalls. Those unconventional methods of yours won't work in such a traditional company."

"Those unconventional methods are just what Eternity needs. Less tradition, not more." He turned to Ziara. Might as well put her to the test first thing. "What do you think? Is Eternity's current path leading to success?"

"I…I…" Her almond-shaped eyes flicked back and forth between him and her mentor, panic darkening their chocolate color. After a moment she said, "Our designers do beautiful work, enough to build a loyal following. Families come here generation after generation to commission their dresses. Our motto, our focus has built a legacy. I have no proof otherwise."

Test number one: fail.

Vivian echoed Ziara's words. "Eternity Designs is truly *where tradition and style forever align*."

Quoting the company's motto as a defense ramped up Sloan's anger. He needed to save this business. His father had worked hard to build it. He'd loved it just as Sloan did. Despite their differences at the time of his death, the 40 percent he'd gifted to Sloan in his will told him his father had wanted him to have some small part of his family's heritage. He had to believe that, had to believe Vivian hadn't poisoned every ounce of their father-son bond.

He glared at them both. "Maybe our motto needs to change."

Ziara held very still, the only movement the frantic pulse beating at the base of that silky throat. But Vivian sighed heavily, with a touch of drama. She would have called it flair. He knew he wouldn't like what came next.

"I've been thinking about options to get us through this little slump. I have a few friends who might know potential backers. That should tide us over until spring."

Shock immobilized Sloan for a moment. Then a sharp spike of panic sliced through the numbness. Then another...and another. "We're not letting an outsider buy into this company."

"I'll do what I have to in order to save Eternity."

"Except call in the one man whose skills would provide the lifeline? Did you honestly think I'd sit back, mouth shut, while you let Eternity go out of the family?" He straightened, the hardball negotiator stepping onto the court. "You know me better than that, Vivian."

With a blink, uncertainty leaked into Vivian's eyes. "I truly don't understand why you'd care."

He shook his head slowly, sorrow over the state of his relationship with his late father leaking underneath the anger. "That right there proves how little you know me...or knew my father. This place was his life—" in the end more than even his son "—I want nothing more than for his life's work to continue, to prove to his memory I'm more than you made me out to be. A hard worker, capable of contributing to the family dream, instead of a slacker who cares about nothing but myself. You're still looking at me as a grieving kid, Vivian. Not the man I've actually become, the man my father saw in me before he died."

But the tightening around her mouth told him she'd never see it that way. After years of convincing her husband that his only son was impulsive and undependable, repeatedly citing his teenage antics, his father had left *her* with the majority ownership of Eternity Designs. That's all she cared about.

"Sloan, I would prefer to keep this inside family lines, such as they are. So I'll stand by my word and give you a chance. But in the meantime, I'll be working on a backup plan."

It wasn't much of a compromise, as they went, but he'd take what he could get. He needed carte blanche over the fall line. Because if Vivian knew the plans gathering mass in his mind, she'd shut him down in a heartbeat.

Her mouth pulled into a strained smile. "Just don't go forgetting who is in charge around here."

"I won't. We'll pretend you're in charge while I become the linchpin holding everything together."

It was a low blow, but he was beyond caring. Vivian straightened, her shoulders squaring as the pinching around her mouth deepened. Then a calculating look slid across her face, warning him he was about to pay for his disrespect.

"I have a caveat of my own. If you should happen to walk away before the fall line is presented—" her tone said she could happily run him off with a shotgun "—then Eternity Designs will become solely mine."

Two

*N*othing like a new challenge and a gorgeous woman to work with.

Sloan listened to Ziara's movements in the outer office as he sat at his desk. He'd wondered whether she'd postpone coming in until the last minute, but here she was thirty minutes early, moving into her new office.

Yesterday she'd both confounded and fascinated him. Her exotic, Indian beauty stirred many un-bosslike urges. Her attempts to keep that beauty under wraps teased his senses. Did she think pulling her luxurious dark hair tight into a bun and covering those shapely legs made her a better employee? It probably did in Vivian's eyes, but Sloan was a whole other matter.

Something she'd learn soon enough, and hopefully enjoy. Though he'd never seduced any of his employees—he spent more time running from than running after—he wasn't above using this mutual attraction as one more tool to secure control of Eternity Designs. He would need her help to understand how things worked around here, to facilitate his relationships with the other employees after being shut out in the cold since his father's death. If tempting her loyalty in his direction meant the reports to Vivian became fewer and further between, or even stopped, all the better.

Crossing the room with a heightened sense of anticipation, he eased through without alerting her to his entrance. She stood behind the desk, the chair pushed aside to give her room to reallocate her personal stuff. Her movements were elegant but efficient as she placed pens and papers in the desk drawers. Her careful concentration told him she had a precise way she wanted things and she'd find a way to create order in this new space.

He barely held back laughter as he sized her up. He was a red-blooded male and his body naturally heated despite her choice of clothes. She'd opted for a longer skirt and boxier jacket, as if that would hide the curvy shape of her hips and ass. But it was the scarf he found most amusing. From the back, he could see the curl of material around her neck. Did it merely cover her throat in the front, or had she gone all out to hide every single hint of bare skin, tucking the ends into her jacket?

Didn't she realize that *don't touch me* attitude set her up as his own personal challenge?

"Settling in okay?" he asked.

Her jerk of surprise should have made him feel guilty, but he suspected he had to sneak up on this one before she cut him off at the knees with her stern librarian attitude.

"Yes," she said. "I'm almost ready."

"No hurry," he murmured, tracking the glide of her fingers over a few pictures. No people that he could see, just atmospheric photographs of simple wooden bridges, each in a different season. She arranged them carefully along the top of the nearby shelf, then reached into the remaining cardboard box once more.

Pulling out an object wrapped in cotton batting, she uncovered it layer by layer. She steadily revealed a glass object inscribed with words that she rubbed over a few times with the wrapping.

Too quick for her to stop him, he lifted the object from her hands for a closer look. "What's this?" he asked.

"Be careful."

"Ziara, you wound me," he said with a cheesy helping of drama. "I promise not to drop it."

The cut-glass award was shaped in the outline of a flowing gown, inscribed with the date and Employee of the Year. Ziara Divan. "Employee of the Year, huh?"

"I've worked hard to get where I am."

"And where is that exactly?"

"If all goes well, I'll be promoted to Vivian's personal assistant when Abigail retires next spring."

"Wow, a full-fledged executive assistant at the tender age of—"

She drew a deep breath, as if he were a toddler trying her patience. "Twenty-seven."

"So young to be so buttoned-down." He aimed a pointed look at her scarf, which did indeed drape down to cover that delectable collarbone and upper chest.

"There are worse things to be."

"Like what?"

For a moment it looked like she would speak, but then those full lips pressed tight. Her hand extended, palm up, and her perfectly manicured fingertips curled in a *give it to me* gesture. "Behave, please."

He stepped closer, moving past her invisible *keep away* signs. "Let's get something straight here, Ziara. You're playing by my rules now. I'd imagine I have seriously different requirements for becoming *Employee of the Year*."

She swallowed hard. "Excuse me?"

She reached for the award, moving her body even closer to him, and he used the opportunity to snag an edge of the scarf. Luckily for him, it was only loosely twisted and unraveled like a dream from around her neck and into his hands.

Award forgotten, her hands clamped to her bare neckline, then she glared at him. "What do you think you're doing?"

"A little employee training." He rubbed the material between his fingers but resisted the urge to lift it to his nose and find out if it smelled like her. Vanilla and cinnamon spice. "I'm not nearly as stuffy as Vivian. I don't run my office that way."

"Mr. Creighton—"

"Uh-uh. Sloan."

He was surprised she could talk through teeth that tightly clenched. "Sloan, your behavior is inappropriate in the extreme."

"Is it? Are you going to charge me with sexual harassment?"

That cool eyebrow lifted in condemnation. "If I have to."

Her response was so unexpected, he almost choked. Man, he sure enjoyed a woman with spice, but she didn't need to know that. Yet. "Oh, I don't think you will."

She opened her mouth, but he continued on. "I know Vivian gave you this job for a reason." He leaned even closer to her, watching her heartbeat speed up in the well of her collarbone. "And not just because you're organized and can turn in paperwork on time. After all, she knows something about assistants and their access to—how can I say this diplomatically—company secrets."

Not even an attempt at a response this time.

He pushed a little harder. "Isn't that right, Vivian's little spy?"

"That's insulting."

But she didn't look insulted. The waver of her gaze and uncertain look meant one thing: guilt. "There's no point in pretending, Ziara. Vivian put you here to keep an eye on me, and report back everything she needs—or doesn't need—to know. But that's okay."

Her eyes jerked back to his, widening to give him a great view of chocolate irises shot with gold sparks.

"Just remember," he said, "forewarned is forearmed."

For long seconds neither of them moved, gazes locked in either a worthy battle or forbidden attraction, he wasn't sure. All he felt was the blood pumping hard in his veins and an excitement he hadn't brought to a job in many, many years.

With shaking hands she finally pulled the award from his

grasp and turned to place it on the corner of her desk. Then, she pulled out a thick folder from a drawer of the filing cabinet. "Here is information on the current preparations for the fall line. I thought—"

He lifted the file from her unsteady hands, resentment that he had to rely on her for information mixing with the other emotions roiling through him. "What do we have here?"

She managed to maintain an outward calm. Almost. "Actually, I thought you might like me to familiarize myself with the project *you're here for*."

Her eyes begged, a moment of peace, but he wasn't in the mood for mercy. "Let's take this discussion into my office."

A spy, he'd said. She'd never really thought about it that way.

How had she been promoted from executive assistant in training to spy in one morning? Proving herself to Vivian had been a long-held goal, but doing it now could put her in a very awkward position.

One last glance at her Employee of the Year award stilled her spinning universe. Looking at it, her uneasiness and frustration melted away and her resolve strengthened.

This is what I want. I'm almost there. Becoming executive assistant to the CEO of a major design firm had been her goal from her first day at Eternity Designs. At twenty-seven, the finish line loomed much closer than she'd dared to hope, despite the lack of money for anything other than a trade school degree.

She'd grown up with nothing—no, less than nothing. Oh, they'd technically had enough to live on, but every spare cent had gone for slutty clothes and accessories for her mother to attract the newer, better sugar daddy around the corner.

She'd dreamed of escaping from the trash that still stained her heart into her own office situated right outside of her role model Vivian Creighton's. But would the price be worth this sacrifice?

Vivian and Sloan are playing a game and I'm stuck in the middle.

Ziara was smart enough to realize it. Her firm loyalty to

Vivian notwithstanding, her choices from here on out had to be dedicated to what was best for Eternity Designs. That was her only guarantee of keeping a clear conscience.

Vivian had given her a long lecture on all things Sloan yesterday afternoon. *He's not to be trusted. Why wouldn't his father have just given him the business if he wanted him to run it? He's up to something, I know it.* Ziara had questions of her own, concerns about a man who spent his life reviving companies but completely ignored his family heritage until it was almost too late. If Sloan truly sought to ruin the company, as Vivian had also suggested…well, she wasn't about to let him put anything over on her.

She'd just watch closely and learn to deal with him. She'd always been a stellar student. If she hesitated before crossing the threshold into his office, it didn't mean anything. Drawing in a deep breath, she straightened her shoulders. A little over three months and her training period would be complete. This was simply a small bump on a long road.

She pushed the dilemmas from her mind and entered the room.

Sloan had chosen a corner office at the opposite end of the building from Vivian's, his windows overlooking the sidewalk and shops that lined the streets in this part of town. Quaint, with a touch of subdued elegance, Ziara had always thought, and easily accessible through a MARTA stop only a few blocks away.

Instead of the soothing cream carpet prevalent in the rest of the offices, the flooring here had been replaced with dark wood planks. A desk just a shade or two darker dominated one corner, facing out so that Sloan could see the entire room, from the door to the floor-to-ceiling windows. He crossed the thick blue-and-burgundy rug to stand before them now, hands in his pockets, looking down from the fifth-story view.

For long moments he remained silhouetted against the lightened windows. His strong shoulders spoke of strength and shelter. The line tapered down to his waist, where his hands in his pockets drew the material of his dress pants across the high, firm cheeks of his backside.

Ziara shook her head slightly, grateful he couldn't see her. Being close to this overwhelmingly masculine presence on a daily basis had the potential to open up a whole host of dark desires she preferred to keep locked deep inside. Choosing a leather chair a safe distance away, she sat, primly crossing her legs at the ankles. She held herself rigid as she prepared to take notes, make phone calls, whatever he wanted of her.

"Did you know this was once my father's office?"

Surprise skittered through Ziara's controlled pose. "No," she murmured.

"I used to play right here on a rug while he worked," Sloan said. "I used to watch him stare out these same windows, while he worked out problems."

His voice was easy, soft with memory. He started to pace, firm steps along the length of the windows. Two glorious views. Candy for her sweet-starved eyes.

But warning lights started flashing through her brain as she thought about his words. She'd never had any type of loving parental relationships, and had cut all ties with her mother at the age of seventeen. But Sloan seemed to feel very passionately about his father, despite Vivian's insistence that Mr. Creighton had found his son a huge disappointment. Why had Sloan—

No. Thinking about Sloan's private life—his childhood, wishes, regrets—could not lead to anything good. Personalizing him outside of their business interactions would weaken her objectivity. She had to focus on work, not skipping through fantasyland.

After a minute or two, he clasped his hands behind his back, his long fingers tapping against his palms. "First things first," he murmured. "Where to start—"

"I've got a list here from Mrs. Creighton, and—"

His laughter echoed through the room, the sound truly amused rather than the nasty version she'd heard in Vivian's office. He paused in his imaginary trek to catch his breath and clutched his chest in mock astonishment. "Surely you jest. I don't think so, sweetheart. We'll be doing this my way."

Well, that's reassuring. Ziara had a feeling she was about to get a lesson in all things Sloan—and it would turn everything she'd planned for on its ear. She pulled out her handy-dandy tablet to take notes, since that seemed to be her only function here.

"We'll need new ideas, new designs, definitely a new designer," he said, his voice so matter-of-fact that she blinked for a moment, unable to handle the transition from sexy hunk to demanding boss that quickly. But she managed to pull herself together.

Then his words truly registered. Yikes! A new designer definitely would not go over well.

Sloan continued. "Something splashy. Something to draw in big buyers, get people talking, get them curious..."

He dropped into the chair behind his desk. "Presenting the line, one buyer at a time in the studio, is standard fare. We need a fireworks show, not a firecracker...I've got it!" Sloan jerked to his feet, palms slapping on his desk with enough force to startle her. "We'll bring fashion week right here to Atlanta, Georgia. We'll put on a fashion show." He started to pace, throwing ideas out with such enthusiasm that she found herself pulled into the spirit without even realizing it. Before she knew it, he had location ideas, preshow party ideas, guest list suggestions, and on and on until he ran out of steam about an hour later.

Ziara's fingers ached from typing so fast; even she had to concede to Sloan's intelligence. Once he latched onto an idea, he thought through every angle—catch, plus and minus. Very impressive. If he truly had plans to destroy Eternity Designs, he was going about it the wrong way.

Glancing up in the sudden silence, she found Sloan staring directly at her. She should have been alarmed, afraid of what he might see, but she had sunk so deeply under the spell of his voice that she merely floated.

His eyes widened at whatever he saw in her own, then

flashed with a heat that echoed deep inside her core. The connection remained taut for long moments as the heat gained momentum like a house afire.

Only when it threatened to burst out of control did Ziara panic. She bent her head to focus on the tablet still sitting in her lap. Though she felt hot enough for her fingers to burn it, the tablet was miraculously unsinged.

A new kind of heat enveloped her—embarrassment. As Sloan approached, her teeth worried her lower lip. Would he say something? Think she'd changed her mind about him? Think that she was silently asking him to come on to her? With her limited experience, she wasn't even sure what kind of message she'd just sent. As her imagination picked up speed, Sloan paused a few steps away.

Then he continued around his desk and sat with a squeak of leather. Out of the corner of her eye, she saw his elbows settle onto the arms of the chair as if familiar with the pose, his fingers forming a peak with his fingertips. Relief swept through her, a cooling breeze, though it couldn't extinguish the fire altogether. She chose to ignore it.

"So we'll be putting on a fall fashion show this year. You'll need to book the venue and start construction on the backdrop. Some plans can't be finalized until closer to the actual date, but pick out invitations, contact the modeling agency so we can line up models, all that stuff."

He leaned forward, his gaze seeing into the distance. "My focus will be on finding the right designer to carry out my ideas."

That was a discussion she'd prefer to postpone for, oh, forever. A new designer would shake the foundations of Eternity, regardless of how wonderful he was.

"And what would those ideas be?" she asked, poised to type. How was she going to tell Vivian all of this? Ziara was excited by some of the plans, but change was definitely not Vivian's forte.

Sloan grinned, resorting to his ample sex appeal in the blink of an eye. "Uh-uh. I'm not giving it up that easily."

Their eyes met and held. In the aftermath of their earlier connection, his bright blue gaze unnerved her more than ever. Not only did it threaten her internal control, it made her want to clamp the top of her jacket closed to hide every hint of cleavage. She pressed her thighs together in a purely feminine gesture of defense.

Slowly he rose and circled the desk, leaning his hips against the front. The angle allowed him to tower over her, while inadvertently giving her a level view of—

No, she wouldn't look. Her fight-or-flight instincts kicked in with a rush. She needed a few moments away from this man's disturbing sensuality. Heck, a few hours would be better. Rising to her feet, she said, "If that's all, I'll start—"

"Ziara."

Her fingers fiddled with her tablet while her gaze examined the polished floorboards.

"I expect hard work out of all my employees. I don't think that will be a problem with you. But trust…trust has to be earned, doesn't it?"

The guilt burned deep inside, because she knew she'd have to tell what she'd learned to Vivian—sooner rather than later. But it was her strong work ethic that just might tear her in two. Her dedication demanded she do what was right for Eternity Designs; her loyalty demanded she do anything Vivian asked of her.

"Though hiring and firing is Vivian's department for now," he continued, his voice deceptively benign, "be aware you wouldn't be in this office if I didn't want you to be." He stopped an arm's length from her, bringing the icy heat of his gaze closer, stinging her conscience. "You have your own reasons for being loyal to Vivian."

She heard the implied question behind his statement. She swallowed, the urge to speak unnerving. How could she describe all Vivian had done for her, the hands-on coaching and molding of her abilities? She opted for short and sweet.

"Vivian saw my willingness to do a job right, even as a simple secretary. To uphold the ideals of this company."

"Where tradition and style forever align," Sloan murmured.

A slight smile tugged her lips. Her chin lifted. She knew her intentions here were right, no matter what anyone else thought. Pride in her hard work, in pulling herself up from the bottom rung of the ladder, refused to let him condemn her loyalties. "Yes."

Sloan stepped even closer. The urge to retreat exploded in her belly. Her muscles jumped to high alert, tightening in preparation for flight.

"I, too, value hard work, initiative and loyalty." He paused, as if choosing his words carefully. "Just don't forget who you work for now."

The pressure of his stare proved too much with Vivian's expectations still flashing neon in Ziara's brain. Her gaze fell, grazing his fit body to the tips of his Gucci dress shoes. A short nod was all she could manage.

She wasn't likely to forget anything about Sloan.

Still, the need to push back rose. "Wanting to uphold the values of this company isn't a bad thing. After all, it is the way your father wanted this business run." She ignored the twinge of her conscience. The truth hurt. This time, she leaned closer to him. "People other than you are allowed to care about this place, you know."

Something flashed across his face that she couldn't quite read, but it encouraged her to push harder. Not for Vivian. Not for her job. For Eternity Designs. "If you would just tell me what you're trying to do here instead of leaving me in the dark, then maybe I could help."

He met her halfway, crowding into her personal space with a sexy grin. "You'll have to try harder than that to access my… secrets."

Three

Sloan took a deep breath and wrestled with his libido for a moment before managing to lock it down. How could the simple sounds of Ziara at her desk turn him into a dirty old man? Well, not quite old, if the level of urgency he felt was anything to go by.

They had a long day ahead—he was pretty sure she was going to hate him by the time he was done, but as the saying went, he had to get rid of the old to make room for the new.

He would need Ziara's help to carry out his plans without permanent damage. Robert and Anthony were indeed good designers, but designers who needed a serious shake-up. Vivian had offered Ziara for her expertise and he planned to conquer a large portion of his new territory today.

After a moment of silence, Ziara peeked around the door. "Do you need me for anything this morning, Mr. Creighton?"

Oh, honey, I need you for something really bad. Even though it was totally inappropriate, he couldn't tame the thought. Once again Ziara was wrapped in a narrow skirt and suit jacket, although this one was a dark chocolate-brown that complemented her eyes, bringing out the golden flecks with a glimpse of a silky gold camisole. A little better, though seeing her abundant hair pinned to the nape of her neck just made his hands itch to let it all loose.

He shifted in his seat. "I've got a full agenda today. Where do we stand so far?"

Ziara's efficiency impressed him. Not only had she started contacting people and places yesterday, she'd made a detailed list of the facts so he could compare easily and make decisions.

Old business out of the way, he straightened his shoulders, preparing to face the hardest part of the day. "Let's take a trip down to the design floor and see what's what with the Old Brigade."

The *Old Brigade* was the employees' term for the two main designers who headed and vetted all the dress designs for the company. Though by no means original, they'd each been with the company for over fifteen years.

Ziara hesitated, frozen for a moment like a deer caught in headlights at dusk; then she gathered her tablet and smoothed down her skirt.

He let her maintain her silence as they crossed into the hall, but he couldn't afford for her to hold back. Everything might as well be out in the open.

He stopped in the middle of the deserted hallway. "Look, Ziara," he said, turning to face her. "One of the reasons you're here is to help me with intercompany relations, schedules, procedures, et cetera. Right?"

"Yes, Mr. Creighton."

The prim purse of her full mouth had his brows rising, a grin tugging at his lips. "Didn't we decide on Sloan? After all, over the next three months, we're going to be spending a helluva lot of time together."

Her lips tightened a touch more before she conceded. "Yes, Sloan."

Teasing her out of that "strictly business" attitude was way too much fun. "Now, I can't do my job if you don't do your job—"

A weighty protest formed in her eyes, though her face remained calm. This woman's responses were seriously under wraps. He had to look very closely to catch the signals, but they told him some genuinely hot emotions hid beneath the surface. "Don't get me wrong, you've been very helpful. But I need an honest rundown of what I'm facing on the design floor today."

"I—I—"

"Honesty. Right now. Got it?"

"Why do you need my opinion? You said you'd been here often as a child."

"And as a child I noticed the person most important to me—my father, and the place I spent the most time—his office. The rest? Not so much. I haven't set foot on the design floor since I was ten."

Her gaze zeroed in on his face for a moment, then she spoke. "Anthony and Robert are very talented designers."

Keeping his irritation from showing proved a little easier beneath her disapproving glare.

"The trouble will come from Robert—he's ruled the design floor through talent and overpowering personality for years. Anthony's a sweetheart, but don't take his lack of attitude for subservience. He's soaking it all in, processing it in his own time and making his own decisions."

He grinned. "That wasn't so bad, was it?"

The low growl from her throat surprised him, sending a shock of sensation right where he didn't need it. *Keep it light. Best to just move on.* "Let's go." But he was getting a really good idea how to provoke her into an honest response.

Just irritate her beyond measure.

The elevator took them down to the third floor and they stepped out onto the observation deck. The design department occupied most of the second floor, but the large exhibition space below could be viewed and accessed from the open walkway they now occupied.

As he and Ziara made their way down the spiral staircase, Ziara's heels clicking on the metal steps, the designers appeared to be gearing up for the day.

"Ziara," Robert exclaimed as she descended the last two steps. "What brings you to our little kingdom?"

Anthony simply smiled and wrapped her in a half hug. Her smile was natural and easy, but she didn't return the touch. *Interesting.*

"I wanted to introduce y'all to Mrs. Creighton's stepson, Sloan Creighton."

The designers exchanged a look, but it didn't display as much alarm as Sloan had anticipated. Nor resignation, either. His Spidey senses started to tingle.

"Yes, yes," Robert said, leading the way by offering his hand. "I believe I remember James mentioning you to us, *Dieu ait son âme.*"

God rest his soul, indeed. Out of the corner of his eye, Sloan could see Ziara glance his way. Since it was obvious from their benign reception that neither designer had a clue what was coming down the pike, Sloan decided to play along.

"Vivian tells me you two are working on the fall line. I'd love to see the best of Eternity's upcoming designs," he said, ignoring Ziara's sudden stare.

The men were only too happy to show off. Too bad they didn't realize they were arming him to take them both down. They exchanged excited glances, then walked toward the display boards in unison.

Sloan stepped closer to Ziara as they followed. "Just relax and follow my lead," he murmured from the corner of his mouth.

After listening to Robert expound on the sketches for over half an hour, Sloan was definitely unimpressed. Just as he imagined their buyer had been.

When Robert finally wound down, Sloan's voice filled the stillness. "Did you listen to anything that buyer said?"

The men stiffened, but there wasn't anything they could say in their own defense.

Sloan pushed forward. "She said the designs were stale. She said the dresses were old-fashioned. Not classic. Not retro. Those are buzz words. Compliments. Stale is not." He gestured toward the stack of drawings. "Nothing has changed here. Nothing. I can find this same thing in any bridal magazine—from ten years ago."

"How would you know what the buyer said?" Anthony asked, his voice sounding weak after the booming quality of Robert's.

"And who do you think you are, to come in here and criticize our work?" Robert added.

"I am now the creative director of Eternity Designs's fall line. From here on out, all decisions from this department must be approved solely by me."

The silence was so absolute it rang loud in his ears. Robert's face gradually turned a shade of purple and Anthony's eyes flicked back and forth between the other people in the room as if he expected someone to tell him what was really going on here.

Finally Robert spoke, his voice coming from deep in his barreled chest. "Ziara, if this is a joke, it isn't funny."

"He isn't kidding, Robert," she said in her most soothing voice.

"Look," Sloan said, impatient with the theatrics. "We have a lot to do and a very short time to do it in. Whether you were informed of this decision previously is not my problem. Getting Eternity Designs back on track is—and I'll be doing it my way."

"Why would we need—"

"Are you truly going to pretend you don't know why I'm here?" Sloan met Robert's blustery gaze directly. "You may not pay much attention to financial statements while you're down here in fantasyland, but I know for a fact you were present when the Bridal Boutique buyer ripped your designs apart. Would you like me to go into more detail, or do you remember it for yourself?"

Anthony again joined the conversation. "No, we remember it well enough."

"Good. I am here to get Eternity back in the black and at

the forefront of the wedding apparel industry. So for the next three months you will answer to me—and only me."

"We won't do it," Robert insisted. "After thirty years as a designer, I refuse to have my ideas approved by an amateur."

"Then I'll bring in someone who will."

Harsh. But he knew from his own history that sometimes the hardest lessons were the most memorable...if you used them to your advantage. Just like he'd turned his father's rejection into professional success.

Moving swiftly across the space, Sloan lifted the entire stack of drawings and dumped them into a nearby trash can. "Start over."

Ziara and Anthony gasped at the same time. But it was Robert he continued to focus on, the leader of this little group. Bring him to heel and the rest would follow.

Robert sputtered his indignation while Anthony's face crumpled as if he was going to cry. How in the world could he get through to these yahoos?

Sloan didn't anticipate Ziara's sudden tight grip on his arm. She pulled him out of hearing range and turned to face him.

"Do you really think this is the way to gain their cooperation?"

He tried to focus on her words, but his own frustration quickly morphed into desire as she moved close enough for them to hear each other without eavesdroppers. All that solid, testosterone-induced drive melted into liquid desire that pounded in his veins with a thrumming rhythm. Lord have mercy, how had this woman gotten under his skin so quickly?

"I don't need their cooperation. If they don't do what I tell them, they're out of here."

A repressive frown marred those full lips. "Robert and Anthony have always been the stars of Eternity Designs. You should treat them with more respect."

How could those lips, pressed tight like a disapproving schoolmarm's, still come across as sexy? He was actually struggling to follow her words. Him. The king of keeping things professional.

"Don't you see, Ziara, that's the problem," he finally managed. "They've had people kissing their asses for years, with no challenges to their work. They think they can give a minimal effort and still be put on a pedestal. And Eternity suffers for it."

"They do work—"

He could almost kiss her for the concern in the dark depths of her eyes but it was misplaced. "Not enough. Where's the market research, the fresh, new ideas? They don't just happen by playing around all day. Continued success takes more effort."

Understanding made a reluctant appearance in her gorgeous brown eyes. For some reason it made all the difference in the world to him. "I know I sound harsh. But they're grown men who've been catered to for years. A polite request isn't going to even make a dent." Reaching out, he brushed his thumb along the softened curve of her jaw. "I do have a method behind my madness, I promise."

The feel of her silky skin beneath his touch was magic, along with the warmth and subtle catch of her breath. They both froze in surprise for a moment. It was all Sloan could do to resist brushing his lips over the same spot.

Whoa. This was the design floor, not a nightclub…not even the privacy of his office. And judging by the utter silence laced with antagonism behind his back, Sloan knew *Robert* wouldn't hesitate to throw around accusations of sexual misconduct. With Ziara's approval or without it.

He took a careful step back, letting his hand drop to his side. "Just remember something—I wouldn't be here if they'd been doing their jobs right in the first place. Okay?"

Her nod was firm, though her eyes were still a little dazed.

This meeting needed to get back on track. "Ziara," he snapped, but with a little less bite than he'd used on the men. "The tablet, please."

She hurried to obey, giving him a moment to regain his focus before turning back to the others. When she handed over the device, he noticed the care she took not to touch him again.

After a moment of tapping on the smooth surface, he paused, looking up at the group around him.

"Current trends favor retro designs, new twists on the old, avant-garde as well as classic." During his recent research, he'd seen some unique retro looks in the fashion and wedding magazines, and they had sparked his own creative imagination.

"In less than three months, I'll be showcasing our newest designs during a professional fashion show. We're going to bring fashion week right here to Atlanta. It'll be an exclusive, invitation-only event that I want people talking about for months."

As Sloan continued to explain the fall show, excitement crept over the anger that had tightened the designers' faces. He might have punctured their egos earlier, but now he was tempting them.

Lifting the tablet, he turned it around to face them. "Every event needs a theme, a focal point. This is ours."

"A car? Are you insane?" Robert yelled, returning to his angry disbelief.

"Not just any car, a Rolls-Royce. A classic car epitomizing the elegance, sleek design and subtle sensuality of the late 1930s. An era where women flaunted sexy curves, draped their bodies with fabrics that showcased their femininity, and set out to entice the opposite sex. Think of the actresses of the time—Marlene Dietrich, Mae West, Vivian Leigh. The dresses they wore—the draped material, exposed backs..."

He caught a glimmer of understanding in Ziara's eyes. Knowledge of where he was going with this idea.

"Ridiculous," Robert insisted. "This is the stupidest thing I've heard in my lifetime."

Sloan wasn't backing down. "We're going to do this and do it right. Get on board, or jump overboard. Your choice."

When had work started feeling like a taffy puller?

Ziara waited until Sloan left the building for lunch before heading to Vivian's office. Her stomach cramped, knowing Vivian would have already heard about the upcoming show, but also knowing she couldn't blatantly walk out of Sloan's office straight to his stepmother's.

Observing Sloan for two days had taught her one thing already—he wasn't playing. His knowledge this morning showed he had done his homework on the market, design, themes, even fashion shows. He'd been calm but firm, occasionally harsh, with Robert and Anthony. Stepping solidly into a leadership role, even if he had to do it by force.

Most disturbing of all, his ideas for the show intrigued her.

With some organization, this could be an incredibly successful event, one the upper classes of Atlanta society would flock to in droves. Eternity Designs would be on the tip of everyone's tongues and the front page in the society section. Notable brides would once again be drawn to the showroom for one-of-a-kind dresses.

But to her shame, Sloan's appeal continued to taunt her on a more physical level. Vivian had insisted she was the last woman who would be tempted by Sloan's charm, but the need that had crawled into her body at his singular touch frightened her. She'd seen her mother move from man to man, taking whatever they could give her, using her body to manipulate them. Mixing business with pleasure was the last thing Ziara wanted in her life. The level of temptation here actually scared her bone deep.

Abigail gave her a sympathetic look as she entered the room. "She's waiting on you, Ziara."

I bet she is. Her hand pausing on the doorknob, Ziara only let herself hesitate a second before going in.

"Ah, Ziara," Vivian said from behind her antique desk. "I see you have finally deigned to bring me news."

Vivian gestured for her to sit. The walk across the room distracted Ziara from the uneasiness caused by Vivian's words. "I felt it appropriate to wait until Sloan left for lunch—"

"Why? He's surely aware that one of your jobs is to keep me informed. Next time I want to hear it from you, rather than the office grapevine."

Yes, but I couldn't bring myself to rub my choices in his face.

She'd probably heard from the Old Brigade, who'd run to Vivian to tattle the minute they'd realized they were losing control.

Ziara wondered if they remembered Vivian had once been a mere secretary—and how long it had taken them to accept the new order of things when she took over. Given the evidence from this morning, Ziara didn't think acceptance had come quickly.

"I'm very excited about this new idea for the line's presentation," she started.

"Ah yes, the fashion show. I hate to admit it, but I'm seeing the merits of this plan myself. I want a full report."

"I've just started working on the details. I'm looking into venues, modeling agencies and such."

"Keep me informed as everything takes shape."

Ziara murmured, "Yes, ma'am," under her breath, but Vivian was already moving on.

"Make it good. Getting some choice buyers in here will make this the must-have ticket of the fall season. I'll have Abigail get you a list of contacts, and I want to know as soon as the RSVPs come in."

If Sloan was a train squishing her on the tracks, Vivian was a wrecking ball, destroying Ziara's calm handling of this difficult assignment. Her mentor ran through a laundry list of items she wanted Ziara to check into, almost doubling the amount of work Sloan had given her. She saw quite a few late nights in her near future.

"Since you will be in the thick of all of this, Ziara—" Vivian's spine straightened as if bracing herself for what was to come "—you should know…if our largest buyer pulls her orders, as she has threatened if the line doesn't move in a more modern, unique direction, it will put the company in a very disadvantageous financial position."

Even Vivian's attempt at genteel diplomacy couldn't hide the facts: Eternity Designs was in deep financial trouble. The confirmation of the actual problem had Ziara's stomach dropping like it would on a roller coaster, a ride she avoided getting on at all costs.

Coming to work here, helping to build some of the finest dresses and dreams, had been like finding her true home. She wasn't ready to leave.

Vivian's fingers spun her wedding band in an endless circle. "So you can see how very important it is for the fall line to be not just good, but spectacular. By putting you in his office, I can let Sloan think he's in charge until we see what he decides to do with the fall line." Vivian's heeled pump set up a twitchy rhythm. "I've known him for a long time. He's sneaky, deceptive. His mother's lower-class roots are showing, I guess."

Ziara controlled the surprise that threatened to bloom on her face. Social standing had always been important to Vivian, but Ziara had never before seen evidence of prejudice.

"I know you said he was rebellious as a teenager." Perfectly normal, in Ziara's opinion. "Why would you think he's up to something now?"

Being on the receiving end of Vivian's glare wasn't comfortable.

"Haven't you ever heard that a leopard never changes its spots?" Vivian asked. "Besides, there are rumors that he uses some rather ruthless tactics to get his way these days." Her pen tapped against her desk. One thump, then two. "He's up to something," she continued. "And I need to stay on top of it. *You* need to stay on top of it."

Ziara wasn't sure if the turmoil gaining ground in her gut was troubled conscience or the guilt of temptation, but she couldn't simply ignore it. "Vivian, I really, well, I simply think that someone else might be more suited to working with Sl—Mr. Creighton. I could easily coordinate the show details from—"

"His office. That's where I put you and that's where you will stay. Or is there some reason you would request a change?"

The last thing Ziara wanted to do was explain the ins and outs of the past two days. If only she could make Vivian understand... "Honestly, I don't feel very comfortable with the position I'm in. If you think Sloan will stop anything he's doing because of me, well, he won't. I just—"

Vivian's head tilted slightly to the side, her brown eyes studying Ziara with sudden intensity. For the first time in a long time, Ziara wanted to hide from her boss, to squirrel away the reactions she had to Sloan just as she had the secrets of her past. Vivian would never accept her if she knew either one.

"Have I not done enough for you, Ziara?"

Not expecting the attack, Ziara found herself speechless.

"Have I not taught you all that I can about running this business, about behaving professionally, about coming out ahead of those not willing to put every ounce of effort into their jobs?"

"Yes, ma'am. You've been more than generous."

"Then why do I suddenly feel like all of that effort has been wasted on the wrong person?"

Panic shot deep, mixing with the fear Ziara carried on a daily basis: that one day, everything she'd worked so hard for would crash down into a pile of rubble. She would not go back to being the uneducated girl condemned by everyone around her.

"I certainly don't want you to feel that way," Ziara said over the pounding of her heart. "I'm very grateful—"

"I see plenty, Ziara," Vivian snapped, her eyes as harsh as her tone. "And what I'm seeing isn't gratitude, understand?"

Knowing she'd overstepped Vivian's invisible limit, Ziara conceded quickly. "Yes, ma'am."

"You've worked very hard to get where you are, Ziara. That's why I chose you to succeed Abigail as my executive assistant when she retires later this year."

At the praise, a glow bloomed beneath her fear. She'd yearned to be recognized for her accomplishments for as long as she could remember. First at school, then at community college, from her first job till now. Though she hadn't found validation at home, her move to Atlanta had been the start of a whole new life.

"I'm confident that you'll do what's best for Eternity Designs." Vivian stood, her posture and classically tailored business suit a picture of authority. Ziara moved quickly to join her.

"This position, though difficult, will also be excellent training for you, and I don't have to worry about the Creighton good looks turning your head like some of the less dedicated girls around here. Do I?"

Ziara realized the question was rhetorical, so she simply shook her head, keeping her growing doubts to herself. Oh, she had no intention of falling into bed with a man like Sloan Creighton. On the other hand, how did she keep his charm and obvious business smarts from influencing her away from what Vivian wanted?

Vivian moved on, unaware of Ziara's fears. "By the time we come out of this, Eternity Designs will be set for the future. I'll be in charge, and you'll have that job as my E.A."

Ziara shifted in her heels. "But what if he succeeds? How can you risk him gaining a majority's ownership if you don't trust him?"

Vivian turned away, her face hidden as she crossed to the window. "Don't worry," she said, twisting her wedding ring around her finger again. "I'll take care of that."

Knowing she'd been dismissed, Ziara retreated to the safety of the outer office, where Abigail waited with a kind smile and some lists.

"Thank you, Abigail."

"No problem, sweetie. Just let me know if you have any questions."

How about, *Will I make it through this without losing my freakin' mind?* Or, *Is everyone going to hate me before this show is over?* But she said nothing, conscious for once of exactly how alone she was.

Walking through the doorway, she found Sloan leaning against her desk. Her stomach dropped to her toes and a flush suffused her cheeks. The guilt was probably glaring out from her downcast gaze and shifting feet.

Where was this guilt coming from? A shot of surprise jolted through her at the answer. The guilt didn't stem from tattling like a four-year-old. That was the best thing for Eternity Designs…for now. She simply didn't want to face him knowing she'd tried to get out of working with him. Her feet stuttered to stillness and she swallowed, praying her voice would work at this point. "May I help you with something, Mr. Creighton?"

Those bright blue eyes, so full of life earlier today, were now cold enough to freeze the devil himself in his tracks. His mouth crooked up on one side, his boyish good looks now brittle around the edges. Oh yeah, he knew what she was up to, and there was no defense against that knowledge.

"I don't know why I'm surprised."

For some unknown reason, she couldn't brush this moment aside with professionalism or tactful confusion. "I don't know, either. You told me you understood my duties here."

"That doesn't mean I have to like it."

Me, either.

Ziara struggled to return to that place where she was strictly a secretary performing an assigned task, but she couldn't. Some kind of barrier had been breached with his touch earlier today, and she was very afraid there was no going back from it.

She had the distinct feeling he wouldn't let her go back even if she tried. His next words confirmed her suspicions. "Too bad I can't give you what you really deserve."

"And what would that be?" she asked, though the naughty mischief melting the iceberg should have warned her she'd moved into dangerous territory.

"A spanking."

Four

The next few days went by relatively smoothly as Ziara discovered the ins and outs of working for Sloan Creighton.

He liked his coffee black with just a touch of sugar for sweetness, but he only drank it in the morning. After eleven, he switched to Mountain Dew. He came into the office around nine-thirty every morning, smelling of citrus and a spicy undertone after his daily game of racquetball. He paced while he dictated letters, his long legs performing for her benefit alone. While dreaming up new show ideas, he liked to lean back in his chair with his Gucci-clad feet propped on the edge of the desk.

She often caught a glimpse of him standing at those floor-to-ceiling windows watching people walk by five stories below, deep enough in thought that she'd close the door behind her with extra force to remind him of her presence.

She was getting to know him way too well.

This new knowledge was uncomfortable, but not as uncomfortable as the suspicion that he was cataloging some things about her, as well. Those damn eyes! Not to mention the occasional spicy remark, like that spanking comment, that she pretended to ignore no matter how outrageous he got. The last thing he needed was encouragement.

Today shattered the routine when Sloan hit the outer door like a bull. She hadn't seen that controlled anger since his first day, that contained heat he'd wielded against Vivian like a fine-tuned weapon.

"I've got a lot of calls to make, Ziara. Don't bother me."

"Yes, Mr. Creighton," she said reverting to formality in her confusion. She watched those long strides carry him into his office, the door slamming behind him. Definitely a good day to keep her head down and work on clearing the clutter from her desk.

A few hours of muffled yelling and banging later, she decided now was probably a good time to escape. She made her way through the corridors to the design floor. Anthony met her a few feet in with a quick and quiet hug. He knew exactly why she was here. Leading her across the room, he showed her the new shipment of sample materials scattered across a large table.

"Robert is very upset with me," he said. "He thinks I'm a sellout."

Ziara glanced over his shoulder at the normally boisterous man now sitting quietly at a drafting table. "Why would he think that?" she asked, keeping her voice low to match Anthony's.

He gestured toward the materials. "Because I ordered these."

Ziara took in the mixtures of cream, pinks, barely there blues and an almost yellow color on a display table that was normally white, white and white. "Hmm. I can see where that would be a problem."

"I've tried to move Robert in new directions for years now, especially as grumblings surfaced from the buyers. But he just won't listen."

"I don't think Mr. Creighton will give him that option."

"Well, maybe he will succeed where I have failed." With a sad smile, he wandered back across the room, leaving Ziara alone for what he knew was her favorite pastime.

Picking up the nearby invoices, she started matching the

materials on the table with the names and prices on the sheets of paper. She studied the fresh array of colors, the textures, drape and a myriad of other things.

In an ideal world—where she would have had a supportive family, scholarships and no need to be her own sole support immediately after getting her GED—she would have been a supplier, searching out the finest materials, the best deals for the entire company in accessories, gemstones, beading, lining, everything. As it was, she could spend hours immersed in the research but allowed herself only small windows here and there. Luckily Anthony wasn't threatened by her presence or interest, so he'd spent many a minute teaching her bits and pieces. Bless his heart.

"Enjoying yourself?"

Ziara froze, her hand buried in a pile of pink-tinged satin. To her knowledge, Vivian didn't know about her little visits here. Yet it hadn't taken Sloan a week to uncover her secret.

"I'm sorry, Mr. Creigh—um, Sloan. Did you need me for something?"

When he squeezed the back of his neck as if to relieve the tension gathered there, she couldn't help but sympathize.

"I definitely need you, Ziara. Don't you know that?"

Her gaze zeroed in on his face, searching for the intention behind the words. His bright blue eyes were now tired, but a shiver of awareness still snuck down her spine. No matter how he looked, no matter what he said, she felt he was bringing her to an awareness of him as a man—and herself as a woman.

She murmured, "I'm happy to oblige." Then cringed inside at the many ways her words could be misinterpreted. She straightened as he moved closer. He reached toward her stomach, which tightened in anticipation—but his hand bypassed her to explore the materials on the table beyond.

A smoky-blue chiffon, almost gray, held his attention. "Very nice," he murmured, the sound almost seductive, as though he was encouraging…something. He lifted the material, testing the feel, weight and drape.

His hands fascinated her, the long fingers with their neatly clipped nails a sharp contrast to the fragile-looking material. But his eyes drew her, too. Those bright blues had darkened as if he were looking inward rather than at the material he handled so skillfully.

"What is this?" he asked.

"It's a light chiffon, mostly used for accents and layering," she said.

Snapping out of his thoughts, he glanced at her in surprise. "Been studying your materials, have you?"

Warmth flooded into her cheeks and chest. "Anthony has been teaching me."

Rather than the condemnation she'd expected, his eyes softened in appreciation. "Show me."

Sloan found himself entranced as Ziara explained the contrasts between silks, chiffons, satins and numerous other materials used in dressmaking. Not over the information itself, even though it was appreciated, but the unguarded spark in her eyes.

Then there was the show: her slender arms lifting each material to demonstrate its ability to drape, the thickness and what it might be used for.

"You could have been a supplier," he said, drawn in by her enthusiasm.

The stillness that invaded her body told him he'd hit a sore spot, even though her lowered lashes hid her expression from him. Not quite understanding, he asked, "Why didn't you? This stuff obviously interests you."

The muscles around her mouth tightened, then she raised her guarded gaze. "Fashion production and supply chain management degrees don't come cheap." She started sorting the material by color. "Tuition was nonexistent for me, so that type of dream wasn't even on the table. I looked at my options and chose what worked with my skills. It wasn't until I came here that I realized how interesting this side of the business could be."

"Your parents weren't able to help?"

Her mouth twisted. "Not even close. It was just my mother and me, anyway. She didn't think school was worth much."

"What about your guidance counselor? If your grades were good, scholarships could have helped."

"Maybe in another life."

The spark of curiosity that ran through his body was exciting but dangerous. He took the leap, anyway. "Why?"

Finally she stopped rearranging the material so she could glare at him. "Look. I came from a really small town, even more southern than Atlanta, with not enough money and very few options. I worked my way through secretarial school with two jobs, eating peanut butter from a spoon every night. Not everyone needs a high salary and trust fund to be successful."

That should have stung—and it did, but not in the personal way he expected. He could see how hard she must have worked to attain her level of success at such a young age—which meant this wasn't just a job to her.

She wasn't just Vivian's pet.

He couldn't think about what that meant to his plans. So he let his mind conjure pictures of her caressing the fabric. Within seconds, he began to visualize designs: a sleek gown of pale pink satin, almost bright against her dark skin, drifting low over her naked back, accented with white diamonds and silver thread. The smoky chiffon shaped into three-dimensional flowers at the shoulders of a structured gray, almost silver, silk dress. The creamy yellow draped tight across her torso in tiny pleats that met at the curve of her hip, then released into a waterfall of softly lilting, creamy white feathers.

All of them made exclusively for the incredible body before him.

His horrible morning dissolved under the rush of creative energy.

"What are you thinking?" he heard her say, her voice echoing slightly as she pulled him from his own head, that place where he created all the things he needed, wanted, with the easy strokes of his mind.

It didn't matter whether it was building plans, an office design, extensive renovations...or, apparently, wedding dresses. He had only to envision it and the lines appeared in the forefront of his mind. It was very helpful, incredibly productive and totally intoxicating.

Which was the only explanation he had for what he did next. Reaching around her to the desk, he snagged paper and a drawing pencil. The move brought him flush with her side, prompting a surge of heat wherever their bodies met, though he forced himself to move away quickly.

He could tell she felt it, too, by the widening of her eyes and the way she held her breath. He shoved the materials on the table aside and started to draw. Within minutes, he had a simple outline of the pink satin dress he'd imagined, though he kept the distinctive characteristics of the model vague.

"Wow," she breathed. "That's gorgeous."

"Thank you."

Her smile warmed him, intoxicating in its sincerity. He often had the feeling that she simply responded to him the way she should, the way an assistant was expected to respond to her boss. Not this time.

Fire lurked beneath the surface of this buttoned-down babe, and he desperately wanted to release it—even if he was her boss.

"I mean it," he continued, anxious to avoid the temptation of his thoughts. "You've shown me exactly what I need."

Before he could do something stupid like kiss those full red lips, he pivoted on his heel and walked away. Now that he had a direction, he knew just how to carry it out.

Eternity Designs would never be the same.

Sloan stalked down the hall toward the elevators, the adrenaline still thrumming through his veins. Pictures of Ziara racing through his mind.

"How's your new assistant working out, Sloan?"

Damn it. He'd been so close to the open doorway!

He pivoted to find Vivian standing in the shadows. Had she been waiting for him to walk by? Had she watched as he and Ziara talked?

"Great choice, Vivian. She'll serve me just fine, I think."

Vivian studied him with the same barely tolerant expression she'd used after many of his teenage escapades. "What's wrong?"

Ah, the pitfalls of working with someone who'd watched him grow up. He moved a few steps closer. Lowering his voice, he tightened his control over the high levels of excitement, frustration and arousal still surging through his veins.

"It won't work, Vivian. Whatever reason you have for planting Ziara in my office—it won't work. I'm still going to do what I think is best for Eternity."

Patronizing was the only way to describe her smile. "I know exactly where Ziara's loyalties lie. She'll do the job I gave her."

"I'm going ahead with my plans, regardless." The feel of the sketch held securely in his grasp brought a surge of certainty. He was on the right path; now he needed the one person who would help him carry it out.

"So you've talked the Old Brigade into actually carrying out your crazy theme?" she asked, concern dampening her smug demeanor. Ah, she'd be so happy if he was stuck working with her two lackeys, wouldn't she?

"Robert and Anthony will fall in line soon enough." His chest tightened as all his earlier frustration rushed forward again.

She shook her head slowly. "Not according to Robert—I believe his exact words were 'over my dead body.'"

Her smug expression shattered his control like nothing else could have. "I wouldn't get too tickled if I were you."

"And why is that?"

"I'm about to turn Eternity Designs upside down."

The *ding* of the elevator signaled his escape. Sloan strode through the doors and turned back to see Vivian's perplexed expression just as they closed.

Five

Ziara dished up her quick version of paella into an oversize, bright green bowl, pausing a moment to inhale the spicy scent of peppers, andouille sausage and shrimp. Padding across to the table, she savored the coolness of the tiled kitchen floor on her bare feet.

After a long, deep drink of sweetened tea, she picked up her book in one hand and her fork in the other. Having survived her rough day at work, her mind craved the relaxing and safe surroundings of home. An early start to her weekend.

She'd worked so hard for her house and turned it into her very own sanctuary. Most important, it was as far from the environment she'd grown up in as possible.

Only here could she let down the defenses. She could safely indulge her passion for cooking, love of reading and flair for color.

She desperately needed that in the aftermath of her confusing response to her boss. Sloan was flirty, no doubt about it, but she'd always held herself to a higher standard. To think a few smiles, some genuine listening and one hot touch could turn her sensible head made her very angry—with herself.

The first bite of paella ignited a burn on her tongue that spread like flash fire up the walls of her mouth to the roof and inner edge of her lips. Yummy, but she suspected her turbulent thoughts had made her heavy-handed with the spices.

Ziara jumped at the jangle of the doorbell. She rarely had visitors—no family, no close friends. It was only five, so it was still fairly light out. Daylight savings time wouldn't hit for another month. Maybe it was a salesman or one of the neighbors' kids fund-raising for school. She sighed.

Traversing the short hallway linking the kitchen with the living room, Ziara paused to glance through the small window that ran down the side of the door. She wasn't above pretending she wasn't home.

The silhouette on the other side didn't quite register at first except to look vaguely familiar. Then, in an instant, it felt as if the heat from the paella exploded at the base of her neck and spread along her skull. Surely that wasn't Sloan so casually posed in the shade of her front porch?

She jerked back, suddenly vulnerable in her cotton yoga pants and old T-shirt, so thin it offered little to no coverage.

Cringing when the doorbell rang again, she looked up to find Sloan blocking the view from the window. Well, he knew she was here. Good manners insisted she open the door and see what he wanted. Muttering under her breath, she decided she now had a very personal reason for being irritated.

Grasping the cool metal of the knob, she pulled the door open just enough to see his handsome face.

"Sloan," she said, her voice more a question than an acknowledgment. She didn't issue an invitation, but apparently he didn't need one. Placing his palm flat on the door, he pushed inside, walking by her as if coming in was his right. She stood dumbfounded for a moment, then closed the door and leaned back against it, her arms crossed beneath breasts that tingled in his presence—without her permission.

"To what do I owe the pleasure?"

Her tone implied that seeing him was as far from a pleasure as she could get. She'd been well on the road to relaxation, but now her back was military straight and the muscles on each side of her neck tightened in protest. Even worse, she couldn't decide if it was because she didn't want him here... or because she did.

"Hi." He flashed his usual confident smile.

Up went her brow. He studied her expression with interest before his gaze moved to his surroundings.

A sense of invasion rose from the pit of her stomach, overriding the awareness that always seemed to come with his presence. She shifted uneasily as he walked around the room, gliding a finger along her favorite fleece throw and pausing to examine the exotic lines of the dancer in the picture over the mantel.

"Sloan," she said when the tension ratcheted up to an unbearable high, "what are you doing here?"

He faced her, his calm expression mocking the tremble that had slipped into her voice.

"I'll tell you," he said, "if you give me a plate of whatever smells so good. Suddenly I'm very hungry."

No, her mind screamed. She didn't want his presence lingering in her home, but short of pushing him back out the door, she had no idea how to refuse.

Sucking in a deep breath, she led the way back to the kitchen, ultraconscious as she passed him of the air grazing her bare arms and the gentle slap of her feet on the uncarpeted floors.

Crossing to the cabinet, she decided she might as well comply and find out what was going on. With efficient movements, she fixed him a plate and drink before settling him at the opposite end of the table from her. She ignored the smirk on his face as she returned to her seat.

He lifted his fork, then sniffed appreciatively before meeting her eyes.

"I know the perfect designer."

"I wasn't aware we needed one. We already have two." His

knowing look had her admitting, "Okay, we have at least one willing to help."

"But I've figured out the one person who can bring my vision to life."

His epiphany obviously accounted for the change in his mood, but not his presence—his most unwanted presence—here. "I'm glad. Couldn't this have waited until Monday?"

He shook his head, then hefted a heaping forkful of rice and spicy meat to his mouth. It had to be a sin to watch those sculpted lips close around anything, even something as innocent as a fork.

She didn't warn him about the heat. He'd probably just blow it off with some macho line. Besides, he was part of what had led to all that spice in the first place.

Suddenly his eyes widened and he coughed, just managing to keep the food in his mouth long enough to swallow. She leaned back with a feeling of satisfaction as his hand shot out for his glass. That would teach him not to push his way in where he wasn't wanted.

"Wow," he said after a long drink of iced tea, "that packs a wallop."

Watching him dig back in without a hint of hesitation, she thought, *Yes, it does*. "I'm glad you like it," she murmured, instead.

He cleared most of his plate, all the while studying her with intent looks that burned more than the food burned her mouth. Goose bumps spread along her skin despite the heat of the food.

She pushed her long hair back behind her shoulders, licking her dry, spicy lips. "Does Vivian approve of the new designer?"

"On the contrary, she'd have a very genteel hissy fit if she knew who he was."

She hesitated. Her gaze locked on her nearly empty plate before braving another glance at him. "So you haven't discussed this with her?"

He shook his head, waves of dark blond hair caressing the masculine angles of his face. "I don't plan to clue her in anytime soon." He leaned forward. "Do you?"

She leaned forward, too. "Let's get one thing straight. Whatever actions I take are for the good of the company. Convince me of the merits of your plan, and you won't have to worry about where my loyalties lie."

He stood, prowling around the sunny kitchen. His cool good looks blended with the greens and golds, the blue accents a reflection of his eyes, the pine cabinets just a touch lighter than his hair. He looked as if he belonged in this room.

He was testing her, but instead of resentment, an excited rush sizzled inside.

"This place isn't anything like I'd imagined," he said out of the blue.

As he took in the kitchen and her in one sweep, she wished for the ability to snap her fingers and be wearing a business suit instead of her relax-and-cook gear.

In an attempt to repress more personal discussions, she said, "I can't think why you'd wonder about it at all."

He stalked across the room and reached out to touch a strand of her loose hair that had fallen forward over her shoulder. "Who knew you had so much to hide."

Her quick intake of breath was her only outward response, but inside she mentally retreated. She couldn't afford to let him in on her secrets if she wanted to remain a respectable part of his business. Knowing would change everything. It always did. The few she'd told her deepest feelings to had turned their backs on her in an instant, and then she'd learned the golden rule of silence.

Standing, she stalked back down the hall and pulled the door open, not so discreetly inviting him to leave.

He followed, the soft-soled boots he wore silent on the wood floor, his face unreadable. Pulling a card from his wallet, he scribbled on the back. "Here's my cell phone number in case you need to contact me."

She stared blankly at the card in his hand. "Aren't you coming into the office on Monday?"

"No," he said. "And neither are you."

"Why not?"

That sexy grin was back. "Pack your bags. We're going to Vegas."

Six

Sloan arrived at the airport with plenty of time to spare. He eased through security, then settled in to wait. Ziara seemed the type to arrive early, but after last night he realized he didn't know a thing about her. Not the real Ziara. Underneath that cool, businesslike exterior lurked a woman he suspected burned as hot as her paella. That intrigued him. What intrigued him more was the *why*.

Why was she so different at work? This wasn't a case of the same woman just acting on a more professional level. No, this was two totally different women.

The rich, resonant colors in the living room—burgundy, flaming oranges and yellows, deep purple accented with gold— seemed such a natural setting for her dark beauty. Why would she dress down in drab grays, browns and navies?

That hair, soft around her face, a silky waterfall draping her chest and shoulders, made him want to spread it across a pillow or, better yet, across his chest. Of course, if she was hoping to disguise her thick, satin glory, she'd failed. Pulling it up to the crown of her head as she did at work only emphasized the exotic slant of her eyes and the exquisite lines of her cheekbones.

Did she get her spicy, riveting beauty from her mother? In all the simple elegance of her home, Sloan hadn't seen one personal photograph on display—not one of Ziara or any family, which struck him as odd.

He glanced over to see her standing in line for security. Looking at his watch, he realized she'd waited until the last moment to arrive. He smiled. Now that he knew what was inside, he wouldn't let her revert back to "all business."

A familiar ache built throughout his body as he watched her progress across the waiting area. The whoosh of adrenaline was similar to the rush of creativity, only a thousand times stronger. He no longer just wanted this woman—he *had* to have her. Which was a problem, because he was technically her boss. Temporarily. Although, if she was also his lover, then he'd know exactly where her loyalties lay. He could live with that…couldn't he?

"Good morning, Sloan," she said, settling into a seat across the aisle from him.

He frowned as she pulled out her mobile phone and searched for a number. "Don't you know it's rude to ignore someone to talk on the phone?"

"Not when it's business."

"What's business?"

She motioned between the two of them. "This trip." Waving the phone for a minute, she continued, "And this call."

Oh, no she didn't. "What kind of business call could you possibly be making on a Saturday morning?"

"I'm calling Vivian. It was too late to call her last night and I should let her know where we'll be. You didn't give me nearly enough time pack and get ready and call her this morning."

And I'm not about to give you a chance now, either. He eyed her stiff shoulders and the haughty tilt to her chin as she studied the screen. She wore her defiance like a uniform—one he wanted to remove inch by inch. "Don't, Ziara."

"Why not?"

"Seriously? What good is it going to do?"

"It just might preserve my job when all this is over," she said, those chocolate eyes finally meeting his head-on. "Or did you forget that someone else has a stake in this besides you?"

Ouch. He knew it, even when he wished he didn't. *Not everyone needs a high salary and trust fund to be successful.* She needed her job. If everything didn't work out, he'd help her find a new one.

Standing, he loomed over her, hearing the call to board blast from the speakers around them. "Still, I'm in charge on this trip. Remember?"

With a quick snatch, he grabbed her phone and stored it deep in the pocket of his khakis. Still within reach...barely.

"Give that back," she demanded, her voice shaking.

"No. But you are welcome to come get it, if you want."

The anger that exploded over her face didn't hide the hint of interest that surfaced. Enjoying a touch of satisfaction, he grabbed his carry-on and strolled across the waiting area to board the flight. The whole time he could feel her glare directly between his shoulder blades.

This would be a fun flight.

On the plane, she lowered into the seat next to him with exquisite care, her tense jaw signaling extreme displeasure. He really shouldn't be enjoying this so much.

"Give back my phone."

"No," he said, giving a little jiggle of his pocket. "Look at it this way—at least you'll have an excuse when she asks why you didn't call."

If he had to guess, he'd say he was seeing his assistant go supernova. Not a sound was made, but the air almost shook around her before she closed her eyes and drew in a deep breath. As they started to taxi, she took out a paperback and began to read. Clearly all avoidance tactics were in full effect now, probably for his own safety. He grinned. Biding his time was a talent he'd long ago acquired.

He allowed her to avoid him until they'd reached cruising

altitude. Then his nimble fingers plucked the book from hers before she knew what was coming.

"Hey," she protested. "Are you planning to make stealing a habit?"

"I don't know. Haven't you learned yet it's rude to ignore the person you're traveling with?"

She angled herself toward the window, leaving him with a devastating view of her elegant nose and full lips, not to mention thick lashes that added to the mystery of her eyes. "I didn't want you to feel you had to entertain me."

He handed back the book, murmuring, "I'll just bet you did."

She shot him a sharp look but tucked the book into her purse for safekeeping. Settling back in her seat, she folded her hands in her lap like the prim woman he suspected she wasn't. If she only knew what that contradiction did to him. Actually, it was probably a good thing she didn't. Ten thousand feet up in an airplane wasn't the ideal place for arousal.

"Aren't you curious about the designer we're going to see?"

She tilted her head toward him, the sun through the window highlighting the curve of her jaw and the smooth caramel skin of her neck. He bet she'd taste just as sweet.

"Okay," she said, drawing out the word. "I'll bite. Who is it?"

Sloan accepted a drink from the flight attendant. Passing Ziara one of the small glasses, he deliberately brushed his fingers along hers. Her quick retreat confirmed his suspicions. She wasn't as immune to him as she'd like. If he played his cards right on this trip, Ziara's loyalties to him would far outweigh any hold Vivian had on her.

"Patrick was my college roommate. He was a fashion design major while I stuck it out on the business track." He paused a moment at her considering look. "I immediately thought of him when I decided to do this project, but he turned me down."

"Then why are we on a plane to Las Vegas?"

"I'm going to change his mind."

* * *

Great. She wasn't on a flight to Las Vegas to meet their new designer but to court one. A reluctant one.

She shouldn't be surprised that Sloan wouldn't take no for an answer. Keeping that in mind in her own dealings with him would be smart. After all, hadn't he just shown her in graphic detail how opposed he was to a little phone call? If he thought she was going to go diving into his pants for her phone—or tell Vivian exactly where said phone had been—he was gravely mistaken.

Maybe she could dig into his plans before he realized what she was doing and shut her out completely.

"I don't know of any big wedding dress designers based in Vegas. Who does he work for?"

Sloan's smirk didn't answer any questions; it only created more. "You won't believe it until you see it."

She sighed in frustration. "What does that mean?"

He leaned toward her, his eyes meeting hers head-on. Her stomach jumped, but she told herself it was from turbulence.

"Ziara, we're on our way to Las Vegas. Relax and enjoy a little pleasure with your business."

Alarm skittered through Ziara when her mental walls didn't go up immediately. She actually wanted to give in to the attraction tempting her, but knew doing so would cost her all she'd worked so hard for, so she pulled back.

"I'm just here to work," she said, hoping she sounded like an old, repressive aunt. "What do you think it will take to convince this friend of yours to change his mind?"

He frowned, collapsing back in his seat. She couldn't help but admire the ease he seemed to feel in his body. "Probably something I'm not going to want to give."

"Why?"

"Because he knows me too well."

She angled toward him in her small seat. "So you must have been really close and stayed in touch all this time."

He shrugged. "We have similar interests."

What did that mean? Ziara wanted to pull her hair in frustration. Or better yet, shake Sloan until all the answers she wanted just tumbled out. His secretive, *I don't trust you* attitude was getting really old, really quick. If he couldn't trust her, that was his problem. Though she should probably be happy she wasn't dealing with a flirty, sexy boss, instead.

"Is there anything you'd like to do in Vegas?" Sloan asked out of the blue. "A show? Shopping?" His gaze slid over her, heating her flesh even through her sensible pantsuit. "Dance with a sexy stranger?"

From anyone else, the question would have seemed presumptuous and sleazy, but from Sloan it was, well, presumptuous and tempting. What would it be like to dance secure in his arms, to give herself up to his lead without having to worry where he'd take her? Without having to worry how he'd feel about her in the morning?

She'd never chance it. This time she leaned forward, meeting him head-on so there would be no mistakes. This tactic had worked time and again in the past. Attitude was everything, though the lock on her bedroom door had come in handy too.

She might be physically tempted like never before, but it wouldn't show. She wouldn't allow it.

"Let's get this straight," she said in a calm, nonthreatening sort of way. "I have no interest outside of helping you find your designer and launch the fall line. I'm here to do my job. Period."

Instead of backtracking or scrambling for excuses like all the men before him under her no-nonsense glare, Sloan simply watched her lips as she formed the words, his gaze tracing every curve. The urge to moisten them with a slip of her tongue grew strong.

A satisfied expression crossed his face, as if he'd stumbled upon a secret she hid deep inside. "We'll see," he said simply, then leaned back in his chair and closed his eyes, leaving her to stew in her amazement at his audacity.

We'll see. *We'll see?* He'd see nothing more than her hand making contact with his face if he tried to pull anything on her.

She knew far too much about the ways of men and the

lengths they'd go to have a woman. She'd seen every trick before; nothing impressed her now. They all ended up looking at you like trash once you gave in. She'd vowed a long time ago that she'd never endure that. Respect meant everything to her. If she couldn't have it romantically, she'd earn it through hard work and initiative in her career.

She never let herself down. That was the only thing she could count on.

Seven

Ziara kept reminding herself of that until the plane touched down late that afternoon. The Nevada heat drained her. Just walking from the airport to the taxi sparked a thirst that for once had nothing to do with Sloan.

They checked into the hotel with relative ease. The elegant suite, thankfully complete with two bedrooms with locking doors, offered an enticing view from Ziara's balcony. Despite her resolve to focus on work, Ziara couldn't deny the little tendrils of excitement spreading through her veins. Vegas was an animal all its own and it tempted her curiosity almost as much as Sloan and his mystery designer.

As the sunset crept over the horizon and lights sparked on, she didn't care about the reputation of Sin City; she just wanted to indulge in a little color and stimulation.

She tried to dig some information out of Sloan during dinner in their sitting area. Knowing his plans would grant her more control and distract her from Sloan's good looks. He'd changed into a lightweight tan suit that brought out the blond highlights in his thick hair. The blue dress shirt, with the top buttons undone, echoed the icy blue of his eyes. He projected an aura of sophisticated relaxation. She couldn't help but envy that cool attitude.

Distraction, that's what she needed. "What is the itinerary while we're here?"

Sloan didn't even look up from his filet mignon. "I'm not sure."

She stifled a sigh. "Do we have an appointment to meet with your friend?"

"I'm afraid not." He paused to chew a bite of crunchy fried potatoes.

How did he eat like that and still maintain those lean muscles without an ounce of extra flesh?

"This trip was a spur-of-the-moment decision."

Really? She could feel her frustration tightening the muscles along her neck. Hadn't he planned any part of this little jaunt? Planning was her modus operandi. Besides, if the designer refused to meet with Sloan, this entire trip would be a complete waste of time.

"So is there at least a plan of attack?"

Realizing her frustration was beginning to ooze through the cracks in her calm facade, she cringed. Maybe she should just concentrate on the juicy chicken Alfredo on her plate. Then she quit caring altogether as she noticed the shake in Sloan's shoulders.

Tilting her head, she caught a glimpse of his laughing mouth. She barely restrained the urge to kick his shin with her pointy dress pumps. Taking a deep breath, instead, she applied herself to her food in outward silence, but inside her mind was calling him every name in the book. And she knew quite a few more than people imagined.

Sloan must have decided he'd tested her type A personality quite enough, because he broke the silence. "I bought tickets for a show here tonight. Since we won't be able to catch up with Patrick until later, we might as well enjoy ourselves."

He studied her as if expecting a protest, but she decided to ease off the hall monitor bit for a little while. Heck, everyone needed a day off. Including her. If he wanted to take her out—strictly as her boss—then who was she to complain?

After finishing their meal, Sloan cleared everything to the room service cart and rolled it outside the door. Ziara changed into the only nonbusiness outfit she'd brought. The plain summer skirt and lack of a suit jacket evoked a sense of freedom from her responsibilities. Paired with a light summer sweater, she was ready to be entertained. The assessing look in Sloan's eyes had her reluctantly standing a bit straighter.

Exiting the elevators, they crossed through the hotel lobby toward the theater. Passing the opening to the casino, various restaurants and shops, Ziara caught the excitement of tourists and let herself slowly slip into the mood, just a little.

A burgundy-uniformed usher led them to seats close to the front, slightly left of the center aisle. Sloan must have pulled strings to get such good seats at the last minute. As the lights lowered and the stage came alive, Ziara's breath caught in her throat. She felt close enough to be part of the action, yet isolated in the dark, alone, with only the warmth of Sloan's arm next to hers anchoring her.

The show was a compilation of variety acts. As Sloan's laughter rumbled in his chest at the comedian, Ziara let herself join in. She held her breath, awed over the awesome acrobatics and stunts in various sketches.

At one point Sloan stretched out his long legs, the brush of material against the bare skin of her calf setting off goose bumps. His gaze branded her like a heat-seeking missile, taking in her reactions to the various acts onstage, reminding her to temper her laughter or excitement.

She thoroughly enjoyed the evening until the next-to-last act. As a scantily clad woman gracefully crossed the stage and burst into song, Ziara cringed in her seat.

She knew the song well—it had been one of her mother's favorites. The scene was from a musical about a prostitute who'd found Mr. Right and hoped he'd look past her profession to the woman within. As fellow "call girls" made their way onto the stage to join in the chorus, Ziara shifted in her seat.

Like a neon sign right before her face, the scene reminded her of all she had to lose if she gave in to her attraction to Sloan. Her past and future colliding in one tempting, disastrous physical attraction. Each word of the song pounded at her temples, reawakening her anger and resolution.

She wasn't her mother and never would be. But she knew from experience that people, especially men, treated her differently when they found out about her childhood. Their attitudes changed. Their words changed. Above all, their eyes changed.

Vivian would definitely change if Ziara's past found the light of day.

Abruptly Sloan stood, grasping her hand to pull her to her feet, then guide her up the aisle to the muted lighting of the foyer. As he paused outside the auditorium doors, she turned to him, acutely conscious of his hand still wrapped around hers. She blinked, her vision adjusting to the faint light, bright after the darkness of the theater.

"What is it?" she asked, withdrawing slightly as he studied her with uncomfortable intensity. That gaze didn't miss much, and she felt as vulnerable as an open book right now.

"You seemed to have lost interest, so I thought it was time to go," Sloan said, a question in his voice.

She shifted, firmly drawing her hand from his grasp. "What makes you say that?"

Stupid! Her defensiveness would surely make him even more curious. Too bad she didn't have a real zipper in her mouth like she'd pretended to as a child, then she could zip her lips shut so nothing incriminating could leak out.

He stepped closer, as if to regain any ground lost by letting go of her hand. She checked the urge to retreat. "You kept wiggling. You seemed uncomfortable and weren't watching the stage despite the excellent performances."

He reached out and pushed an errant strand of hair back behind her ear. Her flesh tingled at the contact, speeding up her heartbeat.

"Was it the performance or the content?"

Now her heart pounded in her chest, drowning out any

sound around her. She made the mistake of meeting his gaze; those cool, steady eyes coaxing her to spill her secrets. But if he knew, knew what her mother had been, those eyes would change. They would glitter, hard as ice, as he condemned her just like her classmates and the townspeople of good ol' Macon, Georgia. Only this time, the life she'd built would be at stake, not just her heart.

"We've got somewhere to be," he said, turning away without waiting for an answer. Had he drawn his own conclusions?

As she followed him down several hallways, she pulled herself back into professional mode, sharp and on alert around Sloan's prying eyes.

Her first inkling that all was not as she suspected came when Sloan led her through a nondescript door that opened into a back corridor near the theater. After several minutes of walking, they came to a door marked Backstage with a doorman keeping a close eye on things. Sloan pulled something from his jacket pocket and the man waved him in.

Going through that door was like entering another dimension. Whereas earlier Ziara had been dazzled by the lights, sounds and effortless flow of the production, now she was amazed that such beauty came from such chaos.

Performers stood in groups chatting or rushing to and from who knows where. Stagehands attended to curtains, props and other mysterious tasks, sidestepping anyone or anything in their way. But it was nearly silent chaos, for the tone of the noise remained low and soft, ever aware of the audience and performance not too far away.

Sloan led her deeper into the backstage area, through rooms containing waiting performers. Here the noise level rose, protected from the stage by distance. Finally they came to a long, narrow room lined with dressing tables. Sloan didn't even blink at the number of women—very toned, well-built women—in various stages of undress, though several certainly noticed him.

He made a beeline to the far end of the room with Ziara cautiously following, awkward under the eyes tracking their progress. Finally Sloan stopped, moving slightly to one side so that Ziara came up even with him. Before them stood one of the performers, a showgirl decked out in a wisp of spandex and sequins. Ziara's gaze trailed down the outfit to catch sight of a man crouched behind the girl, one hand inside the bottom of her outfit and a needle and thread in the other. His spiky blond hair was just level with her rear end, as he leaned close to repair a seam.

"Ziara," Sloan said, "I'd like you to meet Patrick Vinalay, my roommate from college."

Ziara's heart stopped at the shock, then resumed beating again triple time.

This would definitely not go over well. Vivian would throw a true hissy fit if Sloan hired this man to design her wedding dresses. Ziara managed a sickly smile as Sloan introduced her to Patrick's assistant, who was standing nearby.

"Welcome to the drudgery behind the glamour," Patrick said, waving a hand around them at the glittering chaos.

"It's nice to meet you," she murmured, at a loss for anything else to say. Fortunately he turned to Sloan, relieving her of the need for small talk. Her brain couldn't form a coherent sentence; she was still shell-shocked by the bomb Sloan had dropped on her.

What had he been thinking, to offer a man with this background first chance to modernize their line? Patrick was probably great at what he did, but that was the problem. What bride wanted to look like a Vegas showgirl on her wedding day? Eternity Designs was known for its elegance, subtle beauty... not tacky sequins.

Patrick stood, dropping the needle and thread on a table behind him. "So what brings you to Vegas, Sloan? I guess if you brought your assistant, you aren't here for a little *wink-wink*." Patrick accompanied the words with the matching motion. Then his eyes widened. "Or are you?"

The sound of distress—all Ziara could manage—had both men turning toward her. Patrick quickly backtracked. "I'm just kidding! A little off-color college humor between buddies. I'll try to remember my audience in the future."

But the serious consideration she caught lurking in Sloan's gaze sent heat rushing to her face. And the knowledge that some physical recreation hadn't been far from her mind from the moment she'd laid eyes on Sloan Creighton.

Moving closer, he cupped a hand on Patrick's shoulder. "I'm actually here on business."

A knowing, exasperated look crossed Patrick's face. "This wouldn't be about the design position, would it?"

"Of course. Why else would I take time out of my busy schedule to come to Sin City?"

"Oh, how about the glamour? The excitement?"

"Do I look like I have time for all that?" Sloan asked without a change of expression.

Patrick prodded some more. "Sexy women and high-stakes gambling?"

As a waiting showgirl called to Patrick, Sloan laughed. "I don't need all that. I just need a designer."

Shaking his head, Patrick gestured toward the girl in front of him. "Look, I've got to get this done before she has to be onstage for the final number. We'll talk after the curtain falls. Now get out of here," he said with a stern look around the dressing room. "You're distracting the girls."

Patrick's assistant peeked around his boss's shoulder. "And the boys," he said, his tone flirty.

Ziara tensed, unsure how Sloan would feel about this turn of events, but he simply threw a look at Patrick.

"Don't bother," Patrick said. "He's not interested, much to the disappointment of many of my friends throughout the years."

He favored Ziara with another cheeky wink, then crouched behind the woman once more. Ziara pulled Sloan by his arm into a darkened, abandoned corner. "Have you totally lost your mind?" she asked, her tone surprisingly calm and steady, though she was shaking on the inside. Her controlled voice and out-of-control words prompted a laugh from Sloan.

Knowing by now that honesty was the best way to reach him, she continued, "Do you have a death wish? Because Vivian will certainly kill you if you try to bring a costume designer in to work on our wedding dress line."

Sloan's eyes narrowed, his back stiffening in a way that made her swallow, hard. "Our? If I don't step up now, before Bridal Boutique sees the fall designs, there won't be a business left to save. This isn't a game to me, Ziara."

He loomed closer, his broad shoulders inducing a feeling of claustrophobia in the dusty space, leaving her vulnerable to his size. "Since it isn't Vivian's reputation on the line, I don't give a damn what she thinks."

"I understand your urgency, just not your secrecy. This wild idea is exactly why you need someone to provide balance," Ziara said.

"For the record, I'm keeping it quiet because I don't want her shooting down a plan that has nothing to do with her. Understand?"

Ziara drew in a deep breath, choking a little on the dry, dusty air. She knew exactly what Sloan meant. Vivian would do everything in her power to stop this, even if it lost them the Bridal Boutique account. Reputation was everything to her, as Ziara well knew.

"I don't agree with this choice." Ziara waved a hand in Patrick's general direction. "I understand why you are trying so hard to fix this problem. But why him?"

"Because he knows what he's doing," Sloan said.

"That's right," Patrick said from over Sloan's right shoulder, making Ziara jump. "I do know what I'm doing. Besides a degree in fashion design, I know my way around a booty, as you can see." He quirked a grin. "That should come in handy designing lingerie."

Ziara's chest tightened, cutting off her breath for a moment. Sloan's body remained close enough that she could feel the half laugh, half groan he choked back, but when she looked up, his face was still.

Her heart knew this wasn't a joke. Vivian had sensed all

along that Sloan was holding something back, that he might try something crazy. She'd had good reason to be concerned, because this was big. A lingerie line, no matter how tastefully done, would shatter Eternity's conservative reputation forever.

"You're adding a lingerie line," she said with a soft undertone of conviction. "No wonder you've been... You certainly did have something to hide."

Sloan's chin jutted forward, his aggressive stance for once matching his personality. "Are you going to run to Vivian and tattle like a good little girl?"

"Vivian. Good God!" Patrick said with an exaggerated shiver. "If she's involved, that's just one more reason to turn you down. That woman could intimidate the Pope."

Sloan ignored him, his gaze locked with Ziara's. He reached out to once more trace her jawline, his fingers gently abrasive against her sensitive skin.

"Which will it be, Ziara? Friend or foe?"

Eight

Sloan watched as Ziara struggled not to fidget during brunch the next morning. He knew exactly what the problem was, but putting her out of her misery by laying out a plan for the day wouldn't be nearly as fun as his current torture tactics.

She bided her time through coffee, waffles, eggs, mimosas and filet mignon, until she looked like the words would burst through her locked lips at the slightest provocation. He waited just a minute more, but she beat him to it.

"Are we seeing Patrick today?"

"I'm not entirely sure of his plans. We'll have to play it by ear." He could see uncertainty roll over her like a bumpy log. Any minute now steam would come billowing out of her ears. How could it be more fun to torture this woman than it was to sleep with other women? How had he even reached the point where he would ask himself that question?

"So are you excited about the lingerie line?" Sloan asked, a grin finally breaking free.

"Look," she said, that disapproving librarian look making a reappearance. "This is not some kind of game like you seem to think it is. Start talking, or I'll be on the phone to Vivian in two minutes."

He felt his mouth drop open, unable to believe she would adopt his own overbearing approach. Yet aroused by it, just the same.

"I want to understand, Sloan. I really do. But lingerie? Please explain this to me."

He drew in a deep breath before starting. "It's all about marketability—" His hand shot up to stop her from interrupting. "Let me explain." He wiped his mouth with the cloth napkin, then tossed it onto his plate.

"Vivian is focused on making the least amount of change that she can to get by." Standing, he worked off his restless energy by pacing to the glass balcony doors. "Hell if I know why. But that's not how to run a profitable business that will remain stable for the foreseeable future."

He saw logical understanding in her eyes but not the spark of passion he hoped for. He found himself wanting her to understand, needing her to understand. "Modern designs are great. Any willing designer can make those changes." His pacing picked up speed. "But I want a whole new approach—something different, a big splash to make us stand out from the crowd."

Halting, he found himself across the room from her. She sat at the table, her hands folded loosely on the smooth black top. His mind filled with an image of her dressed in lace and pearls for her wedding day, the epitome of elegance.

He mused aloud. "Most women shopping for their weddings already associate Eternity Designs's brand with their big day. Why not expand their thinking to their wedding night, too?"

She shifted. Fear battled with a growing interest in her eyes.

Suddenly he stepped forward, approaching her at a slow stalk. Her throat worked as she swallowed hard. He circled around, pausing behind her. The sweet scent of vanilla swirled in the air. Her personal scent. His gaze branded her at the vulnerable base of her neck.

"Think about it, Ziara—" Just like he was. "There you are,

preparing to put on the dress of your dreams. What do you wear underneath it?"

Leaning forward, he caged her in with an arm on each side. The glimpse of her face lured him to push her further. "Do you want to squeeze into a too-tight piece of Lycra? Itchy lace? Ugly beige?"

Her brows drew together over her now-closed eyes. Following his body's instincts, he lowered his voice, hoping to evoke the images in her mind.

"Or would you rather stand before the mirror in something just as sexy and beautiful as your dress, confident that your husband-to-be will be just as happy when your dress comes off as when he sees you walking down that aisle?"

He shifted closer, his own mind exploding with visions of her in flaming red satin, dark purple silk and then nothing at all. He barely covered a groan.

"Think about a silky smooth body shaper trimmed in soft lace, the same cream color as the dress. No ugly stitching and oxygen-stealing constriction. A strapless bra the perfect shape for your dress's neckline, with smooth, shaped cups and peek-a-boo netting."

A grimace twisted her lips.

"What was that?" he whispered, speaking very close to her right ear. Shivers raced across her skin.

"Nothing," she said, but her voice choked on its way out.

"Ah, methinks the lady has a small problem with sensual..."

Her breath paused just as he did.

"...clothes."

With a whoosh, she started to breathe again. *Dangerous territory,* his mind whispered. She wasn't just resisting because of Vivian—she shied away because something was making her uneasy. Why was a woman whose home was filled with color and spice afraid of the same when she was in his presence?

"You know what?" he asked, backing away as a plan took shape in his brain.

He circled around to stand beside her. Though what came next would probably be the last thing on her agenda, he refused to ask. Only demand. He wanted to know *why*. "We'll perform a little experiment."

"Experiment?" Her high-pitched squeak sent a hot flush through him.

"Yep, time for a field trip." He grabbed her hand, urging her to her feet when she would have resisted. "Let's go."

Oh, this situation had just escalated from bad idea to worse.

The elevator offered her no protection from his probing gaze. She shifted from foot to foot, as if she was a naughty schoolgirl on her way to the principal's office.

He took advantage of their isolation to push her a little further. "Why are you so judgmental of the lingerie idea? Is it the notion of change or the lingerie itself?"

She kept her gaze resolutely fixed on the numbers marking their downward journey. "I'm simply worried about my job," she said. "Vivian would not appreciate having Eternity Designs associated with…that…"

"Ah, so it's the lingerie itself."

"What?" she asked with a gasp, only to look at him and catch his satisfied grin. "I did not say that."

The grin widened. "You didn't have to."

He didn't speak again, but instead let the silence build until she rushed to fill it. "I think it's just, you know." Her hand gestured toward her body in an awkward jerk.

"I don't know. What?" He drew the word out.

"It just seems dirty."

"Seen a lot of it, have you?"

Ziara gave a simple shrug of her shoulders, but the red that rushed up her chest and into her cheeks told a whole different story. And had him licking his lips.

"Obviously not," he said as the elevator doors slid open on the ground floor. "It's time for your education."

Ziara struggled not to choke on her hot embarrassment as she stood beside Sloan. Not even her Indian heritage could hide this blush.

Around my mom's house, I saw it all the time. But she wasn't about to detail her mother's favorite business wear. That woman had never made a secret of what she did for a living—at home or away from it.

Ziara followed Sloan at a trot as he strode through the bustling indoor avenues that traversed the ground floor of their hotel. At first she suspected they were heading for the casino floor with its scantily clad waitresses or even another show. Instead, they silently traveled quite a distance to an indoor promenade fashioned as a replica of a high-end Parisian shopping district lined with quaint, expensive little shops.

Now they stood facing one and she was deathly afraid of what he would demand next.

A lingerie store.

If he expected her to tour a place like that with him at her side, the heat might rise to explosive temperatures. Tremors radiated from her thighs to her calves. It could have been the fast pace of the walk, but she suspected it was dread of what loomed on her horizon.

Sloan made no immediate demands. Instead, he planted his feet, crossed his arms over his chest and studied the delicate ironwork framing the front windows. "What do you see, Ziara?"

The stuff of my nightmares. She settled for, "A store."

The sound grumbling low in his throat could have been disapproval...or a threat. "Look closer. Describe it to me."

Taking a deep breath, she brought her focus to the windows.

The wince was involuntary, a force of habit as she glimpsed the barely there bra-and-panty sets, the sheer teddies, the lace-only gowns. So she turned her attention to the framework—aged wrought iron in fancy curlicues decorating the windows as if they were paintings—

"Out loud," Sloan said, breaking into her thoughts. His voice remained soft, but there was no mistaking the steel undertone. "Describe it to me, Ziara."

Swallowing anger at his high-handedness, she said, "The windows remind me of pictures, feminine and delicate. The pink-and-brown decor is also feminine, like candy and chocolate, but classy, like a sophisticated chocolatier."

"Very good. Go on."

She let her eyes slip to the lingerie, then quickly pulled back. "I don't know. It's underwear." Or outerwear, depending on the woman.

Silence engulfed them in the midst of the eddying crowd. As the seconds ticked by, Ziara's internal tension wound tighter and tighter. Whatever this test was, she was obviously failing.

"Ziara, I want you to go inside."

Yikes.

"Go inside and see for yourself. And I mean really look. Lingerie does not have to be slutty."

She scoffed. "Tell that to—" Her teeth clamped shut.

"To who?" he asked, his voice barely loud enough to be heard above the noise from the crowds.

The shake of her head was sharp, a reflection of the anger building inside of her. She had no idea where it came from or why it filled her so quickly. But it had to stop. *She* had to stop. The cracks would get too wide and then she'd never be able to repair them.

"I can't do this, Sloan." Turning on her heel, she was stopped by two strong hands with the softest of holds on her upper arms.

"Wait, Ziara," he said, his voice once more soft, speaking into her ear just as he had in the privacy of their suite. Here, it was just as intimate. "You can do this. I know you can. You simply have to trust me."

"You don't know," she whispered, not even sure he could hear her.

"Whatever it is, I want you to lock it away."

She thought she had, but not well enough.

"Lock it away and go in with fresh eyes. Use those gorgeously sensitive fingers to explore, to discover. Trust me."

If only I could... But she couldn't say that out loud, so she simply nodded her head. His hands slid down her arms, then defected to her waist, leaving tingles of awareness in their wake. Then he turned her to once again face the storefront. "Go in."

She was halfway to the door when the fear took hold of her. Glancing over her shoulder, her eyes met his. Without a word, he urged her forward. Without a word, she followed his command.

The fabrics were beautiful, tempting her to touch, to stroke, to explore the texture and feel. But each time she reached out, she could sense Sloan tracking her progress from display to display. His gaze blanketed her in warmth, strength. She could almost feel him surrounding her, pushing her, enticing her.

A nightgown, pale gray and silky smooth, slid over her fingertips. She could imagine it against her skin, caressing her hips, the sensitive tips of her breasts. Sloan's gaze had her wondering if he imagined her in the silvery fabric, too.

Somehow the nightie and a matching robe found their way into her hands. A spot of the same silvery gray color caught her eye from a nearby table. Panties had always been utilitarian for her. Waistband and shape were chosen for comfort.

But with the first stroke she imagined wearing them for Sloan's hot gaze. She couldn't begin to see herself in a thong, but the dramatic curve of the high-cut briefs would line the edges of her backside with sheer lace. The phantom feel of his fingers tracing the edges brought a shiver along her spine, daring her to look over her shoulder through the outer windows.

She couldn't, wouldn't, but she scooped several colors into her hands and moved to the register before she could think any more about it. All the while, Sloan's presence called to her from just outside the door. His tracking gaze should have induced embarrassment. Instead, every glimpse of him through those wide windows brought the warm reminder of comfort, encouragement and, yes, trust. Along with a desire to be a woman she was not.

Without him she'd have never even spared this store a glance.

Her rush out the door slowed as she noticed a corner set off from the rest of the store. A quick glance made her think, *Wedding night,* prompting her to pause, to wonder.

A younger woman held up a thigh-length confection of cream satin, lace and pearls. Her companion, who was old enough to be her mother and probably was, smiled, whispering something that encouraged a nod from the daughter. They walked toward the dressing rooms, leaving Ziara watching them with loneliness creeping into her heart.

And confusion.

At first she'd been convinced Sloan was out of his mind. But maybe, just maybe, he was on the right track.

Getting married was a precious vow. She knew that even though she'd never witnessed or wanted that happily ever after herself. What if Sloan could extend the traditions of Eternity Designs to the private celebrations of marriage and not just the public ones?

For an instant the desire to experience a love deep enough for that kind of commitment overwhelmed her, settling at the pit of her stomach in a tide of need. She'd been alone so long, depending only on herself, the only person she could trust. What would it be like to give in to those feelings of overwhelming attraction, to trust someone to understand your needs rather than judge you for them?

She shook her head. With unerring accuracy, she turned to the windows and met Sloan's bright blue gaze once more. Deliberately lowering her lashes, she forced her thoughts to the lasting image of the mother's smile. She would never experience the feminine bond of shopping for her wedding night. Even though her mother wasn't dead, shopping for lingerie with a prostitute was a whole different experience from what she'd just witnessed. She knew. She'd lived it.

Nine

Following Sloan back into the cool air-conditioning of the hotel suite, Ziara noticed the sweat coating her neck and scalp as she took her purchases to her room. A pounding headache—whether from the building tension or lingering emotions—throbbed in her temples and down along her jaw. A few minutes alone, that's all she needed. Time away from Sloan's probing gaze and questioning looks.

He'd watched her closely as she returned to him on the promenade, his eyes flicking between her face and the bag in her hands. That's when the arousal had hit her, this time piercing and sharp. Almost painful. It would be a long time before she forgot that particular sensation.

In the bathroom she pulled the pins from her hair, allowing the heavy weight to fall below her shoulders. She ran a quick brush through the mass. Sometimes just letting it down was enough to ease her tension headaches.

Walking into her bedroom, she moved to close her door so she could rest for a while, but the phone rang. Not hearing any sound in the suite outside, she crossed to the extension beside her bed, stretching her neck from side to side as she went. Taking a deep breath, she answered.

"Hello?"

"Ziara?" Vivian's voice rang in her ear, stealing her breath for a moment. A wealth of suspicion and condemnation resided in that one word.

"Yes, Vivian?"

"Would you like to explain to me what you are doing in Sloan's hotel room?"

For a moment, Ziara's head swirled. Her own concerns mixed with remembered insults and insinuations from the past. She forced herself to breathe, remembering Vivian knew nothing about her past. And never would if she had anything to say about it.

"Actually," Ziara said, grateful her voice came out calm and even, "I'm in my own room. Sloan booked us into a suite so we'd have a common area for working."

Vivian didn't answer immediately, as if pondering Ziara's explanation. This time her voice was a little less tight. "Good. I'd hate to see your reputation compromised by Sloan's charm."

Words rushed to Ziara's lips in her own defense, but she held them back. They would sound like token protests. Besides, hadn't she been tempted? Like Eve by the snake.

"Thank you for your concern," she murmured.

"Ziara, why didn't you contact me about this trip? Why didn't you keep me informed as I instructed?"

Because my phone was resting a little too close to your stepson's privates for me to comfortably make a phone call.

She could have made the phone call after getting to the hotel, but by that time she'd convinced herself that Monday was soon enough to let Vivian know.

Oh, wouldn't that go over well? She decided on a half-truth. "By the time I realized we were going, it was too late to call. I mistakenly thought I could inform you of everything when I returned."

Maybe her growing attraction for Sloan was corroding the responsible part of her brain, but she just hadn't been able to call without his consent. Her mind had justified the need for more information, more…something.

Now she had more of the facts, and she was starting to see Sloan's point of view. Scary, but holding back seemed to be the right plan. For now. Besides, Vivian would faint dead away if she knew who Sloan was here to see.

"I'm truly sorry, Vivian." She used her most placating tone, the one reserved for unhappy clients. "I had to rush to be ready for an early flight Saturday morning."

There wasn't any need to tell her Sloan had come to her house. Vivian would find that move totally unprofessional.

"I see. That does sound like a stunt he would pull. We all know he wants me kept in the dark as long as possible."

Thankfully, that statement was totally true.

"Well, on a personal level, let me warn you, if I may." Vivian's tone didn't sound like a gentle warning. More like a harsh command. "Be careful. You don't want to end up like all the rest of Sloan's assistants, now do you?"

"What do you mean?"

"He has a history of going through them like Kleenex. Oh, he says the feelings, the misconceptions are all their faults. But I know that they are drawn in by his charm, and when he's used them, he discards them with little thought."

Aren't you glad that attitude didn't run in the family? Ziara knew the thought was petty, but Vivian's comments disturbed her on many levels. She didn't want to believe, but then again, what if Vivian spoke the truth? Didn't Sloan flirt and tease her? Hadn't he just taken her to a lingerie store?

Ziara's goal for her entire adult life had been an honorable career. She wanted an employer who respected her for who she was, what she was capable of, not a series of dirty, no-meaning encounters that would put her back in the ugliness of her childhood. Especially if she did it with her boss.

"I promise to keep that in mind."

"Good. I'm only trying to look out for you," Vivian said in an overly sweet tone. "As your mentor, and someone who knows Sloan very well, I don't want to see you get hurt."

"I understand, Vivian."

Even as she spoke, Ziara could feel guilt creeping in. Vivian had done so much for her. Her loyalties toward the woman who had nurtured her career and Eternity Designs were being ripped apart, piece by piece, by her growing attraction to Sloan, reinforcing the doubt Vivian planted in her mind.

"Now," Vivian's voice intruded, "I assume you've gone to Las Vegas to court a designer, though why he'd be there I have no clue. And why we need one is lost on me."

Yet another topic fraught with minefields. "Yes, Sloan is looking into a designer here, but I don't think anything definitive has been decided."

"Hmm, does he look any good? What do you think of his work?"

Well, if you are into tassels and sequins... "Actually I haven't had the chance to see any of his work yet," she said, hiding behind another little lie. Because if Vivian knew Sloan wanted a costume designer, she'd be on the first plane headed anywhere near Las Vegas. Ziara wasn't ready for that—yet. "I've only briefly met him. I think Sloan is hoping for a more formal meeting tonight."

She could hear the *tap, tap, tap* of Vivian's gold pen against her desk. That habit always indicated she was thinking hard.

"Well, I guess it wouldn't do any good to tell him I called. Is there anything else you think I need to know?"

Ziara's stomach tightened. Her legs went shaky. This was a big step, putting her own career on the line. But some small niggle in the pit of her stomach said Sloan might be on to something with this lingerie idea. He certainly wasn't going to get a lot of cooperation from Robert. She had to know for sure before she could decide where her *company* loyalty lay.

"No. Right now there's nothing more to tell."

Another tension-filled pause. Did Vivian suspect she knew more than she was letting on? "Very well. Keep me informed."

Ziara stifled a sigh and said simply, "Yes, ma'am."

After disconnecting, Ziara sank to the bed, her wobbly knees no longer able to support her traitorous stand.

Had she just made an irrevocable decision based on her physical response to the wrong man, a man who could never be more than her boss, instead of practical career considerations? She hoped not, because if Vivian learned she'd hid something so important from her, her career with Eternity Designs would be over.

Was making the fall line a success more important than her own need for security? The answers weren't so clear-cut anymore—no matter who ended up controlling the company. Hopefully, Vivian would never know at what point Ziara discovered the truth.

Like any dangerous pilgrimage, moving forward was the only option. She had to see where Sloan was heading with what she now knew were two new lines. Rising to her feet, she straightened her clothes, then turned toward the door, all thoughts of a nap now abolished from her mind.

Sloan stood in the doorway.

Ziara froze, absorbing his powerful presence, though he leaned casually against the doorframe with his arms crossed over his chest. His face had softened into a slight smile, but his eyes tracked her every move.

The contrast threw her off once more. On the outside he appeared approachable, carefree and happy, but those intense blue eyes alerted her to the hunter within. Pushing away from the frame, he stalked toward her, the tired lines on his face becoming faintly visible. This quest was wearing on him, as well. Her fingers itched to trace the weariness with her fingertips, soothing it away like she would a wrinkle out of fabric, but she forced her hands to remain still.

Stopping so close that a deep breath would bring his chest into contact with hers, he slid his hands into her hair and covered her lips with his own.

Ziara's widened eyes closed as the explosion of sensation from her lips connected with the feel of his hands in the tumble of her hair. He kneaded her scalp as if to massage away the tension hiding there, and she melted into his embrace. Reason and logic disappeared. He could do whatever he wanted. *Just don't stop touching me.*

Never one to do things by half measures, Sloan's tongue plunged through her parted lips, sweeping across her own, igniting a flash of longing through her body. Long after the last of her intelligence had leaked from her brain, he pulled back a fraction. His hands remained anchored in her hair, his minty breath fanning across her face.

Forcing her heavy lids upward, her eyes met his. "What was that for?" she asked, embarrassed by the husky whisper of her voice.

His hands tightened against her head for a moment as if to draw her forward for another kiss but, instead, he spoke. "For keeping my secrets."

They stood immobile for long minutes, afraid to move and bring reality back into their fragile peace. Ziara had never experienced anything like their kiss. Everything before had been a simple match set to flame, but this time fireworks exploded.

She needed to back away, but she didn't.

Slowly his hands drew the silky weight of her hair forward and over her shoulders. "Beautiful," he whispered, though his eyes never left hers.

An urge unlike any she'd ever experienced swept through her. No previous desire, no previous need felt real compared to the intensity of this moment. With no thought, she leaned forward, eager to taste his kiss once more. He didn't back away.

Until a knock sounded on the door.

Sloan escaped to the outer room, leaving Ziara behind. One deep breath followed another. If he could just get his head in gear and think this through, he'd make the right choice. When he opened the door, a courier brought in a simple white box, fairly long and thick in size, tied with a deep purple bow.

Sloan closed the door and turned to catch sight of Ziara standing in her bedroom doorway. She hugged herself loosely across her middle, warning him that awkwardness had set in. Good thing he had something to break the ice.

He drew in another deep breath, willing his heart to stop racing. His response to her was unbelievably strong. "You have a delivery," he said.

"Me?"

As she walked to the table, he noted her hair swinging midway down her back. His hands itched to bury themselves in the dark, silky fullness again. He'd always suspected her hair would be extravagant when set free from the constraint of that bun thing, but the sight and feel of it surpassed his tantalizing dreams.

He watched her delicately untie the bow, her care and precision not surprising him. But her restraint had a different quality to it, something more than just her normal reserve.

He studied her movements. The contained excitement on her face, the slight parting of her lips. Did she ever receive surprises? Was there no one in her life to offer those happy moments, big or small? With an unexpected spike of jealousy, he hoped there wasn't another man. He'd seen no evidence of anyone at her house.

Was her family the reason she'd closed herself off from the sensual parts of life? Had someone hurt her, damaged her?

She lifted the lid slowly, then pushed aside the tissue covering the contents. Her eyes widened, that sweet mouth opening in a silent O. She didn't remove whatever was inside, simply caressed it with exploring fingertips just as he'd seen her do with the lingerie and design fabrics.

Before those luscious strokes could completely shatter his control, Sloan walked forward to peer into the box himself. At first all he could see were layers upon layers of sheer, brightly colored fabric before he realized an expensive dress lay inside.

Sloan's suspicions were confirmed when Ziara pulled out the card tucked among the golden tissue.

"Patrick. But why?" she asked, turning to face him, though one hand remained resting amid the folds of the dress.

He opened the note. "We're invited to a party Patrick is hosting tonight. He wants you to wear this," he said, handing the paper over for her to read. His earlier jealousy settled like a lead brick in his stomach because Sloan himself hadn't been the one to make her eyes light up like stars.

She gazed back into the box but still didn't lift the dress. "I can't believe he did that." She looked at Sloan, a frown drawing those elegantly arched brows together. "Is this appropriate? I don't want to give the wrong impression."

"You worry too much. Of course it's okay to accept a gift. I'd say it's a sign we're headed in the right direction." Reaching in, he found the straps and lifted the dress, shaking it out to its full length. "Exquisite," he murmured.

Patrick's mind must have run along similar lines as Sloan's. The vibrant, flaming colors would be a stunning complement to Ziara's dark caramel skin and black hair. The soft, handkerchief layers of the skirt echoed her femininity, as did the cut pieces attached to the form-revealing bodice. His lips pressed together as he slipped into creative mode.

"I don't think I can wear this."

Sloan surfaced from his thoughts at the sound of Ziara's shaky voice. "Of course you can. This dress was made for you."

She shook her head, those soft waves of hair framing her face. "No, I can't. I'd feel too exposed."

Exposed? The dress did have only single straps across the shoulders, though they were thicker than spaghetti straps. The scoop of the neckline would reveal a little bit of cleavage, leaving her chest and arms bare. His mouth watered at the thought of all that delectable skin on display for his starving imagination.

He eyed the jacket she was wearing—her standard office fare. He remembered the T-shirt with its three-quarter-length sleeves that she wore in the middle of a hot Southern summer. Maybe there was more to her clothing than just an overblown sense of professionalism. If she was going to be stubborn about this—a grim smile slipped out—he had the perfect ammo for fighting back.

"Don't be stupid. You're wearing it."

"No." Her arms folded around her waist as if to anchor her clothes. Did she think he would strip her naked to force her to wear it? The tightening in his groin reminded him his thoughts were moving into dangerous territory.

He pulled back immediately, but pushing *her* out of her comfort zone would be good for her. The sensuous, open woman he'd glimpsed at her house needed releasing. If he benefited at the same time, all the better.

He tossed the dress toward the box, crowding forward to tower over her. "You don't get it, do you?" He connected his gaze with hers, insuring he had her full attention. This wasn't about business for him…his descent from lofty goals was gaining speed. But business was what she understood, so that's the reasoning he'd use.

"I want Patrick as my designer, and I'll do whatever I have to for him to agree. So if he sent a garbage bag with holes for the head and arms, you would be wearing that."

Her back stiffened and those lush lips thinned. Still he drove his point home. "We'll do whatever Patrick wants. Don't forget who's the boss around here."

Her eyes narrowed to a glare, her softly pointed chin edging up a notch.

"Now," he said, before he could give in to the temptation to kiss her pretty pout away, "go hang the dress up. We've got a party to get ready for."

"What are you talking about?" she asked. "The party isn't until eight tonight, and it's just now three."

God, her anger made her that much more beautiful and awoke an urge to channel it into a more mutually beneficial emotion.

"Trust me," he said. "We'll make every minute count."

Ten

Ziara's knees developed a tremor as she stared at herself in the mirror, making her unsteady on high-heeled gold sandals.

Sloan had instructed the hairdresser to leave her hair down, though she'd tucked one side up with a comb behind Ziara's ear. The orange, red and purple swirls of the dress and glint of gold threads hinted at a gypsy look, overlaid with Moroccan belly dancer.

The movement of the dress was reminiscent of veils, which emphasized the impression, along with her muted Indian heritage. Her skin seemed darker, more exotic. Her eyes more mysterious and shadowed. Her bearing more regal, like a princess tucked away in a harem—sensual, yet above approach.

The tremors grew, taking on a life of their own. Reminding herself that as Sloan's date, she didn't have to worry about anyone harassing her, she forced herself to walk to the door. But then, Sloan couldn't protect her from her own weaknesses, could he?

When she finally found the courage to leave her room, Sloan waited near the glass balcony doors. He turned to face her, his body a long, lean silhouette against the glittering backdrop of the city, whiskey tumbler in hand. An ache bloomed within her, a desire to meet him as an equal—strong, passionate and confident instead of closed off and broken.

He moved slowly into the light as he drank from the tumbler. His tongue slid across his lips, catching the last trace of amber alcohol. She followed the movement with her eyes, wishing she could lick the same path. He watched her, his light eyes sparking with desire as his gaze devoured the length of her body. These two days with him had attuned her to a whole level of herself she'd never known.

She stepped forward, conscious of the skirt, sheer from right above her knee down to the handkerchief points. Fear or revulsion should have set in, but neither did. Just a need to feel the heat of his mouth once again covering hers, her pulse pounding throughout the secret places of her body.

He stopped only inches away, forcing her to look up to see his face. The smooth line of his jaw, the taut muscles along his neck worked as he swallowed, making her own mouth water. But he didn't dip his head to indulge; instead, his eyes narrowed as a sexy grin spread across his full lips.

"I knew Patrick was the right designer for the job. He certainly knows what he's doing. This dress makes you look like magic."

His praise prompted her to stand a little straighter, ache to move a little closer, so she pulled back.

After clearing his throat, he said, "There was something else in the box."

"More?" She gestured to herself. "This is way too generous."

Sloan shrugged, his strong shoulders rippling under the slippery thin material of his button-down shirt. The blue made his eyes even more electric. Reaching into the pocket of his usual khaki pants, he pulled out a glittering length of golden circles. "He's a designer," Sloan said. "They want the look to be complete."

Ziara's mouth drained of moisture. Anxiety pounded at the

base of her throat, even though logic told her there wasn't any need for nerves. Then Sloan moved to put the chain around her throat.

"No." The force in her voice wasn't necessary, but she couldn't control it. Moderating a little, she continued, "No, please. I don't really like jewelry. It makes me uncomfortable."

"Why?" he asked with a frown.

Knowing any protest would just give him an opportunity to argue, she turned away. Moving to the balcony door of the suite, she escaped into the hallway with quick steps.

The limousine took them to a modest estate a short distance from the Strip. Ziara stepped out into night air that carried the tinkling sound of a center courtyard fountain. Through the open veranda windows drifted a soft rock song. The melody sounded vaguely familiar.

Sloan slipped up next to her, then tucked her hand into the crook of his arm. The gesture was a bit old-fashioned, part possessive, part protective. Despite her usual "no touching" rule, this calmed her nerves as they made their way up the stone steps.

They hadn't moved ten feet from the car before Patrick appeared through one of the arched doorways. The open floor plan of the house allowed glimpses of the adjoining rooms through the repeated arches.

"Ziara, you look exquisite," Patrick said, inspecting his creation and her in it. "Of course, I knew you would." Though his gaze lingered at her bare throat, he didn't mention the jewelry.

She smiled. "Thank you. And thank you for sending the dress." She fingered the skirt with her free hand, glancing down at the flaming swirl of material. "It's so beautiful."

Having stood silent long enough, Sloan said, "I knew you had talent, but this proves it. I'm tempted to up my offer."

Patrick frowned. "Sloan, no business. This is a party. Don't you remember how to have fun?" He pulled Ziara gently into his own grasp. "Let's mingle and meet about a hundred of my closest friends."

Ziara laughed, surprised the sound floated from her so

freely. The loosening of her control was almost a physical sensation.

Then she simply let herself follow Patrick's lead. He took them from group to group, making introductions. He didn't mention Ziara's status as Sloan's assistant. Her instinct was to correct him the first time, but something stopped her at the last minute. She didn't want to be that person right now, which was both scary and exhilarating.

Would the universe fall apart if she loosened up for just this one night?

They finally settled in with a small group of Patrick's theater buddies, one or two of whom had also known Sloan since college. After a period of catching up, one of the men turned to her. "And what do you do, Ziara?"

Unsure how much she should reveal, she answered, "I'm an executive assistant in training at a wedding gown design firm."

"Hey, Sloan, doesn't your family own one of those?" one of the men asked.

"Yep."

"Which is why I'm in training—to keep him on track," she said, unable to resist teasing.

Everyone chuckled. Before Sloan could make a snappy reply, Patrick stepped into the gap between them. "Could I borrow my buddies here for a few minutes? There's something I think they'd like to see."

Ziara nodded, smiling as the men stepped away. The women around her chatted about the wedding dress industry, distracting her from a sudden sense of vulnerability. With a deep breath, she remembered she could take care of herself. She'd been doing it every day since a very early age.

After chatting for a while, she excused herself to hunt down a drink. Despite the variety of alcohol at the bar, the parched Nevada air had put Ziara in desperate need of plain old water. When the waiter gave her the bottle, she opened it gratefully. The chilly liquid soothed her dry throat.

Someone bumped into her from behind, hard. Grimacing as

cold water splashed across her bodice, she tightened her grip on her drink and spun around.

"I'm sorry," said a man in a navy suit with a loosened tie, the top three buttons of his shirt undone. His gaze wavered and he took precise care in pronouncing his words. He was obviously drunk but trying to hide it.

"No harm done," she said, brushing at the water spots darkening her dress. She replaced the lid on her bottle for good measure. "It's just water. It'll dry."

He stared at her a moment before a pseudo-charming smile tightened his loose lips. "That's nice."

Her tension mounted as he closed the gap between them. She told herself he wouldn't attempt anything in a room full of people, but she'd seen enough drunks to know they were unpredictable.

"You're really pretty," he said, only slurring the words a little. His slight adjustment to his tie and straightening of his shoulders reinforced his attempt at being suave. It wasn't working for her.

"Thank you." She moved back a few steps before forcing herself to stop. *Stand your ground.*

"I think such beauty deserves a kiss." As the man advanced, Ziara held up her hands to maintain distance between them. Her water bottle dropped to the floor.

"Stop right there," she said, remembered panic adding force to her words. "I'm not interested, so you can just back away."

He paused. "What do you mean, not interested? I bet you're just saying that. Women who look like you are always interested."

His assumption punctured her normally impenetrable armor. Her arms wavered long enough for him to slip through. Grabbing her, he dragged her body closer. "I'll just have a taste of the goods for sale."

If his earlier words were a pinprick, these were a knife to the heart. The pain that lanced through her provided the strength to slam her foot down on his toes as he leaned forward to touch his lips to hers. Then she shoved him back, straight into Patrick's chest.

Sloan's friend surveyed the situation with wide eyes behind his designer wire-rimmed glasses. Sliding an arm around the man's shoulders, he said, "Come on, Michael. Let's get you into a taxi before my friend here decides to find the nearest meat grinder."

As Patrick led the drunk away, Sloan moved close to study her but kept his hands to himself. Her contrary body protested, aching for his touch.

"Are you okay?" he asked, his face tight.

"I'm fine," she said, struggling to control the sudden shake in her voice. She reached down for her water bottle. "No big deal."

He leaned forward until his eyes were level with hers. "Really? Because I don't think that guy's foot would agree with you."

A glance in that direction showed Patrick and the drunk had disappeared. "I'm sorry I made a scene at Patrick's party. I'll certainly apologize and smooth things over when he returns."

Sloan clasped her wrist, using it to guide her to a secluded corner. "I don't give a damn about any scene. That guy's lucky I didn't coldcock him. I'm kind of jealous that you handled it without me."

Though his mouth remained serious, his eyes smiled into hers. She was never so glad to see the crinkles along the sides.

"Well, a woman has to do what a woman has to do. This is the twenty-first century, you know."

"Does that mean I can't lead while we dance?" They shared a smile, then he bent close to her ear, his breath ruffling her hair. "I have the odd compulsion to throw a blanket over you. But I doubt you need me for protection."

She shivered, afraid of her sudden yearning for connection. Her body felt as if it was attached to an electric pulse. She'd never had this reaction to the few lovers she'd previously accepted, men she'd chosen very carefully for their safe auras.

The two who'd made it to the sexual stage hadn't been worth a repeat performance.

She had an inkling being with Sloan would be the performance of her life.

"Let's dance," he said in a husky whisper.

She stiffened, trying to pull back as he led her through the crowded rooms to the patio. "I don't think that's a good idea, Sloan. I've never danced before."

He paused. "Never?"

She shook her head.

"Not on a date?"

"No."

"Not even at a school dance?"

She shook her head again, not about to tell him she'd gone extra lengths to stay away from the guys around her school. Her mother's reputation wasn't a secret in her small hometown. Ziara had been harassed on more than one occasion by boys and girls alike—boys who expected something from her, girls who judged her for the same reason.

Sloan's trademark sexy grin slid into place, softening his face and sparking in those intent eyes. "Then I'll be the first."

They stepped onto the back patio, an oasis in the desert. Framed by potted and hanging plants, the stone mosaic floor created texture and color. Soft lighting from outdoor torches combined with the stars overhead, giving the feel of vast open space despite the others dancing and talking around them.

As a slow song floated on the air, Sloan chuckled. "Great. This will be an easy start."

With trepidation, Ziara let him pull her into his arms. Her fears—of giving in, of him seeing how she reacted and completely humiliating herself—kept her stiff. But when he settled her chest against his, their bodies in complete alignment, her muscles relaxed without her permission.

Her body openly rejoiced in Sloan's nearness, letting the earlier encounter fade from memory. The nervous shivers radiating from deep inside were chased away by his proximity—heat, height and a touch of humor.

She instinctively moved in time with him. He didn't lead her into anything fancy, but he didn't just shuffle his feet, either. Other than holding her firm and close, he didn't make any other move to touch her. He didn't have to. She responded fluidly to every brush, every breath. And she didn't have to wonder if she was the only one feeling this, because the hardness of his body made it very clear he was along for the ride.

As one song blended into the next, Sloan pulled back enough to see her face illuminated in the soft glow of the torches. "Better now?" he asked.

"Of course," she said, hoping to brush aside any further references to the earlier upset.

"Those smooth moves made it look like you have experience defending yourself."

He'd never know how much. Instead, she shrugged. "Self-defense course at the Y."

He nodded but continued to watch her. At least she thought he did. Looking down, his face hovered over her in shadow, leaving her guessing. It should have been a relief to not see that intense purpose in his eyes, but instead the mysterious darkness both drew and scared her.

She knew just the way to redirect her thoughts.

"I'm starting to see what you mean. You talk a good game about company direction and expanding on buyers' demands, but...thank you for showing me."

His mouth opened as if he would speak, but then he brushed a soft kiss against her temple. "You're welcome."

As the song shifted into something a little rowdier, Sloan guided her off the dance floor to a secluded corner of the patio. The dry air was noticeably cooler, bringing gooseflesh to the surface of her skin. But the incredible view of the moon riding low in the sky over distant mountains distracted her.

"Ziara," Sloan said, his voice low and intimate. "I realize Vivian doesn't trust me—" The hand he raised to stop her words compelled her to pause. "I understand why she doesn't. Considering our history, she shouldn't. But I do actually know what I'm doing. Maybe the design part is new to me, but I've been buying companies and rebuilding them, sometimes after devastating setbacks, for more years than I care to count. I *can* do this."

His focus shifted out into the night. He leaned forward, resting his elbows on the stone balustrade. "But more than that, my father meant a lot to me. She thinks she's cornered the market on those emotions, but she hasn't."

Ziara recognized the ache in his voice from that first encounter in his father's office. "This really does mean a lot to you, doesn't it?" she asked, her voice barely above a whisper.

His head dipped as if in defeat, though she couldn't imagine him being defeated by anything—even Vivian's determined animosity.

"My childhood was wonderful until my mother died."

Ziara couldn't imagine how different her life would have been without her mother, how much better. "How old were you?"

"Fourteen."

She winced. "That's a bad age for major upheaval."

"Yes," he said with a slow nod as he looked out at the desert sky. "Her death was quick, only six weeks after she was diagnosed with a brain tumor." His pause was heavy with memories. "I had a new stepmother within a year."

What had his father been thinking? "It must have been hard for him to be alone."

"He wasn't alone. He had me." His deep sigh blew away any sounds of self-pity. "My father changed after he married Vivian," he said, the words slow but gaining speed. "Life became all about his new wife—her demands, her needs, her desires. What little was left went to his company, not to a fifteen-year-old boy in need of reassurance after losing his mother to cancer."

The picture of isolation he painted was nearly as bad as her own teenage years, living in her mother's house but not really *living* with her mother.

"She told my father I was lazy, unmotivated. But instead of wondering why, he simply condemned me. Any protests were considered a teenager's way of trying to weasel out of the consequences."

"And things never got better, even after you became an adult?"

"Not with Vivian poisoning his brain. At least, not that I could tell." He turned to her, the movement bringing them almost as close as they'd been on the dance floor. "He died from a heart attack, you know. Very unexpected."

Ziara had known, but he seemed to need to talk so she let him.

"When the lawyer read his will, I could hear Vivian screaming in frustration even though she never uttered a sound. The fact that he left me any part of Eternity Designs completely shocked her."

As if he needed some connection with Ziara, his hands reached out to rub up and down her arms, warming her from the outside in. "But that forty percent meant more to me than all the money, houses and stuff Vivian inherited. I could have sold it, resented it. But it made me think that in some small way, he had truly seen what I'd made of my life and was telling me that he believed in me."

An alien urge to wrap her arms around his waist and snuggle close swept through her. She just barely kept herself from acting. "Then why did you stay away so long?" If the company had meant so much to him, why had he left Vivian to it?

Laughter rumbled in his chest, the vibration echoing in her own and setting off all kinds of sparks under her skin. "You've seen how well Vivian works with me. For Eternity's own well-being, I stepped back from the running of it. She wanted free rein. I gave it to her."

"But you knew the time would come…"

"I knew without strong business acumen, Vivian probably couldn't keep the firm afloat. So I waited, and showed up when she didn't have a choice but to let me step in."

His cold calculation should disturb her, but what choice had he been given?

"Vivian should have known I wouldn't walk away forever," Sloan said. "Eternity is the only part of my father that I have left."

Which said all she needed to hear.

Eleven

Retracing their steps back through the house, Sloan found Patrick in the front room surrounded by people laughing. He gestured, letting his friend know he needed a moment.

Patrick approached with a casual, lanky stride. If he'd been into computers, he'd have been a geek, but he'd been designing clothes and dressing those around him for most of his life. He and Sloan had bonded as young men over the neglect of their home lives. Despite their many differences, Patrick was always the person to shake Sloan out of his anger, force him to look in a new direction or simply bust his chops until he could solve his problems. Sloan offered the same support, and they took every opportunity to dog each other about relationships, jobs and various life issues, just like the brothers they should have been.

Now Sloan needed something more than camaraderie. His thoughts must have shown, because Patrick flashed a rueful grin. "Do-or-die time, huh?" he said.

Sloan didn't disappoint. "Yep."

With a gesture Patrick directed them to his office. As Ziara moved into the space, she gasped. Sloan watched with a warm feeling in his chest as an almost childlike excitement burst over her face. He certainly understood.

The room was completely out of character with the rest of the house except for the pale walls and arches over the double windows. Otherwise, overflowing bookshelves lined every other wall, with more shelves jutting out to create aisles and hidden nooks. There were several oversize leather chairs with huge ottomans and a table-style desk supported by intertwined pieces of wood that formed the legs. It was slick, modern, but washed with an antique feel. An incredible contrast that Ziara obviously loved.

"This is so unique," she breathed.

"Patrick would live in here if everyone would leave him alone," Sloan said, earning a sucker punch in his upper arm.

"Would not."

"Would, too, you little recluse."

Ziara looked back at them in surprise, then glanced at the door separating them from the party.

"That's right, Ziara. Sloan calls me a recluse, but look at the parties I put on. He's clearly delusional. As is perfectly evident by his insistence that I join him in this crazy designing venture."

"I'm not giving up, Patrick. You have to give me an honest chance at talking you into this."

His friend waved toward the closed door, and the lavish house and glittering guests beyond it. "Why would I want to leave all this?"

"You know you get bored easily. This is just an opportunity for a new challenge." He might as well start off simple.

"You think working with fifty cast members and a demanding director isn't challenging?"

"How about—to teach an old nemesis she doesn't know what's best?"

Sloan noticed Ziara stiffen out of the corner of his eyes. Though her back was turned politely to them as she perused a nearby bookshelf, he still couldn't dismiss the connection he had to her every emotion.

His jaw tightened as he remembered seeing her fight off that drunk. Granted, the guy wouldn't get too far in a crowded party, but something about the practiced way Ziara had handled him made Sloan uneasy. What had happened to her that she needed to know how to defend herself? Classes at the Y, his ass!

He forced his attention back to Patrick. "Look, it's time to step up to the plate, buddy. We're leaving tomorrow. Are you following me or not?"

"I'd have to be crazy to sign on to pull together a show in less than three months."

Sloan grinned. "But think of the thrill."

"Vivian is not going to like this," Patrick said with a careful glance at Ziara. "The last time I did something she didn't like, she threatened to have me arrested."

Ziara gasped. "What did you do?" she asked.

Patrick had the grace to look away. "Well, we snuck into the liquor cabinet when she wasn't home and guzzled half the bottles down."

Ziara frowned.

"Give us a break," Sloan said. "We were only nineteen at the time. And how were we to know she had guests coming over for drinks the next day?"

Both men laughed, which felt good to Sloan. He missed those simpler times, when his struggles with Vivian only impacted himself and sometimes Patrick instead of the livelihood of close to a hundred people.

"It made an impression, that's for sure," Patrick said with a shudder. "Her expression…"

Sloan tried again. "So view this as the chance to show Vivian you've grown up from a spoiled little rich boy to an extremely talented designer."

"Flattery will get you everywhere," Patrick said. He rocked back on his heels, indicating to Sloan he was finally considering his offer without saying a word.

"I'm serious," Sloan said, stepping forward. "You don't need flattery. You know what you're capable of. You work on these live shows because it gives you something to do and an excuse to be here. Just give it a shot. If nothing else, just get me through this show."

This time Patrick leaned forward to meet him head-on. "I want final say on all designs."

Sloan shook his head. "Robert and Anthony would come unglued. They've been there forever. It wouldn't be right, Patrick. Besides, you would only be tweaking the main line with modern elements, not actually designing the clothes completely."

But Patrick wasn't swayed. "This isn't a power trip, Sloan. It's the only way I can have two lines finalized by fashion week." He glanced carefully around the room. "You do want the lingerie line ready for the show, too?"

Not looking at Ziara, Sloan inclined his head. He simply had to trust that this weekend had taught her all she needed to know. And that she'd stand by him—or at least near him—if Vivian went ballistic. "You would have complete control over that line. I want to open with both in two months."

Patrick stared at him for a long moment, then shook his head. "I can't believe I'm saying this, but yes—I'll do it. You are going to make it worth my while?"

"Always," Sloan agreed.

"Then I'll see you on Wednesday." Still muttering to himself, he left them to attend to his other guests.

Mission accomplished, Sloan's instincts set their sights on another prey, another conquest. As he and Ziara settled into the limo, his senses were attuned solely to her, the soft whisper of her breath, the smooth swish of her skirts as she crossed her legs, the spicy scent of her skin mixed with some illusive floral perfume.

His mind drifted back to this morning, watching her through the windows of the lingerie store. When she'd first entered, she stood almost paralyzed, looking so lost and unsure. So unlike herself. He'd almost dragged her back out rather than strip her of her usual strength.

But the point had been more important than protecting her. And now, he had the image of her explorations burned into his brain.

He was downright hooked.

Shame filled him as he remembered his casual thoughts about getting close to her in order to gain her loyalty. All it had taken was a true glimpse of her response and this game had become strictly personal.

Sloan slumped back in the seat, staring out the window of their limo. Getting Eternity Designs back on track was kicking his ass.

Ziara spoke into the darkness. "Well, you did it."

He couldn't tell from her tone whether she approved or not. Probably not. He wasn't worried. She was a walking example of what Patrick was capable of—the proof was in his design.

But Sloan didn't want to think about work. He'd rather have her in front of him so he could touch her, stroke her breasts until her nipples peaked—

"Yep," he finally got around to replying, his tone ironic but showing his fatigue.

"I hope Patrick knows what he's getting into. This time frame will mean a lot of late nights."

"He won't mind me working him like a dog," Sloan joked, chuckling when she looked askance at him. "Patrick may come from money, but he worked hard in school and at his job. He'll come through for us."

She nodded, but he still sensed her hesitation. There wasn't anything he could do about that. She'd see in time.

Her silhouette, profiled against the night, accelerated the beating of his heart. Sloan breathed deep, forcing calm to cover his growing need. He noted the slope and angles of Ziara's cheekbones. A model's face. Why did she work so hard to hide her beauty? He was more determined than ever to find out.

The conviction that she would be his surged deep in his soul.

He wanted to unravel the mystery, find what she hid beneath the surface so well. Why she hid at all.

"This is an interesting place," she said, her eyes focused on the approaching city lights.

He studied the thick dark lashes concealing her thoughts from him. "I'm glad you like it. Patrick takes a lot of pride in his work *and* play."

"It shows. But I didn't mean just tonight. More like Las Vegas in general." She absently rubbed the material of her dress between two fingers. "A combination of decadence, debauchery and the everyday. Kind of like life."

He scooted closer, gaining ground until he could touch her hair with the hand resting across the back of the seat. "How so?"

She dropped her head back so that it landed in his palm, but she didn't seem to notice. The silky weight of her hair made him want to run his hands through it, massage her scalp until she moaned, use handfuls of it to guide her mouth to all the places where he wanted to feel that wet warmth.

"Well," she went on, "maybe not everyone's life, but at least mine. My old life."

The opportunity opened before him like a lit doorway. Adrenaline aftershock, sleepiness and the shakedown of her natural barriers were lowering her inhibitions. The facade was melting away.

He told himself he should hold back, but they'd shot way past a professional relationship at this point. As he caressed her scalp, he knew deep down he would get to the bottom of the contradictions in her personality that had him tied in knots. For all the wrong reasons.

The intimacy of the limo, shrouded in gray shadows, invited him to explore the secret places, the dark desires beneath her surface. It would surely be the experience of his life.

"Rough childhood?" he asked.

Her eyes closed a moment as she shuddered. "You have no idea."

She turned toward him, those dark eyes sucking him away

from the voice of reason. "My mother..." She paused, biting her lip as if afraid to say more. "My mother was so wrapped up in her own needs, her little games, that she didn't care about what happened to me. She abandoned me."

Though he'd heard quite a few tales of childhood woe in his time, the desolation darkening Ziara's face ignited a protective streak in the pit of his stomach. "How old were you?"

Her fingers worried the fabric now. "Officially? Seventeen. Unofficially? So long before that I can't remember when."

Thoughts tumbled through his mind about what could happen to a seventeen-year-old girl who looked like Ziara without anyone to protect her.

"What about your dad?" he asked.

Her fingers jerked then went still. "I wouldn't know. I never met him." A few minutes passed before she said, "I think I could use a drink now."

Reaching out, he trailed his fingers down the back of her tense hand. "I don't think you need alcohol."

"Yes. I do."

"Why?" Sloan asked, taking the risk of looking straight into those tempting eyes. Half-mast lids were sleepy, sultry. Sexy. Man, if she decided to drink, who knew where they'd end up?

Her desire to let go had him shaking. It must be worse than he thought for her to resort to booze. "Why?" he repeated, hoping conversation would distract him from his thoughts and rapidly escalating erection.

"Because without it I'll never do this." She twisted, her lips brushing his, though she stopped short of a firm kiss.

The fire that burst through him burned away his inhibitions with one clean flare. "Ziara," he said, pulling her gaze to his. "You don't need liquid courage to do that."

Something perverse inside of him exulted in her making the first move, so he remained still. A quick lick of her lips sent a shiver of anticipation through him. Her lashes lowered as she pressed closer. Her lips barely met his before he took the reins back.

Burying both his hands in the soft fall of her hair, he stormed her mouth, sliding his tongue inside. Without further invitation, he explored the moist heat within before returning to caress her lips with his own. So soft, yet meeting him halfway, she beckoned and commanded his response without a word.

A flash of lights outside the windows eased Sloan from the cocoon of intimacy they shared. Though they were behind tinted windows and privacy glass, they were still in a public place.

And he wanted to do something they could be arrested for in public. Even in Las Vegas.

Resigning himself to a snail's pace, Sloan resumed his exploration of Ziara's mouth. He resisted the urgency surging under his skin. Their first time together shouldn't be in the back of a limo with a driver on the other side of the glass.

But he couldn't stop himself from exploring the boundaries a little. Drawing his hands down the side of her neck, he pulled her mouth closer, letting one hand travel to cup her breast. The soft weight overflowing his palm made him groan, but her electric response had him swearing.

Luckily at that moment they came to a stop in front of their hotel. Sloan opened the door himself and pulled Ziara out behind him. He rushed through the lobby and into the elevator with her a few steps behind. His hands trembled as he swept the key card through the lock, then pulled her into the suite with less finesse than demand.

The dim light of the suite was barely enough to silhouette Ziara's beautiful face. The stillness in the room as the door clicked shut only accentuated the pounding of the blood in his veins. He stalked forward, using their still-clasped hands to draw her near. He was pleased to see she didn't cower from him, from the intensity of his desire.

"Ziara, I need you."

This time it was she who anchored her hands in his hair. "And I need you," she choked out. "I really do."

Her voice shook at first but quickly firmed, though she sounded surprised. Whether at the need or the admission, he wasn't sure, but he didn't question his good fortune. Letting her pull his head down, he met her swollen lips once more, tasting the sweet burn he now associated with Ziara herself.

Allowing his hands free rein, they roamed her body, cupping those full breasts and squeezing them gently together. Her nipples hardened into peaks he could feel through the layers of fabric.

He followed the curve of her waist to the flare of her hips, finally drawing her tight against his erection.

Ziara bit lightly against his lower lip, sending Sloan's body and mind flying apart. Grabbing the zipper hidden along her side, he jerked it down, then the dress. Ziara gasped, but he didn't care. He just needed to touch her skin with his.

Instinct took over. His lips only left hers long enough to pull his shirt over his head. Drawing her against him, he groaned at the sensation of flesh against flesh, hotter than he could ever remember being. His head fell back, only to drop forward again to bury in her neck.

Her sweet, spicy scent drove him to taste her skin. Working his way down, he licked and nibbled the smooth column of her neck and the curve of her collarbone. He fell to his knees so he could savor the textures of her breasts and nipples.

Only then did he become aware of her panting breath, too jagged for passion. Releasing her sweet flesh, he looked up, catching the glint of moisture on her cheeks in the lights filtering through the far windows. "Ziara?"

"Please stop."

Twelve

Ziara stayed in her room the next morning until the last possible minute. Hiding wasn't the noblest of behaviors, but she simply couldn't face Sloan after calling a halt to...whatever last night had been.

How would she ever explain why she'd led him on, then left him hanging like that? How could she ever look herself in the eyes again and not remember her actions? Behavior that brought memories of her mother flooding to the surface. No matter how much her mind insisted she wasn't using Sloan, the fact that he was her boss couldn't be ignored. She refused to participate in anything reminiscent of her mother's life, built on sex, money and scheming for everything she could get.

Drawing in a deep breath, she smoothed her hair back into its usual bun. More aware than ever of the facade she presented in her business suit, she grabbed the handle of her rolling suitcase and opened the door. Sloan stood silent near the outer door, his own luggage not far away, remains of breakfast littering the table near the window.

Keeping her chin lifted and her eyes focused over his shoulder, she somehow crossed the room without stumbling or being sick. By the time she neared Sloan, his hand rested on the doorknob, but he made no move to leave. She could actually feel him looking at her, and her insides shivered. Part of her cowered in humiliation; the other part flared back to life with arousal.

For long moments Sloan didn't move, keeping them locked in a silent battle. The tension ate away at her composure.

"I just have one question," he finally said, his voice strained and husky. "Why?"

She spit out the words she'd rehearsed during the long, dragging hours of the night. "You're my boss. It just isn't right."

She must have managed the right level of conviction, because he opened the door and led the way outside. Watching him stride away struck her as bittersweet.

The flight home, long and silent, was punctuated by agonizingly polite phrases like "Excuse me" and "Would you like a drink?" Her body pulled in on itself, making her wish she could shrink into oblivion. But she couldn't. Not yet. Soon, though.

Unfortunately, Ziara was left with lots of time to think over what had occurred between them, as if she hadn't replayed it a hundred times in the dark of night. His kiss had been seductive in more than the obvious sense. It had made her blossom with beauty, power and wantonness. Therein lay the rub. She wanted to revel in the passion Sloan evoked, whether they were sparring or kissing. But she couldn't because it might lead to becoming the one thing she'd promised herself she never would.

As for work, she couldn't fathom how she'd ever behave normally again. Why did it have to be this particular man who affected her like this? The one man who could tear down the respectable career she'd worked so long and hard for with just a few words.

Deciding to bite the bullet as they stood at the luggage carousel, she turned and said, "Would you like me to pick up some lunch on my way to work?"

"Go home," he said.

Ziara's body froze with her emotions. She couldn't see for

a moment. Everything went blurry. When her vision cleared, Sloan was propping her suitcase in front of her. Was he so fed up, so desperate to be rid of her, he would fire her despite Vivian's insistence that they work together? Not that Vivian would oppose him once she found out what Ziara had done.

"Rest today," he said, his voice a little softer this time. His gaze inventoried her face, probably noting the swelling under her eyes and the red rims she'd been unable to cover this morning. "The real work starts tomorrow."

He turned and walked away without looking back, leaving confusion and an achy longing behind.

Desperately needing something to distract herself, Ziara tried to catch up on things she probably wouldn't have a chance to do in the weeks to come unless Sloan changed his mind about firing her before tomorrow. Deep cleaning the house and weeding the flower beds were always good for keeping her hands busy. Too bad her mind didn't want to cooperate.

But even if he didn't fire her, she knew in her heart she'd have to move on as soon as the show was over. Even if Vivian graciously extended the offer to be her executive assistant to Ziara, just knowing Sloan was right around the corner and could appear at any minute would keep her on edge.

It looked like she'd end up losing, after all. Her heart tightened, grieving as much for the loss of her beloved position within this company as it did for the necessity of keeping Sloan at arm's length. She hadn't just worked for Eternity Designs, she'd believed in its values, its purpose, and had hoped security could be found within its ranks.

As she went inside to clean up, she couldn't hold the tears back any longer. They mingled with the streaming water of the shower, invisible enough that she could dismiss her shame.

What was happening to her? All these emotions, so long buried deep inside, were erupting at every twist and turn. This was exactly why she didn't want them—because she couldn't control them. Or maybe she grieved because she did want them yet couldn't express them.

Guess she could add confusion to the messy pile.

Tears spent, she dried off, shaking away the last vestiges of depression and guilt. She dressed casually in khaki capris and a fuchsia T-shirt, then brushed out her hair in front of the bathroom vanity. Everyone was allowed one colossal mistake in their lifetime, right? This was hers. At least her conscience was clear. Her mistake wouldn't hurt anyone but herself.

Padding into the kitchen, she immersed herself in cooking dinner. Something as far from paella as she could get.

She threw together a quick southwestern chicken panini, which she coupled simply with apple and orange sections. Delicious as it was, she'd only managed to choke down half when the doorbell rang. Grateful for an excuse to give up on the pretense of eating, she straightened her T-shirt on the way to the door.

Shock sizzled through her when the door swung open to reveal Vivian. Without waiting for an invitation, her mentor glided inside. Ziara remained speechless for a moment. In the six years she'd been working for Eternity Designs, she'd never seen the Creightons outside the office. Now in the space of a week, both of them had shown up unannounced at her house.

After a thorough glance around the room, Vivian turned to face Ziara. "Is he here?"

Though Ziara understood, she still asked, "Who?"

"Sloan, of course."

Ziara easily pulled her facade into place, almost amazed at how well she could handle the accusation. But then again, she didn't have anything left to lose. "Sloan is not here, Vivian, and I resent the implication that he would be."

Vivian studied her for a moment, brows raised as if surprised Ziara would stand up for herself. Then her chin dipped in a slow nod of acknowledgment. Luckily Ziara found she could meet Vivian's eyes without a problem. A glimmer of compassion streaked through her as she noted Vivian's disarray, in contrast to her usually immaculate appearance.

"Perhaps we could sit and talk," Ziara said. She gestured Vivian into the sitting area facing the fireplace. The overstuffed chair and chaise weren't necessarily elegant, but they were comfortable and their deep burgundy hue complemented the fire-glazed tiles covering the hearth. "Can I get you something to drink? Coffee? Sweet tea?"

Vivian shook her head, a trembling sigh escaping her coppery brown lips. "That's what I so like about you, Ziara," she said. "Always cool under pressure, knowing just the right thing to say."

Ziara perched on the edge of the chaise opposite Vivian, wishing the same were true in her relationship with Sloan. *Business.* Business relationship with Sloan. They didn't have anything outside of that...anymore.

"I know my accusation was rude. But considering Sloan's history with assistants and this trip to Vegas..." She made a vague gesture with her hand, her diamond rings glittering in the soft evening light. "I assumed something I shouldn't have, knowing you. You are far too smart a girl to get mixed up with a smooth talker like my stepson."

Ziara prudently kept her mouth shut and her face impassive.

"Did Sloan procure a designer?"

Ziara now wished they'd go back to the sex issue. There were a lot less mines in that field.

Vivian grimaced. "Ziara, I'm going to find out eventually. I'd rather be informed now than surprised in front of my employees."

Ziara was too emotionally exhausted to come up with a clever sidestep. "He's hired Patrick Vinalay."

Vivian stood immediately, the *click* of her heels rapping on the wood floor. "I should have known Patrick would be the one to take him up on the offer. But it will put a kink in my plans."

Ziara frowned. "What do you mean?"

Vivian turned to face her, the pale cream of her skin contrasting with the bold colors of Ziara's home. "I thought I could get around whatever he might do by influencing Robert to cause a few delays until I could find a backer to bail me out, but having someone else on the design floor will change that."

With a jolt, Ziara realized how serious Vivian was about

this. Her mentor, the woman who had taught her the meaning of professionalism, had actually considered sabotaging her own company. Delays in production could have bogged down the rest of the process, resulting in major issues at showtime. Maybe even cancellation.

Unaware of Ziara's growing alarm, Vivian smiled and said, "I'll just have to find another way to get what I want."

Sloan paused for a moment after exiting the elevator, his pulse pounding as he stared at the door to his office suite down the hall. How ironic that after years of sidestepping persistently amorous employees, he now found himself on the other end, wondering how he could go back to acting like a normal boss. Especially when all he wanted was to lay Ziara across his desk and— He coughed to clear his throat. *This wasn't helping.*

If only he hadn't seen those red-rimmed eyes. Knowing how much he'd upset her, when she could usually be counted on as the calm one, put those boundaries firmly back into place. Determined not to cause any embarrassment, he marched forward.

"Good morning, Ziara," he said as he swept by her desk. "Could you get me the location contract, please?"

"Sure," she mumbled.

He took that for as good a sign as he was gonna get. They spent the morning focused on the push for the show, smoothing out location details and ordering fabrics Sloan already knew they needed.

Ziara left for lunch at 11:30 a.m. on the dot, but Sloan stayed behind, trying to breathe after a morning of straining to act normal and, honestly, trying to hide his erection. Once he had himself under control, he figured it might be a good idea if he headed down and gave the Old Brigade a heads-up. Patrick was due to be in sometime today, but he hadn't texted Sloan to let him know when.

Exiting on the third floor, he heard raised voices. *Oops. This visit was just a little too late.* He eased onto the overlook. Remaining back in the shadows, he studied the scene below. Patrick had arrived and no one was happy about it. Seeing

Ziara standing to one side of the fray, he made his way down the staircase and slipped up behind her.

Unable to resist, he leaned in close to her ear. "Did I miss the start of the war?"

In his chest, he felt the shivers that moved down her spine, urging him to press closer. How quickly his resolve was shaken by the temptation of almost touching that caramel skin.

His mind focused on the heat from the exposed curve of her neck and the vanilla scent drifting from the tamed confection of her hair.

"I ran into Patrick at the door," she murmured. "And made the mistake of letting him in."

Patrick was throwing out orders as if he owned the place, which didn't surprise Sloan in the least. Patrick knew how to captivate a room, but true resistance didn't bring out the best in him. No one appeared to be playing nicely.

"This is my studio and it will run the way I say," Robert bellowed.

Patrick folded his arms over his chest. "Really? When I signed on it was with the express understanding that final say would be mine."

Robert gasped, his hand clasping his heart, in contrast to Anthony, who stood silently in the background, watching the scene before him with somber eyes. "Say it isn't so!"

Patrick chuckled, prompting Robert to launch into a litany of French while Anthony's face turned red to the point of glowing. Sloan feared the way he bottled things up might cause a heart attack.

Taking control, Sloan let his voice boom out across the massive room, bringing everything to a halt. "That's enough."

Ziara jumped as he moved away from her, stepping forward from his position on the sidelines. "Patrick is here to modernize the line."

"But we don't need him," Robert insisted.

Sloan went on as if he hadn't spoken. "He will take the basic designs you put together and adjust or add to them as needed.

I have given him final say in the overall designs for the fall line to speed things up."

As Robert sputtered, Sloan pinned him with a look. "Do you want this studio to close?"

"No," Robert said, resignation in the very lines of his face.

"Then I suggest you find a way to make this work."

Not as diplomatic as he could have handled it, but effective. Sloan let his gaze sweep the whole group. "You two will put together the basic designs we've already approved, with Patrick adding what he believes is necessary. He'll have his hands full between that and his additional line."

"Additional line?" They all jumped as Vivian's voice erupted from behind them. "And what would that be?"

She walked toward the men, bypassing Ziara with barely a glance. Sloan's blood started to pound through his veins, that instinct to clash rising to the fore. But he checked himself, his curiosity starting to stir. How much had his little assistant given away already? He'd been with her most of the morning, but he couldn't account for every phone call, every second in the office. Or out of it.

"Still causing trouble, I see, Patrick," she said.

"Vivian." Patrick grinned. "As lovely and cold as ever."

She frowned but let the comment pass as her eyes swept over the men to rest on Sloan. "What do you mean, another line? We'll have a hard enough time coming up with one." She turned to examine Patrick from under raised brows. "Don't tell me he's going to do some kind of trashy, glitzy gowns. Surely taste hasn't gone that far downhill."

Why was she ignoring Ziara? He didn't want to believe that Ziara would rat him out, but Vivian was her mentor. Was Vivian testing him? Did she already know what was coming? The thought nibbled at the back of his brain. Ziara stood at the rear of the group, her brows lowered, arms crossed tightly over her stomach. Noting every curve, every shift, he still couldn't tell if she was transmitting nerves or guilt. He remembered her tortured expression as she'd asked him to stop—*please don't let it be guilt.* Deep inside, he needed her to be innocent, needed someone to be on his side.

"Actually, Vivian, it won't involve wedding dresses at all," Sloan said, going on the offensive.

Vivian stiffened. Enjoying himself, he let a smirk slip onto his lips. Even though Ziara's silent stare weighed heavy on him.

"Then what is it?" Vivian asked.

"He'll be launching our new lingerie line."

Sloan may have delivered the news with just a bit too much relish. The room became so still that from several feet away he heard Vivian's ragged intake of breath.

"Absolutely not!"

The furious look she threw Ziara definitively answered his questions—the woman he'd held in his arms, who clung so tightly to her professionalism that she would turn away from the inferno they created together, had stood her ground. Or rather, his ground. She'd kept his secret, despite the risk of losing the career Vivian held in the palm of her hand.

Now—if he didn't succeed, he wouldn't just lose the company. Ziara would lose everything she'd worked so hard to achieve.

Thirteen

Sloan and Patrick holed up in his office for most of the afternoon while Ziara practically collapsed at her desk. Work was beyond her for the first time in her life.

As if in slow motion, she relived Vivian turning until her accusing eyes met Ziara's. She knew Vivian would forever hold her responsible for not telling her about the lingerie line the day before. Her stomach clenched as the ramifications of her actions hit her. When Vivian turned and left without a word, Ziara had said her final goodbyes to the position she'd worked so hard to attain.

Vivian would never give it to someone she couldn't trust.

But would Sloan believe her now if Ziara came to him with the truth? She'd been trying all day to find the right time to tell him about Vivian's threat, but each time she'd hesitated. They'd maintained a strictly professional attitude toward each other that she'd been afraid to upset. That balance was so fragile. What would happen if she brought up such a personal subject?

"Wish me luck, sweet cheeks," Patrick said, sweeping by her toward the suite doors. "I'm off to face Mutt and Jeff."

She frowned, her strained emotions too heavy to hide. "Their names are Robert and Anthony."

He leaned against the doorframe. "It was just a joke."

"I know. But Robert and Anthony are going to have a difficult time adjusting to this. They've devoted many years to this company. Joking might not be the way to go."

A light grin tugged his lips. "I can take a hint. Just remember, I'm making the best of a situation they created."

Hoping her expression told him she understood, she nodded and watched him slip out the door. Then she dropped her head into her hands as the roller coaster of emotions of the past few days—heck, the past few hours—got the better of her.

She'd lost so much—her direction, her focus—and for what? Where would she go from here? Once Sloan got through the fall show she'd have to leave. But how could she find a job that would mean as much to her as this one?

"Ziara."

She heard Sloan's husky voice at the same moment that his heated palm cupped the back of her neck. She sensed him kneeling beside her chair, but she couldn't bring herself to raise her head, because she knew her face would be an open book at the moment.

"Ziara," he tried again. "Are you okay?"

No, she wanted to cry. Instead, she wiped the emotion from her face as she would tears, then sat up straight. She nodded shortly. "Yes. I'm just tired."

Skirting around her, he propped himself on the edge of her desk. She tried hard not to notice the sculpted muscles of his thigh, revealed by the pull of his slacks.

That husky drawl came again. "Do you need to go home?"

Like the snap of a twig, the pressure broke her prized control. She tilted her head to the side in order to face him. "Why are you being so nice to me?"

He choked on a laugh, those electric eyes widening. "Am I not supposed to be?"

"No. I mean, after…" She shook her head. "I'm not handling this very well."

"Me, either," he said, his voice deepening as he slid off the desk, then lifted her to stand before him. Using her arms to draw her against his chest, he bent to take her lips in a kiss that made no mistake as to his needs.

To Ziara's shame, she couldn't pull away, even knowing they were at the office. Her lips opened with a groan and her mind shut down. On a purely physical level, she met him pant for pant, kiss for kiss, lick for lick. Sloan's hands tightened to the point of pain on her arms, but it was one more sensation in the flood. Her control completely evaporating, she allowed him to lead her wherever he wanted to go.

Suddenly he pulled away, staring down at her, leaving her dazed and panting. "Not one word. Just go in my office."

Confused, Ziara thought he was speaking to her until she caught a glimpse of Patrick sweeping past. Her eyes snapped shut, her head dropping forward in shame. How could she have let this happen? Here of all places.

With a nudge of his fingers under her chin, Sloan raised her face. Opening her eyes, she noted his expression numbly at first, then with growing awe.

Instead of the crazed lust or judgment she'd expected, his eyes sparked with honest desire and a touch of tenderness. A reverence she'd never expected to receive from a man warmed the icy blue of his eyes. The look sent her own need into hyperdrive.

"I guess we'll have to put this discussion on hold," he said, tracing her moist lips with his thumb. His eyes narrowed in resolve. "But we will talk, Ziara, because neither of us is going to be able to ignore what's happening here."

Turning, he entered his office and shut the door behind him, leaving her to wilt into her chair. She should be worrying about Patrick—what he'd seen, what he assumed. She should be worrying about Vivian and her own future. Instead, she trembled inside, thinking only of Sloan's parting words.

Sloan and Patrick remained in conference so long that Ziara took the opportunity to slip out and head home. She desperately needed some time to herself, time to sort through her feelings.

As she concentrated on assembling lasagna for dinner, hoping the tedious layering would help her focus, she acknowledged that she'd had other reasons for calling a halt to things in Las Vegas. Reasons much deeper than Sloan being her boss.

Because, deep down, the thing she feared most was what might come the morning after. She didn't know how to do more, or whether he would want to do more...or if he would even care about the consequences. But every time he looked at her with that mixture of passion and admiration, she came a foot closer to crossing that inevitable line. She forced her mind to give it a rest as she focused on the task at hand. Sauce, noodles, sauce, ricotta cheese, mozzarella, then noodles again. Swaying slightly to the sultry jazz music playing through the house's sound system, she savored the feel of the cool tile beneath her bare feet. Breathing deep, she pulled in the smell of tomatoes and oregano enriching the air around her, blending with the darkness creeping down outside to cool the summer heat.

She'd just grated a small block of Parmesan onto the top and put the pan in the oven when the doorbell rang. An uncharacteristic expletive slipped out as she wiped her hands. The sound of her own doorbell now filled her with dread.

She barely got the lock turned when the door burst open. Sloan stalked through, slamming it shut behind him. Holding her gaze, he slipped the lock back into place, then strode across the small foyer to where she'd backed up against the love seat.

Without a word, his hands anchored in her hair, dragging her mouth to his. She had a brief moment to wonder about his obsession with her hair before surrendering to the dark current of desire.

Her body melted into his, her head automatically tilting to

the side to accommodate his mouth. When she made no protest, his hands slid from her hair over her shoulders and along her spine to cup her rear end, pulling her forward to meet his erection. With a groan, he pushed into the cradle of her hips. Her body arched, rising to meet his demands.

Before she could think, her shirt was unbuttoned. He peeled it open to reveal her breasts. Pulling back just the upper part of his body, Sloan spent moments memorizing the view. The pressure from below reassured her that he liked what he saw.

She wished she could see his hands as they cupped her through her bra, but she couldn't tear her gaze away from his face. Thoughts of losing his respect fled in the wake of the awe glowing in his expression, the utter pleasure he took in touching her.

Pride intensified her response. She wanted to revel in his reactions. Pushing herself farther into his hands, she shivered as a zing shot from her nipples to that all-important point between her thighs. The pressure there was heavenly yet growing more urgent with his every touch.

Allowing her head to fall back, she lost all strength as he sucked and licked his way along her neck. He anchored her to his body with his arm around her hips.

After pausing for a moment to savor the rapid pulse at the vulnerable base of her neck, he lifted her into his arms and carried her down the hallway. As if by instinct, he strode past several rooms with barely a glance, pausing outside only one.

"I should have known," he murmured, then strode across the room to lay her on the bed. Soft illumination from the doorway and a candle lit earlier glinted off the gold threads in the purple bedspread, the silky material caressing her bare skin when Sloan laid her down. After stripping her, he stood and tore off his own clothes, his gaze never leaving hers as he quickly slid on protection.

The sight of his body took her breath away. Long, lean muscles. Smooth, firm chest. Strong, tight thighs. Her core ached for the steely length between them. She wanted to touch him, savor every new discovery. But he was already crawling onto the bed and spreading her trembling thighs to his gaze.

The flash of vulnerability surprised her. She knew he wouldn't hurt her, wouldn't humiliate her. But the fears still lingered.

"Sloan, slow down," she gasped.

He stretched to take her mouth in a hard kiss before resting his forehead against hers. His panting breath sounded loud in the quiet. Only faint music could be heard from down the hall.

"I can't, Ziara," he said. "I've waited too long, wanted too hard. Please let me in now."

She hesitated, knowing that if she did, there would be no turning back. Already her hands and thighs shook with the effort of holding herself together, but her need was too great. She had to meet him all the way. As she'd feared, there would be no half measures.

And hopefully no regrets.

She groaned, her thighs sliding apart. Reaching down with a boldness that surprised her, she took him in her hand and guided him to her hot, wet entrance. He pushed inside with one plunge.

His body in hers sparked a tingly firestorm that burned between her thighs and spread outward to every point of her body. To the tips of her fingers, the top of her head. She could feel him imprinting on every part of her.

As he moved, the fire built higher and hotter. She'd never yearned to let go like this. Even though warnings screamed inside her brain, for once she thrust them away, so she could revel in how he made her feel.

She was drunk—not off wine, but off the sensation of having him so deep inside her, having him devour her with his gaze, having him stroke and praise her. His possession went straight to her head like tiny champagne bubbles.

With a cry, a sharp peak overcame her, but his whispered words in her ear brought her quickly to another.

The contractions were intense and powerful but not satisfying. As he levered onto his arms and pounded between her thighs, her body writhed, lifting to meet him, demanding more and more until she finally exploded in an outward expansion. Thousands of pieces flying out, a moment of nothingness, then floating back to make her whole again.

As she collapsed into the softness of the comforter, she heard Sloan shout. He buried himself hard within her body, holding stone still as he emptied himself.

A part of her, she dimly thought, then accepted him into her arms when he collapsed. Absently she stroked the slick muscles of his back, wanting only to keep this connection from fading so reality couldn't enter.

He groaned and moved against her but didn't try to leave. His mouth traveled up her neck, settling below her ear as he nuzzled close. Sensation stabbed into her nipples, and her hips lifted in response.

With an appreciative chuckle, he slowly pulled away, then disappeared into the bathroom with his pants after a quick brush of his lips over hers. Who knew when sex worked, really worked, that there were so many shocks along the way? With this man, only this one, sex had been one incredible sensation after another.

She lay in the bed, absorbing the quiet, but as she stared at the chiffon strips of material that formed her canopy, tension rapidly spilled back into her system.

What was she doing here? In the rush of sensations, thinking had been beyond her. As panic set in, she jerked to her feet, rushing through the room to grab clothes and drag them back on.

Her regular clothes didn't feel nearly secure enough, so she pulled a sweater from the closet and slid her arms inside, tightening its hold on her like a straitjacket. She stared into the dark depths of the closet, grateful for the nothingness for a moment.

Until her gaze focused in on her work clothes: suit jackets, A-line skirts, dress pants, severe button-down shirts. Work. She was a different person there. He was a different person—her boss.

The panic spread, making it hard to breathe. She didn't even hear Sloan until he was right behind her. "Ziara, are you okay?"

She didn't respond. She couldn't with her throat closing. When his arms reached around to circle her waist, she jumped, whirling toward him, then backing into the darkness of the closet in a misguided effort at hiding.

"Hey, it's all right," he said, his voice still as husky as when he'd been moaning in her bed. "What's the matter?"

Her head started to shake back and forth. "I can't do this. I really can't. We just can't do this."

She realized her eyes had closed, enfolding her in the darkness. After a deep breath, she opened them to focus on Sloan's face just inches from hers. His breath warmed her cheek.

"Talk to me, Ziara."

Sucking in air seemed a herculean task, but she managed, calling on years of maintaining a perfectly calm demeanor. When she could finally focus on Sloan in front of her, she took in his pale features without the protection of her normal walls. The thought almost started the panic again, but she shoved it away, tucking it down in a teeny tiny box to deal with later. Much later.

"I'm s-sorry..." she stuttered. "I've never had, whatever that was..."

"I think you had a panic attack," Sloan said. His shoulders dropped as he relaxed, though his hands continued to cup her face. "Are you okay?"

"I think so." *No, absolutely not.*

"Want to tell me what brought that on?"

"I...I..." Just one more deep breath. "I guess it just hit me. What happened. What—what we'd done."

He nodded as if her stream of consciousness made any sense at all. "Come here," he said.

When she started to follow him, she realized her muscles had turned into Twizzlers. She walked, but it took all her concentration to keep everything from wiggling all over the place. Wow. Since when did sex turn people completely unstable? Of course, she'd felt that way ever since she'd met Sloan, so this wasn't something new.

He led her to the overstuffed reading chair in the corner of the bedroom, where he settled and pulled her into his lap, all in one motion. Protest wasn't an option. He simply did what he wanted.

Unconsciously her fingers made short, light strokes across the top of his pecs, exploring the light smattering of hair that rested beneath them.

"I'm going to ask one more time," he said gently. "What's going on in that little worry factory in your head?"

Any other time, she would have smiled at the analogy, because it was pretty close to accurate. But right now she couldn't. "Sloan, this is completely wrong—"

"Doesn't feel that way," he said, his mouth nuzzling into the crook of her neck.

The shivers he elicited felt so good, but she gallantly reached for control. "Stop," she said, proud of her firm, no-nonsense tone, though her attempts to stand were promptly thwarted. "Sloan, you're my boss. I can't believe I lost my head long enough to forget that."

"I can." She didn't appreciate his grin. Her stern stare changed his tune. "Look. I understand this is a little unusual. But the fact is, I'm not technically your employer. Vivian is. And—" he continued a little louder when she would have argued "—I'm working with you temporarily. Once Abigail retires, you'll go back to working in Vivian's office."

Her frown drew tighter as she realized he hadn't come to the same conclusions she had. Vivian wasn't going to keep her on, no matter what. Better to change tactics. "You'll abandon the company?"

Luckily Sloan kept a hold on her when he jerked to his feet or she would have fallen. But he quickly let go to pace several feet away. He didn't give her a chance to get steady before he started speaking, his voice rough and low. "What the hell? Why would you think that?"

"I...I didn't mean..." Maybe it would be better to keep her

mouth shut. She truly wasn't sure where the question had come from, except she knew Vivian hadn't been worried about Sloan being around long-term. She chose the safe route. "I know you have other companies, other projects."

"Yes, but my father's company means a hell of a lot more to me than those."

Immediately guilt settled in Ziara's stomach. In her own panic, she'd forgotten the whole reason Sloan was even at Eternity Designs. "I'm sorry, Sloan."

For a moment he didn't move, his tall body a looming tower, his head lowered as if in grief. But when his head lifted once more, none of that emotion showed on his face. He crossed the short space between them to take her once more in his arms. "Look, this will be fine. I'm only your boss for a couple more months, at the most. Until then we'll keep this strictly out of the office."

She couldn't help but wonder if she accepted his reasoning simply to give herself permission to stay right where she was, burrowed deep in his warmth and masculine scent. But for once she was going to do what she wanted, not what the job required. "Agreed," she whispered.

After a thorough kiss, Sloan cocked his head to one side. His nostrils flared as he breathed deep.

"What's that smell?" he asked.

Sniffing, Ziara caught a whiff of Sloan's citrusy scent, followed quickly by the sharp tang of burning cheese.

"Oh, no," she said, rushing toward the hall. "The lasagna."

Fourteen

Ziara was able to salvage most of dinner because only the outer edges had burned. Sloan found this very amusing and teased her as they ate.

"You are a great cook," he finally said. "Who taught you?"

She picked up their plates and crossed to the sink, feeling a little too vulnerable still to face him. "I taught myself." Turning on the water, she rinsed the plates. "My mom…worked a lot. I had to either cook or live off cheese and crackers."

Not wanting to elaborate, she concentrated on cleaning up. Ever since her brain had come down from its mind-numbing high, she'd been struggling with conflicting emotions. She didn't want to enjoy being with Sloan, and the fact that she did—although *enjoy* was way too mild a word for how she was feeling—was something she might not be ready to face. Being with him intimately hadn't been dirty or sordid or even ordinary. And it wasn't just the sex she'd enjoyed, it was the eating and talking and laughing….

Ziara was so lost in thought that she didn't notice Sloan approaching until his warmth cradled her back. "What are you doing?" he asked, his hands resting on her hips. His moist lips nuzzled through her hair to the back of her neck.

More than anything she wanted to melt into his warmth, to experience again the joy of being a part of him.

"I—I'm cleaning up. What does it look like?"

"What if I want some more?"

Twisting in his grip, she tried to see his face. "Why didn't you say something? You can have another plate."

He closed in, his hips tight against her backside, giving her an unmistakable impression of his hardness. "I didn't mean more food."

Her breathing accelerated, currents of excitement jumping from his hands straight between her thighs. She wanted to stroke back and forth, letting every inch of her back discover every inch of his front. Then she'd turn and repeat the moves all over.

He was an addiction. A tempting treat. She could discover every texture and taste of his body, branding him as hers with her scent and touch. As his hands traveled from her hips to her breasts, she wondered if she was losing her mind.

At least she was enjoying the ride.

He turned her to face him, claiming her mouth with his. Slowly unbuttoning and unzipping her capris, he allowed them to slide down to the floor around her feet, followed quickly by her panties.

With a flex of his biceps, he lifted her onto the tile counter. A squeal rang out as her bare bottom met the chilled surface. He chuckled.

"That's sadistic," she accused.

He grinned, his dark gold hair falling softly from the crown of his head to frame his devilish good looks, reminding her of a Hollywood bad boy.

"I'm all about the sensations," he said.

The grin quickly melted into a more serious look, making her feel like prey. Her heartbeat picked up again, and she tried to pull him to her, but he didn't budge. Layers disappeared:

her sweater and cotton T-shirt, followed by the tank she'd put on in lieu of a bra.

He kissed her thoroughly, letting his hands trail down her arms, which he guided behind her and propped on the counter.

When he released her mouth, she found herself leaning back on her braced arms, her body on display for him to peruse at his leisure. Instantly awkwardness swept in. How could she let him see every little part that she'd kept hidden for so long?

When she tried to lift herself up, his hands on her shoulders held her still. After one dark look, his gaze moved down... along with his hands. She should have felt shamed, wanton in this position, especially when he pushed between her legs and propped her feet on his hips. There was absolutely nowhere to hide.

She let her head fall back and her eyes close. Therein lay her only protection from his onslaught.

Before he finally entered her, he had explored each and every part of her body with thorough intent, branding her with his touch.

She didn't recognize the moans and whimpers erupting from her mouth. She only knew if she didn't have him, she couldn't make it through the next few minutes. His body in hers was a momentary relief, but when he thrust deep, the fire returned ten times hotter. She exploded within minutes, Sloan following close behind.

With their ragged breathing echoing off the tile, she didn't even care about being put back together again.

Pulling himself out of Ziara's bed at two-thirty the next morning wasn't an easy or pleasant task for Sloan, but he forced himself to return to his own house. They needed to slow down—and certainly needed to downplay anything that smacked of a relationship, sexual or otherwise.

He'd tossed aside Ziara's concerns last night and he stood by his decision on both counts. But he knew no matter what he'd told her earlier, Vivian would kick her to the curb the minute she discovered they were sleeping together. She was only barely tolerating Ziara after learning about the lingerie line.

So he'd stay in control. They'd be careful. He could have her and protect her—somehow.

When he'd suspected a mystery lay beneath Ziara's cool exterior, he hadn't known the half of it. He felt like he'd cracked that hard surface and found the richest pool of tempting dark chocolate, so deep he could drown in her.

Willingly.

That was the scary part. Her loyalty, her integrity, her professionalism—all wrapped up in the sexiest package he'd ever touched. It made him want the very thing he was trying to hide: a chance just to be with her. He couldn't articulate the why of it. It was just Ziara.

Coming through the door to his office suite seven hours later, he barely controlled his double take. There sat Ziara, looking as calm, crisp and professional as she always did. He couldn't reconcile it with the woman who'd wrapped her silky, toned legs around his waist while he gave her multiple orgasms the night before.

Looking at her now, he wanted to kiss color into her lips and cheeks. Better yet, make her eyes glint with mischievous passion. But that was in direct violation of their agreement. He barely controlled the impulse to rip every last pin out of her hair until it fell in a black cascade down her back.

Wouldn't Vivian just love that?

As if sensing a presence, she glanced up from her desk, eyebrow raised in inquiry. A tentative smile peeked from her lips—not her normal professional greeting, but a small, secretive smile full of the knowledge of what they'd done to each other the night before.

He stalked to her desk and leaned forward onto his hands. "I want to tear your clothes off."

Her eyes widened a bit before returning to normal. Her lips pressed together as if to contain a laugh, though it didn't disguise their sensual fullness. "Shh, not in the office. Besides,

Abigail called to say Vivian wanted you on the design floor in twenty minutes. A reporter is coming to interview y'all."

He cursed under his breath. "Guess I'll have to put my plans on hold until tonight then. The least you can do is come along and protect me from the big, bad dragon lady."

He paused, giving her a moment to back out. Her subdued "Sure" swept through him like a victory dance. He wouldn't jeopardize her reputation here at work, but he had to have her again. Soon.

Fatigue hovered at the edges of Sloan's consciousness a few hours later. The reporter had been excited about something new and different to feature in an upcoming society page, and had snapped at least a hundred pictures of the design floor.

Ziara had tried a few times to head back up to the office, but Sloan or Patrick always distracted her before she could get away. Constantly conferring with her over details of the actual show and even some of the fabric choices had kept her in close range—exactly where Sloan wanted her.

But she'd definitely started to lag at the end, her normally calm tone growing short and her posture tight. The most trying thing, the one thing that seemed to tap her energy while revving up Sloan's, had been Vivian's disapproving stare. Oh, she'd managed to keep it out of range of the camera, but Sloan could feel the bad vibes emanating from her on more than one occasion. At least she seemed to be an equal opportunity dispenser of disapproval. No one but the reporter and Robert could do any right this morning.

Sloan just wanted to crawl back under the covers and sleep, right up against his naked assistant. Problem was, lunchtime had barely arrived.

"Check out the feature in the Sunday paper on the seventeenth," the reporter threw back over her shoulder as she and the cameraman swept from the room.

Sloan could see his own weariness reflected back at him in Patrick. "Is it just me," his friend asked, "or was that woman way too perky for anytime before lunch?"

A giggle slipped from Ziara's lips, but she quickly went silent under Vivian's disapproving gaze.

"Considering how quickly we're trying to pull this together, we should be grateful for all the publicity we can get," the stern matron said.

Ziara backed slowly away, disquiet leaking through the cracks of her professional facade. Patrick simply raised a brow and turned away, letting the comment slide over him like water off a raincoat.

"Ziara," Sloan said, ready to get away from the old witch himself. "Let's head back upstairs and get some work done before the whole day is gone."

They arrived at the elevators together, slipping in just as the door opened, not realizing Vivian had joined them until they turned back to face the closing door. *Damn it. Would this day never end?*

"Since I realize a written report is a bit too much to expect from you, Sloan, why don't you bring me up-to-date on where we stand at the moment?" she said.

Not seeing the point of haggling, Sloan gave her a quick rundown of the current budget and status on the design work. By the time he finished, they were in the upper hallway and Ziara was eyeing the door leading toward their office—and away from Vivian—with desperate yearning. Sloan couldn't blame her. Vivian's shoulders tightened the longer Sloan spoke, even though he presented the facts in a clear, dry manner. Any minute now she was gonna blow her top.

"And when are you planning to show me the designs for the...lingerie?" Vivian asked, making the word sound like trash to be picked up from the side of the road. *Ah, here it came.* "Or were you planning on surprising me, just as you did with Patrick?"

"I didn't realize you expected me to run every idea by you, especially since your approval isn't necessary," Sloan replied.

Ziara pressed her lips together, her tension palpable. This did have all the makings of a pissing match and for once he'd rather be anywhere else. Like in Ziara's cozy, colorful bedroom.

"I simply think that running things by me would show a little decency, since I am still the majority owner of this establishment."

Sloan kept it short, but not sweet. "Decency isn't part of our agreement."

"You mean not a part of your agreement—or hers, I'm learning."

"That's enough, Vivian."

She chose to ignore Sloan's warning, turning the full force of her ire on Ziara. "You were supposed to be keeping an eye out on him, keeping me informed."

"I did," Ziara said with quiet dignity, though Sloan read unease in her carefully guarded expression.

"About everything?"

"Ziara is doing what she thinks is right for this company," Sloan interrupted. "She loves Eternity Designs and wants to see it regain its rightful place in the market, just as I do."

Vivian shot another glare over Sloan's shoulder, so palpable it probably burned Ziara's skin. "What's best for Eternity isn't her decision to make. It's mine."

"Typical of you, Vivian. Last I remember, your decisions ran this place into the ground." Sloan's voice was laced with so much venom he was surprised any of them were left standing. Years of resentment and loneliness surged inside him, anger over losing his father breaking through the surface. "Drop it. Ziara's doing a damn good job bringing this show to life. She can't do that and be at your beck and call all the time. Or don't you remember how much work that really is?"

If anything, Vivian's gaze turned positively glacial. "What I remember is all the work I've put into keeping this company afloat. Your father's dream has kept me going since his death."

"And you've shut me out," Sloan fought back. He was in rare form today. "But that's what you wanted, wasn't it?"

"I did what I thought was best, what *your father* would have wanted."

Sloan stalked closer, the carpeting muffling his steps. "If

Father wanted me out, why would he have bothered leaving me forty percent?"

"How would it have looked if he'd left his son with nothing?"

"You know, Vivian," he said, "I don't think he cared about how things looked nearly as much as you do."

The truth hit really hard, and Vivian's face flushed a mottled red. "I will not let you ruin me."

"If I wanted to, you couldn't stop me."

Sloan turned and walked away, calling Ziara to follow him. But the memory of Vivian's face remained with him for the rest of the afternoon.

Outrage? Yes. Anger? Yes. But something else, something underneath that hinted at desperation. What would Vivian do if she felt that Sloan had backed her into a corner? If he succeeded, would Vivian rejoice in Eternity Designs's success or ruin it for the chance to keep her position as its CEO?

And did his lover have any idea what might be coming their way?

Fifteen

A few days later, Ziara stalked down the hall after a frustrating hour mediating between the two-ton egos on the design floor downstairs. As if her emotions weren't shaky enough! She could barely restrain herself from yelling, *Behave like the adults you are or I'll send you to time-out like you deserve.*

But she'd managed to keep her prized cool. Just barely.

Since their confrontation with Vivian, the cracks in her professional facade started by Sloan's lovemaking had widened. Vivian's rejection hurt, more than the taunts of her childhood, but she'd pushed through to do whatever she could to make this show a success. She owed Eternity Designs and Vivian that much, even if Vivian didn't want it.

Deep inside she'd convinced herself that Vivian would change her mind once Eternity Designs regained stable footing. She'd understand Ziara's decisions, instead of condemning her—and somehow Ziara would be able to remain a part of this home away from home.

Somehow.

Finally reaching her desk, she sank into the seat and swiveled to face the desktop. Exhaustion lowered over her like a heavy mantle. The long days of tension and emotional turmoil—good and bad—were taking their toll. As she dropped her head into her hands, her elbow connected with something on her desk. Glancing down, she found a long, rectangular present wrapped in iridescent paper. Her mind remained blank for long moments, but slowly trickles of excitement filtered in.

Gifts were few and far between in her life. The small Christmas presents exchanged in the office and with a couple of neighbors were the extent of her experience. She almost couldn't believe someone had gotten her something special, something just for her.

Lifting the box, she found a piece of Sloan's personal stationary underneath: "Enjoy, Sloan." With delicate care, she peeled back the paper, revealing a flat, black jeweler's box with feminine gold lettering: Par Excellence, Las Vegas.

Old fears made her drop the box like she'd discovered a big, hairy tarantula was living inside it. The simple package filled her with dread despite her commonsense knowledge that it was just a box, a small gift of appreciation. Giving herself a firm talking-to, she reached out to pick it up with a fairly steady hand.

Her heart started freezing before she even had the lid open. By the time the teardrop diamond pendant, hung on a delicate gold chain, came into view, she'd gone completely numb.

"Is that from your trip to Vegas?"

The unexpected sound of Vivian's voice made Ziara jump. She almost never came to Sloan's office, preferring to send Abigail when she needed something. What sin had Ziara committed to condemn her to Vivian's presence at just this moment? The layer of distaste underlying Vivian's tone compounded her own churning emotions.

"I suppose so," Ziara said, too shaken to play defense. With a deep breath, she looked up at her former mentor.

Vivian watched her for a moment, her gaze then moving to the sparkling necklace. "You are a dedicated employee with the tact and control to excel as an executive assistant, Ziara.

I've been extremely concerned by your behavior since you took this position."

"I don't understand," Ziara said, her words more forceful than she would normally have used with her employer. She shook her head. "I thought you trusted my judgment? You are the one who put me here."

Vivian nodded. "That's because I thought you had the ability to fulfill the position where others had failed. Without becoming personally involved. Now I know I was wrong."

"I thought you wanted me to insure Eternity's success— that's what I'm trying to do."

"By worming your way into Sloan's bed?"

The words stole Ziara's breath, cutting through the cold, but Vivian wasn't through with her.

"Oh, I know how this works. I was even accused of it myself. No one understood what my husband and I had, how we felt about each other." She raked her eyes over Ziara's trembling body, encased in a perfect pink suit, with harsh judgment. "But I never stooped to using my body to get what I wanted."

If she could have doubled over in pain, Ziara would have. Instead, she felt locked in a swirling fog that mixed old accusations with new ones. Vivian turned toward the door but paused before leaving. "Ziara," she said without turning around. "Rest assured, if Sloan doesn't get rid of you when he's done, then I will. There's no place at Eternity Designs for smut like you."

Her exit was as quiet as her arrival.

With an unnatural calm, Ziara put the lid back on the box. The memories called up by the piece of jewelry had more power to hurt her than even the threat of losing her position here. Under normal circumstances, she could have buried them quickly and gone about her day, but these weren't normal circumstances.

Rising to her feet, she walked into Sloan's office without her usual knock. He looked up in surprise from the papers he'd been perusing on the desktop. "Was that Vivian I heard out there?" he asked.

He glanced from her face to the box in her hand. "I saw that in Vegas. I hope you like it."

Leaning forward, she placed the box squarely on his desk in a parody of the way she'd found it. He looked up in confusion, allowing her to meet his gaze straight on.

"Just so you know," she said, her voice calm but hollow, "I don't require payment for services rendered."

Then she turned on her heel and stalked out.

As dusk deepened to full dark several hours later, Ziara heard Sloan's Mercedes purr into her driveway. She'd been half expecting it, half dreading it. The stubbornness of his personality wouldn't let him leave her alone after their earlier scene.

And she wasn't anywhere near ready for him to be here.

Her eyes were probably still puffy from crying on the way home. She hadn't cried in a long time, but twice in a month was unheard-of. The emotional release after everything that had happened proved inescapable.

The loss of control bothered her because it wasn't *her*. She was the cool one, stable, clearheaded. But today she'd turned into a crying, hurting mess, desperate to close the door on a past that had reared its ugly head despite her attempts to get as far away as possible.

And it was All. His. Fault.

Not waiting for him to knock, she jerked the door open as he marched up the stone walkway. Pressure built inside as her anger swelled. Anger at him. At Vivian and her accusations. At the gift. At her lack of control. At her need for him, even after everything.

Catching sight of her in the doorway, he stopped short in surprise. "What do you want?" Because if he thought he was getting sex, he was sadly mistaken. No matter that her body clamored at the sight of him. The latent desire added another layer of dirt to her already soiled soul.

"Can I come in?"

Those commonplace, even words destroyed the last of her manners. Turning away, she left the door open for him to enter if he wanted to—she had no doubt that he would, even though she made it clear he wasn't welcome.

She stopped moving in the middle of the living room. Turning to face him, her arms instinctively crossed over her stomach to protect herself from any ugliness to come. She thought she'd escaped all the drama when she'd finally moved from her mother's house. But like her shadow, it had a way of catching up with her.

Sloan carefully—too carefully—closed the door, then approached her with cautious steps.

"Do you want to tell me what's going on?" He paused, and when she didn't answer, he continued. "Or am I going to have to drag it out of you?"

The anger that crept through her like lava spurred her to speak. It strengthened her backbone and lifted her chin. "I thought I made myself clear at the office."

"You think I'm paying you for sex?" His incredulous tone jarred her.

"I'm your employee. We…slept together. Then you gave me expensive jewelry. What am I supposed to think?"

That full mouth twisted. "Oh, maybe that it's a *gift?*"

"Vivian certainly didn't think that."

His eyes widened when he heard his stepmother's name. Ziara squeezed her arms tighter, hoping to hold in the tide of hurt and anger. She should have known going for a guy outside the safe zone would leave her feeling like a slut. So her self-image was a little skewed—years of bullying at home and school would do that. But Vivian's words had convinced her that she was repeating history.

Everything she'd felt for Sloan up until now—the dizzying rush of desire, need and freedom—wasn't pure at all. Just shameful. No one really needed another person that strongly. It had to be a mirage, a fantasy.

"What does Vivian have to do with this?" He stepped closer, one measured movement at a time. Ziara retreated until the back of her knees hit the side of the chaise.

"She came in while I was opening the box."

"Convenient, seeing as how she rarely comes to my office."

She glanced away. The logistics didn't matter now. Just the broken pieces left behind.

He reached out to tilt her face up, giving her no choice but to look at him. "She accused you of sleeping with me." His mouth tightened, compressing his lips and whitening the edges. "I don't care what Vivian said. She has no proof," he continued when she neither confirmed nor denied it. "Her view is a little skewed, black-and-white in a world of gray. She sees me as some kind of playboy, when the opposite is actually true."

Ziara couldn't stop her eyebrows from lifting.

Sloan chuckled. "Yes, I know it's hard to believe, but I've actually had to let three assistants go because they pursued me, not the other way around. This—" he gestured between the two of them "—is new to me, believe it or not."

He slid onto the chaise, pulling her back until her shoulders met his solid chest. "This isn't about me taking advantage of you because you are an employee, you're convenient or even because you're so damn hot. I thought…"

She leaned into his warmth, her spine too weak to keep her upright. Even though she knew it was wrong, her chest ached with her need to believe him. "So what is it about?"

"I don't know," he said, reaching around to cup her cheek in the warmth of his hand. "But I sure want to find out."

His kiss was gentle with a touch of erotic edge. She melted into him, afraid to believe, yet afraid not to. Old fears were hard to kill off. Like horror movie villains, they seemed to rise constantly from the dead.

Finally he pulled back. Standing, he picked her up, then resettled them both onto the chaise with her firmly planted on his lap. "I saw the necklace in Las Vegas," he said, his hands already burrowing into her hair to excavate the pins confining it. "I don't know why I bought it. I just knew it would look stunning nestled right here." He brushed his knuckle across the hollow at the base of her throat. "Bright against your skin."

She shifted, swallowing hard. "Then why give it to me today? We agreed to keep this out of the office."

He laughed softly, a kind of exasperated sound that rumbled against her chest. "I honestly didn't think about it. I thought it might be a nice gesture after all the hard work you've done, and, well, Vivian hasn't been easy on you. I wanted to do something nice for you."

He felt so good, so solid beneath her hands. Looking up, she let her eyes meet his, the bright blue mesmerizing in the near darkness. Would it hurt anyone but her if she believed him, just for a little while? She'd lost everything else during this debacle. Why should she have to give him up this soon? Surrendering with a sigh, she melted into the crook of his shoulder. "I'm sorry."

He shrugged. "What made you think I intended it as a payoff?"

She knew she shouldn't say it. But the words snuck out of their own volition—without her consent.

"There was an...incident when I was younger."

"What happened?"

She shouldn't tell, she couldn't. No one in the intervening ten years had ever known.

As if he were listening to her thoughts, he pressed a soft kiss to her temple and murmured, "I'll trade you. Tell me something about you, and I'll swap it for something about me."

The temptation, coupled with the darkening shadows in the room, coaxed the rest of the story from her.

"When I was a teenager, one of my mother's many...boyfriends...showed up at the house one day while she wasn't home. He said he was there to see me, to give me a present."

She snuggled closer, seeking Sloan's protection. "He gave me a beautiful ruby necklace. It was gorgeous, but even at that age I knew something wasn't right about him giving it to me." Her stomach clenched in remembered dread.

"Just then my mother came home. When she saw the necklace in my hand, she had a fit."

The accusations had been the worst—much worse than getting slapped and having the "gift" snatched from her hand. Her mother had accused her of trying to steal her client, not listening to a word Ziara said in her own defense. "Finally, he convinced her it didn't mean anything, but I stayed out of his way from then on. The way he watched me…"

Sloan's body absorbed her shudder. It felt so good not to be by herself anymore. She'd been alone, entirely alone, since that day so long ago.

Despite his promises to her mother, that man had tried to come into her bedroom one night. But she'd managed to slip out the window before he'd finished picking the simple lock.

Under cover of night, she'd watched him walk around her bedroom, touching her things. The next day she'd made a trip to a local hardware store, where a nice old man had sold her everything she'd needed to install a dead bolt. Ziara relied on herself alone after that. Until the day of her seventeenth birthday, when she'd left home without a forwarding address.

Ziara looked up at Sloan. Those memories from long ago influenced her current decisions more than she'd like to admit. "I shouldn't have jumped to conclusions."

"Just remember, not everyone thinks like Vivian does. Just look at Patrick. He's always telling me how great you are." He smiled, though his eyes didn't warm in color, and carried her to bed. "It's been a long week. Let's get some rest."

Gently, he stripped them both. Leaning over, he settled them against the pillows in a move that seemed natural to him. Ziara remained stiff for long moments before gradually relaxing into his hold. Never had she lain in another person's embrace, not even the loving hold of a parent. Until Sloan. Here with him, like this, felt like home. Warm, secure, safe… The final bit of awkwardness melted away.

"Tell me something now," she said, eager to shift the focus. "Tell me about your father."

She'd never had one, couldn't even imagine what it would be like to have a man in the house. Her mother's men had just been visitors who had brought nothing but indifference at best, anger and pain at worst.

Sloan's hands rubbed up and down her arms, lulling her into a drowsy state. "My father was always laughing, always happy, until my mother died. They were very much in love through it all." His hand started to squeeze, massaging up and around her shoulder. "I'll never forget, one time when she was really bad off with the cancer, he took me with him on a business trip."

"Where did you go?"

"I don't even remember, but I know we went to some kind of trade show. I remember following him through walls of people, listening to his voice as he talked to other men, having him introduce me like I was one of the adults, soaking it all in as he explained stuff to me."

His heartbeat thudded evenly under her cheek. "Did you learn a lot?"

"I was thirteen years old. I still remember every word."

As she drifted to sleep, the happy wistfulness in his voice brought on dreams of a family she'd never had.

Sixteen

The fast-approaching deadline for the fall show escalated the rush to complete the two lines, so the days got busy and the nights even busier.

She ran messages back and forth between Sloan and the design team and mediated a few squabbles, though the three designers had formed an uneasy truce among them. Vivian lay low as the time for the fall show approached. Ziara occasionally wondered how she felt, but no longer had an in to inquire how Vivian was doing.

She and Sloan spent most nights together, always at her place, with Sloan never staying all night. She didn't protest. What was the point of trying to force him into something he didn't want?

Only one night did they deviate from the pattern.

Sloan and Patrick had been holed up in a conference until about forty minutes past normal shutdown time. Ziara knew she could leave, but her greedy feminine nature urged her to wait. She could ask Sloan if he wanted her to cook dinner. If he'd like to unwind with a drink, a hot shower, a... She groaned, allowing her head to fall forward into her hands. Shameless. She was utterly shameless.

"Night, sweet cheeks."

She jerked upright, returning Patrick's smile as he sauntered out the door. Blushing, she turned to find Sloan leaning against the doorframe connecting their offices.

"You look tired," he said, his gaze scanning her face. "Am I driving you too hard?"

His sensual tone added deeper meaning to his words. She shook her head, her throat too tight to speak.

He reached for her arms, rubbing his hands along them in light, comforting strokes. "Why don't you go ahead home?" He nodded toward his open office door. "I still have some work that needs to be finished tonight."

She knew she should do exactly that. She should go home, rest and have a good night's sleep. Nibbling on her lower lip, she realized she didn't want to do what she *should*. That wasn't how she wanted to spend her evening. Studying the fatigue darkening Sloan's normally vibrant eyes, she realized she wanted to take care of him. Ease a little of the strain he was under. She chose not to wonder why but to just act.

"Why don't I go get something for dinner and bring it back here?"

As surprise lightened his eyes, she spoke faster. "It would save you some time. You wouldn't have to stop working as long and could get done sooner. I don't mind—"

The rush of words ended when he placed his lips over hers. She leaned into the gentle kiss for a moment. He pulled back until their lips barely brushed against each other.

"That sounds great," he breathed.

Her chest flooded with warmth as he pressed his mouth over hers once more, then returned to his office.

She tried not to be overly pleased as she raced home and changed into a gypsy skirt and tunic that she belted low on her hips. Though she never went out anywhere without her hair confined in some way, tonight she let it down and brushed it, the long strokes heightening her anticipation.

Sloan's obsession with her hair only grew. He was constantly touching it, burying his hands in it, especially as he rode her to climax. She was anxious to see how he reacted to her wearing it down at the office, even if it was after hours.

She stopped by a replica fifties diner near the office and ordered the deluxe burger and fries Sloan indulged in every so often, with a chicken salad sandwich for herself, before rushing back. When she walked through the office door, his eyes scanned her slowly from the tips of her strappy heels to the crown of her jet-colored hair. His gaze narrowed as it returned to her face.

"Oh, you so don't play fair," he said.

Her laughter floated around them as they spread the food on the small table in Sloan's sitting area. They ate in silence, staring out the floor-to-ceiling windows at the city lights. His eyes frequently rested on her hair. It felt so good to be free, to enjoy the moment.

"Why do you and Vivian fight so much?" Ziara asked, her earlier concern about the older woman still lingering in her mind. "It isn't just the business, either. You two seem at odds about most everything."

Sloan took his time chewing and swallowing. Ziara thought he wouldn't answer, though his face remained relaxed and open.

"She married my father when I was a teenager. I'm sure that rough adjustment period set some bad patterns in how we relate to each other."

He took another bite, chewing slowly, distracted by his thoughts. Her eyes strayed to the working muscles of his jaw and throat.

"My dad and I had a pretty laid-back arrangement until she came along. I don't know if she told him to take me in hand or what, but after their marriage it was rules, rules, rules and 'this is how we expect you to act.'"

"At the risk of sounding clichéd, at least someone cared," she said, forcing any self-pity from her voice.

Besides the dead bolt she'd installed on her door, she'd

stayed as far from home as possible. Often she ended up being at the public library until closing. She'd gotten a job at the local drugstore at sixteen, working her way up to assistant manager, saving every penny until she could leave town and lose herself in Atlanta. Her mother hadn't cared about her while she was home. She probably cared even less now.

His eyes snapped in her direction. "Do you know how Patrick and I met?"

"You said you met in high school."

He nodded shortly. "And he was my roommate in college. I was assigned to that room because I listed my original major as fashion design."

Ziara frowned. "I didn't realize—"

He broke in. "Vivian hated the idea. She told my father that I'd need a business degree if I wanted to run the company one day. He decided if I didn't change my major, he'd cut me off."

And he still hadn't gotten to run the company. The urge to defend his younger self rose, but she choked it back. "You and Patrick remained friends?"

"I know Vivian thought it was to spite her—and we got a kick out of rubbing her nose in it." He grinned. "But Patrick and I had become close by then. He taught me a lot about the design business that my father never did."

Just as Ziara was learning a lot more with Sloan than Vivian had ever taught her. "And he was the first person you turned to when you needed…a designer," she said, standing up to gather their trash.

"And he expects nothing more of me than to be myself and work hard to create success. I respect that."

As he came up behind her and kissed her on the neck, she wondered if he'd added the last bit for her benefit. Was he telling her what he needed out of a relationship?

No expectations? No commitment?

She frowned. She wouldn't be one of those women who turned into a clinging vine the minute a man showed any interest. As she shifted in Sloan's arms, she vowed to do the same as Patrick. She would enjoy the part of Sloan she had for as long as she had him.

She savored his hold until his guiding touch turned her toward him.

"I've waited long enough," he said.

He pulled her over next to him on the leather couch. She had a quick thought that she must have truly lost perspective to be doing this in his office before she could only focus on Sloan and his hands in her hair.

Later, much later, she woke alone on the couch. Disoriented, she sat up. Cool air caressing her skin reminded her of her nakedness. She grabbed the blanket Sloan must have covered her with and wrapped it over her shoulders.

Glancing around, she spotted Sloan hunched over his father's drafting table near the window, absorbed in the paper before him. He didn't look up as she hastily dressed, noting the clock read nearly one in the morning.

Walking to where Sloan stood, she peeked around his shoulder. To her surprise, the drawing was one of the designs for the fall show. The lingerie designs.

The table was covered with drawings in various stages of completion. They were classically beautiful—delicate, colorful and feminine—not slutty as she'd feared from the first. The designs were delicately sexy, with an exotic flavor that drew her.

"These are beautiful, Sloan," she said.

He grunted, seeming lost in thought. "What they need to be is finished."

She smiled. If she knew anyone who thrived under the pressure, it was Sloan. He might dislike—okay, hate—external expectations, but when it came to his expectations of himself, he didn't just meet them. He exceeded them.

But she was surprised by these drawings. They were his. Sloan's. Not Patrick's. Not Robert's. Not Anthony's. Sloan drew with sure strokes, bringing the design to life by catching the fluidity of the fabric, the lace detail and the fit against the body beneath. Compared to the one design sketch he'd shown her before, these were easily Picassos. And he'd kept them secret from her all this time.

She felt blown away—a bit sad that he hadn't told her before now—but blown away, nonetheless.

The scratch of pencil on paper continued a moment; then he froze. With extra care his eyes lifted to meet hers.

"Hey there," she said, residual emotions sharpening her tone just a bit. "Remember me?"

His jaw worked, allowing her to gauge the tension gripping him. Keeping her voice calm and free of accusation, she asked, "Were you ever going to tell me?"

"I don't know."

Um, ouch.

Something of her reaction must have caught his eye because he started throwing out excuses. And they actually made sense. "I've always drawn, always wanted to learn more about design, but never got the chance once I changed my major. After Dad died and Vivian forced me out of the company, I didn't see the point. But I've always wanted to try."

"Is Patrick some kind of front?"

His smile was a bit lopsided. "Hell, no. He's had to give me a crash course ever since he came home. Without him this would be a disaster. I've drawn up building plans for years." He looked over the pages before him, a kind of fascinated pride brightening his already light eyes.

"But why keep it a secret?" She struggled to keep disappointment out of her voice.

His mouth twisted. "You've seen how Vivian reacted to Patrick. Do you think she'd have signed any kind of agreement if she even remotely knew I would be in on the actual designs? Hell, my ideas for the show were shot to hell and back, but in the end she had no choice but to accept it." His naked shoulders lifted in a shrug, drawing her attention away from his sardonic grin for a moment. "It was one less battle to fight."

Which made sense, but she couldn't help wondering why he

hadn't told her. Didn't he think she'd understand after everything they'd said to each other, done with each other?

Maybe he didn't trust her as much as she'd thought he did.

Returning to the scared-rabbit mentality of her childhood had never been one of Ziara's life goals, but these days she found herself fearing the world around her like that lost, lonely child once more.

She wasn't entirely sure how to stop it. Throughout the next week, anxiety rolled over her whenever Sloan wasn't with her. Even though it was a stupid, feminine insecurity, she realized she wasn't as immune to the disease as she would have hoped.

Which was why she was awake at seven o'clock on a Sunday morning instead of curled up in the arms of the only man to ever inspire her to snuggle. He'd slipped into her bed after a really late night at the office and slept the morning away. But here she was trudging to the kitchen for some coffee, rather than waking him up.

When a knock sounded on her door, her heart jumped. *Please don't let that be Vivian.* All she needed was to confirm Vivian's already glaring accusations by having Sloan walk out from her bedroom in his favorite pajamas—his birthday suit.

When she opened the door, she stood for a moment in puzzlement. The woman's face wasn't familiar to her, but one look at her clothes and Ziara almost had a heart attack.

"Mom?" she croaked.

Her mother cracked her gum in the same way she'd been doing all her life. "I told you not to call me that, remember?"

I've done my best to forget. "Sorry. What can I do for you, Vera?"

"Aren't you going to let me in?" she asked.

Ziara didn't move, but shock kept her from shutting the door in her mother's face. She'd never prepared for this scenario, never dreamed her mother would track her here to Atlanta—or even care enough to want to find out where she was. This situation was completely alien, but anger started to seep around the edges of her confusion.

She wasn't about to taint her home with even a hint of bad memories. Pushing forward, she met her mother on the porch and closed the door firmly behind her. "What are you doing here?"

Vera knew Ziara better than to play the loving-mother card. "Well, I saw your picture in the newspaper, looking all fancy, prim and proper. Almost didn't recognize you."

Probably because she hadn't seen Ziara, truly seen her, since before she'd hit puberty. "That doesn't explain what you're doing here, at my house."

"Well, if you wanted to hide, you shouldn't put Z. Divan in the phone book. I picked up on that right off."

As her mother prowled the porch, Ziara performed her own inspection. The years hadn't been kind, by any means. Not surprising, since her mother had started binge drinking about a year before Ziara left for good. Her once-thick, shiny hair had been teased to lift its lifelessness. Wrinkles radiated from her mouth as if she'd taken up smoking, hard. But one thing remained the same: her clothes. The skintight animal prints hadn't looked good ten years ago, much less now.

"Right nice place you've got here, Ziara." She paused to peek inside the window along the side of the door. "Right nice. I always knew you would land on your feet."

I certainly did, with no help from you.

As Vera droned on about the house, Ziara found it easy to shut her out. There were no excuses, no changes her mother could make to establish a relationship between them—if that's what she was looking for here. Seventeen years had been opportunity enough. Even if it made her a bad person, she wasn't going to soften her heart for a woman who would put men and money ahead of her own child.

A child who had been haunted by those choices for her entire lifetime.

"Yep, you've done good. Better than I expected."

"I know." Anger seeped into Ziara's voice, making it hard and cold.

Vera stopped in her tracks as if just now getting the message. Her eyes homed in on Ziara, almost closing from all the mascara gooped on her lashes. "Guess you did get some of my genes, after all."

"Excuse me?"

Reaching into her cleavage, Vera pulled out a crumpled piece of newspaper to wave in front of her. With a quick snatch, Ziara was staring at the picture. In the foreground stood Vivian and Robert, discussing something with the reporter, but it was the background that caught her attention.

She and Sloan faced each other across one of the fabric tables. She looked as circumspect as she always did at work, but it was his expression that gave away the true nature of their relationship. She could just imagine the wolfish comment that would accompany that look on his face. Someone would have to be searching to notice, but she was pretty sure Vivian would look closely if given the chance.

Vera turned back toward the window. "That boss of yours looked like he could eat you up. Judging on his looks and money, I'd let him if I were you."

A shudder worked its way down Ziara's spine, the picture of Sloan even now sleeping in her bed burning in her mind. Despite the differences in their incomes, Vera and Vivian probably viewed this situation in a very similar manner. But what she felt for Sloan couldn't be reduced to a simple paycheck.

"Why are you really here, Vera?"

The other woman's back stiffened. "Well, I figure I fed and clothed you for seventeen years. Now that you're on your feet, payback would be the grateful thing to do. I've had a few setbacks lately, and I can't work—"

I just bet you can't. "Actually, Mother, the state paid for my raising. I took the checks to the bank every month, remember? I bought the groceries with the food stamps I managed to salvage from your purse. *I* raised me. Not you."

Anger sparked in the other woman's faded brown eyes. "I don't think so, you ungrateful brat. I worked on my back every day, something you never appreciated. And now you're going to make sure I never have to worry about money again."

Ziara crossed her arms over her chest. "This is ridiculous. Why would I give you money?"

"Because you want your next job to last longer than this one."

She froze. "What is that supposed to mean?"

"I could pay your boss a little visit. Put a little bee in his ear. After all, you certainly didn't earn those skills on your own. And I can do the same to your next boss, and your next, and your next. I'll follow you around like a bad penny until I get what I want."

Even though it was something she'd feared her entire adult life, she found herself saying, "They won't all hold me responsible for your actions."

"No, but they can hold you responsible for yours. After all, you did sleep with your boss, didn't you, dearie?"

And wasn't that the pickle she'd put herself in? Vera couldn't prove anything, but Sloan would know the truth. She had slept with him. Could she make him understand it was for love...not for money? Feeling sick, imagining what this woman would say to Sloan, she sank against the brick wall. "What do you want?" she mumbled.

"A salary of my own. You'll pay me every month to keep my mouth shut and stay at home. A nice home, not that nasty trailer I'm living in now."

Anger returned with the strength of a lightning bolt. "Like hell I will." She stalked closer, now the hunter rather than the hunted. "I'm not going to pay you a dime, *Vera*. I've paid enough for being your child. I'll just go to the police—you know blackmail is a federal crime, don't you?" Ziara wasn't sure whether it was or not, but her mother wouldn't know the difference.

Vera paled, backing toward the door. "You can't do that."

"Oh, I can and I will. Who do you think they'll believe, Mother? Me or you?" Securing Vera's arm with a firm grasp, Ziara led her off the porch and around to the driveway. A beat-up Chevy Cavalier rested at the curb, looking barely capable of going twenty miles, much less the eighty-five between Macon and Atlanta.

"Just remember this." Ziara turned Vera to look at her. Staring into those brown, sad eyes, Ziara felt her heart softening but forced steel into her voice. "I will not be manipulated. Neither will Sloan. So get back in your car and drive south. I don't want or need a mother anymore. I never did."

She waited until Vera pulled away before returning to the house. Once inside with the door firmly locked, she rested her head against the solid wood. She wouldn't cry—Vera had lost that hold on her a long time ago. She wouldn't worry—surely her mother wouldn't risk prosecution in order to get money from her. She wouldn't relent—Vera had made her bed a long time ago.

It would just be nice if she didn't have to stand her ground all alone.

Then a warm heat covered her back as Sloan brushed her hair aside to rain quick kisses across the base of her neck. "Good morning, gorgeous," he whispered against her skin. Her entire body came alive under his touch. "Did I hear you talking?" Ziara's heart started to pound, a dragging *thud, thud* that physically hurt in her chest. No matter how much bravery she could manage to Vera's face, telling Sloan the truth wasn't what she wanted. If he never knew her dirty, rank secrets, he would never look at her with pity or indifference or judgment. Even she wasn't that brave.

"A neighbor," she mumbled. "Just a neighbor who dropped by. Want some coffee?"

He growled, teeth scraping her skin this time. "I want something—but the coffee can wait until later."

Seventeen

"I think I'll head back to the office until you finish throwing your little temper tantrum."

Sloan winced as Ziara's words rang throughout the design floor, then turned to watch her dramatic exit, her body moving with the grace of a runway model and the irritation of a woman putting up with a difficult man. He'd snapped yet another order at her, one time too many, and apparently she'd had enough. He knew he took on bearish qualities the closer he got to a deadline. It hadn't bothered him before now.

But it wasn't simply the pressure that had him up in arms.

Ziara had been distant since their night here at the office. As he turned to Patrick to discuss the finer points of an orange flame pajama set, he remembered again the pure rightness of having her sleep in his arms before tearing himself away. A sense of inevitability colored every intimate moment they spent together. He couldn't decide if he was sinking fast or had already drowned—which only upped his grizzly bear aura of the moment.

Hell, there wasn't time to examine his life. He had a show to put on. Looking up, he found Patrick watching him. "What?" he demanded, not bothering to mitigate his irritable tone with his closest friend.

Patrick's face cleared. "Showing her the designs, huh? I thought you weren't big on anyone seeing them until they were done?"

Sloan shrugged, wishing Ziara hadn't let that little tidbit slip. "She was working late with me." He cringed at once again sounding like an uncaring ass, but he didn't have to explain himself.

"Does Vivian know?" Patrick asked, though his tone said he already knew the answer.

"Hell, no. I don't have to report my love life to her."

"Not about you, maybe," Patrick said, his tone unconvinced. "But she'd be interested in Ziara. You're poaching on her territory, professionally speaking. And she could make Ziara's life mighty uncomfortable after you leave."

"She already has, though Ziara admitted nothing."

"Please tell me you aren't going to leave her to face the old dragon alone when all this is over?"

"Who says I'm going anywhere?" he asked, then walked away without waiting for an answer. He knew he'd woven a complicated web. And he knew staying away from Ziara wasn't an option.

There would be plenty of time to fix all that *after* the show. Ziara's job was important to her, but he could always find her another one if he needed to keep them together. But he worried, deep down, that the approaching show was the reason behind Ziara's slowly rising wall. Was she afraid he would dump her after she was done being useful?

Deciding a quick exit was best for everyone involved, Sloan headed straight for the door instead of back upstairs to his office. He could get things done just as well from home and he wasn't in the mood to deal with interruptions. A brisk walk to his car would help with the thoughts crowding his brain.

The voice calling his name didn't register at first as the list of everything he needed to handle this afternoon ran through his mind. When he finally heard it, he turned back but didn't see anyone he recognized on the lightly populated sidewalk. A woman detached herself from the background to approach, but she wasn't familiar.

Her shaky smile revealed yellowed teeth from cigarette smoking if the bitter smell was any indication. Her clothes would have been indecent on a woman thirty years her junior, but on her... He kept his gaze trained on her face to spare them both any embarrassment.

"Are you *the* Sloan Creighton?"

Great. Media coverage could benefit a project, but it could also bring out the crazies. "Yes. How may I help you?"

The preening seemed instinctive for her, but it had Sloan shifting in his suede shoes. He glanced around—was he being pranked?

"My name is Vera, Vera Divan. I wanted to talk to you about my daughter."

Daughter? Surely not— "You mean—"

"Ziara? That's the one! She's turned into a right pretty thang, hasn't she?"

A part of him frowned in disbelief, though he made sure it didn't spread to his face. Judging by how she measured up against him, she was probably a couple of inches shorter than Ziara and the distinctly exotic flair was definitely missing. Maybe Ziara's father had been Indian, because it certainly hadn't come from her mother, whose thin, mousy-brown hair lacked her daughter's vibrant color. But a glance at her clothes revealed that they'd seen better days, sparking a moment of sympathy.

"Did you want to see Ziara, Mrs. Divan?"

"Oh, it's *Miss*. I'm not married, never have been—and I'm definitely available."

Sloan had been in many uncomfortable situations over the years, but this was one he doubted he'd forget.

"No, I didn't come to see Ziara. I came to see you after I found this." Reaching into a flashy, bright pink tote bag, she pulled out a newspaper clipping. Yet another article about their interview, but not from a newspaper that he recognized. He examined the photo. The look on his face as he talked to Ziara had him choking. They stood in the background, but the camera had still captured what was obviously a very intimate exchange.

"I'm pretty sure you get why I'd want to have a little chat, right?"

That caught his attention real quick. Though he had a feeling he wasn't dealing with a lady, he acted the part of the gentleman. With a sweep of his hand, he gestured for her to join him. "Would you care to walk with me? I'm heading to the parking garage."

Her grin was way too happy for his taste. Sloan wasn't fooled. Better to get down to business if this was headed where he thought. "What can I do for you, Miss Divan?" he asked, stumbling over the name.

One of her overly arched brows lifted even higher at his directness. "Well," she hedged, "I was just surprised as all get-out to see that picture in our local paper." She glanced sideways as they walked. "I'm from Macon, you know."

He didn't. Ziara rarely talked about her past, her family. The few tidbits he'd gleaned while in Vegas and since then hadn't painted a pretty picture, so he didn't push for more. He certainly couldn't imagine this creature giving birth to Ziara's exquisite perfection.

"But I know men," she was saying, "and a man only looks at a woman that way when he wants one thing."

Sloan jerked to a stop, swiveling to face her with tightly leashed aggression. "What the hell are you saying?"

"Not that I blame you," she said, her tone sweetly placating. "Ziara grew up around that kind of stuff. I'm glad to see she learned how to take care of herself and get what she needs. Guess she was paying attention after all. Too bad she has trouble with the follow-through."

Sloan's stomach went into a nosedive, swirling on the roller coaster before he could get off the ride. Please, please let her not be saying what he thought she was saying. He took another thorough look—short skirt, top unbuttoned enough to reveal more than the edges of her bra and abnormally high heels. In that instant, something in his memory clicked, and he recalled the woman he'd seen walking down Ziara's driveway last Sunday.

Ziara had said she'd been speaking with a neighbor. And he'd believed her. After all, he'd only seen the woman from the back—a quick glimpse out the bedroom window.

"Are you saying—"

One short, manicured finger scraped from one of his shirt buttons to the next, making his skin crawl. "That's right, honey. I'm good. Ziara learned from the best, all right. And now she wants you to pay up."

Anger started to build, low and deep. He'd spent the past five years since his father's death determined to take back from Vivian what he thought she'd stolen from him—the only piece of his father he had left. But Ziara proved even more ruthless than him.

Her mother was a prostitute. Had she truly followed in her footsteps?

There was no mistaking the insinuation. The woman before him lived the lifestyle, whether she simply used men for their money or actually walked a street corner. Ziara went in the opposite direction, had buttoned down every part of her personality. That would be why she'd latched onto Vivian, the exact opposite of the woman who'd raised her. Dressing to fit the part so she could catch even bigger fish.

The enormity of what she had done hit Sloan in the gut like a physical blow. He just prayed he didn't spew all over her mother's imitation designer shoes.

"Why isn't she here, asking for whatever the hell it is you want, herself?"

"Well, she's still a little soft when it comes to closing the deal. Not quite enough experience. When she asked me for help, I knew I'd have to step in. You'll do just as I ask." She waved the picture under his narrowed gaze. "This picture tells me most of what I need to know. Not to mention the words from Ziara's own mouth. That little trip to Las Vegas got things off to a right start, didn't they? I wonder how your stepmother would respond to accusations of sexual, um, what's that called?"

"Sexual harassment," he mumbled.

Though he knew she was wrong, and had defended his actions in the comfort of his own mind, there wasn't a whole lot he could say in his defense if charges were brought against him. And Ziara knew it.

"What, exactly, are you trying to exploit from me here?" he asked.

"Now, you don't have to say it like that." She glanced around the cool darkness inside the parking garage. "It's more like, you scratch her back, then well, you scratch my back. You've already gotten your scratch, I'm sure."

Her rough laughter had the bile rising in the back of his throat again. How could Ziara have viewed their time together as a business deal? As a bargaining chip? "Why not just come to me if she needed money?"

"Oh, money isn't what we want. Yet."

He waited, welcome numbness starting to creep through his limbs. For the first time in his life, he couldn't summon his hardball negotiator side.

"This little show you're working on? You're gonna walk away before it's done."

If the first demand hadn't shut him down, this one would have immobilized him. "Why would you want that?"

"Ziara knows it means a lot to you, but having Miss Vivian in charge means a whole lot more. Ziara owes her for all she's done, and with Miss Vivian as a boss, she'll have an executive assistant job locked down for years to come. Better deal than working for you until you get tired of her."

With each word, his disbelief was chipped away into nothing. Only one person could have told her those personal details—Ziara herself. As much as he didn't want to believe, it looked like he didn't have much choice.

"What difference does it make to you?" he asked.

"Well, it means a lot to me." She rubbed her fingers together in an age-old expression of greed. "With Ziara's status, I'll get myself a whole new makeover and access to an upscale client list." Her yellow-toothed grin said she believed this delusion. There wasn't enough plastic surgery and cosmetic dentistry in the world.... "Then we'll both be living large." She sidled a little closer, forcing him to back up flush with his car. "A woman my age could use a little retirement fund, so to speak. Of course, if I had someone like you in my life, I wouldn't need one, would I?"

"And if I refuse?" There was always a catch.

"Well, you wouldn't want Ziara's secrets to get out, now would you? With your reputation, how many people wouldn't believe claims of you takin' advantage of the hired help? Those big-money contracts wouldn't come your way nearly as often, if people around here didn't want to be associated with you, huh?"

He wasn't going to show how unnerved that made him. If Atlanta was suddenly filled with accusations of sexual harassment at his father's company, no one would risk hiring him. Ziara and Eternity would look like the victims, thus keeping their reputations solidly intact while his crumbled.

One of her nails tapped the newspaper clipping. "So what do you say?"

He struggled to find a way out of this mess, but his brain remained stuck on the picture of Ziara, sleeping so innocently on the couch in his office. Disbelief still hung around because he did care, didn't he? He'd fought it, hid from it, pretended it wasn't there.

But it was.

Knowing she had him backed against a wall, he conceded. "Done."

Ziara took a deep breath of cool air, savoring the softening fall weather, before pushing through the revolving door into the Eternity Designs building early on a Thursday morning. She felt much lighter after a good night's sleep, although she'd missed Sloan's warm body curved around her as she drifted off. Amazing how quickly she'd gotten used to that.

Now she was ready to face the Abominable Snowman again.

A soft laugh escaped as she crossed to the elevator. Sloan's attitude had finally pushed her over her limit, but when she'd smarted off in return, she'd felt a surge of adrenaline. Matching wits with him energized her, made her feel alive like she hadn't in her entire life.

She smiled as she trekked down the hallway toward Sloan's office, remembering a similar walk several months ago. Now, instead of dreading seeing him, she couldn't wait. Instead of resenting her attraction to him, she reveled in it.

Turning a corner, she spied Patrick standing in the doorway to her office. He gestured for her to hurry.

"Ziara, get in here."

Ziara rolled her eyes. Patrick tended toward the melodramatic, but she accelerated in anticipation of seeing Sloan. Even when he acted like a bear, he was a lovable bear.

At the thought, her body froze, her heart seeming to stop, then start again twice as fast. She could almost feel the shell encasing her heart give one last crack before bursting into a million tiny pieces. Left behind was a pure red, bigger, more feeling muscle that beat with the certain knowledge of her feelings for Sloan.

How did she even know what she felt? It wasn't that she'd ever been in love before. Or loved anyone at all that she could remember. Maybe her mother at some point, but she retained few memories from her early childhood. She remembered very little before her tenth birthday. After that Ziara supposed she'd lost hope of it ever being returned, so whatever love she might have had died a painful death.

The only love she'd ever felt had been for her job.

Maybe that's how she knew this was love—she'd never felt like this before, about anyone. She'd never felt so exposed, so vulnerable. So alive.

Patrick practically vibrated with irritation. "Come. On."

Ziara jumped, then picked up speed as she moved toward him. "What?" she hissed.

Patrick started dragging her across the office before she could even finish the word. "You have to stop him—"

Her heels skidded as she halted just inside Sloan's office. He stood in what she thought of as his "thinking" position: facing the floor-to-ceiling windows, head down as he contemplated those scurrying below him, his shoulders broad and square, hands clasped loosely behind his back. The surveyor of his domain.

After a moment, she took in various boxes littered around the room, file drawers gaping, the top of his desk wiped clean.

Her head swiveled from one end of the room to the other, not comprehending the chaos before her.

"He's leaving."

Ziara turned to find Vivian, the jolt of shock racing through her brain down into her body. "What?" She heard her voice but never felt her lips move.

"He's leaving." Vivian's tiny smile smacked of smug superiority. "Even though this means he'll lose everything, he's decided 'everything' is no longer worth his time."

"That's not what I said at all, Vivian," Sloan growled, though he didn't turn from the window.

Vivian practically purred in her victory. "But it's what you meant, isn't it, dear?"

"I told you, I have another project that needs urgent attention. There's only so much of me to go around." His voice sounded tight, no hint of emotion seeping through.

What? Ziara's brain could barely process what was happening. Another project? What about his father's legacy? His connection?

Her gaze fell on the drafting table in the corner where she'd watched Sloan, his golden head bent forward in the lamplight, hair long enough to obscure his face. Those drawings weren't the work of someone who didn't care, someone who could simply walk away.

Pivoting slowly, she faced Sloan, who stood just as he had when she came into the room, completely oblivious to anything happening around him.

At first he didn't move, but his back straightened, becoming more rigid. Something she hadn't dreamed possible. His hands tightened around each other. Could he feel the weight of her stare between his shoulder blades?

She waited for some sign that the man she loved at least gave a damn about something, about the people involved here. Unlike Vivian. "Was it all just some kind of game?" Ziara asked. "Didn't it mean anything to you?"

He twisted, marching down on her like a bull, forcing her to retreat. "You don't get to ask questions, got it?"

He turned to Vivian, facing her with a mixture of anger and despair like nothing Ziara had ever seen. "You got what you wanted, Vivian. Now get out. If I see you again, I might just change my mind."

Vivian's voice rumbled in the background, but Ziara couldn't make out the actual words. It didn't matter. Only Sloan mattered. The sound of the office door shutting with harsh finality shook her composure.

She was left in the room with someone she didn't know, didn't recognize underneath the stone cold facade. Oh, she should recognize him, remembering Sloan's first confrontation with Vivian. But that harsh strength had never been used against her.

Never.

With the numbness slowly creeping over every part of her body, she remained frozen as he approached once more.

"I hope this is all worth it for you, Ziara."

She shook her head. "What?"

"All the lies and deception. Why would you pretend to be something you're not? Why would you present yourself as this—" his hand gestured down her body, encased in a conservative black suit "—professional, moral woman, when deep down, that's not who you really are at all?"

Ziara felt her head start to spin. The words coming from his mouth had an eerie similarity to thoughts that had whirled through her brain for ten years. She'd told herself that she was a better person, a stronger person, than the trash heap she'd crawled out of— But sometimes it seemed she hadn't shaken it at all.

How had he learned her secret?

Her voice a little shaky, she said, "I don't know what you're talking about, Sloan."

Reaching out, he pulled a thick strand of hair from her loose updo, twisting it around his fingers like he had hundreds of times before today. Only this time, his touch had an edge to it, a slight pull on the roots that communicated his anger. "Really? Are you sure, Ziara? Didn't you know this would get to me a lot quicker than dressing like a tramp?" he asked, stepping close enough for her to feel his breath across her forehead. Those icy blue eyes gave no mercy, showed no love. In light of her own recent revelation, his lack of emotion hurt all the more.

Why was he doing this?

"I met someone yesterday," he murmured, the usually seductive tone now hard as a rock. "I met your mother, Ziara. Are you sure you have nothing to tell me?"

She almost choked, but forced out, "My mother?"

"Oh, I understand why you wouldn't volunteer the information. After all, this is a rockin' body you've got going on. Wouldn't want me to get a clue too soon."

He thought she'd used him for—what? Sex? Hadn't all those late nights and intimate conversations, all the hard work she'd put into building her reputation and work ethic, meant anything? "It is not what you think."

"Oh, she spelled it out pretty plain for me…unless you have a different explanation?"

"My mother is—" In that moment, under his hard stare, years of shame and fear kept her from saying the word *prostitute*. His obvious disgust told her he'd already come to his own conclusions. Knowing her mother, she'd given him every reason to believe Ziara had followed in her footsteps. And living in a small town had taught her that most people enjoyed believing the worst about others. She'd hoped he'd see her differently than other men.

But he hadn't.

"Sloan, please understand—"

"Oh, I understand. I understand that you used me to get what you wanted."

What?

"Or should I say what you and Vivian wanted? I guess I can live with the fact that no matter what happens, I'm the one who actually lifted this place back onto its feet." He turned back to the drafting table, running a hand along its edge. "The only person whose recognition I've ever wanted is long gone. So why should I bother seeing this through? After all, I've gotten everything I wanted from you. And plenty of it."

"Sloan," she moaned. How could this be happening? How could her worst nightmares be coming true?

"Get. Out."

Hardly able to breathe, she backed slowly toward the outer door.

Sloan turned slightly to glance at her over his shoulder. "And don't worry. You won't have to prostitute yourself to me ever again. I'm long gone."

The words hurt, but what she saw in his eyes cemented the numbness spreading through her limbs.

She'd told herself all along, from the moment he'd seen her in the designer dress in Las Vegas, that she could do this as long as he looked at her a certain way—or any way except how men used to look at her mother. A mixture of lust, disgust and superiority. As long as that didn't show up on Sloan's face, she could put away all her insecurities and just be with him.

But now his eyes, those pale, electric blue eyes, were icy and cold, free of any emotion. His blank stare sliced through her, but she felt no pain.

She realized in that split second that as much as she wanted respectability and stability, had pushed herself to win Vivian's regard and respect, she couldn't care less about it in this moment. She didn't care that she'd lost everything.

All she cared about was Sloan.

But he didn't care about her. His willingness to walk away without a word, without listening to an explanation, told her everything she needed to know. That it had all been a lie.

Tears pushed into her eyes and she lowered her lids. She would not show vulnerability here, in this room that had seen the most sensual loving in her life. Now it was just a room. Cold and distant. She'd stay strong and protect herself, just as she'd been doing since she was a teenager.

The boxes once again caught her eye. Watching him pack up and leave, knowing he'd leave her behind without a twinge of regret, might just strip her of the stupor dulling everything—inside and out.

Ignoring him, she turned back to her own office. Luckily she hadn't put her purse away. The straps remained tightly clasped in one of her hands.

She wandered down the hallway as if in a trance. Nearing the turn, she heard Patrick's voice behind her. "Ziara, are you all right?"

She didn't acknowledge him, didn't even glance his way. For once she didn't care if it was her job to make things as easy as possible for her boss. Instinct said run, so she did—stepping into the elevator that opened before her like the doors to a haven.

Two days later Ziara lay motionless on her couch, staring up at the ceiling. The lights remained off, but she knew she would look a mess if anyone saw her. She'd managed to enter her bedroom only once and that had been to change out of her work clothes. She'd avoided it—and the memories of hours spent in her colorful bed with Sloan—since then.

She hadn't moved except to blink for two hours. Her mind whirled, reexamining the same questions over and over again. The one image that rose repeatedly was the look in Sloan's eyes when he'd glanced over his shoulder at her.

The blankness, so reminiscent of her life now.

She hurt too deeply to cry, to even move. So she held still and prayed it would all go away. She'd always been a doer, the type of person to take charge in a crisis, capable of handling most anything from her teen years on.

Now she simply endured.

Unable to face the office, she'd called the next day and spoken with Abigail, whose gentle voice had almost been her undoing. But then Vivian had come on the line.

"Though I'm disappointed, I completely understand how you could find yourself in this situation, Ziara," her mentor had said, her attitude far more subdued than in previous conversations. "Take a couple of days, but then we need you back in the office. The show is only seven days away and we can't afford for you to be absent longer than that. After the show, we'll talk."

Which probably meant: *I need you to get me through this event, but then you are fired.* Good or bad, she'd meet her obligations for the same reason she'd started working with Sloan—because she cared enough about Eternity Designs to see it succeed.

What she'd do after that, she didn't know.

Eighteen

Sloan stared at the blueprints for his newest reconstruction of an historic office building, but his thoughts turned again and again to the sketch of an imperial-style nightgown he knew was hiding underneath.

He should have moved on by now, but he couldn't. The show was tomorrow and he should be there, making sure everything ran smoothly, damn it.

His mind kept replaying Ziara's stiff back and shattered expression before she'd walked out of his office. Had he made a huge mistake? Had he let his pride mislead him from the truth?

She'd felt something for him. If he'd doubted it before that moment, he hadn't since. He didn't blame her for not saying it, for holding back. Not after seeing what she'd endured as a child.

He couldn't stop himself—he'd dug into Ziara's past the minute he'd returned to his old office. She'd come from a less than reputable family. Her mother had gotten pregnant with her very young—at seventeen. The same age at which Ziara had left home.

The father seemed to have been in the picture enough to

sign the birth certificate, but records indicated he'd left Macon not long after Ziara was born. His name hinted that he was the source of Ziara's exotic beauty—an Indian who had moved back to India five years ago after failing to make much of himself here in the U.S.

Vera's police record for prostitution started when Ziara was eight, with only a few arrests, but a quick conversation with an officer in Macon indicated she was well-known for her trade and generally left alone until some wife made a fuss. That same officer had told him Ziara left town as soon as she'd earned her GED, after years of being tormented by schoolmates who were well aware of her mother's profession.

But the information had only reinforced his decision to walk away. He didn't know where Vera Divan had gotten her information, or why she had confronted him that day—at least, not for sure. Suspicions lurked at the back of his mind, but honestly, the problem with Ziara meant more to him now than the business. He would not make Ziara pay any more than she already had for her upbringing. His physical relationship with her had given Vera the ammunition she'd needed to interfere in her daughter's life. What would stop her from doing it again? What if his suspicions were wrong?

Sloan sighed, running rough hands through his hair. It sucked when you realized you were in love with someone as you walked away from them.

Looking back, he could see that Ziara was ashamed, not just of her past, but of the things her mother did for money. So she'd run as far in the other direction as she could.

The buzz of the doorbell pulled Sloan's thoughts away from the scenarios swirling through his brain. Striding the length of the house, he jerked the door open. "Yes?"

"Don't have to be so short about it, Sloan."

Frowning at Patrick, whose incessant phone calls had about driven him crazy, he turned away without a word.

"Love you, too, jackass," his friend called out behind him. He didn't let Sloan's reticence stop him from coming in and making himself at home.

"What are you doing here?"

"Well, since you stopped answering my calls, what choice did I have?"

"You could have just stopped calling me. Or gone home. After all, you don't have a job here anymore."

"And let you throw away something you've worked damn hard for? Not a chance." Patrick just kept on coming. "And I do have a job, thanks to a certain someone whose name you forbid me to say."

"What happened?"

"If you wanted to know, you should have answered my phone calls."

Sloan glared, torn between curiosity and the pain of hearing her name. Patrick simply stood there with a smirk on his face, humming a few bars of "That's What Friends Are For." Infuriated, Sloan stomped through the house to the kitchen, jerking open the fridge to snag a Mountain Dew.

"I told you," Sloan said after returning and taking a long drink, "I have no interest in coming back. I'm certainly not wanted or needed there."

"According to who?"

"Vivian, for a start."

"Since when has her opinion ever counted for anything? In fact, it usually makes you do the opposite."

"Not this time."

"Why?" Patrick moved closer. "Sorry, bro, excuses are not gonna cut it."

"I told you what happened. She wouldn't even defend herself."

"Did you give her a chance or did you just railroad her with that overbearing attitude you get sometimes? Did you even tell her what you told me? What her mother said? I doubt she even knew what she was defending herself against. I told you that you were wrong…and this time, I can prove it."

"How?"

"Ziara went to bat for you—against Vivian."

Something tingled in Sloan's chest, but he ignored it. "What do you mean?"

"The lingerie line. Vivian wanted to cut it—and me—from the show. Ziara kept production moving until Vivian got wind of it, then she argued that it should stay. And so should I."

"How?" Sloan asked again, his throat tightening too much to get anything else out.

"The same argument you used, plus pointing out that a few choice tidbits have already been leaked to the press. Hints of a completely new direction for Eternity that has the RSVPs pouring in like water in a spring flood."

He was almost afraid of the answer. "Who alerted the press?"

"Not me. Not Robert or Anthony, who were surprisingly supportive of her arguments, by the way."

"Yeah?"

Patrick nodded. "So I'm guessing that only leaves one choice. Unless you did it yourself?"

"No way." Sloan's hands lifted in a hands-off gesture. "I want nothing to do with this show. Nothing."

Patrick leaned closer, his knowing look pinning Sloan where he stood. "You sure? You haven't been looking at any designs, thinking about fabric or drape or weight?" He wiggled his eyebrows. "It's very sexy when a woman comes to her man's defense."

"I'm not her man."

"Deep down, you know Ziara had nothing to do with her mother's blackmail threat. Time to admit you were wrong."

Sloan turned to face the bay window, staring out over his wooded backyard. "What if I'm not?"

"Don't you want to be?"

"Yes," Sloan said. It was harder to admit than he'd thought it would be, but it was the truth. He wanted Ziara to be innocent; he wanted that shattered look on her face to be real—not some kind of act that she'd learned from her conniving mother.

"Then don't worry about it. I, personally, am pinning my money on Vivian," Patrick said, his voice deepening in disgust.

"But I have no proof."

"And you'll never get it brooding around your house. Get back in the game, you coward."

Sloan would never have tolerated it from anyone else, but from Patrick, he knew those words were the honest truth. It was time to put his protective armor aside, face the fact that he loved Ziara and give her a chance to prove her innocence.

"Vivian will fire Ziara after this," Sloan said. "She's never tolerated me being a part of anything."

Patrick nodded. "With or without you, I think that's already her plan."

When Ziara arrived at the fashion show venue, it was a scene of organized chaos. Watching for one last quiet moment, an achy sadness spread through her. After tonight, her job at Eternity Designs would be done and she'd be on her own again. The loneliness had started creeping in earlier this week, an extension of Sloan's absence.

Spotting Patrick, she eagerly walked down the aisle, anxious not to be alone with her thoughts.

"It's beautiful," she breathed, staring at the simulated 1930s nightclub, elegant in its classic simplicity, sexy with silver and black details. The colors of the dresses and lingerie would look amazing against that backdrop. Peeking from a side wing, as if it had just dropped off guests at the show, was a 1930s silver Rolls-Royce classic car.

"Isn't it, doll?" Patrick said. "And the background changes colors." He paused. "But I guess you already knew that."

"Yes, I did," she said with a sad smile as she remembered the day she and Sloan had picked it out, together. Tucking away the pain, she turned all business. "Time to get ready for opening night, huh?"

By early evening she was a weird combination of tired and wired, with a long night still ahead of them. She didn't attend the preshow hors d'oeuvres, but she watched the crowd arrive for the event. Vivian was in her element, glimmering in a golden lace overlay gown as she smiled and conversed with members of Atlanta's elite.

No, not just Atlanta's, or even Georgia's. Ziara recognized a few of the surrounding states' political figures, not to mention the buyers for their usual venues and a few New York buyers, too.

Her heart fluttered, her stomach tightening like a fist. So much rode on this event for Eternity Designs and Sloan, even though he didn't seem to care anymore. Surely all the hard work and turmoil would be worthwhile.

Surely her heartache wouldn't be for nothing.

Ziara took her gown backstage to change. It was the same dress Patrick had sent her to wear for his party, topped with a sheer wrap in deference to the cooler fall nights.

Coming out of the dressing room, she had to walk through the space they'd set aside to prep the models. It was already filling up with half-naked women who had Ziara looking askance. A smile tugged at her mouth as she came across Patrick, kneeling behind a scantily clad model wearing a gorgeous burnt-orange negligee." Isn't this how we met?"

He grinned up at her before finishing the last few stitches. Then he stood. "I'm done, Jennifer. Thanks." He turned to her as the model walked away. "You look stunning in that dress, Ziara."

"Thank you. The designer did an incredible job." She leaned over to brush a kiss on his cheek, only to jump when someone said, "What's this?"

Hearing Sloan's voice was a little surreal. Turning, she was at a loss for words as she faced those bright blue eyes.

Patrick spoke from behind her. "You sure know how to make an entrance, buddy."

Sloan's grin made her heart ache, but she couldn't stop looking. The cool, calm facade she'd rebuilt over the past week cracked under his stare.

"Why...why are you here, Sloan?" she asked, clearing her throat in an attempt to get the words out.

"I'd like to know that myself." Vivian's voice drew their

gazes as she stormed through the curtain. "I was told you had arrived, but I have no idea for what purpose." Her eyes swept over their little group before resting back on her stepson. "I'm waiting, Sloan."

Ziara felt herself take a step back, afraid of the coming storm. Fights between Sloan and Vivian were notoriously intense, and she really wasn't up to enduring one at the moment.

"Then you'll be waiting a long time, Vivian," Sloan said. "I don't answer to you. Nor do I need an invite to my own show."

Vivian sputtered, "It's not your show."

"Oh, it is. Unless you'd like me to confiscate every dress, every item I had a hand in creating, carrying them to my car right through the front door. Your guests would love that, and we'd certainly make the society pages. And you'd still have a few left to show, I guess." The charming grin that got Ziara every time made an appearance. "Just not the best ones."

"You wouldn't dare." His charm was definitely lost on Vivian.

"Oh, I would. I assure you." He rubbed those incredibly skilled hands together. "I'm back in."

Nineteen

"Excuse me?" The high-pitched squeal in her voice would have mortified Vivian if she'd been more aware of it.

"You heard me," Sloan said, enjoying Vivian's distress. His eyes remained on her, but his senses were searching out Ziara's reactions to his presence. Now, just like the first time, she distracted him. Everything that made him a man told him to end this argument so he could sweep her away to a back room somewhere. But it was too soon for that.

Too much unfinished business between them.

"Oh no, Sloan. You left of your own accord," Vivian said.

"I prefer to think of it as a vacation."

The frustration reddening her face wasn't pretty. "That's simply semantics. It won't hold up in court."

"Wanna bet? Besides, I'm pretty sure Patrick will testify that I've been in touch with him over the past few days about final details. In my opinion, that counts." Thank goodness for Patrick's pestering. "This is simply a courtesy notice. I'll see you on the stage later." With a wink at his friend and Ziara, he turned toward the stage exit.

"So you decided you believed the little slut after all? What did she do, beg you to take her back?"

Sloan halted in midstride. He heard Ziara's gasp behind him, but forced himself to focus on Vivian alone. If she wanted to do this out in the open, let her hang herself with her own rope.

She kept right on talking. "I didn't count on that idealistic streak of your father's running through you as well, so the sexual harassment angle was definitely the way to go. I guess love didn't mean much in the face of prosecution."

Sloan pivoted slowly, his body tensing into standard negotiation mode. He'd thought the hardest part of regaining his father's company would be bluffing his way back into the deal. He'd never imagined Vivian would admit to having met Vera Divan first.

Ziara stood directly in his line of vision, her eyes trained on Vivian. Her olive skin now held a pale undertone and her gaze was hazy, unfocused, as she absorbed a blow he should have protected her from.

Patrick stepped in this time. "How did you even get Vera Divan to approach Sloan?"

"People like that will do anything for money, unlike us." Vivian kept speaking, digging the hole deeper and deeper. "She's just the daughter of a whore, Sloan. Or are you finally ready to sink to their level? Your mother's lower-class roots making themselves known."

That was all he needed. Stalking across the floor, he leaned in, dwarfing her with his size and his anger. His voice, when he spoke, was cool and deadly, but Vivian didn't seem to notice. "Actually I'm back here because my father's idealism runs strong through my veins. I want his dream to grow and thrive, not become some kind of shrine to the marriage you wanted but could never have. You always knew you were second-best, which is why you turned my father against me."

"You were simply a reminder of *her,* all free spirit and no responsibilities. The memories are what kept him from moving forward. He could have loved me just as much, given time."

"But there just wasn't enough time for you to mold him

into what you wanted, was there?" Sloan asked, his breath speeding up as he remembered the pain of the wedge Vivian drove between them. "As for Ziara, watch how you speak about her," he said. "She's not the daughter of a whore. She's a strong woman, who inspires me to be the person my father wanted me to be. She's worked hard to get where she is. She chose respectability when she could have given up, followed in her mother's footsteps. That's an example of refinement you'll never understand."

Vivian's eyes widened, fear creeping in at the edges.

Digging deep, Sloan remembered that last special moment with his father—his memories of following the taller man as he pushed through the crowd with sure steps. Sloan forged ahead. "I value traditions just as much as my father did, and he was right about one thing—you and I can't work together. So I think it would be best if you retire when Abigail does. I would hate for word to leak out about your shady dealings with Ziara's mother."

"You couldn't do that without telling people about Ziara's past."

"Who gives a damn? I certainly don't care what people think. She's not her mother—in any way. And anyone who dare speaks even her name wrong will have to deal with me. Personally."

This time Sloan's exit was straight and true. He walked out with a new connection to his father and a woman he still needed to seduce—this time into happily ever after.

Ziara glanced down at her hands, the slight vibration a little surprising. She wasn't sure if it was from witnessing the confrontation between Sloan and Vivian, or the sheer shock from seeing him again. In her heart, she knew he was only here for the business, for his father's memory. His surprising defense of her made her wish for something else, for something more personal, more private.

As she watched the glamorous throng being urged to their seats, she knew it wouldn't happen. Now that the truth was out, she'd never fit into this world. Vivian would make sure of that. And Sloan would never want to fit into hers.

As everyone settled and the lights dimmed, Ziara took a deep breath. This was it. The moment of truth. The reception of these lines would make or break Eternity Designs.

Things went well from the beginning. Guests oohed and aahed in all the right places as the wedding gowns graced the spotlight. The tightness coiled deep inside Ziara loosened as the first model for the transitional lingerie line made her entrance. Her dark coloring set off the white, slim-fitting gown against the now-pale pink backdrop.

As the emcee explained the nature of the material and the gown's function, Ziara heard whispers, and flashbulbs exploded. Just at that moment one of the runners stuck his head around the side door and motioned for Ziara.

As she approached, he whispered, "Miss Ziara, we need you."

Duty called.

Ziara and Patrick arrived back in the side wing just as Sloan started his speech. Tears in need of release ached in Ziara's throat. But she'd gotten through tonight, just as she would get through whatever lay ahead. Even if it meant starting over somewhere else.

Drinking in Sloan's confident, cocky grin as he addressed the crowd, she wished her future would keep her with Sloan.

Patrick left her side to join the other designers as Sloan introduced them. They looked like a melting pot of styles side by side, but the combination had been wildly successful. The standing ovation was proof positive.

Standing alone in the wings, Ziara's heart warmed with gratitude. Sloan had attained success, just as he deserved. He'd been right and she and Vivian had been wrong. In the end he'd saved the company they all loved.

Catching a change in Sloan's voice drew her focus back to him.

"There's one other person I must thank for making tonight

the success it is. Not only did she work tirelessly behind the scenes, she played mediator, organizer and even stagehand."

Ziara's heart thumped so loudly Sloan's next words were almost blocked out. "But most importantly, she served as the inspiration behind some of my new lingerie pieces. She taught me a very important lesson—the most amazing thing you can do in life is to be true to yourself. Not what people want you to be, the mold they shove you into, but to be what you want in life. That's the greatest challenge. She encouraged me to create some of the designs you saw tonight, and it's one of the most fulfilling things I've ever done. I hope my father would be proud."

He turned, staring straight at the spot where she trembled backstage. Gooseflesh prickled her bare arms as she listened.

"Please welcome Ziara Divan, my executive assistant at Eternity Designs."

When his hand extended toward her, she knew he meant for her to join him. Her mind was numb, yet she forced one leaden foot in front of another. As she stepped from the shadows out into the bright lights and applause, her mind came alive, racing with a dozen questions.

She ignored them, intent on reaching Sloan's side to slip her shaking hand into his outstretched one. Leaning down, he buried his head once again in the hair near her ear. "I love you, Ziara."

She shook her head, pulling back to stare with wonder into those glittering blue eyes. "What about—" she began in fear.

Sloan silenced her with one warm finger against her lips.

She heard the crowd erupt into applause, but she could only lose herself in Sloan's hot gaze and hope the fears would disappear like mist under the heat of his desire.

Later that night, long after the last guest was gone and the last dress packed away, Sloan found himself enjoying a very different kind of show in the privacy of his luxurious bathroom.

"Sloan, I really can't do this."

"Ziara, look at me." Sloan gently cupped her chin, guiding it up so she could watch the two of them in the full-length mirror. He knew she didn't want to see herself, but he wasn't going to let her hide. His gaze devoured her sensuous curves in the coppery silk. He probably shouldn't push her tonight, after everything she'd been through at the show, but part of him needed her to see the truth.

When he'd said she had been the inspiration for his lingerie pieces, he hadn't been lying. But this particular piece had been created for her—and him—alone. Like layered veils of transparent copper, burnt-orange, pale yellow and gold, the floor-length sheath both covered and revealed the curves of her body. Tempting him with her exotic beauty, showcasing the woman she was meant to be.

"Are you your mother?"

Her sharp intake of breath threatened to strain the zipper, but he wasn't backing down.

"Answer me."

"No, not even a little bit," she said, her assurance translating to her body. Her shoulders straightened. Her tension dissolved.

"Are you a beautiful woman who deserves to wear pretty things? Who wants to see how strong and sexy she is?"

Swallowing hard, her constrained voice came out a whisper. "Yes."

"Then wear this. For me."

Sloan let his eyes wander down her reflection. Luscious mounds of plump flesh overflowed the cups. While the effect wasn't quite pornographic, his body responded by tightening immediately, hard and throbbing. He'd fantasized about Ziara in various pieces of the lingerie he'd designed, but they hadn't gotten around to her wearing any for him. The reality was more spectacular than he'd imagined.

Unable to wait any longer, he did the one thing he'd been dying to since he'd seen her backstage earlier that evening—covered her lips with his own.

She pulled back way too soon. "Please understand, I didn't do this for any other reason—" He could almost hear her throat close, hear the fear she hid inside.

He knew of only one way to convince her of his love, to prove how much she deserved to be cherished and respected. That he wanted to be with her for an entire lifetime. Only one way to break through her barriers and convince the woman within.

He eased his hands up her back. When he buried his hands in her hair, pins clattered to the tile floor. He ran his fingers through the thick silk, searching for any remaining pins, then massaged her scalp until she relaxed, tension easing from her muscles. She melted against him. Tipping her face up to meet his, he was surprised to find silent tears trailing down her cheeks.

"Oh, baby, don't cry," he murmured.

"I'm not," she insisted. Swiping a hand at her cheeks, she stared at the moisture on her fingers in disbelief. He barely caught her whisper. "I've never cried, not since I was fourteen years old. Until I met you."

He guided her gaze up to meet his with a finger under her chin. "There's no need to, because I believe you. I believe *in* you."

A hopeful expression lit her darkened eyes just as her legs gave out. He clasped her to him, picking her up and striding down the passageway toward his bedroom.

He laid her on the bed, then explored her slowly, tracing every tantalizing curve through the soft fabric—her shoulders, neck, hips, calves, then back up to her stomach and breasts. Every hitch of her breath, every tremble in her limbs drew him closer, tightening the connection that bound them together—mind, body and soul.

"I can't believe how this feels," she whispered. "How you feel. I never want it to end."

"Me, either," he said before burying his face between her breasts. The round, soft weights tempted him, and were almost as distracting as her dark, tight nipples. Pulling the cups aside, he savored them as much as he did her silent declaration. One day she'd be ready to speak her true feelings. Though he had a reputation for pushing to get what he wanted, this time he'd wait as long as necessary.

Finally, widening her thighs with his knee, he settled over her.

"Now I know why having you is so different for me," he said, lifting his gaze to watch her in the shadowed moonlight.

"Why?"

"Because I love you." With those words, he pressed inside her, savoring the slick heat of her body, the arch of her back and the gasp from her lips.

No other words were spoken between them as they strove for release, each giving as much as taking until the world exploded around them. Long moments later, Sloan opened his eyes to find Ziara staring at him. He quirked a lazy eyebrow, savoring their still-connected bodies. "What is it?"

Her words were hushed, as if in reverence to the intimate connection between them. "I can't believe you believe me, after all she must have said to you. How can you still love me?"

He thought for a moment, choosing his words with care. "I should have remembered that Vivian has her own kind of ruthlessness. I'd already started to suspect, but never dreamed she'd lose her cool enough to admit her involvement with your mother." He looked into eyes surrounded by the thickest lashes he'd ever seen. "I never dreamed I'd be stupid enough to fall for it."

Trailing his knuckle along the curve of her cheek, he said, "My father was right."

"About what?"

"He said loving my mother was pure magic."

He felt her awe in the softening of her body, the tiny smile that visited her lips. As he settled once more within her arms, his hand stroked along her thigh. His mind soaked in her presence. "I love you, Ziara," he said.

"I love you, too, Sloan."

Joy burst under his skin. He brushed a tender kiss along her temple, pausing a moment to savor her declaration. Tonight truly was magic. He'd fought for what he believed in and won. As he whispered erotic intentions in her ear, he vowed to turn their dreams into reality.

For all eternity.

* * * * *

MILLS & BOON®

Fancy some more Mills & Boon books?

Well, good news!

We're giving you

15% OFF

your next eBook or paperback book purchase
on the Mills & Boon website.

So hurry, visit the website today and type **GIFT15**
in at the checkout for your exclusive 15% discount.

www.millsandboon.co.uk/gift15

MILLS & BOON®

Buy the Regency Society Collection today and get 4 BOOKS FREE!

Scandal and seduction in this fantastic twelve-book collection from top Historical authors.

Submerge yourself in the lavish world of Regency rakes and the ballroom gossip they create.

Visit the Mills & Boon website today to take advantage of this spectacular offer!

www.millsandboon.co.uk/regency

MILLS & BOON®

Why not subscribe?
Never miss a title and save money too!

Here's what's available to you if you join the exclusive **Mills & Boon Book Club** today:

- *Titles up to a month ahead of the shops*
- *Amazing discounts*
- *Free P&P*
- *Earn Bonus Book points that can be redeemed against other titles and gifts*
- *Choose from monthly or pre-paid plans*

Still want more?
Well, if you join today we'll even give you
50% OFF your first parcel!

So visit **www.millsandboon.co.uk/subs**
or call Customer Relations on **020 8288 2888**
to be a part of this exclusive Book Club!

MILLS & BOON®

Why shop at millsandboon.co.uk?

Each year, thousands of romance readers find their perfect read at millsandboon.co.uk. That's because we're passionate about bringing you the very best romantic fiction. Here are some of the advantages of shopping at www.millsandboon.co.uk:

* **Get new books first**—you'll be able to buy your favourite books one month before they hit the shops

* **Get exclusive discounts**—you'll also be able to buy our specially created monthly collections, with up to 50% off the RRP

* **Find your favourite authors**—latest news, interviews and new releases for all your favourite authors and series on our website, plus ideas for what to try next

* **Join in**—once you've bought your favourite books, don't forget to register with us to rate, review and join in the discussions

Visit **www.millsandboon.co.uk**
for all this and more today!